ABSENT ON SCHOOL PICTURE DAY

◆━━━━━━━━━━━━━━━━━━━━━━━━━━━━━◆

A. HOLLIS

For Robert

Acknowledgements

My alpha reader, Christopher

Past and present students, faculty, and staff of Douglas County
High School

With a special acknowledgement to my editor:

Jessica L. Lanham, MA

Douglas County High School Class of 1998

Ms. Lanham is a professional technical writer based in
Richmond, Virginia.

Table of Contents

One: Anne
February 2, 1998 11:40 AM Douglas County High School 1

Two: Judy
August 15, 1994 8:20 AM Douglas County High School 21

Three: David
May 19, 2006 4:40 PM Chicago, Illinois 37

Four: Anne
January 6, 1998 4:14 PM Douglasville, Georgia... 57

Five: Jeremy
December 27, 1998 9:09 AM Douglasville, Georgia.. 75

Six: Crystal
April 24, 1997 10:51 AM Douglas County High School 91

Seven: Matt
October 18, 2005 9:10 AM Las Vegas, Nevada... 109

Eight: Melissa
October 31, 1997 11:15AM Douglas County High School 127

Nine: Michelle
December 3, 1997 7:00 AM Perry, Georgia 147

Ten: Seth
October 1, 1994 11:55 PM Chattahoochee National Forest, Georgia 167

Eleven: Jennifer
March 6, 2009 5:12 AM Atlanta, Georgia.. 183

Twelve: Emma
November 20, 2012 10:57 AM Douglasville, Georgia 203

Thirteen: Nicole
January 25, 1995 6:35 PM Douglasville, Georgia.. 223

Fourteen: Justin
March 1, 2010 6:01 AM Lithia Springs, Georgia 243

Fifteen: Tommy
October 18, 1996 6:50 PM Fairplay, Georgia 261

Sixteen: Alicia
July 1, 2000 4:20 PM Paradise City Beach, Florida.................................... 281

Seventeen: Anne
  April 17, 1998 8:08 AM Jekyll Island, Georgia.............................301

Eighteen: Michael
  December 18, 1999 5:15 PM Douglasville, Georgia......................319

Nineteen: Jason
  March 1, 1992 4:57 PM Douglasville, Georgia............................337

Twenty: Ryan
  September 9, 1996 9:09 AM Douglas County High School 355

Twenty-One: Stephanie
  June 14, 2008 6:21 PM Atlanta, Georgia....................................375

Twenty-Two: Brittany
  December 19, 2000 4:18 PM Atlanta, Georgia............................397

Twenty-Three: Will
  April 5, 2003 9:10 AM Charleston, South Carolina 419

Twenty-Four: Robert
  January 1, 1999 5:34 PM Douglasville, Georgia.........................437

Twenty-Five: Preeti
  June 14, 2008 5:05 PM Atlanta, Georgia 457

Twenty-Six: Amanda
  March 30, 2016 12:57 PM Carrollton, Georgia...........................477

Twenty-Seven: Anne
  February 2, 1998 10:50 AM Douglas County High School 495

Twenty-Eight: Penny
  October 2, 2014 3:24 PM Villa Rica, Georgia..............................515

Twenty-Nine: Heather
  September 19, 2009 8:36 PM Athens, Georgia............................533

Thirty: Brian
  May 18, 1996 4:54 PM Mableton, Georgia 549

Thirty-One: Joe
  June 14, 1990 3:12 PM Douglasville, Georgia 565

Thirty-Two: Julian
  December 23, 2020 4:44 PM Winston, Georgia 579

Thirty-Three: Anne
  February 2, 1998 12:07 PM Douglas County High School..........597

One: Anne

◆━━━━━━━━━━━━━━━━━━━━━━━━◆

February 2, 1998 11:40 AM
Douglas County High School

In the Deep South, the humidity is a sedulous presence that methodically chips away at wood, exterior paint, people's sanity, and their manners. On any small town street corner, our eyes bear witness to wet oppression. Testimony evidenced by dilapidated buildings, peeling paint, and rusty fences.

My father blames the heat and humidity for summer crime waves that surge and crest in downtown Atlanta. Waves of criminals, weapons, drugs, and money flow out into the suburban counties. The Douglas County Sheriff's Department makes certain that the waves crash at the county line. Douglasville is the shoreline between the urban rancor of Atlanta and the rest of the decent people of Georgia.

Growing up, everyone thinks that their schools and families are normal; at least, that is what most of the Douglas County High School Class of 1998 thought until two minutes ago. Now, a select few of us have crossed the teenage-to-adulthood threshold because of what happened in Mrs. Couch's English class today. In fact, there are serious allegations of cheating, lust, money, and betrayal, and all of that is in addition to whatever fictional characters we were discussing this week. The characters could not have been very compelling. I have already forgotten who they are. I feel numb...is this feeling shock?

"Wait. What was that, Anne? David, what happened? Where is Jeremy?" Jennifer mumbles. She is feigning discretion while partially covering her braces' neon bands. We are walking out of our College Level (CL) senior English classroom towards the cafeteria for our twenty-minute lunch. My mind is a flurry of information and disbelief.

I glance over at our one male friend, David. He is trying to keep pace while poorly hiding a nasty flask of Surge in an inner pocket his puffer coat. He almost drops the container falling up the stairs on our way from Lower Banks to Upper Banks. He lurches over his own feet and is dangerously clumsy. But, then again, our teacher is just as gauche too. Her lack of tact and grace intensifies her words rather than her actions.

Douglas County High School is a maze of inter-connected building additions. Portions burn and are re-built using rose-colored memories rather than architectural blueprints. That is what happens when your school is built and re-built over the decades. My luck: going to the oldest, most dilapidated, yet most prestigious, high school in the county. It feels as though I am at the peak of an empire, and I do not know how much further I will have to climb to find the summit. A mental fog covers and invades my summit.

In a dazed voice, David says, "I've never seen anything like that. It was unholy. I don't think I can play a round of *Magic* after that. What will we do about lunch? I can't eat after that."

I turn to my two closest classmates and confidants. I whisper, "We can't, y'all. We can't pretend that we were absent, just now. We can't go to lunch and act like we're okay. I'm not okay, guys. Are you okay? My head is throbbing. I don't feel good. I'm going to barf."

"Don't faint on us again, Anne! That's all we need: an ambulance showing up today. You need to sit down, sweetie. Where's a good place?" Jennifer says.

My best friend grabs my elbow and guides me through the second-story windowed walkway to Mashburn. Once inside the massive hall, the soothing eggplant color works its magic on me. Miniature white lights line the high arched ceiling in a constellation pattern. Focusing on the fabricated stars helps me breathe easier. The heat and air conditioning work best in Mashburn because the administrators' offices are here. I feel a burning heat all over my body and cannot tell if it is hot or cold outside.

David says, "Our only options are the library, theater, office, or –"

"The career center. Let's go make friends with Mrs. Graham." Jennifer blurts out. She wrangles me by the elbow. She knows that I have only been off my Prozac for a few days. I am woozy. I can feel the stress building in my veins. I do not like uncertainty.

I keep a granola bar handy for emergencies, and today is the most unexpected emergency of my life. I have a dream of creating a delicious granola bar one day that does not melt in my purse. Like me, my bag is constantly exposed to the West Georgian heat and humidity. There are other, more important, dreams that I had too; that is, until a few minutes ago.

My childhood is slipping away like fine grains of sands through my fingers. I want it back. I would prefer to be naïve. I have never heard an adult rampage like that. I want to cry and be alone. The worst place in the world to have this feeling is at high school.

With limited options, we walk into the career center. The room feels airy with tall windows and an unobstructed view of the unpro-tected outside world of Campbellton Street. It seems fitting that it is at the front of campus, nearest to the outside world of adults. We are not quite adults yet; at least, legally. In less than four months, we will be tossed into the outside world and expected to be adults or something.

I do not understand what is expected of us now. Oh no. I feel a panic starting in my throat. Something is swelling. I cannot breathe. Why will this cold air not force its way into my lungs? I feel like my body is a house of cards that is collapsing.

"Anneewakee, you'll hyperventilate." Mrs. Graham, the career center counselor, says walking over to the six-person table where we are sitting.

The bookshelf walls behind me are choking with college prospectuses from all over the United States. I have not heard of many of them. I will soon know my admission status to the one university I applied. If it does not work out, I need to pull a backup plan from a proverbial magic hat. Adults have backup plans. I think this ugly, horrible world has made an adult of me today.

Mrs. Graham looks at us with kind eyes, "Well. I haven't seen you all in here too much; but, you're seniors. I'm glad you're here. Do I need to print out a transcript for any of you? Do you know what your majors will be? What colleges have you applied to?"

"Anne and I applied to Georgia Tech." David mutters. "Jennifer wants to go somewhere far away. But not so far that the HOPE Scholarship does not cover it. Do you have anything like that?"

No. David has already started sipping his Surge. He will be a caffeinated mess in a few minutes. In my intrapersonal hurricane of thoughts, it occurs to me that he will need to come up with a better plan to sneak around Coke products when winter ends. Puffer jackets are too hot for July. Now that I think about it, he will not be smuggling carbonated beverages in July. We will all be free by then.

Jennifer shamelessly takes off her sweatshirt to reveal an illegal-at-school spaghetti-strap tank top. She pretends to flirt with both myself and David as she passes us to go towards the prospectus wall. Unlike her twin, Jennifer has not yet decided where to apply to college.

"I want a college near a beach where I can wear tank tops all year round. I want to be tan and, honestly, I don't care what I major in. I'll pick something that looks good in the table of contents. I'm going to join a sorority and party until the break of dawn." Jennifer says.

At that moment, we notice two more students sitting at the table with us. They are in our CL English class. I knew Michelle Worthan very well growing up, but I had not gotten to know Will Eason any more this school year than in our previous three together. Both were wearing head-to-toe black and carrying extra-insulated industrial-sized lunchboxes labeled *vegan.*

An awkward silence creeps up. I am uncertain if they found Jennifer's bare shoulders to be offensive to their religion. Actually, I do not know what their religion is at the moment. What is a vegan? Last year Michelle was Baptist for the first half of the year and then Hindu for the second half. Or was it Buddhist? Neither of the two vegans ever smiled, and we had nicknamed them "the beatniks" as if they were from our parents' generation.

"You all are so ill-prepared for the real world." Will says. He barks at us as if it were an accusation and final judgment at the same time.

"Who frickin' wants to live in the real world? The real world is boring. *Ha.* The *Real World* is boring. You're boring. I want to shake my tail and become the next hot intern to catch the eye of a powerful man. I'll be on CNN before I'm twenty." Jennifer says.

Without warning, Jennifer hops up onto a navy plastic chair with metal legs. It does not creak under her modest weight. She starts to shake her butt in a faux striptease with one leg on the back of the chair. Suddenly, the back breaks and she tumbles to the ground uneasily. There is no blood, yet.

Burning with embarrassment, I grab Jennifer's elbow and help her to the table before Mrs. Graham comes back from printing out a transcript. Each transcript is twenty or more pages long and takes almost a half hour to print on her auto-feed dot matrix printer. At least half of the school has dot-matrix printers, but Mrs. Graham's is the oldest because her department is least funded. Even though school athletes often sign assorted college contracts in the career center, it is rare for students to visit without cause.

I think today is my second or third time here. I knew Mrs. Graham from her required visits to our classes over the years. The school counselors visit each English class every semester to update us on opportunities and what we should be doing. English is the only subject area that Georgia students are required to take all four years. Many students graduate with only three years of science, math, and social studies. More Douglas County citizens would have high school degrees if twelfth-grade English was not a graduation requirement. Senior English is the most challenging class in the entire school, and we have the most arduous teacher.

Michelle sneers at us and says, "You'll kill yourself before you're twenty, Jenny. Did any of you hear what Mrs. Couch said in class? Did you take any of it to heart? Or do you even have hearts? Are children born with hearts, Will? Or do they merely whine and break chairs?"

I feel color draining from my burning cheeks. I want to slap the beatnik attitude out of Michelle and Will. Thoughts about accusations of assault and battery added to the senseless hurricane in my brain. I swear it is like James Joyce has taken over my brain and removed all the punctuation.

I am stunned into silence by the girl that had gifted me an extra-large Conair curling iron at my tenth birthday party. In those days, all of us wanted spiral perms like the teenagers in our neighborhoods but were not quite old enough yet. We had to settle for the high heat of the metallic fuchsia iron. Michelle and I have a complicated history. I blame Tommy more than Michelle but Michelle was not a victim, nor was I.

Michelle's path had parted from mine long ago, and she grew up before I did. But, unlike her, I did not see any reason to race into adulthood like we were thoroughbreds running the Kentucky Derby. Fancy folks drink mint juleps at the Kentucky Derby. I wonder if mint juleps are vegan. Michelle would sneak illicit food on campus then claim religious exemption or something strange.

"Anneewakee, what are you thinking about?" Mrs. Graham was suddenly standing over me.

Mrs. Graham was bending over me with a fake smile. Her breath smells like the fresh broccoli from Burger's Market on Highway 78. We were intruding on her lunch break. She welcomed all students during all periods, especially the seniors, but I do not sense the typical welcome. At this moment, she feels less hospitable than normal.

"Nothing," I lie. "I'm not thinking about anything."

"Now, come on. I'd like to help." Mrs. Graham cajoles.

"Oh, *uh*, mint juleps and The Kentucky Derby," I answer.

I know that I look like an idiot. I have no saving grace at this table of fools. They all laugh. Mrs. Graham giggles a little. That giggle turns into a covert snicker and loud snort. She is a dear, sweet counselor and very much like one of the fairy godmothers in Sleeping Beauty. Even a teacher could not help but laugh at me. Mrs. Graham must have overheard Mrs. Couch talking about me.

"I don't have a brochure for that, Anne. Maybe you would like to work with horses; but, oh dear, me, that's not a real career, now is it? There are practically no more farms left in the county."

"No, ma'am. But, I've already applied to Tech." I say. I lower my eyes.

"Whatever did you choose? You're a dreamer, Anneewakee. You need to find a good, practical career suitable for a young woman of your generation. You could be a teacher or nurse. You would be a lot of good to our society. All of us at Douglas County would be proud if you applied yourself."

I am embarrassed. I want to do well for our community. I place my head in my hands for a moment. Will and Michelle chime in together taunting me like comical twins on some random Comedy Central show, "Airhead! Airhead! All you're good for is to lie in bed."

There is a lump in my throat. I cannot find my voice. David is side-glancing at me like he does not know me. I know I cannot count on him for a verbal rescue. He is counting cards in his specially built *Magic* deck. Some days I want to be like David and have a one-track mind, almost like a racehorse.

I take a deep breath and say, "I'm going to be a programmer, like my father. I mean, not exactly like my father. But, he did it before me. I mean before I was..."

Yes, I blanked and went for a variation on a classic *Star Wars* line. Everyone now knows that I am a complete geek. I am the only female science-fiction fan in the entire school. Fine, it is better to be a geek than admit, like Jennifer, that my goal in life is to be an intern with vague connections to the President. Besides, the President said on television that he did not have sexual relations with that woman.

I believe him. Government officials cannot lie. That would be dishonest, and they are not allowed.

I wonder what *she* wants to be when she grows up; that is, the questionable intern on television. My thoughts are flying around here and there without ever touching the ground or reality. In a flash, I realize that everyone is staring at me. They look startled and stoic.

"Well, veritably, that is a good career choice. I don't know what a programmer is, but it sounds like something that makes money. It's better than being a florist, right?" Will says in a complimentary tone. Despite his tone, he made a small dig at my part-time job. I dislike working at Beautiful Lee-Dunn. The business is corrupt and evil; at least by floral shop standards.

Jennifer sits down next to me with a hard thud. She has unzipped and rolled up her Adidas athletic pants to wipe a trickle of blood off her knee. She is dramatic and flamboyant, but she is a lightning rod for bad luck. Jennifer is sturdy in her own way. She always feels the need to compensate for being blessed with the genetic gift of being a natural blonde.

"Well, the robots spoke. Leave Anne to it. She'll cure juvenile diabetes or something. David, you're going to have to pull back from the bottle, my friend. You've kissed the green fairy too much. You're bound to break the seal soon." Jennifer says without drawing attention to her bloody knee, but I see it. I see the blood.

David chokes on his contraband Surge. His eyes flush red from violent coughing. In a soft voice, he says, "What does that even mean? It sounds grotesque. Is that Edgar Allen Poe? What *seal*?"

"Oh, goodness, no. Darling, Poe was so last year. So, Am Lit 101. I'm Irish. When I turn twenty-one, I'll drink like I'm Irish. That's it, Mrs. Graham. I want to unearth a hidden gem of a college where I can drink like I'm Irish." Jennifer says and slams her palms on the table.

Mrs. Graham's eyes sparkle. She says, "I've got it! I know precisely the college for you, dear."

The beatniks, David, and I all look at each other equally puzzled at Mrs. Graham's revelation. David sits with his mouth open for a moment before speaking. He says, "So, you think being Irish entitles you to drink? Because, if you think you're Irish, then I'm German. I could outdrink you any day; especially in Coke products."

"You're all disgusting, undeserving filth!" Michelle says as she tightens her too-loose cardigan around her flat chest.

Pointing to Jennifer with an accusatory index finger she yelps, "You are not Irish. You're from some Carroll County trailer park. I think you and that fat ass brother of yours are Irish travelers. You're not really Douglas County. You're merely passing through. And, David, you're from some lonely place in the backwoods of this horrid county. Anneewakee's family and my family live at least ten miles closer to civilization than yours. Have you ever even been to

Atlanta? The perimeter is fifteen miles away. Educate yourself! Try leaving the county every once in a while; you don't need a passport."

Deep emotional pain crisscrosses Jennifer's face in the form of displaced wrinkles and an ill-timed curl in her lip. It is an unspoken rule that you never say anything to anyone who has ever lived in a trailer park. TP residents have a tendency to become defensive.

They are even more defensive in an age of rapid new growth. Half-million dollar homes are popping up on floodplain land that was cattle pasture three months prior. By some magical Southern formula, people who have lived in trailer parks always seem to be able to spot other people that have lived in trailer parks. They all protect each other's interests like an unofficial gang.

In a flash, Jennifer leaps across the table at Michelle. When she grabs Michelle's left hand, a spork full of mush falls. Jennifer says, "You loose-lipped, tiny-tittied heifer! Your mouth is full of decayed teeth and your soul of decayed ambitions."

David looks at the mush like it is radioactive material. Will rolls his eyes. *Blech.* I try not to vomit.

Mrs. Graham's face goes pale when she sees us. We pause. She says, "I know what you're thinking. By the way: Bravo on quoting James Joyce. If you want to go drinking, then you want to go to the University of Georgia. But, a few students each year...oh, about two or three...go south. They go to Georgia Southern or a tiny college near the coast called Armstrong. Armstrong became a real university a few months ago. They have a professor there that specializes in Irish studies. Oh, dear, if you're interested in Irish studies, go to Savannah. It's a better life-pursuit than landing in the county jail due to your hot temper."

While I was holding Jennifer back from the beatniks by the waist, the principal happens to walk by the door. The timing of which, once again, proves that Jennifer is phenomenally unlucky. He grits his teeth and says, "Hey, you! Girl! No public displays of affection. Wait 'til after school for the love-fest."

Jennifer looks at him intently. She extends both of her middle fingers. She yells, "Yeah, go ahead and put me in ISS one more time, Principal Daniell. I'm a drunk Irish Catholic lesbian. I have civil rights."

Principal Daniell had been walking away. I wish he had kept walking, but he did not. He spins on his feet and walks backward a few steps. In one swoop, he jerks Jennifer out of my arms. My brain is working in a dense fog. I must have clung a little too tightly because I did not want her to go to in-school suspension again.

There are clear advantages to going to ISS right now. She likes the quiet and solitude of ISS, and it did make the other girls afraid of her. On any given day, there were twelve or so boys in ISS, but only one or two girls. The predominantly male administrators often excuse girls for being emotional teens.

Principal Daniell says, "You will learn to control your mouth and your attitude, JJ. You and your girlfriend will not make it in the real world. Anne, I expected better out of you. DCHS expects better out of all of its CL and gifted students. Our future depends on the lot of you. I don't know what happened in that classroom, but I received a complaint. What is going on in there? Are you torturing Mrs. Couch? That woman has been through enough this year. Now, before I write your slip up, remind me which of the J's you are."

I do not want to show my weakness, but a rogue tear escapes. It feels like all of the school staff, especially our teachers, are working together to get across the message to our class that we need to straighten up before being released into the real world. We have been raised in a protected bubble. We know we were separate from the real world, but none of us fully understand what it was like, not really.

We are tagged, and our school is graded based on our performance; not only this year but for the rest of our lives. Principal Daniell leaves us and walks away with a swift step and his eye towards the Banks building. We speak of things in vague whispers when the adults are not watching.

"I'm Jennifer. My brother is Jeremy. He is probably off in some bathroom sulking. Feel free to write us both up, Principal Daniell. We'll tag-team our way to double trouble in ISS." Jennifer mouths off.

Jennifer and Jeremy are fraternal twins but closer than many identical twins I have known throughout the years. Unlike the majority of DCHS students, our little subset of gifted and college-track students have been in classes together for four years with few additional students coming in or going out. Jennifer and Jeremy are always together. As a result, they even share the "JJ" nickname.

"I know you're not a lesbian, Annie," Michelle says from behind her long bangs and empty lunchbox. "That would make you cool, and you're not cool."

Mrs. Graham bustles over to me with her long skirt hitting the ultra-short industrial carpet in a rhythmic pattern. "Here, give this to, *uh*, what's her name? She is one of the two JJ twins. Yes, Jennifer, when she's back from the bathroom or wherever she disappeared to now."

I look down at my hands and see paperwork for an application to attend Armstrong Atlantic State University in Savannah. I appreciate the help for Jennifer, even if she does not. But, I am not quite sure that Jennifer is interested in Irish Studies simply because her great- grandparents three times removed, or something like that, came to the United States before the potato famine.

I squeak as Mrs. Graham was walking away, "Can I have another application?"

David quits sorting his *Magic* deck. He looks at me with shock. Mrs. Graham appears equally surprised.

Mrs. Graham says, "Why? Do you think she'll rip up the original? I'll keep it if that's the case. These original applications don't grow on trees. Are you going to lose it? Are you interested in Irish Studies too, dear? I only have one application, but I could make a photocopy. I think they would accept that."

"You know, only if you don't mind," I reply in a low voice. My lungs feel like a vacuum. The bell rings extra loud inside the small career center. "I could submit an application on the Internet too."

"What? The Internet? No. That's not suitable for college applications. No one would ever do that. That's not safe," Mrs. Graham says. "Who would want an internet applicant? How disgraceful, Anne! No respectable university would do that."

"Of course," I think silently. "What a ridiculous question."

I cannot believe that I asked too much of Mrs. Graham. I do not want her to think that I am snotty. I accept my blank photocopy application with a fake smile. I show my teeth in an awkward fashion when I fake smile. I should practice it more. It is an unfortunate, but necessary, skill for young women in the South.

David and I walk behind the beatniks on our way back to English. My feet feel leaden, and my elbow aches. I miss Jennifer. I do not want to go back to CL English class. I want to hide in the girls' room with Jennifer. If I join her, the teachers will know that it is not a coincidence, and we will be written up for skipping class.

Not wanting to jeopardize either of us, I take in a deep breath and exhale.

"Did you ever think about what we're going to do when we go back in there?" I ask David.

"What? No, all that mess happened, didn't it?" David says. He is shaking and holding his flask.

Principal Daniell is waiting outside our classroom door. The beatniks, David, and I had a shorter walk back down to Lower Banks from our lunch break than everyone else who was in the cafeteria. The rest of the class starts filling in the empty spots behind us near a closed book closet adjacent to our classroom.

The classroom is dark. The door is locked. We can see some light shining through the exterior windows that overlook the football field and weight room near the stadium. There are students scurrying along the outer sidewalk to get some last minute fresh air before enduring the rest of our long block period. I ache for underclassman years when we had seven short classes a day, instead of four long ones. Even after a full year of block scheduling, teachers and students still seem to hate it.

The principal stares off into space like Forrest Gump on the stairs of the Lincoln Memorial. He picks an unknown point on the bland beige painted concrete hall wall three feet away, focuses his eyes there, and says, "Mrs. Couch needs some time off. She's not coming back today. I'll be staying with you for the rest of the block."

A thousand questions pop-up from my fifteen fellow students. I cannot think of any words. Well, the words are there, in my head, swirling. I have too many questions to formulate a proper sentence. I place the college applications in my backpack purse with extra care. I am swirling now too.

David's eyes dilate. He stutters, "But, but, but. But, she can't leave. She's the teacher. She can't leave. Who does that? There are no other humans qualified to teach us according to her. She's the department chair."

David is not managing this unforeseen divergence from routine very well. From my point of view, almost everything today has been unexpected. If the bogeyman jumped through the concrete wall right now I doubt my pulse would, or could, go any faster. I put my hand on David's shoulder to comfort him, but he is twitching and bouncing up and down a little bit.

The principal looks at David with narrowed brows, "You're fidgeting. Are you on drugs, son?"

"No," I shout. I hide behind David and his puffer jacket hood.

Principal Daniell and my fellow students stare at me. Like James Joyce's *Ulysses*, my mind hops, skips, and jumps from thought to thought. My brain seems to short-circuit.

Gold bracelet hot chain linked fence brown grass gray sky dirt sink dustpan room empty chair locked-up lockers emptiness applications college essays narratives compositions questions journal answers thesis essays arguments support Joyce decayed soul Savannah candy sugar flask decayed teeth flask empty tank empty water hot blood envelopes Macbeth

I want to be small and invisible. Instead, I melt into the unusually clean hallway laminate tile. I slither over to the blue lockers against the wall opposite of our classroom door. I see tight-lipped mouths with loose tongues whisper speculations.

Suddenly, I remembered I had not eaten the granola bar. The hallway is crowded and hot. It is sweltering. How did it get so hot in here? I cannot breathe. The bright artificial lights begin to flicker in the hallway then dim, only to repeat the pattern over and over.

The light flickering pattern is wonky; it is off. The lights are brighter toward the middle but dim on the sides. The tile rises to meet me. It feels refreshing against my head. I am floating. I wish I could still hear, but everyone's voices are muffled and then, after a few seconds, on mute.

Two: Judy

$$\blacklozenge\!\!\!-\!\!\!-\!\!\!-\!\!\!-\!\!\!-\!\!\!-\!\!\!-\!\!\!-\!\!\!-\!\!\!-\!\!\!\blacklozenge$$

August 15, 1994 8:20 AM
Douglas County High School

Walking down the hall of Lower Banks, I halt two steps short of a noisy school room. A noisy classroom is a disorganized classroom, in my book, and lacks critical leadership. Twenty-three years of teaching at Douglas County High School tells me that this exact room is less than three-quarters of capacity. I can tell by the way the voices bounce off the concrete walls.

Officially tested and designated gifted students from Douglas County middle schools, but predominately Stewart and Chapel Hill, may apply to take individual gifted classes in high school. As a result, the gifted classes are more elite and offer a more challenging curriculum for our brightest students. These specific twenty-seven students began their high school careers less than five minutes ago. I have already memorized their names, and I am not even their classroom instructor this academic year. The Class of 1998 starts high school today. Their language arts education is in my care. It is a job that I value and take very seriously.

This ragtag bunch of insipid pupils will be mine in two years. I will keep most of them for the final two years of their high school career here. While any enrolled student with decent enough grades could apply for my combined senior British Literature and College

Level English and Composition class, I am very particular about which students I admit. After a deep breath, I notice that my nervous habit of flicking my fingernails against each other has ensued without my conscious permission.

One of my least competent co-workers is undoubtedly botching the entire English language; more for her indolent benefit than that of the benighted little beasts that are sitting doe-eyed in the back rows of the almost empty classroom. I could get more classroom inspiration with a walk through Cub Foods on a Saturday afternoon. Peeking around the doorway, I observe the barren walls. Her lack of creativity in putting up the pretense that she cares about her job bothers me. I should have protested more vehemently when her application for employment slipped through the cracks while I was out on medical leave last spring. My heart aches. These students will require so much more of me in two years.

Eavesdropping with the utmost discretion, I lean against the painted concrete blocks that form the hallway. I hear a student ask a question, "How is our class different than the other ninth grade English classes? Last year we were pulled out of class for enrichment but still responsible for all of the classwork and homework that happened while we were out. Do we do that again?"

Bile knocks at the back of my throat as I hear the high-pitch squall that is this banshee teacher's voice. Banshee insults the students, "*Geez-o-pete*, kids! Get your ink pens out. We'll read the syllabus together. You are going to have ninth-grade language arts like everyone else, but we'll be doing more during the same time frame. You'll have more questions at the end of the chapters. I'll expect more from you, lookit."

A boy, whose voice had not changed yet, asks, "It says here that we're reading *A Raisin in the Sun* today. How are we going to accomplish that without our textbooks? Do we have a copy to take home?"

"Cripes Almighty! I don't know. My department chair didn't say anything about how we were going to do all of this. She had someone else hand out the syllabus. Everything is already lined up for my five other classes. All of their work is normal." Banshee says in an impatient tone.

I suck in my inner cheek lining and an involuntary tightness puckers around my eyes. Banshee's sloughing off of her responsibilities on me is centuries of inappropriateness. Her unprofessional manner has worn my nerves thin in the past two minutes that I have been observing her. If I do not nip her lackadaisical attitude in the bud, I will be the one that has to pay for her lack of teaching skills in the years to come. This self-important banshee is not allowed to tinker with my 1998 College Level scores. The CL scores are a reflection on my teaching and abilities even though I will only have two years to whip these primitive freshmen into shape. Colleges are giving education degrees to any youthful slag these days.

While holding the long length of my dress, I rush inside the classroom like Lady Macbeth. In an accusatory tone, I say, "It is the teacher's responsibility to procure her classes' textbooks from the resource closet two days before the start of classes. Are you not capable of fulfilling your responsibilities?"

"Who are you?" Banshee says. She looks like a wide mouth bass with a hook in her mouth.

"That's Mrs. Couch!" says one of the boys in the class. I think I know him. His name is Matt. "Look, lady, this is my first day of high school, but everyone in this room knows not to mess with her. Our eighth-grade teachers told us all about Mrs. Couch. We're to be on our best behavior. We cannot use first person narrative in our essays. She has a functioning guillotine in her classroom!"

I place him. Matt is a Boy Scout. I bought popcorn from him one year after Brian dropped out of scouts. I walked him around our neighborhood. Matt is trying to smooth out the situation, but I cannot let him know that I appreciate his efforts; remembering and using his first name should suffice for now. Besides, the fact that Matt is wearing a baseball cap inside the school aggravates the tar out of me. The banshee must be taught.

"You should always address Mrs. Couch as 'ma'am' in the class-room," Ryan says. "Or, madam."

I feel as though I have known Ryan's family since the dawn of time itself. I forgot this was his first day of high school. I should have remembered. I have not felt like myself since February, and my social graces have slipped these past six months. I will ring his mother this afternoon.

"Charming to see that my reputation precedes me, Matt and Ryan," I say without smiling.

"Our Program Challenge teacher at Chapel Hill told us never to use pronouns in my essays for Mrs. Couch. She told us that we would turn to stone!" One girl says.

The nameless girl is sporting not-to-dress-code white jean shorts with a sleeveless button-down collar shirt. Bless this child. The girl has not had her first period yet. Time and hormones will take care of those white Daisy Duke shorts. She belongs in a rodeo, not a classroom. She is positively unrefined.

"Lookit, what's your name?" The banshee squeaks to the student.

"Nicole." She answers while scrunching down into her seat. "Nicole Samantha Thigpen."

"Go with Mrs. Couch to the closet and get the books, will ya?" Banshee says in an exasperated voice. Her disorganization and tone will not do. "I don't care what your middle names are. You're only here until June."

The girl sitting beside Nicole is wearing her cheerleading camp shirt from this past summer. It will be interesting to see where her academic potential lies. The cheerleader grabs Nicole's hand. They rush to the door of the classroom. I will take the two pets with me and finish doing this teacher's job for her; just this once. I will share every ounce of my patience this one time, and then after that, she will need to go to another school. She needs to be in another state; maybe Alabama. They have low expectations. Stars fell on Alabama and hit them in the head.

At the end of the hall, I walk into the open book closet and come up with a last-minute proposition for the girls. "Give me three adjectives to describe yourselves. Go!"

"I am resourceful, independent, and flexible." The cheerleader says. She's confident. "I'm Heather."

"My adjectives are reliable, responsible, and conservative." Nicole finishes quickly. She is nervous. Good.

"May I take the two of you into my confidence?" I say. They nod in a labored fashion. "I need to have eyes and ears in that fresh-man-level gifted English class of yours. In exchange for giving me minor information about your assignments and what you are doing in class, I will tutor you for twenty minutes each week.

"Come and see me during your lunch period on Fridays. You two will be, bar none, the two best English composers in this county for your generation. Did either of you happen to slip out a copy of the syllabus? I will need a copy of that as well. Usually, the teach-ers use the ditto machine. I get a copy. Your teacher seems to have printed something out from a word processor."

Heather hands me Nicole's copy of the syllabus, which she had tucked in her hand when she grabbed Nicole's hand. She will be a valuable asset. Heather reminds me a lot of myself when I was her age. She may not have much natural talent when it comes to language arts, but she wants to work hard and is willing to learn. Heather can see the long game. Nicole seems confused, but I see her potential too.

"That was slick," I comment with a sneer. "Can you tell me five things I need to know about the other students in the class? Remember, you all will be my students in two years."

"The boys are behind the girls. Our middle school teachers were soft on them; not only English but in all subjects. The gifted boys feel more entitled than the girls. Everyone thinks that they're going to grow up to my great scholars, doctors, lawyers, or politicians. They want to ride their parents' coattails into a quick mention on the evening news. But, the girls work exceptionally hard. Almost all of the girls have gone to writing camp or had extra tutoring; except Anne." Heather says. She spills her emotions coolly.

"What's wrong with Anne? Does she want to be an hourly worker in some factory?" I ask. I have not heard of this student yet. She must not have any older siblings. Her parents are not in politics.

"Anne is," Nicole starts. "Well, not always well. She does the best that she can. She was on the yearbook and newspaper staffs in middle school. She makes us laugh. She's witty and charming. She gets along with everyone. She doesn't hang around with the rest of us as much as she used to, you know, before she got sick. She has diabetes. Her blood sugar is weird. She faints."

"Dear me," I say with genuine sympathy. "That is sad. It's always sad when someone is sick, but it feels worse when someone is young and chronically ill. So, is that it? Is she smart but sickly? Does she have to rest? Is she okay to start high school? The gifted program is stressful. We're striving for an International Baccalaureate program one day. It's in my personal and professional ten-year plan."

"Yes, ma'am, it's something like that," Heather says looking down at her shoes. Her shoes were probably new at the beginning of the summer, but not now. Girls always wear new shoes for the first day of high school. I wonder what Heather's story is. Did her mother not take her back-to-school shopping?

Rather than burdening the girls with the large Prentice Hall textbooks, I hand them twenty-five individually bound copies of *A Raisin in the Sun*. I smile to myself. I have a plan.

I relay a small snippet of advice for the girls, "If your teacher, and I use that term loosely, is going to treat you like toddlers, then I imagine that you'll be reading this aloud in class. Let one of the boys read the role of Walter."

"Okay," Nicole says looking perplexed. These next few years will be tedious with this one. "Wouldn't one of the boys read the role of Walter anyway?"

"Walter isn't just any old part. He uses certain colorful language that you nice young ladies may find objectionable." I lead.

"Most excellent," Heather says. She understands. She was a boom after Nicole was a bust.

"Now, if you were to pick a boy in class for Walter. Who would you choose?" I coax.

Nicole grins, "I don't know all of them yet, but I would choose that awful boy in the back with the big belly. He smells like French fries and gym sock sweat."

"Who? David? No. His mother works here. Try again." I lead them further. "Think of someone that you may not want to spend the next four years in English with, ladies. If he finds the class too difficult, or emotional, then maybe he will see where his real talents lie. Some talents lie elsewhere, I'm sure."

"Tommy," Heather says, sounding promising. "He's good at everything because his mom does everything for him. But, she's always contributed to advertising and fundraising for the football team; well, the cheerleaders too. I don't want to be mean, but he doesn't understand a lot of things about academics in general. He may have an easier time in regular ninth grade English."

"Don't say *Tommy*," chides Nicole. "That would break Michelle's heart. Why isn't she sitting next to him today? Did something happen over the summer?"

"No," I say with authority. "If you notice, there is a clear-cut distinction in your class. All of the boys are sitting on the side of the room facing the football field. All of the girls are sitting on the side with the classroom door. It's the same way every year. All the boys want to be out on the field and all the girls want to exit the class quickly to get to the water closet before the line gets to be too long."

"How smart!" Nicole says with a startling surprised look on her face.

Closing my eyes, I whisper a silent prayer that my future daughter-in-law will not be named Nicole, Heather, Jessica, Amanda, or Kimberly. The chances are fair that she is somewhere on campus right now, enduring her first day of high school. My future daughter-in-law needs to receive a quality education this academic year, and every year for the next eight years, if she will get anywhere in life.

I need a sophisticated, educated daughter-in-law to grant me my heart's desire: beautiful, smart grandchildren. If she were a British exchange student, that would be terrific but beyond all reasonable hope. I blame my son's mediocre prospects on his father's predisposition to a wandering pecker, complicated by straying eyes, and a beating heart of stone.

Nicole looks a little like a scared chipmunk, although I would never tell her that. I am sure someone will tell her before high school is over. If they thought middle school was mean, high school is even worse. Douglas County High School is full of cruel kids with means. Or, rather, the means make the kids meaner. The entire county was poor three or four years ago. We do not know what to with new-found money but spend it foolishly and on undeserving teenagers that have not earned anything.

"Any other boys? Brian is mine, of course. I know David, Matt, and Ryan. Mr. Couch is related to Ryan's family. I have known them since we were in high school here," I say.

"Oh? Ryan won a PTA contest for the past two years. It may have been for writing. I'm not certain." Nicole says. At least the cowgirl has a little bit of memory. She will be helpful in that way.

"Ryan's family has money. Have you girls not figured that out yet? One of the fundamental truths of life is that rich folks get what they want when they want. I imagine that Ryan's parents were the largest donors to some PTA campaign, so he was awarded local level prizes, naturally."

"His fiction placed at the state level. How rich are they?" Heather asks.

"Well, I should have held my tongue; maybe he does have some talent if he went from school to county to regionals to state level," I admit. I will keep an eye on Ryan.

"Be strong, girls," I encourage. "Don't forget to bring your lunch on Fridays. Several of the upperclassmen girls, even a few graduates, join me on Fridays. Wear nice clothes, be pleasant, and learn to listen with a critical ear. These girls are well connected and will teach you how to navigate high school. It's far better than any issue of *Seventeen* magazine could ever aspire to be."

With a few copies of *Raisin* in my left hand, I lead the girls back to the classroom. It sounds like this generation will be slim pickings. I will need a few minutes to review the syllabus before I can root out the weaknesses. Banshee has come to the wrong dominion to play her games. These children will grow into adults by the time they leave these halls. Their ability to perform in the outside world is a direct reflection on my underling teaching team and me.

Banshee is sitting in a circle of ninth grade student desks; what a hippie. They have started discussing the syllabus, but I can overhear their variegated conversations. I can tell that this teacher does not have the respect of her students. Banshee does not have the command and respect of her students. She is ill-fitted for this motley crew of hormones and hopefuls.

I was never that young. I was never that inexperienced. I did not need mentoring. I came out of college ready to teach.

My students have always been the cream of the crop, and I have only had to make them better. These students are at a critical point. They will find enlightened success, or they will flounder. The price for floundering may not seem like much for a year; but, if you multiply that by decades, then the price is indeed steep. Careers are won and lost in this hall.

The room falls silent as I approach Banshee. I say, "If you had looked ahead of time, you would know that the required reading of *A Raisin in the Sun* is not in the textbooks. You can send some of the boys from class down later to get them for everyone.

"In the meantime, I have brought you our printed book-bound copies of the play. Students, please be careful. You will notice that the books belong to the county. They are indeed antediluvian. Some pages may be missing." I say as Heather and Nicole begin to hand them out.

"This was printed before I was born!" A girl screeches in an owl-like tone.

"Mine smells like dog urine!" A tall, gangly boy cries out.

"And, how exactly, would you know what dog urine smells like?" I quip in reply.

"They're simply coming unglued, Justin." A pale girl says to the boy. I wonder if she's Anne. Pale Girl does not look like she has a strong constitution but is optimistic. "We can use craft glue to fix them up."

"Do you have one more copy, Mrs. Couch?" the snide Banshee fakes a smile.

"No. You may have to be creative and give up your copy." I say with firm resolve. She can learn how to work this teaching gig herself. The county does not pay me to babysit the adults.

"We can share," says a blonde-haired girl.

The blonde's cheeks are full of freckles, but her teeth are too big for her mouth. She will probably grow another foot while in high school. Her accent indicates that she is from one of the more rural western counties. She smiles at a boy across the room. They are the same height, weight, and have matching freckles. *Ah*, they are probably twins. She will not be overly verbose like so many of the other girls. She will be accustomed to sharing the teacher's attention. Excellent.

"Well, it looks like I won't even have to go to the bookstore for a copy. How about that?" Banshee says. She is tip-toeing on having her lunch in the faculty lounge thrown away through some odd misfortune.

"Please keep in mind that I require my students to do no less than an essay a week by the time they reach twelfth grade. I require an essay every ten days from my juniors. You will need to get these students writing original essays. Those idiotic questions at the back of the book are for the academically lazy. They are for the general population. Impress me." I say. I challenge the Banshee.

"An essay every week?" David questions me from the back of the classroom.

"You can do it, David. I'm not asking you to do that this year. You will work your way up to it. I will give you assignments over the summer. Your mom can help you." I encourage him out of ear-shot of the other boys. I imagine that he will be teased a great deal this year. Going to the school where your mother works is not an easy task.

"Okay, it sounds like a lot. It feels like a lot of pressure. Today is our first class of the day. I already have a backpack full of stuff for my mom to help me with tonight. I think it's too much. Maybe I'm not smart enough to be in gifted anymore." David confides in me.

"If you stick with this program, your high school transcripts are going to be amazing. Colleges will see that you chose to take the most difficult classes to advance yourself and give you credit for that when they calculate your admission status.

"With the HOPE Scholarship in Georgia now, there is no reason why you couldn't go to University of Georgia, West Georgia, or anywhere else that you wanted to go. Getting a college degree from a good university will open a whole new tier of career opportunities for you and your family too. Don't you have a little sister that is looking up to you? I won't beg you to try so this is the last time that I will say that to you." I say and turn away from David.

"Oh, and that is a friendly reminder to all of you other new students today." I increase my volume and go into my typical teaching cadence. "Your high school transcripts have to start sometime and, for you, that time is today. Do your best every year, and in all of your classes, so you're not scrambling the second semester of your senior year to try and get a college-worthy GPA. Cramming works, if you start on the first day."

"Any other pearls of wisdom?" The snide Banshee taunts me flipping through a yellow book.

"If I recall, the reading role of Walter in *Raisin in the Sun* is grammatically challenging. Since you're from the Midwest, maybe you can recreate an authentic accent as a treat for the children today. You know, really bring Chicago to this humble Georgia classroom. Boys and girls, listen judiciously." I say with a smile as I gently close the door.

With a slight nervous twitch, I fiddle with my large set of English Department Chair keys in my right hand. My heel spurs have started acting up. I walk cautiously back to my classroom and office.

Well, class of 1998, let us see what you have for me, Douglas County High School's own Lady Macbeth, two years from now. Most of you will learn to drive by then and will have experienced heartbreak at least once. You will have read Shakespeare for the first time. You will go on field trips not available to the other students; let us see how they enrich you. I know I should not get too attached, but I am a bit smitten with this group already. It is only natural under the complicated circumstances in which I find myself this year.

Three: David

May 19, 2006 4:40 PM
Chicago, Illinois

When I was in high school, I never thought, *Hey, Baggett! Do you want to be a salesman when you grow up?* To be truthful, I am the only person to blame for my limited job prospects. After not completing college, I drank and drugged my way out West and back again. Through a series of miracles, I do not have a criminal record.

Even though I am working, I feel like I am not a whole adult without having the expected college degree. My entire family thought that I would be the first person in my family to earn a college degree, but it was my sister instead. Our parents dumped thousands on my rehab and ended up bankrupt earlier this year from my medical bills. I was an unemployed and uninsured drug addict. What can I say? I want to excuse my behavior but finding the right words for my present situation eludes me.

In high school, I had wasted my time on classes that were too difficult or impractical in high school; life is too short. I know a fortnight is fourteen days and nights; so what? At one point I knew all of the U.S. presidents. Do I get a gold medal for remembering that? No. I used all kinds of drugs to anesthetize my brain into forgetting. Now I quote Shakespeare to impress potential clients, especially the ladies.

I am selling customizable jump drives at a sociology conference in Chicago. This is my first day in Chicago, ever. We only
learned a little about Chicago and Illinois in school. Our social studies curriculum glossed over geography and city histories, except
Atlanta. Chicago makes me think about Mrs. Couch and her stunt
with our ninth grade English teacher, Miss Michigan Face or whatever, with *Raisin in the Sun*. Miss Michigan never came back from
Thanksgiving break. I wonder what happened to her.

Ideally, I am looking for large university orders. My sales pitch
goes along the lines, "Wouldn't you like to purchase ten thousand
units for your incoming freshmen? Wouldn't that impress your
alumni association or foundation?"

I would like to be a part of an alumni association. High schools
do not have alumni associations. The closest thing that Douglas
County High School has to an alumni event is football homecoming once a year. I never attended a homecoming as a student, why
would I now? Fat single guys get no slack back home.

While flipping through an extra catalog, a short brunette girl
with a pleasant look on her face approaches me. She says, "Hey! Do
you want to skip the reception tonight? There's a few of us going
to the Navy Pier. Our universities hardly ever let us out of the academic cage. I mean, how often are we going to be in Chicago? Unless
you're a Chicago native, David, are you?"

Skipping the opening night reception would be a missed networking opportunity. But, this small group of people could turn into clients. I should strike while the iron is hot and develop a more personal relationship with this group rather than swimming with a thousand other vendor sharks inside the hotel fish bowl. I take a chance.

I slow my thoughts and say, "Sure. I'm game. I flew in from Atlanta. I've only read about Chicago before today. It was part of that play *A Raisin in the Sun*, right? My ninth grade English teacher got into trouble over that book, and that's all I remember about it. What's your name? I don't see your conference tag."

The mystery client giggles with the laugh that reminded me of one of my sister's childhood toys. She says, "I'm Carrie. I'm from Florida so I'm not used to the cold weather. It's under my coat; at least I brought a coat! I never knew that mid-May could be so cold. I know a little bit more about Chicago than you, but I haven't been here before either. It's funny that you remember ninth grade English. I don't remember high school at all."

We are in Rosemont and walk the block or so to the 'L' train. While walking toward the train we pass by an empty Dunkin' Donuts inside the station. I cannot believe there is food at the station. I do not see any gang signs. The sun is lowering in the sky but everyone seems calm and secure in our togetherness. If this were

Georgia, at least three-quarters of these people would be carrying a gun or knife.

I attempt conversation, "I have never seen such clean, safe mass transit. The 'L' is not like Atlanta's MARTA at all. You'll get murdered on MARTA if you get off at the wrong station."

Our little group has fourteen people. We are from around the world but mostly the mid-Atlantic and Deep South. Legitimate Tidewater Virginians were inside the hotel socializing in a structured manner. The rest of us are juvenile and untamed. The Californians are still arriving at Chicago-O'Hare from their day jobs on the West Coast. There is a mixture of students, faculty, and family members. If I judge correctly, all of us are in our twenties and thirties. Not ready to be confined to the conference at the hotel yet, we venture out. Academic conferences are vague. You never knew where you are going to end up when the clock strikes midnight. We are a living social experiment.

I entertain Carrie with some tales from high school and my travels out West. I tell her about Mrs. Couch's nervous breakdown that day in February 1998. I confide about how her words affected all of us and even ended with murder. Couch was never charged in connection to the death but I know what I know.

Carrie thought that I was telling her a tall tale and giggled on occasion as I made light of the situation. I wish that she knew that she was the first person that I had ever told what really happened.

It felt good to unburden my soul and, for the first time since high school, I felt like I could really trust another human being. Douglas County has clouded my heart with suspicion. I always wonder about other people's motives. My mind constantly whispers, "What will they get out of the deal if x, y, or z happens?"

As I enjoy the new company, I discover that sociologists like to people-watch and socialize as much as I do. I never knew that there was a career field that involved the study of human behavior. I wish Mrs. Graham had told us about that back in high school. There are a lot of things that I wish our teachers had told us back in high school but they were so busy using scare tactics that very few of us ended up on the straight and narrow right out of high school.

The talk of the early evening is a relatively new book: *Freakonomics.* Unfortunately, I have not read a book since high school; for business or pleasure. Tonight is one of those nights when I do not feel excluded for not having a college degree but I love the energy of being around people with college degrees. I try not to mention that I am a mere vendor and college drop-out. We are strangers together riding a train to what is, in my mind, the Pleasure Island of the Midwest.

Carrie leans over, "So, David, does your campus have a *Pi Gamma Mu* chapter?"

I love sorority girls. I smile confidently and say, "Well, they all blend together after a while."

"No kidding! If I get one more request from a small but established academic organization, I'm going to scream! I can't sponsor everyone." Carrie says at a near yell, trying to talk over the train.

"Yeah, I'm close to my sponsor." I say.

Shit on a stick! I should not have said that out loud. Why did I say that? What is Phi Gamma Chai? I am sweating despite the cold. My jacket feels big. It feels as big as it did in high school. I feel bloated. I am bloated with secrets and lies. Rather than those secrets eating away at me, they sit along my waistline. My waist is smaller than it was in high school but they are still sitting there, waiting to bulge out over my belt. Suddenly, I am the Eric Cartman of the group and people's glares bore into me.

Carrie looks puzzled. She says, "Are you a student? I thought you were faculty."

The oldest man in our group grabs my left fist. I unclench. In a polite tone, he says, "We won't drink this evening."

Whoever these people are, they are not from Earth. They are certainly not from Douglasville. They do not know me. They do not know what goods I peddle. Yet, they have accepted me with open arms without question. I am going to cry. I am going to cry like I am four-years old. I am breathing. I am trying to breathe.

I softly say, "Thank you. But, please, go ahead and enjoy your beverages tonight. I'm six months, three weeks, and one day sober."

Carrie snuggles next to me to make room for additional passengers at one of the stations. She says to our group, which dominates our section of the train, "No. Certainly, not: You're vulnerable, David. You may not know it. You may not be able to see it right this moment. But, of course, I would have invited you anyway and none of us feel put-out. We all want to support you. We ALL live out our professions supporting other people in their journeys. We want to help you tonight on this leg of your journey."

I put my forehead in my hand and rest my elbow on my knee. I am completely overcome. I have not had this level of solidarity since scouts. My support squad in school was Jennifer, Jeremy, and Anne. We were always commiserating over our teachers' antics and breakdowns.

After another deep breathe, I confess to Carrie, "I'm not even directly connected to the conference. I am a vendor. I sell USB drives and other tech that can be personalized."

The next thing I know we are underground and exiting the blue line at Clark/Lake. It was not until Carrie moved that I understood that her warmth is genuine. She smells like lavender and Florida sunshine. I want to follow her and stay safe in this strange city. She seems very comfortable in her own skin and confident that she will always know what to do. I feel like a bull-in-a-china-shop bungling around this big city.

Holding a small map in her hand, Carrie tells the group, "There's no use in transferring to get to Grand Station. We can walk from here. Follow me."

"Okay, so now I know that you're a professor or something, and you sponsor academic clubs. What do you do?" I say.

I am shyly trying to both make up for my sordid past while not acknowledging the obvious either. I am an addict in recovery. I will always be an addict in recovery; every minute of every hour of every day until I die.

"Me? I'm a mere grad student presenting a paper on the social constructs surrounding rape cases in the court system." She says with a laugh and then accidentally snorts, "It was that or the sexual deviances of Buddhist monks in Thailand. I hope I picked the stronger of the two topics. But, yes, both involve rape. Yes, I'm a feminist."

"I'm not a feminist. My mother raised me to believe that women were always the greater of the two sexes." I say.

I should have said gender instead of sex. Now I cannot stop thinking about sex. I am thinking about degenerate Chicago stranger sex with Carrie. Why did I not pack condoms? I am in recovery. I am not supposed to be seeking out relationships with strangers right now. *Ack!*

We were walking toward a large glass enclosure with palm trees. Carrie definitively lives in Florida because she did not even notice the palm trees. She walks towards a stain glass exhibit. I follow her and stay close. My greatest fear right now is losing her or the group.

Inside the exhibit, time flows in a strange way. We are in there for forever, but forever only is a flash in the pan for me. We stop abruptly in front of a piece featuring nymph-like women dressed as the four seasons.

"In high school, two of my three best friends were girls. They were, I guess, feminists. I suppose I looked up to them more than I realized. I think they helped me be a better brother to my little sister. When you're around the same people all the time, it's easy to miss the details. Like, after tonight, I'll probably never remember that only one of these girls is blonde and the other three in the panel have dark hair."

"You're into blondes?" Carrie banters. "What's a girl to do?"

I gaze at her in disbelief. Half of my mind is on the near-by beer garden. Controlling my urge to go drown myself in alcohol takes up so much of my energy that I barely have any left to respond.

"No. She reminds me of my friend, Jennifer. Jennifer was blonde, Irish, and ended up in suspension a lot because the school staff thought she was a lesbian."

"Being a lesbian isn't illegal," Carrie smiles and tries to be gracious. "What happened to Jennifer? Where is she now? What's her story? Was she too thwarted by the evil Mrs. Couch?"

"Well, to be honest, I don't know. All of us thought that we would stay in touch forever and then after the whole class went through a couple of moves away from home, off to school, back to home again, then apartments; well, we got lost. Some classmates have died already. Bad things have happened. But, Jennifer wasn't a real lesbian. I'm friends with her twin brother, Jeremy. Even if I told you what he does for a living, you would never believe me."

Next, I see that the group has thinned out. We are standing in front of a sign that reads, "Billy Goat Tavern. Cheezborger, cheezborger...no fries...chips!!"

I gulp a little and see "No Pepsi. Coke."

With a glad heart and empty belly, I take the sign as a sign from above. I am supposed to be here, in this beautiful city, on this distinctive pier, tonight; with perfect company. I do not see alcohol on the menu and, glory be, there is Coke up here in Illinois. I order a rib eye steak as fast as I can. Using all my will power to keep away from both the beer garden and Carrie's panties is making me hungry. Carrie is standing in front of me when some people outside our group burst into a little fight.

Not thinking, I maneuver my body between the two fighting men and Carrie. The belligerent group slowly retreats. The two fighting men move along after being yelled at by a cook. We move forward again and order in a disheveled manner. Carrie orders and pays for herself, even though I want to offer. It did not seem right to let a kind and social person pay for herself. But, I do not want to seem too stalker-ish, inappropriate, or anti-feminist.

What am I going to say? "Hi. I just protected you from a fight. Can I buy you a cheeseburger without fries?"

The sun is setting on the other side of the city. The city itself is flat as a pancake. I could run all over this city and not get half as out of breath as I do in Atlanta. The sociologists are talking about their various specialties and topics. I enjoy listening. Even though they disagree on most of the topics, I never saw a happier disagreeing group. This group was the complete opposite of the interaction that I was accustomed to in Mrs. Couch's class.

Mrs. Couch was a pot stirrer. She instigated more fights than she broke up. As a classroom dictator, she punished those who dared question her knowledge or authority. The sociologists are all kind and polite to each other. I see happy people blissfully unengaged in power struggles. There are no personal attacks and they seem to know each other, even though we were merely thrown together tonight in some strange twist of fate. I wish I had a camcorder to record this as evidence. No one back home would believe it.

The man who held my hand earlier on the train sits next to me after a quick trip to the can. He says, "Carrie is an amazing human being. Her topic is not very popular among some of the older, more established faculty. Maybe you could peek in on her presentation tomorrow. It might mean a lot to her to see a familiar face in the crowd. I would go myself but I am presenting in another room at the same time."

My mouth is dry. I realize that I have been slurping on an empty drink container for a few moments too long. I say, "Yeah, maybe I'll do that. So, what's your topic?"

"Braithwaite's Reintegrative Shaming Theory as it applies to repeat drug offenders."

"Okay," I know I look like a deer in headlights. "I don't know what that means. But, I've never been arrested for a DWI. So, I guess, that's a good thing."

"It means that you need to go learn more about social constructs surrounding rape cases in the criminal justice system," the man smiles. "You two have good energy. I can feel it. You need her."

"Excuse me?" Carrie interjects. "Constructs in the court system? It's not known as the second rape for nothing. David, you should go to some of the seminars, even if it's not mine or Hal's."

"I'd like to. I guess now that we've shared a Coke in a foreign land, kind of, it's like we're family while we're here." I say. I feel like I am stumbling on my words. My tongue feels big in my mouth. I like Carrie and I want her to like me too.

With smiles, we all raised our disposable paper cups and toast to a traveling caravan of family. At that moment, I wish I knew what had happened to my high school friends. We were like family.

Maybe I should show up for Carrie's seminar? If it were Jennifer or Anne, I would be there without question.

Last I heard from the Kelly family was that Jennifer is a hot and tacky Hooter's girl in Savannah. I do not know what is going on with her, nor does Jeremy. They are estranged, which is bizarre for twins. At least I know Anne's story. In some ways, she was the author of her own book; in other ways, she had her story stolen from her, only to be told in fragmented pieces while being blind-folded from truth. Lady Justice can kiss my fat Southern ass.

I wonder if Jennifer or Anne would still want to be friends now; if it were possible to do it all over again. I have no idea how I could even start to get in contact with my high school classmates. We were so close, we grew up together, and then everything evapo-rated. *Poof!* Adulthood is like quick sand and I have been flounder-ing and drowning in it for so long. I do not want to drown anymore. I do not want to play Eric Cartman in a four-person comedy. I do not want to be moving from one wretched situation to another like a perpetual victim.

Thinking of Jennifer and Anneewakee, I open my eyes to look at Carrie. I say, "I'm your family right now and I'm here for you. I want to be at the seminar tomorrow. I'll show up early to help you set up your stuff if you want me to. It's kind of what I do. I'm not an academic so I can't help you there. I'll even be your event bouncer if you need it."

Not realizing how hard it was to say what I said, Carrie says, "Yeah, right! Like I need a bouncer for a paper presentation. *Ha!* But, I do have dreams of a streaming multi-media PowerPoint featuring survivor accounts. Are you good with WiFi configurations? The time for set-up between presenters is sixty-seconds and it will take me that long to walk to the podium."

"I'll do it." I commit. I never commit to anything, especially not a day in advance.

In what seems like a single moment, we are walking back toward the 'L station. The night is cooling down. The shop selling UV-activated tee shirts has long closed but I feel bright, charged, and alive for the first time since middle school.

We leave the Navy Pier. Walking at a brisk pace, we turn right on Lake Street near the Chicago Theatre. The sign reads, "The Ultimate Doo Wop Show Saturday May 20 at 7 PM."

I could live here, right? Part of me wants to ask Carrie to stay here with me, forever, in Chicago. I do not want to go back to Douglas County and face my shame and demons on a daily basis.

The Chicago Theatre reminds me of the Fox Theatre back home, if Atlanta is really home. Growing up in a rural area, Atlanta is the big city. But, compared to where I am now, its home too. If anyone tells you they are from Atlanta, be wary. Most people who claim to be from, or live in, Atlanta live somewhere outside the

I-285 perimeter, in a suburb, like me. Everything that I start feeling about myself and my life is feeling fraudulent.

"How did you come across your topic? Was it assigned in class one day?" I ask Carrie. I am so breathless from the walk that I draw attention to myself. I hate when I do that.

There are a few people between us as we walk through the aisles that take us back inside the station. I see a pop art ad for the iPod. Even the black shadow of a person with white earbuds has more personality than me. I do not know who I am. I do not know if there is enough time in the universe for me to find out. I am a person who abandons those closest to him.

"I know it sounds crazy, but I took the first topic that I could find to move me toward graduation. The one instructor that was available to mentor me has worked with different branches of women's justice and rape since the seventies. She was only interested in mentoring someone with the same inclinations. I was interested in graduating so we were a good match." Carrie says with a catty smile.

After a pause, Carrie adds, "Well, all of that is true and I am a survivor too."

"Oh, that's so cool. I've always wanted to be a Survivor too. Oh, man. I would have to lose a little bit of weight. I couldn't survive on dirty water and rice like I am now. Did you meet anyone famous? What season were you on? Was it Guatemala? I missed that one. I was taking a night class."

I said something wrong. Carrie fixes an angry look on me. The train announces that we are at the Western station. I look around to see if anyone else is getting off but they all seem to be looking anywhere but at myself and Carrie.

"David, you seem like a nice guy. Do you really not know what a survivor is? Or, are you making fun of me?"

Cringing, I say, "I'm sorry. My bad. You probably won, and I completely missed it."

"I'm a rape survivor, David. I didn't win a reality TV contest."

Carrie's eyebrows furrow. It reminds me of the look that Mrs. Couch would give me when she found out that I had copied either Anne or Jennifer's homework. I feel put on the spot and I want to run away. I want to run into a bottle of Tequila and never come out. I am the worm at the bottom of the jar.

Breathless with embarrassment, I say, "Oh, Carrie. I really misunderstood what you said. I wasn't listening. It's my fault. I apologize. My teachers were always getting after me about not understanding context. I offended you. I'm sorry."

These wonderful human beings have taken me into their fold and I accidentally disrespected one of their own. I am an outsider; an uneducated guest among the academic elite. There is a reason why the other vendors told me to not even engage them in small talk. I knew that they would talk loops around my head. I am so stupid. I feel stupid and...Anneewakee. Sweet, Annie. Dear, Anne.

"*Uh*, you know? It's okay, David. I get that you're not a sociology major. And, you didn't automatically assume that because I'm a female and making a presentation on rape that it meant that I am a rape survivor. That's cool too."

"Thanks and I'm genuinely sorry." I apologize. Self-consciousness flushes my face.

Before I can catch my breath, we are walking back to the hotel. I do not want to let Carrie down. I ask her for her presentation information but it all blurs together. If all else fails, I will stand up in front of thousands of people and scream for her in the morning. I want to spend time with her but I desperately need to get to the safety of my hotel room so I can call my sponsor.

I am holding someone's well-used copy of *Freakonomics* in my hand. It feels curious to even hold a book again. How do they know I will even read it? I should start it tonight. It will keep my mind off my current predicament of not having sex with Carrie.

Hastily, I flip open my phone before the room door auto-locks behind me. "Hello, Coach? I met this woman in Chicago and I royally screwed up, and -"

"Son, do you know how many drinking stories start with 'I met a woman' and end with someone in jail or with alcohol poisoning? Of course you royally screwed up. You're in recovery!" He says. It is almost midnight on the East Coast.

"But, she's different. Carrie is the most amazing person that I've ever met. Things are rather different up here. She's different. She's funny and smart and very patient!" I say. I am floating. I am in my room, and my feet are not touching the carpet.

"It's the prairie wind. Ignore it. You're almost seven months sober. I don't want to have to cancel your party this fall."

"In some peculiar way, Carrie reminds me of Anneewakee, you know, my Anneewakee, from my class," I say as I lean against the wall and slide down. The rough texture of the spackle leaves a mark on my arm that I cannot feel.

"I know exactly which Anneewakee you're talking about, David."

"What if? I mean, what if? Let's just say, 'what if'? What if I can be redeemed? What if I can get my life together and-"

"And 'what if' the cow jumps over the moon? You need to focus, son, on your next step. Remind me again, what step are you on?"

"*Uh*, I think it's nine. But, I'm kinda stuck on nine because…"

"I know exactly why you're stuck on nine. Let's skip talkin' about nine. She ain't alive, and you don't want to hurt her family neither. I think you've reached step ten. You sound like you're at a ten, David. I'm proud of you. I'm happy for you. I'm going back to bed. The Mrs. is about asleep."

"Yes, sir. Thank you. I think I'm even going to read a book tonight. Someone gave me a book. I want to say that I appreciate everything you've done for me." I mumble with earnest.

"The Mrs. approves of you reading again. Good night, David. Ignore the prairie wind." He says. I am waiting for more advice when hear that the call is disconnected.

I am at step ten; and, right now, that is enough. Rome was not built in a day and no addict has completed all twelve-steps in a day either. For the first time, I want to battle my own demons. I want to slay my own dragons. I do not want my alcoholism to come between me and what I want most.

What I wanted most before tonight was to have my friends back. But, now that I downright know that the impossible cannot be done, I want a real relationship with Carrie. She and I can survive adulthood together; if not, I will find another way to keep my head above water on my own.

My despicable path through adulthood has been too isolated and lonely so far. I feel energized and connected. I open the well-used copy of *Freakonomics*. I have no idea who gave it to me. All I see in my vision is Carrie, looking like a kindhearted angel prepared to rescue me from an island of self-isolation and self-abuse.

In less than an hour, I have read a good bit into the worn text. I feel as though I am a living embodiment of the first chapter. The chapter is on cheating. I am a cheater, past and present. I cheated in school. I am not ready for step-ten. Principal Daniell knew that. I am cheating myself. He was only waiting for me to realize it. I feel deflated and defeated. The recovery journey continues for however long it may. I must rescue myself.

Four: Anne

January 6, 1998 4:14 PM
Douglasville, Georgia

Earlier today, Jennifer and Jeremy invited me to meet them at the new Chapel Hill Road Waffle House to celebrate the Feast of the Epiphany. I have no idea what an epiphany is, but it sounds like it is worth celebrating. Besides, I have an ulterior motive. I need to talk to Crystal and see if I can get her to come back to school.

Where the Waffle House currently stands was a lush forest a few months ago. The mall is slated to be built across the way, down Douglas Boulevard. The mall is the most controversial topic at school right now. Some people say that it will bring jobs to our area and attract shoppers all the way from Alabama. But, others are more cynical.

I am hopeful that the new mall will boost Douglasville's economy. The rest of the school newspaper staff is skeptical. In terms of evidence, now at least one person in our graduating class has gained full-time employment with Chapel Hill Road's expanding retail development. Before interviewing Crystal, I need to double check that her waitressing job is full-time here at this location. I hope they are not splitting her time between the Highway 5, Fairburn Road, Lee Road, or Thornton Road locations.

Chapel Hill Road is mostly trees. Anneewakee Creek is somewhere down there; between the Waffle House and Chapel Hill Baptist. If you go down Chapel Hill Road for forever and a day, you will end up at the Chattahoochee River, which is the southern boundary between Douglas and Fulton counties.

I look suspiciously at the new concrete around the Waffle House. Everything looks incredibly clean and modern. But, then again, even the connected Quick Trip in the parking lot is new. I do not know how this location, or even the gas station, will ever make it. There is nothing out here. No one comes here. Chapel Hill Road is the sticks. It is almost as stark as Post Road, where the Georgia State Patrol office is. All of us had to go out there for our driving learners' permits. It felt like the edge of the known world.

A cool breeze whips past me. If I shutter my eyes tight enough, I can imagine that I am at the ocean, even though I have never been. I savor this singular event in time. I inhale the smell of the freshly poured concrete. I sense the aroma of a gas station that does not smell like gas but, instead, new plastic and a hint of pine sap in the under notes.

I will remember it my whole life. I reflect, "This is what January 1998 in the Blue Ridge foothills feels and tastes like."

After a few moments, twins Jeremy and Jennifer pull up in their car. Jeremy is unusually loud and mouthy as he exits the car. He says, "I do not understand. Why is this section of the road Chapel

Hill but not where the school is? The school is a mile up the road. The country club is down the road, wouldn't it make more sense to name the whole road Chapel Hill and rename Douglas County High School something more chic like Chapel Hill High School?"

Jennifer smokes a Camel cigarette, which she is at least a month too young to purchase, and asks me, "Yeah, what's up with the name Campbellton? You know, since we're renaming everything in Douglasville. The building is out of control over here. We're a land of shopping malls. Thanks, Rita."

"You know who knows?" I say. "Crystal. She knows everything. She's not a know-it-all but it's like she got struck by a knowledge lightning bolt and she somehow synthesizes it all into coherent answers. She should be a teacher or a detective." I try to re-focus our conversation from the snippy county newcomers.

We see Crystal inside the ultra-clean Waffle House. I slip past the counter while she has her back turned. We grab a window booth in the empty restaurant. As Crystal turns to us, we yell, "Surprise!"

Crystal gives us a look of murderous death as we try to smile. To keep me from panicking, I take a seat so I can see the door. Jennifer and Jeremy are oblivious to any special accommodations that I may need and sit down.

Jennifer gets out her pack of Camels and lights another. She exhales a light gray cloud and croaks, "You know what this place needs? A jukebox. That would make it slightly less homely."

Jeremy snorts, "This Waffle House is exactly like every other Waffle House you have ever seen, ever. There's nothing special here. No character at all, in my opinion."

Crystal slowly walks over to us like she is a cowboy. Her blue collared shirt and black apron make her look more mature than us. All of my insecurities about her being the first in our class to grow up and achieve adulthood, and financial independence, flood to the front of my brain.

With heavy footsteps and a haughty air about her, Crystal says, "You're going to kill your freakin' lungs with that. Put that mess out. It makes the dang food taste bad. And, by the freakin' way, Waffle House number 1114 is brand spanking new and we have an A+ on our health inspection. So, there. We're not like all the other Waffle Houses in Douglasville or anywhere else. And, besides, I'm here, so I'm planning to take real good care of her. Jukebox is a comin'."

"But, Crystal, all of this must be so suffocating for you. You are brilliant, and a brilliant mind is a terrible thing to waste!" Jennifer says. Jennifer looks wide-eyed but authentically believes what she was saying. Her intent was to motivate Crystal back to school; but, it had the opposite effect.

"Look, trailer trash Barbie, here's the thing. I made a decision," Crystal says with a strong emphasis on *decision*. "...to leave that mess up yonder behind. Yes, I could have gone to the Academy at West Georgia. But, no, I'm getting my degree. I want to get the hell outta this backward town. It's not for me. It's not what's best for my momma. The minute I turn eighteen, I promise you that I'm going to be at the armed forces recruitment office. I have a plan. I have a plan to serve my country and get my college degree. What's your five-year plan? Die of lung cancer? Lose your golden flax hair to chemo?"

I try to smooth things over and say, "Crystal, you're a survivor. You are a provider and an amazing woman. I want to be like you when I grow up. I do. You're the bomb. If we were Spice Girls, I would want you. I would really, really, really want you. But, Jennifer, is worried. Jeremy and I are too."

"What are you worried about, Anne? Because my American Dream doesn't look like your white girl American dreams? I'm fine. I come from generations of doing fine," our now former class vice president explains to us. In truth, she does not owe us anything, even an explanation.

A cook clears this throat in the background to indicate that we needed to hurry our ordering along. Jeremy browses a menu and orders a pecan waffle for Jennifer and a pork chop Big Deal dinner for himself. We each ask for a vanilla-cherry Coke. I pipe in, as an afterthought, "Oh! And, I'll have a grilled cheese."

"*Jeez*, Anne," Crystal admonishes. "It's like you're a five-year-old. Don't come back again unless you're going to order real food. Grilled cheese is all you and Flannel Guy eat."

My acute shame burns on my cheeks through my dark beige skin as our friend sashays to the grill. Crystal works all day and probably eats real meals while I hardly pick at my food. I was not that hungry but wanted to see Crystal tonight. She has grown distant. She seems light-years older than us.

Jennifer cocks her head to one side and says, "Don't worry about it. It's her funeral. If she's ready to kiss her youth good-bye then let her. She had it all. She probably would have been prom queen or something. If she wants to go all *Native Son* on us then, fine, let her."

"You are too racist to be my twin!" Jeremy barks as though offended. "This is not 1930s Chicago. Crystal is not an impoverished male criminal on trial. Oh, lawd! I need to scoot over to sit with Anne because lightning is about to strike you. You are an ignorant, trailer trash Barbie! How do we share DNA? Remind me."

We were only two months into the school year when Crystal announced that she was dropping out shortly before Homecoming. She was on the newspaper staff with us for a few months. Her assignment had been to cover Princess Diana's fatal accident. When Mother Teresa died too, Crystal had double duty. Jennifer made the call as editor to assign Crystal to that death as well. Crystal was an amazingly talented writer and had written funny, British-style obituaries for the paper in the past. She is tactful and has a mature, dry sense of humor. Jennifer nit-picked Crystal's writing out of spite.

All of us had grand plans for our little *Eye of the Tiger* newspaper. Since our school mascot is a tiger, our advisor had chosen the cheesy eighties title. In her visions of grandeur, Jennifer wanted the most honest and diverse writers in our class. I had suggested carving out a portion of the newspaper for creative writing, like Ryan's, but it was a no-go.

I am not a talented writer, but since we were soccer buddies, I got an extra slot as the copy editor. I do not have any noteworthy writing talents beyond the ability to edit the paper on Adobe PageMaker, which is a software program that no one else was familiar with this school year. The one or two students that knew copy last year did it with literal copies, paste, and scissors.

The first taste of soft drink fizzes in my mouth. I watch Crystal with an editing eye. She moves like a graceful dolphin through her restaurant, very much in command of her body and space. She has soft sable skin and very short natural hair. She could be fifteen-years old, twenty-five, or even fifty. Her timeless, classic features surpass time.

Crystal has double-pierced ears, which my father would never allow me to have. Assorted coaches over the years begged her to play basketball, but she said it never held any appeal for her. She thought it was racist of adults to assume that she would be interested in sports. She was right. She never tried out.

I know that Crystal was the very best and brightest in theater and arts in the entire county. She had cleaned out the awards at the county-level arts fair for years. Her work spoke for itself. She had competed in oratory, original composition, and photography. I feel lost in thought when I notice that she is walking over to us balancing a tray of drinks. I grab Crystal's hand, inappropriately, like we were still in scouts together. I need her to hear me.

"Please! Please take a break and sit down with us. I miss you so much." I say and feel big salty tears welling up in my eyes. "Is there anything that any of us can say or do to get you to come back? I'm sorry if Jennifer gave you a crap article assignment. Ryan was disappointed that his work wasn't published either. You can have my stories. You're welcome to cover the India-Pakistan nuclear escalation. I don't care about it. You've got to come back."

"*Shh*, Anne. It has nothing to do with your little newspaper. I don't want to go to prom. I don't want to go to homecoming or a pep rally. I don't want to paint our nails green and take the SAT together. I'm sick of it all. Small town life maddens me. I want to travel and see the world. I want a flippin' paycheck."

I slide my untouched second glass of Coke over to Crystal. I know it is her favorite. I wanted her to have something nice; even if it was only for four minutes on a random Tuesday night with a Catholic feast.

Then, it dawns on me. I almost stutter when I say, "W-Wait. Does this have to do with the field trip earlier this year to Atlanta? What happened? You were there for most of the play. Then you disappeared."

"Okay. I wanted to go to the play. And, by the way, it was called *Much Ado About Nothing*. It's Shakespeare for goodness sake. Okay, you know what? Fine. That's when I decided. I went to the bathroom during intermission and decided that that was when I knew for sure that I couldn't go back to school. I enjoyed visiting the Tavern. It was lovely. That life, the quasi-college life, is not for me."

"You have a restless and ancient soul," Jennifer says as she unpacks her stolen tarot cards. "I want to give you a free reading. You could be the reincarnation of someone famous, like the Queen of Sheba."

"You crazy, sorceress! I'm not going to let you do witchcraft in my store and bring some awful curse down on this whole dang street! You pack that mess up right now," Crystal reprimands us.

Jennifer has only had the cards since Halloween. She did not come by them honestly. I did not help steal the cards; that is on Jennifer's head. But, I did not do the right thing and go back inside the mall the turn them back in either after Jennifer told me about them. For my part in complacency, I am sorry because now we are in hot water with one of the women I admire most.

"I'm not a witch. I'm Catholic! And, you better be grateful. Jeremy and I add diversity to our class. Without us, no one would ever have any fun," Jennifer says while packing up the cards.

Looking over Jennifer's arm, I see that the card on the top of the deck was a Hierophant. I do not know what it means. I am uncertain if all Catholics universally accepted tarot cards as mere fun.

Douglas County is predominantly Protestant. I had not heard of tarot cards before meeting Jennifer. People line up outside their house early in the morning for Jennifer's cheap readings. The readings bring much-needed cash flow into their home; much to Preeti's chagrin. Preeti fancies herself a real gypsy. She weaseled me into switching essay topics with her earlier this year.

Crystal stands up abruptly, "Jennifer, you think that you and your plump bro here add diversity to our class? *Whew!* I don't have time for this mess. But, yes, I'm so glad that our county now has a few token Catholic families. That matches well with the one or two Presbyterian churches in the county. Maybe you all can play softball against the hundreds of Methodist and Baptist churches here. Oh, *Jeez*, get a life. You're not fun. You're irresponsible. Jeremy is right: you're ignorant too. I think that's worse. "

I do not know what words to speak to make things better, so I remain reticent. Crystal and I were in a Girl Scout troop together for years. She was responsible for making sure that I did not get lost during cookie sales or field trips. Snakes, the Georgia State Patrol, and the Girl Scouts operate on the buddy system, and she is my buddy. Even as a child, she had a street smart about her that no one else in our troops did. Her love had protected me from questionable Santa Claus impersonators and from wandering around too many empty hallways when we visited local nursing homes for service projects. I know that Crystal had seen and experienced unfortunate situations to gain her smarts. But, I am not as naïve as everyone thinks.

Jeremy looks over at his twin, "JJ, are you happy now? You have probably just ruined any desire that Crystal may have had to come back to school. Even if she called me fat, I could tell that she is pissed off. Girls, something happened! What happened? Was it on the field trip? Did I drive on that trip? Was I high?"

My mind is off-topic. I start thinking about the Shakespeare project that we have due in a few weeks. I have not started on it. My topic is to explore the use of traditional makeup and props to further realism in late sixteenth century plays. I have recently discovered that men played the female parts as well. I find that shocking. Cross-dressing is very taboo in Douglas County. No one speaks of it. Besides, why would the Elizabethans not just assign women to play the female roles?

"Ground control to Major Anne!" Jennifer snaps her fingers. My food is getting cold. Crystal had asked a co-worker to bring our food out to us.

Cold grilled cheese is gross. I do not think I can stomach the grilled cheese but eat anyway. I cannot manage my feelings anymore. This all goes back to my counseling sessions and antidepressant prescription. The adults in my life are uncomfortable. I have too many questions.

Last spring, I became embroiled in scandal and no one forgave me for it. I did not forgive myself for it. Now, I am in a state of incessant torpid detachment. It is difficult to write, or even speak, when drugged as I am now.

I walk over to Crystal as she wipes the already clean counters. I plead, "Crystal. I'm sorry that I don't know what I did. I know that you think I'm such a child already. I know you've become too cool for me. But, please know, I care for you like a sister. We survived the mean boys in our confirmation class together. I have missed you so much at lunch. And, it's not only because David is beating me at *Magic: The Gathering.* My white deck is well-stacked against his nonsense. My heart misses your heart."

"Anne," Crystal says as she takes off her apron. "I miss you too. I miss *you,* but I don't miss school. I don't miss the way things were for me there. It's good that I'm here. I'm going to be enlisting between now and November. If I have to move, I want you to have my collection of kids' meal toys from when we were little and used to go after scouts on Thursday nights."

"This is really happening, huh?" I say in a desperate tone. "Don't leave me here, please. Not with the Tweedle twins and mean boys. I feel so lost. You seem so together. When did you grow up? And, can you give a little of that to Jennifer?"

Jennifer has a useless talent for ruffling feathers in most people in our class. She is a survivor too, like Crystal. Jennifer, Jeremy, and their parents survived a 1990 tornado when we were fourth grade. They lost everything. Their insurance did not cover a fraction of what was needed afterward. Jennifer lost all of her childhood toys and family photos. She became a blank slate and had to reinvent herself. None of us knew what she was like when was little.

People say the Kelly family had a beautiful home in Carrollton. But, the four of them ended up living in a trailer park for a year before moving to Douglas County. They moved east to be closer to Atlanta after the 1996 Olympics were announced. As a result of the move, Jennifer and Jeremy were permanently branded as trailer park trash, along with about a third of the other county residents. Crystal's family had a little more money and lived in an apartment complex off Highway 5.

"Anne, don't let her pull you into her witchcraft ways. Jennifer is messing with dark stuff that she doesn't even know about. It's dangerous. Remember what Preacher Dan said about tolerating the occult? Okay. You need to remember. You stay out of trouble." Crystal advises me. She puts her apron back on.

Crystal moves to the pie display. She says, "Now, I remember your sweet brother liked chocolate pie. Goodness! He loved my momma's chocolate pie."

I had been rude without realizing it. "How is your momma? She was the best troop leader we ever had, and she was fun! Do you remember her trying to keep track of all of us in Savannah when we went to the J. Lowe house?"

Crystal giggles while slicing a piece of pie for me to take home. I have my ticket in hand along with a five dollar bill. I dig deeper in my tiny keychain wallet for an extra few coins. Crystal notices my digging, "Don't worry about the pie. It's not for you. I'm the one earning a paycheck right now. Let me get it for Robert. We 'bout killed my momma on that trip. We were all over the place. We were going up and down streets without names. We're lucky we all made it back!"

I laugh too and say, "I think we about ran into a buggy while running away from that strange man. Then we took that long river cruise that was so much fun! That was the best day. The city would have been ruined if they left the state capital there years ago. I want to live there one day."

"And, do what? There are no horses there anymore." Crystal asks with a genuine interest. "You're a horsewoman at heart. I don't know why you waste time and talent at that florist shop."

"Oh, I guess I could do anything. I don't know. I could give tours. Or, take Jennifer's tarot cards from her and set up on a street corner. I could be a gypsy, like Preeti." I say, trying to downplay Crystal's dire warnings about the cards.

"Girl, you could go work in the candy shops down there on River Street. You always made luscious cupcakes for the bake sales at school."

"I bake cupcakes only because I had no other fundraising options, Crystal."

When I ponder for a moment, I recall no fewer than twelve hair-brained ideas that Brittany and I cooked up to raise money for a Model United Nations trip. For our purposes, The Hague is located in Macon. Macon is far enough away to require an overnight hotel stay. Travel to Macon eats into any student fundraising.

Local middle and high school cheerleaders host Krispy Kreme doughnut sales on Saturday mornings near the major intersections, always near a grocery store. Model UN competitions do not have the kind of local support that jumping cheerleaders in short uni-forms do. Douglas County is located between several counties that have colleges, but we do not. Our academics are not as supported as the sports teams. Imagine the math team having a pep rally before a regional competition.

"Crystal, you can do anything," I say. I fiddle with the weak latch on the white Styrofoam container. "Go do whatever it is. Save the world. Please remember to write home about it. I'll keep email-ing you. I'll tell you everything that Mrs. Couch covers so it will be just like you're there."

I glance back at the table where Jennifer and Jeremy are sharing a cigarette. Jennifer is sporting a red tank top; it is in the mid-sixties outside. We have had an El Niño year. It never seems to stop raining. Jennifer could have been a Baywatch Babe if she wanted to, but she is perpetually stuck here in this county with the rest of us.

Jennifer looks at me with earnest and yells, "C'mon, let's go. We'll see Crystal again soon. Waffle House isn't going anywhere."

Crystal and I nod to each other as we exit. We acknowledge what was and what could have been. It feels like we have lost a major ally tonight. It is almost as though we could have turned the tide of the war if Crystal had stayed. But, we are not at war.

None of us know war. For a short time, in elementary school, we had bought yellow ribbons and tiny buttons at gas stations to sup-port the troops. I did not know anyone that knew anyone enlisted in the military. It is a foreign concept that does not affect my daily life. There is a Vietnam veteran that goes to church with us, but I do not know anything about him.

The thought of Crystal joining the military makes me uneasy. I am so glad we are at peace and that all the wars in the world are happening somewhere else. The only contact that I have with firing squads, genocide, invasions, toppling governments, and murder is watching *Channel One News* in the morning at school. May diplomacy ever prevail; at the very least, for Crystal's sake.

Five: Jeremy

December 27, 1998 9:09 AM
Douglasville, Georgia

"Jenny!" I yell for my twin sister as loud as I can. "How many people do we know named Anneewakee?"

The natural light in our parents' kitchen lingers dim at this hour. I am not accustomed to being awake at nine in the morning, thus the life of a happy college kid. I hear Jenny stumbling down the stairs. Her body knocks into the front door as she exits the stairs. She is still drunk from last night. Good. She will need to be drunker before the hour passes.

"What about Anne?" Jenny says with a wide yawn. "I guess we don't know anyone else with her name, Jerm. It's very Douglas County. Anne's parents named her after a Creek Indian Princess whose burial mound was on the banks of the Chattahoochee River. *Whoa.* What is that on the back porch?"

Jennifer rushes to the sliding glass door that opens onto the porch. She runs too fast and hits her nose and forehead. I follow her gaze to see a large screech owl. The owl's large yellow eyes captivate me. I feel entranced. We only know one Anneewakee. It is time to tell Jennifer.

"Dad left the Atlanta Journal-Constitution out." I start, uncertain of how to continue. "Mom didn't even cut out the coupons this week. I thought it was strange because they seem to have only read the front page. I never read the paper, but I did this morning."

"*Hist!* Put it on mute, Jerm. It's quiet in here with Mom and Dad off at mass. It's like the owl can hear our every thought. Mrs. Couch would say that he's an omen of death. I wonder who will die. Is that superstitious of me?"

"Anneewakee was murdered yesterday, Jenny. That's why our sweet girl didn't call you back last night after work." I say. The words stick painfully on my tongue.

Jenny slides down the glass screaming at the top of her lungs. She starts pounding on the glass door and it scares the owl away. I pull her back from the glass, so she does not break it. The last place I need to be is floundering helplessly in a sea of broken glass. Jennifer's face is turning red. She vomits and screams louder. Her tears are flowing hot and fast. She cannot see. I try to help her to the kitchen sink. She has pissed on herself.

Our parents come through the kitchen's side door. Dad flashes past me and picks Jennifer up. He carries her to the living room and lays her on the sofa. Mom picks up the bags Dad dropped at the door. She has enough ginger ale, root beer, and ice cream for a classroom of children.

"I saw the headline, Mom. I told Jenny. I thought you were at mass or something. I didn't know what to do." I say. I know I should be crying but I cannot. I'm too terrified for tears.

"You should have waited on me, JJ! Your dad and I read the article this morning and called the McWhorters. It's all true. Anne's funeral will be in January after they release her body to her family. They are not fit for any company right now, but we'll see them soon." Mom says and bites her lip.

"So, Anne dies, and you go and get ice cream?"

"Well, of course. What else am I supposed to do? I wanted to go to Blockbuster too and get some cartoons for you all to watch, but they open late on Sunday. I thought it might make JJ feel better. We're going to have to look after her this week."

"I don't think she'll get over this by the end of the week," I answer. I think I know my twin better than our mom knows us.

"She's not going to get over it. JJ will have to learn how to manage it. Now get her some saltines and tomato juice. Next, we'll move to coffee and then water."

My mom calls to my dad and sister, "JJ is getting you some saltines. Do you feel like you can manage a ginger ale? Step one is to get sobered up. We need to talk right away."

Not thinking straight, I look in the refrigerator for the box of saltines. I stare for a long moment. There is a small bottle of insulin in the door with about one dose left. It is Anne's. My mind floods with questions. I start asking the block of cheese why Anne died. I shake the milk jug and ask it how. My attention is a million places a once until my mother helps me out of the bottom refrigerator shelf where I was resting my head.

The cold penetrates my body. It makes my legs not work right. I think I forget to breathe for a moment. My mom is mumbling something about delayed shock. I am sitting scrunched up on the loveseat when I warm at last. Without noticing the movement, I see my parents turn off the television and sit down on our stout pine seventies coffee table. Mom is shaking. Dad is crying.

"Anneewakee was murdered yesterday while at work," Dad says with his lip trembling.

"The killer is on the loose. Police don't have anyone in custody. They don't know who did it." Mom adds with a slight sob.

"Well, is the Douglas County Sherriff's Office going to do its job or what?" Jennifer asks in an accusatory tone. "They need to get off their fat pig asses and find-"

"Anne wasn't killed in Douglas County," Dad says. "She's was working-"

"She works off Hospital Drive, Dad. That's the heart of Douglasville." I say.

"Anne was at another location, JJ." My mom answers me. "She was working in Austell. It's the strangest thing. She wasn't scheduled to work at that location until late Friday night. The police can't figure why. The restaurant manager said he was following Anne's wishes."

"I know why," Jennifer speaks up. "But, I'm not telling any of you."

"Jenny, if you know something, you have to talk to the police," I yell at her. She has always been a selfish drama queen. She will make Anne's death all about her. Anne's funeral will be like a morbid prom.

To my great surprise, Jenny stops crying. She goes several minutes in silence. She changes right in front of my eyes. Jenny throws a steely glance my way. She looks like she could rip my heart out and dance a jig on it. I am looking forward to her going back to Savannah. It is too awkward with her here at home. Now that I have had a taste of what it is like to be an only child, I admit that I like it a little.

"JJ, you have to talk to the Cobb County police," Dad says. Jenny shakes her head 'no.'

"You don't have a choice." Mom coaxes. "Don't you want to help Anne?"

Jenny keeps staring straight ahead. She sits up stalk straight and crosses her legs Indian style. As much as Mom and Dad bombard her with questions and flatter her, she will not say a word.

"Can't you see that she's taken a vow of silence?" I say. "She wants this to be all about her. She'll make you pay her money, find her better pot, or pay for her abortions or something."

Without being able to finish properly harassing Jennifer, she leaps at me and starts to try to choke me. This is the Jennifer that I know. She has no respect for humanity. Once I pry her hands from my throat, she starts trying to scratch at my face. She is such a bitch! She still will not say a word, but she is grunting hard. Since I am much larger than her, it is easy to throw her back onto the sofa.

As always, our parents do not know how to break-up the fight. We have gone years without ever addressing Jennifer's impulsive behavior and bad temper. I am glad that they finally witnessed it firsthand. They think I have been exaggerating for years.

"We don't believe in abortions, JJ. Just keep that in mind." Mom says. She is twisting the front section of the newspaper into a tight roll. Maybe she will hit Jennifer on the nose like a naughty puppy.

"Do we need to get a lawyer for you?" Dad asks with his head slumping over. He rubs his knees compulsively.

The fact that he is considering that Jenny's criminal involvement in Anne's death speaks to how little he thinks of her. Jenny remains silent but flips both of our parents off with her middle fingers. Next, she moves her fingers over in my direction. Yes, Jenny, I will screw off after being attacked by you. Whatever, bitch!

Mom clears her throat. She says, "Sweetie, we need to go Cumberland and buy you a black dress. You'll need it for the wake and the funeral. Anne's mom thought you might like to read something-"

"What is a wake?" I interrupt. If Anne were awake, we would not need the funeral.

"Viewing, JJ," Dad answers for Mom. "You kids haven't been to a funeral. When Nanna died, you were too young to go. But, you're adults now. Adults go to both the wake and the funeral. The wake is also known as the viewing. You will show up, be respectful, profess your faith to those that need comfort, and act like you weren't raised in a damn barn. I am tired of everyone in the county thinking that we're trailer trash. We have a lovely house, respectable jobs, and now we deserve to have proper and well-behaved offspring. That is where you two come in. You will wear solemn, modest clothing and not pull any theatrics."

"Even though we were young parents," Mom starts to lay into us. "We gave you both everything. Now the least that you two can do is to get your lives together. I was a mother at your age! I had four mouths to feed. I was happy to do it. Your father wasn't Catholic and wanted me to have an abortion."

"What?" I say with a shrill gasp. "Dad, you wanted to murder us?"

Ashamed, my mom runs into the kitchen and starts unloading the dishwasher. I never knew that Dad was not a born and raised Catholic. How did Mom manage that? How did Mom get pregnant as a teenager? Were they married?

Jennifer runs upstairs. She does not excel in emotional-ly-charged environments where she is not the center of attention. I bet she will be brazen enough to light a roach right in her room. I am sick of taking out our bathroom trash so that my parents will not see her myriad of cheap pregnancy tests. I will not cover for her salty behavior anymore.

Dad looks at me for a moment. He does not know what to say. He tries several times to start to say something. "I'm sorry I wasn't around much when you were young, JJ. I had to work two jobs to-"

"You don't have to apologize, Dad," I say, beating him to the punch.

"I'm not apologizing. I think that the way you turned out has a lot to do with me not being around. I blame myself."

"We're eighteen. We'll get the hang of the funeral. I'll help Jennifer. I'll wear a suit and it will be lovely." I say. I am still lying like a compressed accordion on the loveseat. I move to the sofa so I can stretch out some.

"JJ, I'm concerned that you're going to want to wear a dress like your sister."

"What? Me? No! Never! Why would you ever think that?" I yell before I can sit down.

"Not now, Josh!" My mom screams from the kitchen. "Leave JJ alone. There is already enough tragedy in this house without us telling him about preclusion from grace due to the violation of natural and divine law."

"What could be more tragic that not seeing our son in Heaven, Linda? *Huh*?" Dad yells. "We borrowed your laptop this morning, JJ. Your mom and I were searching to see if we could find out if our Anneewakee had truly passed away. We didn't like what we saw when we opened the blasted thing up. You brought home sin."

"You invaded my privacy! How could you?" I scream. "I had a screen lock on there!"

"You're going to have to think of better passwords, JJ. Your sister knew your password on the first try." Dad says while rubbing his hands together. "She was drunk, asleep, and still knew it."

"So, you're okay with Jennifer and her dalliances in Savannah, spreading her legs for who-knows-what and drinking like a fish, but not with my fiction writing? You are directly funding the mattress on which she lays her head at night while screwing around with strangers, Dad! You are enabling her to do that. I am saving the family money by living at home."

"You can't live at home anymore. I'm sorry. Your mother and I worked too hard for you to build your house on sin. We can't allow it. You're a man now. Your mom and I were going to talk to you about it today anyway. Anne's death was a brief detour in having this conversation."

"Is the sin that you're most concerned about the fact that I'm writing about homosexuality or that you think that I've engaged in it?"

"Both. I have never thought about another man's body in that way. Now, you can take the initiative and go talk to one of the priests."

"No! I know for certain that talking to a priest, at our parish or another, is not going to change my feelings. Besides, I'm a virgin. I'm like the only guy in college that is still a virgin after the first semester. How much more sinless and white do you want me?"

"You may always be a virgin that way but-"

"No! I've never been with anyone sexually, male or female. They're strictly thoughts and fantasies. People pay to visit my website, Dad. I'm making some money. I'm on scholarship and supporting myself. I pay for my textbooks and supplies. You should be kissing the ground that one of your two children turned out to be a success. Jennifer didn't have the GPA for any financial assistance. She went to a faraway college and had to live near campus, but not on campus, because they don't have student housing. She was trying to escape all of us and sow her wild oats."

Dad looks down at his feet. He doubles over on the coffee table. Mom saunters back in the living room. She squeezes Dad's shoulder. Dad limps off to their bedroom, looking defeated. I know that he wishes that another boy was his son. I wish that another man was my father. In that manner, I suppose that we are even.

"I've tried to speak to your father about you staying at home during college. It's really no trouble. I like having you here. Parents joke all the time about getting rid of their children at eighteen, but not me. We can't abide the sin, though. Could you compromise and talk to your father and the, um, stuff you're writing? Tell him that you'll delete it, or something?"

"Why do you treat Jennifer so much better than me? Did you want a girl more?" I say. It's easier to cry in front of Mom. While Jennifer uses her tears to manipulate others, my tears flow sincere.

Mom answers, "Girls are easier later on. Boys are more difficult at first. They get into so much trouble. I thought parenting adult twins would be an easy time period for us, but now things are complicated with JJ giving us the silent treatment too. We loved Anne like another daughter, and now she's gone. I still haven't accepted it yet. I won't admit it until I see her lying in her coffin. I always like to hold out hope until the last minute.

"I'm holding out hope for you too, JJ. I'm holding onto the idea that you'll meet precisely the right girl and have beautiful little blonde-headed angel babies. You would make a great father and husband. That is too much to throw away on lust-filled youthful illusions." Mom says. She stands up to walk away but pauses.

"What were your lust-filled youthful illusions, Mom? What did Jennifer and I destroy?"

"Nothing important, I'm certain. I have enjoyed traveling the path that was laid out before me. But, I did have dreams of being a Hollywood actress and marrying Bruce Jenner. I tried to get an audition for Dallas. Did I ever tell you?"

Laughing, I answer, "No, I missed that dream. That was your seventies version of the American dream?"

"Well, sure," My mom says with a smile. "What are kids dreaming about nowadays?"

"I guess a lot of us are following the dreams that our parents have for us. We did well enough in school to go to college. I did, right? I know you and Dad didn't dream of having a homoerotic fiction writer in the family, but here I am. I don't think I'm going to change, Mom."

"What about the other boys in your class? What are they up to?"

"Well, Brian achieved fatherhood first. Go, Brian. But he never married Alicia. Will, the little Goth boy, ran as fast as he could away from here. He grew up in a broken home, so good on him. David, Ryan, and Matt have been up to no good since 1995. *Ha!* They're going to end up on the TV show *Cops*, and not as police officers. Seth is off at some school in North Carolina after rejecting his HOPE Scholarship, but he has family up there. Tommy is scoring big at UGA. Women, professors, and coaches worship the ground he walks on. Being close to your fan base is good marketing. I work and go to school. Michael works a floor above me. I don't spend my days asking after classmates that I saw six months ago. My number hasn't changed."

"What about that girl? Christy? You two were lovely together. It seemed as though-"

"What about her, Mom? Did you think we were going to get married? She didn't have a date for prom and neither did I. We went because we were cheerleaders together. It was a rough night."

"And, Jeremy Patrick Kelly, I'm so proud of you for giving up certain illegal indulgences, JJ. I was hoping that you weren't going to give up on girls too. I expect more from you. You have to learn to control every little whim. You're an adult and need to be thinking about a real career, settling down, and having a family. Homosexuals are deviants, not family men. They don't have children. Don't you want to be a good husband and father?"

"If you want grandchildren, you should harass Jennifer. Using birth control is as much a sin as writing slash. She'll be pregnant with triplets by the end of the year."

"Don't be dramatic!"

"I'm not. The end of the year is four days away."

For the first time, my mom slaps me. She lays into me for making fun of sinful behavior. She explains to me over and over again how sin is a choice. I wish she had gone to Hollywood, become an actress, and that I had never been born. I think that would have been a far less cruel fate that being born into a makeshift family that did not want you to be alive.

"Think of Anne and her family today! The McWhorters are suffering the consequences of someone else's sin. Try and remember what Anne wanted to be. She was like another sister to you, JJ. I never had the opportunity to cover poetry in high school. I was too busy growing two whiny-ass, ungrateful children in my belly. Go and talk to your sister about what poem or text she'll select. It's the least that you can do."

"What's the least that I can do? I've already done the least. I remained silent when I should have spoken up so much sooner! The only poem that will suffice for Anne is Sidney Lanier's *The Song of the Chattahoochee*." I say in the firmest tone that I can muster.

"That's stupid! I've never even heard of it. It should be something about death."

"You don't know Anne. You don't know what we've been through in school. You don't know what happened to us. You weren't there for us! What? Do you think your GED qualifies you to voice a critique of education?"

For the second time, my mother slaps me. She says, "How dare you! Your father and I worked and worked to buy this house in this neighborhood so you could go to the best school in the county. We are spending money hand over fist for you and your sister's college education. Yes, my GED qualifies me to critique every single detail of the life that you can afford on my dime. Now go pick out a sad poem about death and grieving. Give it to your sister."

Walking up the stairs to Jennifer's room, I can sense that I am now a stranger in my childhood home. My family no longer welcomes me here. My opinion is not valued here. I am and have always been, a burden to my parents. This complex realization is depressing.

I exhale long and loud before knocking on Jennifer's door, but she hears me first and opens it. I say, "You have to pick out a poem to read. I told Mom that it had to be *The Song of the Chattahoochee*."

Jenny considers it for a moment and nods. She begins to close the door gently but changes her mind. She sticks her left hand through and holds mine for a brief crack in time. I see a library copy of *The Picture of Dorian Gray* by Oscar Wilde. It is my favorite book. I have no idea why Jenny is reading it.

"Jerm, did you know Mom is pregnant again?" Jenny says. She speaks with her eyes closed.

"No," I answer.

"She wants another set of twins. She thinks we're screwed up. I guess it is time for her to throw out the old kids and welcome the new." Jennifer snivels.

"I gathered that. Is that why there were a dozen pregnancy tests in the bathroom trash can this winter break?"

"No. Those pregnancy tests were not hers." Jennifer sobs softly. "I am going to stay in Savannah. I don't want to be around the new babies. We can't be bringing home sin or whatever."

"I am going to move out too, Jenny."

"Really? When did you decide that?"

"When you told me Mom is pregnant. There is no reason for a smart young thing like myself to shrivel here is the Atlanta suburbs when there is a gay revolution happening in the city. I will not be wasting away in the attic."

"That does sound a little like *Flowers in the Attic*, doesn't it?" Jenny giggles a little.

"Don't eat any of Mom's doughnuts, okay?" I say. I squeeze her hand. She slowly closes her bedroom door.

There are things left unsaid between us. I hate being a twin. Now, Jenny does too. The river of energy that once flowed between us has dried up. Now the two of us are only connected by our rocky riverbed of a family. No flowers will grow here. We will not blossom where we have been planted. I need to find new, fertile soil and grow into whatever it is that I am destined to become.

Six: Crystal

◆━━━━━━━━━━━━━━━━━━━━━━━━━◆

A typical lunch at Douglas County High School is akin to a fish bowl. The subjects, like me, are always observed by adults that linger on the fringes of the cafeteria. Like animal handlers at the zoo, they are detached from their observed population. The school resource officer, administrators, cafeteria staff, and teachers are prepared to render simultaneous judgment and punishment at a moment's notice. I imagine this is how my family's jail birds feel when they dine in a cafeteria on the inside.

As I sit down at our usual table, I glance over at the slow moving lunch line. You would think that the first period cafeteria shift would move at a more clipped pace, but it does not. Anne looks tired and her hands are full with her salad bar tray. At least now that we are second semester juniors, we get to eat first and everything in the kitchen area is clean when we walk through the doors. The utensil holders and refrigerated milk case are full. There is no gum on the soup ladle or spit on the floor yet.

"My white deck is going to kick your blue deck to the curb, David. Plus, Anne will be here in a minute. I'll tap her manna to get started." I say as I pull out my *Magic* cards.

My opponent and table mate looks over at me, "Crystal, don't get any ketchup on Anne's library. For real! Point of fact, it is my deck. I'm only letting her borrow it today."

This child is getting on my nerves, so I reprimand him, "David, that mess is not even ketchup. That is pizza sauce from this nasty pizza. We have the worst food in the world. Who thinks that you can give growing children pizza, tater tots, and chocolate milk and say that this is a balanced diet?"

"I've never, not once, thought about where this food comes from, Crystal. Do we get to eat better stuff when we graduate? I thought the food was probably the same at every college everywhere. We're all going to college, of course."

"Do you genuinely believe that all three hundred and something of us are going to college? And, that the food is the same everywhere?"

David is sheltered. I should be patient with him. His mom works in the cafeteria here. For all I know he may have school cafeteria food at home for dinner. At least, I bet he has food at home. My mom has been out of work since the Olympics left. Her job was temporary and without benefits. Now that the Olympics are over, the pantry is starting to become empty. It has been like this for seven months.

"What? What the heck is that? Where did that Battlegrace Angel come from? I thought you only had Serra Angels." David says as Anne sat down with her tray.

In the time that it took Anne to get real food and pay with pocket change, David and I have already eaten our free meals. Anne has a very different relationship with food. The wrong food can kill her. David and I do not care. Beggars cannot be choosers. Sweet Anne will never know what it is like to be hungry. I hope she never knows. I cast the thought away as we stack our trays on the large laminate-topped circle table.

"Oh, I found some amazing artifact cards this weekend at the flea market in Bremen," Anne says. She eats her salad quickly.

Anne's soup is getting cold. I would love to have the ability to take something home. I could eat it while walking from the bus to the apartment. There is some comfort in being an only child and not having to sharing food. I know David has to share food with his little sister; but, at least his parents were working and both were in the food industry. Both Anne and David have two parents, lucky dogs.

"That reminds me, Anne. I owe your bro some cards. He helped me fill out my deck when I went to see him at the comic store last week," I say as I flip past some white knights and continue, "He gave me a bunch of strip mines and now I want to give him a Dwarven Hold. With *Magic: The Gathering* fifth-edition coming out last month, the cards have gone down in value. But, I appreciate him."

Heather and Nicole give us a vile look from the popular girl table. I call them *Pop Gulls* because they flock like seagulls. They have been insufferable in American Lit this year. I cannot imagine going through Brit Lit with them next year. On the other hand, I desperately want the college credit that comes along with successfully passing a CL English Exam. Nicole stares at us and gets up with her folded arms and walks away in a huff. I wonder what that witch is up to right now.

Yesterday, I had to read Amy Lowell's *Patterns* the minute we started class. I have not read poetry to an audience before and that poem was a mess. I thought it started off talking about a garden, but Mrs. Couch interrupted me on the third line and told me that I was reading it wrong. She told me that I was only supposed to pause if I saw punctuation. The whole poem ended with me taking the Lord's name in vain. I did not know what to do. I know that we had a discussion about the poem for half an hour after I read it but I have no idea what anyone said. I only heard snickering.

As my thoughts are drifting, I notice David staring at me. I say, "What's up?"

"Don't look behind Anne." David mimes with his mouth.

The principal is standing six inches from the back of Anne's chair. The situation is obvious to me. Nicole fluttered her little butt up to the principal's office. We are going to be reprimanded for something. I do not know how, but Jennifer and I are the only two students in the advanced classes that ever go to ISS or serve detention. And, I swear, our punishments are always for the stupidest reasons.

Last week, I said something about a storyline that I saw on Jerry Springer. I got detention! It was not a bad storyline but it was the fact that I invoked the name *Jerry Springer*. As though saying the celebrity name would act as an incantation to spoil the pretty little white quasi-virgin heifers at DCHS.

For a moment, I thought I could escape. I was planning to take my tray back, slip by the teacher's lounge, and head toward the covered walkway down the hill to Upper Warren-Dorris. Or, alternately, I could fake indigestion and walk up the ones story ramp to the top of Mashburn. I slowly slide my hand toward my cards. *Magic* cards are not free and too valuable to walk away from.

"Stop right there, Crystal. We've had a witchcraft complaint from a random student." Principal Daniell says.

"Bull crap, sir. It was no random student. It was Nicole, that little snot!" I say

"Crystal, please don't make me send you to ISS. I want to give everyone a verbal warning. Here is your warning: You can't play *Magic* out in public, like the school cafeteria."

The principal sits down next to Anne. He looks at the cards and says, "I don't understand this. I'm not even quite sure what y'all are doing. I have young people running to my office day in and out complaining about something or another. It's not why I became a principal. I wanted to inspire a generation. Now, I'm sitting at a table full of decks of cards and it's not poker. Are there any pictures of anything naked in here?"

David is the first to speak up, "Uh, no, sir. Not anymore. There used to be some cards, which I never owned, or brought to school, that had some very artistically stylized figures but they weren't humans."

Principal Daniell sits back in the plastic chair. He looks confused. He says, "Well, how can they be naked if they're not human? How do you know if non-human creatures are naked?"

I thought back to my American Government class. I say, "I think Justice Potter said something about obscenity and knowing when he saw it in *Jacobellis v. Ohio*, sir."

"Crystal, it would be a crime against humanity if you grew up to be anything but a lawyer. I couldn't think of punishing you all for anything with a concise defense like that. When you kids can properly defend your position with legitimate discussion and evidence, I darn near want to cry. It gives me hope in your generation." Principal Daniell says.

I have never received such a high compliment from anyone at any school; ever. The principal, David, and Anne did not know the half of it when it came to verbal self-defense. I try to smile pretty, act nice, and relax my hair but there is a fierce monster that grows inside me when I go home and find my momma with a bottle. She never got over my daddy dying. I try to keep the monster quiet but sometimes it comes out. I do not have a name for the feeling but I know it is there; it is too familiar.

Daddy was sick for years but his death still shocked Momma. Her two younger brothers stepped in and helped out and I am grateful my uncles for what they could do at the time. But, the bottom line is that I am not their responsibility. When I think about it, I am my own responsibility despite not being eighteen-years-old on paper.

It would be nice if my momma could fend for herself a little bit better, but she is my responsibility too. God bless those who love addicts. It is not an easy road, as I have sadly discovered. Momma is my responsibility until she can function better. She has a hard time telling the difference between day and night; when she should or should not shower, or even eat.

Momma and Daddy had a dream to make money during the Olympics. They were going to open a little screen printing business and have kiosks in downtown Atlanta during the games. Plans to help build the *Gone with the Wind* theme park in a nearby county have not panned out yet. Rather than using anything officially licensed for printing, they were going to make the cheapest and most generic shirts possible and then charge half of what the other vendors were charging. Daddy called it a niche market. They got a tiny little storefront across from K-Mart and near our favorite restaurant, Szechuan Village.

One shopping center off Georgia Highway 5 has Hancock Fabric, Blockbuster Video, and Ruby Tuesday. The JCPenney catalog pick-up location used to be in a drug store in the center. Before Wal-Mart opened off Stewart Mill Parkway, it was the western edge of Douglasville. Po' Folks is in the same shopping center's parking lot as well but has officially changed the name to Folks now. We all still call it Po' Folks. At that time, my family and I were not poor folks.

Now, my mood for the rest of the day hangs on either a reprimand or a compliment from a school administrator. My life has become too small. Waves of regret, hope, sadness, and joy wash over me in waves like I am standing at the edge of Lake Lanier. If I stand here, in my mind, any longer then my feet will sink into the ground. I will be Artax instead of Atreyu.

"Well, thank you, sir. I appreciate that." I say to Principal Daniell. He nods.

I look at the *Magic* cards in front of me like they are foreign objects. It dawns on me that I was playing a game. I was playing a portable board game. I had wasted gas, at almost a full dollar a gallon, to go a couple of exits west and buy, sell, and trade *Magic* cards. What was I thinking? Principal Daniell has continued talking to Anne and David about something unimportant. This is a good time to excuse myself to the bathroom.

I pick up my cards, smile at the principal, David, and Anne. I take my tray and leave the cafeteria three minutes early. I run up the stairs to get to the front of Mashburn Hall as quickly as possible. I immediately go to see Mrs. Graham. I catch her eating cherry tomatoes at her desk while the rest of the career center is as silent as a tomb.

Mrs. Graham slowly reaches for her sweet tea. She tries to recall my face. Finally she says, "Hi, sweetheart. Are you a senior this year? Are you getting ready to graduate? Graduation is late this year because we started late because of the Olympics. You have plenty of time to start whatever process you want to start. Do you want to apply to a university?"

"No, ma'am. I'm still a junior. I need a work permit. How do I get one?"

"You fill out a form and have your parents sign permission. What are you doing to do?" She says while looking too puzzled for the conversation. Isn't this an essential part of her job?

"I'm going to be a waitress." I say.

Waitressing is an ill-conceived idea but I know that I can make some tip money off the books and that will help get me started. I have never interviewed for a real job. The most that I have done, until five minutes ago, is participate in Model UN. We have mock trials to practice public speaking but, that is nothing special. I cannot let my fears control my actions, including static from Mrs. Graham.

"Well, where?" Mrs. Graham looked at me strangely. It is like she is trying to read my mind.

"*Um.* You know, I don't have that figured out yet. But, there are about one hundred restaurants in a fifteen-mile radius of our home so I can start with that circle of businesses." I say.

I am completely committed to my plan of action now. I am never going to be poor again. I am going to support myself. I will work my way out of desperation.

"Sweetheart, you may want to envision some things before interviewing. Reflect on how you're going to get to work. Estimate what your hours will be. Consider your base pay. Know that you'll have to pay some taxes. Determine whether the company charges for uniforms. Ask if they have a management training program," Mrs. Graham says.

Much to my surprise, Mrs. Graham clearly has her act down. The fact that I am not the first student to bumble into her career center like this worries me a little. I want to be unique. I do not want to think that I am following in the footsteps of other students before me. What happens to those people? They do not come back to high school. There are no tales of survival to learn from on this front.

Mrs. Graham sits down at a student table. She pats a padded seat next to her. She folds her hands and begins, "Did you read the *Little House on the Prairie* series when you were little?"

"No, ma'am. I didn't. But, I know what it is. I used to watch TBS with my momma during the summers. We didn't have cable. *Little House* came on before *Mama's Family*. *Little House* started at 9:05 AM."

A hesitant smile crosses her face, "Well, sweetheart. The television series is very different from the book series, you see. The two aren't anything alike, really, other than the characters have the same names."

"Why are we talking about *Little House*?"

"In the books, you see, once Laura started earning money; well, she liked earning money."

"Yes, I think prairie girl and I will have something in common," I say and snort.

"Well, she had to use a lot of self-discipline to be able to work one or two jobs and also finish school. Do you have that kind of discipline? We promote the GED program for those that have already dropped out for extenuating circumstances. We have night school as well. I don't think you have that set of circumstances. I would like to see you get a high school degree. I'm sure your parents would like to see you get a high school degree. I think you're on college track, am I right?"

"Yes, Mrs. Graham. I'm sure you're right. I think I have that self-discipline. But, my parents are supportive of my desire to work right now. They believe that it will teach me that discipline I need." I lie.

"Oh, okay, then. Come back later today and pick up your permit."

The bell rings and I join the crowd in Mashburn Hall. I am ready to say goodbye to it all. I think about the Boar's Head Festival a few months ago. I am not a very good entertainer but I was happy to help bus the tables and deliver the food during the festival. I do not have any religious objections to helping to serve a whole hog tied with an apple in its mouth. If I start working I may have to quit chorus and drama club as well. Those were the things that helped me get through these last few years of working with my momma and taking care of things after Daddy died.

I sit down in the medium-sized chairs in the classroom. Suddenly, the desks seem inadequate. The desks are too small to do any real work. I simply do not have enough space. It feels like the idea of my work permit was too much for the desk. I am self-conscious enough to understand that I have become obsessed with the idea of working. I want to earn a real paycheck. I am exhausted with trading cards only to further myself in a fictional game. I want to be in the outside world, with real people, and earning American greenbacks.

Before anyone could say anything, Mrs. Couch sits down at her own student desk at the front of the classroom. She places her massive gradebook in front of her. I have always thought that she would teeter-totter the wrong way if there was ever a time when she did not have it in her hands. I conclude that it would throw off the balance of the invisible force field that binds the universe and the school together.

Mrs. Couch calls on one of her two teacher's pets. Nicole clenches her jaw when she hears the poem she has been assigned. Mrs. Couch, places her reading glasses at the tip of her nose. She is the most generic English teacher that had ever existed since the dawn of mankind. Yet, she is cruel. Her nickname is Lady Macbeth although she strikes me as being more like Hamlet's mother, a queen in the dark.

"Let's move forward with poetry in Realism and the Frontier. Nicole will be reading *Song of the Chattahoochee* by Sidney Lanier."

Nicole quivers as she stands near her desk. She is on the same side of the room as Anne and I, but closer to Mrs. Couch. She cannot make eye contact with the class. She buries her nose deep in her textbook. Her breathing increases and she mumbles, "Out of the hills of...um...Haber...uh...Habersham, Down the valleys of Hall. I hurry a mane. A man? Uh, um. What? Oh. I hurry amain to reach the airplane. I mean, I'm sorry, I mean plain."

Mrs. Couch's eyes grow large and her mouth drops open. She sits there staring at Nicole like she is mythical creature without wings that has stumbled into her classroom. Nicole's read-aloud is in a tailspin. She needs help.

Hesitantly, Mrs. Couch says, "Oh, dear, what shall we do? Start over."

The first stanza drones on. None of us know what is wrong with Nicole. She cannot read aloud to save her life. The worst possible profession for her would be to become a teacher. She is petrified of her own voice, public speaking, or may be illiterate.

When Mrs. Couch talks to us about literature, Nicole seems like she has some sense but there is something wrong with that girl's brain. A wire is loose somewhere. Once, she had a difficult time reading lab instructions in biology. She almost hurt herself.

I raise my hand confidently, "Please, Mrs. Couch. I would like to read."

Mrs. Couch is cautious. She thinks it is a booby trap. "Well, only if it's okay with Nicole."

Nicole nods and concedes the class time to me. I pick up my massive, well-used *American Experience* text. The county has had this series of Prentice Hall books since the fall of 1991 when we started sixth grade. They are stained, well-used, and no longer fresh. Caressing the page, I feel a flair for the dramatic come over me. If I quit school this year, I want to do it on a high note.

Walking over to David, I hold my book in my right hand and say, "All down the hills of Habersham. All through the valleys of Hall."

Straightening my back, I move to Mrs. Couch and lean against the student version of her desk, "The rushes cried *Abide. Abide.* The willful waterweeds held me thrall. The laving laurel turned my tide."

I walk toward Heather. I enunciate with razor precision when I say, "The ferns and the fondling grass said *Stay.* The dewberry dipped for to work delay."

Next, I move to the back of the classroom to Preeti and Stephanie, who are hiding on the fringes. They are embarrassed that I have acknowledged them. So, I grow louder, "And the little reeds sighed *Abide, abide, Here in the hills of Habersham. Here in the valleys of Hall.*"

Matt is in the corner looking half hung-over and half high. I sit on the edge of his desk where he is resting his head on his arms. My butt touches the elbow of his hoodie that he is inexplicably wearing in April.

"High o'er the hills of Habersham, Veiling the valleys of Hall, The hickory told me manifold Fair tales of shade, the poplar tall Wrought me her shadowy self to hold." I say leaning backward into the half-asleep Matt.

Matt groans and I shift to the pod of boys on the other side of the room who sit opposite from myself and Anne. I lick my lips at

Tommy, Seth, Justin, and Will and say, "The chestnut, the oak, the walnut, the pine, Overleaning, with flickering meaning and sign, Said, *Pass not, so cold, these manifold Deep shades of the hills of Habersham, These glades in the valleys of Hall.*"

Jeremy stands up and starts shaking his bottom and snapping his fingers. Mrs. Couch parts her lips even further but no audible noises come out, so I continue, "And oft in the hills of Habersham, And oft in the valleys of Hall, The white quartz shone, and the smooth brooke-stone Did bar me of passage with friendly brawl."

I rub up against Jeremy like a cat and continue, "And many a luminous jewel lone-Crystals clear or a-cloud with mist."

My next audience is the jocks. I lay backward across the top of Tommy's empty desk. Tommy's head, desk, and backpack were all empty. I moan, "Ruby, garnet and amethyst-Made lures with the lights of streaming stone In the clefts of the hills of Habersham, In the beds of the valleys of Hall."

I pause as I rest the large book on my flat stomach. Looking at Jennifer, I say, "But oh, not the hills of Habersham, And oh, no the valleys of Hall."

Studying the ceiling tiles, I sigh. My soul wanted to burst out of the confines of the Lower Banks building and right out of the gifted kids' semi-private hallway. I take a deep breath and exhale, "Avail: I am fain for to water the plain. Downward the voice of Duty call – Downward, to toil and be mixed with the main."

Tommy slips a dollar bill in the waist of my jeans and gives a shrill whistle. I get up and seductively touch the edge of Jeremy's desk with my sandals. I deepen my voice to say, "The dry fields burn, and the mills are to turn, And a myriad flowers mortally yearn."

I snap away from Jeremy's desk and sit in Justin's lap. I am mortifying him but I finish, "And the lordly main from beyond the plain Calls o'er the hills of Habersham, Calls through the valleys of Hall."

Having finished the poem, I walk over to a pale Anne. With all the love in the world for my sister scout, I say, "You're the Chattahoochee, Anne. You flow through people and places. You bind us together. You cross manmade boundaries. You try to always see every side. This poem is for you."

Nicole walks over to the intercom button. She presses it without saying a word. A nameless office lady squeaks over the aging speaker, "Yes, Mrs. Couch?"

"Yes, I need the resource officer to escort Crystal Ryan back to ISS, again."

"I'm sorry, ma'am. We can't hear you. Did you say that you need someone to take Brian?"

"No. Crystal Ryan."

"Your son, Brian, is already in ISS, Mrs. Couch."

"I know that! I said, 'Crystal Ryan.'"

"I'm sorry, Mrs. Couch. The principal has already radioed that he is in your class. We do not have anyone else to send."

My face radiates a strange heat from the dramatic exertion. I feel an arrogance, and fear, that cannot be contained. I swallow hard and see the principal peeping through the small glass window in our closed classroom door. He is smiling. I am smiling. The class is excited. Sidney Lanier is probably more excited than Mrs. Couch, and he is dead. The only people put out by the performance are Mrs. Couch and her two suck-ups, Heather and Nicole.

I feel an airy paternal pride coming from the principal. My performance is a one-time gig and it cost me dearly to perform. I know that there will be other painful forms of retribution from Mrs. Couch. She can make me suffer through my grades and will close all kinds of opportunities to me. I may have jeopardized my work permit for the sake of livening up the class. But, I am an adult now. I weighed the costs and benefits and made my own decision. I stand by it. Heck, I stand by my decision with an extra dollar in my pocket.

Seven: Matt

October 18, 2005 9:10 AM
Las Vegas, Nevada

In that strange, foggy moment between being asleep and awake, I start thinking about Anne, a girl that I went to school with years ago. As if she were lying on the pillow next to me, I feel the warmth from her sun-kissed skin. The decisive warmth of her brown eyes compliments the aroma of grapes and exotic cheeses whose names I cannot pronounce.

In my half-dream, she says, "Matt, do you know the way to the Xanadu? Follow me to where the river caverns end at a sunless sea. There are forests as ancient as the hills. Come on, Matt. Follow me."

The hotel room is dark. I cannot tell what time it is outside. I cannot feel what time it is. Time has abandoned me. We are in a different time zone. The sound of my jaws smacking wake me further. I can tell from the smell of the room that we are west of the Mississippi River.

The desert air is interrupted by a familiar sensation, though. My blood veins cry out, *feed me*. My brain says *you are not starving; you just need a few hits*. Then, I wake up fully, and I can feel my veins talking to me from all over my body. My cravings have followed me here, to Las Vegas, Nevada, along with my gambling habits.

"Hey, David! Know what I'm thinking about right now? It's crazy, right? But I'm thinking about Samuel Taylor Coleridge's *Kubla Khan*. I'm high and thinking about poetry." I say and giggle.

Looking for some water, I have another thought, "Remember that time that I passed out in Mrs. Couch's class, and that girl went off during realism and poetry. Like, remember? She went OFF! Dude! How could I have missed that show? Anne told me all about it afterward. I've been to shows in Vegas, man, but it's nothing personal like that. A free lap show and all. The girls shakin' it out here don't mean anything to me."

Blood starts flowing throw my cold veins as I tip-toe back towards consciousness from my drug-induced haze. The first place the blood visits is my tallywacker. Thinking about the girls loose with their bodies and morals here make me ache for the girls back home. I once stole a glimpse of Anne topless in a swimming pool.

On my honor, I would have given my both my balls to see deeper into the water. I know she was skinny dipping. The cold water made her nipples stand out like cork board push-pins. I wanted to screw her there in the pool, but my body would have none of it. My tallywacker is a Southern Boy. I did not know heated pools existed back in the nineties.

"Matt. You're a stupid whoremonger. Go back to sleep. I can hear you moaning about some girl." David says through a pillow.

"Oh, right. I get it. That insult is a flashback to Brit Lit. I still have no idea how I passed those classes. I'm glad Brian helped me out with our little scheme; because it was his mom and stuff. I am famished. How can I be so hungry? When was the last time we ate, man?"

The room was a regular shape, but the whole set-up feels askew. I do not see any luggage either. I quickly search the room for any sign of snacks. Anything edible would have been fine. The room is unfamiliar. I start walking back and forth to see if I can see anything new each time I make a loop in the room. I look out the window to see that we are rather high up in this hotel's towers. I can see a water fountain below with dancing water jets but no sound. I see the Eiffel frickin' Tower across the street. I also see the Aladdin. I know where I am now, but how did we get here?

I shake David and say, "Hey, man! We gotta go. I don't think this is where our stuff is. I don't know where our stuff is."

David looks pink and vomits over the side of the bed. He is choking. I wish that I could remember anything from all those years of being in scouts. But, in this emergency, everything blends together in my fried brain. I hold David so he will not fall. I throw a sheet on the floor. I instantly start having flashbacks. I do not want to witness another friend die. I cannot do it. Not again. Not so soon. We are only twenty-five. This is some stately pleasure dome that we have found ourselves in today.

A woman walks into the room wearing a wet one-piece athletic style bathing suit. I listen as close as I can to her deep and authoritative voice when she says, "Oh, now that you boys are awake, maybe you could, uh-"

"I'm sorry I don't remember last night. I'm so, so, so sorry. But, my friend David here is really sick. I'm so scared that he's going to die. Is there any way at all that you could find it in your heart to help us? Could you do that for me?" I say and flash her signature smile.

The strange wet woman is unimpressed. She gives me the same look that Mrs. Couch would give me when I dropped Brian off late at night after we smoked a little too much in high school. Unlike the beatniks and other weirdoes, we were not smoking anything filtered. But, I justified screwing around with Mary Jane for a decade by saying that it was all natural. It is mostly natural. Now that I think about it, it is probably unnatural. Natural would have been grown and harvested on our own; like, Farmer in the Dell type of stuff.

The bronzed lean woman in the tight fitting bathing suit has a tight brunette bun. Everything about her is tight. She looks at me seriously and then kicks me. She says, "Listen, white trash, I have no patience for your mess. It's your mess. Clean it up. Leave a tip for the maid after she has to deal with this disgusting scene. I'm calling the cops. You're not twelve-years old. You're responsible for your shit."

I want to find her sexy, but I find her extremely frightening. She has knocked me to the ground. I have no idea what type of sex we may or may not have had last night. I am used to women finding me interesting, attractive, and giving me a lot of space, and meth. This chick is not giving me space or even the benefit of a shadow of a doubt! As a matter of fact, her fingers are moving toward my knee. She is trying to kill me.

"Listen, you trite little beast, I am not impressed by your antics nor your friend's games. You are not cute. You are not cuddly. You're old enough not to be in need. You don't get to act any which way in this world and not have to pay the price. We all have to pay the toll. And, sweetness, you are in arrears right now." She says through gritted teeth. Her lips are pursed and still. She did not flinch or hesitate.

Oh, I would have given anything to believe that she was anything other than a Terminator machine sent from the future to kill us right then. But, I know what I know: she is the Terminator. Soon, this woman would be wailing for her demon-lover. Wait a second: am I the demon-lover?

"My stepmother made Daddy take pity on you when we found you both on the Strip last night. I don't have pity. I lack pity. I think you're an offense to humanity. You're a sack of crap that took my hotel room last night. I want it back. This is my graduation trip, asshole! Now I've had to share my special time with my father and stepmother instead of in my own hotel room. You will never be able to repay me."

My bowels release. I imbulbitate. I do not know what else to do. I have been holding it all night, or maybe even a week.

The woman in the purple suit looks like she could incinerate me with a wave of her hand. The Terminator is going to kill me. David is unconscious next to me. He starts looking gray, but the gray turns to blue. In a few seconds, he is purple. David is dying. It is all happening all over again, like a video playing in a continuous loop. Maybe the third overdose is the charm. He will survive.

The Terminator calls the front desk for an ambulance. She pounds on the wall nearest me, inches above one of the queen bed headboards. She spouts an exaggerated, "Daaaaddddy!"

Principal Daniell skids into the room. He says, "Matt, what happened?"

"Sir, I'm so glad you're here. David's not breathing. Did you time travel here?"

The principal's daughter shoots eye daggers my way and says firmly, "I've already called for help. I think we should make the scout perform CPR. I'm not getting near a dead body."

I do not know how else to help David, so I move his body to the floor. I tart what I can recall of CPR. I could not, under any circumstances, blow air into his lungs. But, this was my mess. I was the first person ever to give David a puff. It was me on that terrible, cold night in December 1998. It was all on me.

My ravening lungs say, "Come and sit here awhile and let us smoke off unspeakable acts and try to float away."

David's addiction is my fault. How could I do this to my fellow scout? Our scoutmaster had been weird. He taught a ridiculous song with which to do the compressions. I start humming the song through the stony silence.

In a moment, like an angel touched him, David throws up again. I roll him to his side and pat his back. I am not certain that I am supposed to do that. He keeps going. He is holding his stomach and his bloodshot eyes open wide. His eyes are red. He looks like something out of a comic book. He is scaring me.

The principal comes over, "Spoon feeding teaches us nothing but the shape of the spoon."

"What? What the hell does that mean, man?" I say. I look around the beautiful ivory room and the previously hygienic bedding that David and I have tainted.

If I died right this second, no one would say anything memorable about me. Friends and family would probably think, "Yeah, Matt was a confirmed loser. The gifted program didn't help. He never got it together. He let his friends die seven years ago, and again five years ago and then he made the same mistake again, but this time he was high on homemade meth instead of street drugs and alcohol."

I hold David's head in my lap and stroke him like he is a kitten, "Dammit. Dude, we gotta get our shit together. What if our principal hadn't found us out? I mean, what are the chances that our damn high school principal would find us out here in Sin City?"

Principal Daniell says, "The chances are decent if I'm taking my family to see Elton John's *Red Piano* at Caesars Palace. You boys were camped out on the Strip. My dear, sweet wife recognized you and begged me to help you both back to the hotel to sleep it off. That woman has a heart of gold. I can't believe you're still wearing the same old loser clothing, Matt. You're not a surfer! You'll never be a surfer. And, the dang cops should have taken you to jail to dry out. People don't play around here. You've got to get clean somewhere."

Terminator looks at me. She kicks my leg and says, "You ruined my graduation gift. You destroyed my vacation. Grow up. I'm not your mama. Your mama doesn't even want to be your mama; for shame!"

David and I have no shame. We have been living in the tunnels beneath Las Vegas. Consistent with my volunteer work in high school, we are both vaguely involved with an underground economy involving sex, drugs, and human relocation services. We share an unzipped sleeping bag that smells like cat urine and anguish.

Every time it rains, we have to start over again. I have a milk crate next to the sleeping bag that contains all of my worldly possessions outside of my mom's Douglasville home. I can never remember what is in there: another dirty shirt, meth, and a phone, I think, business cards, perhaps? We cannot leave alcohol lying around. People steal even the smallest bottles of water or alcohol without hesitation.

Emergency medical technicians tap on the open door. Two very fit men whisk David onto a stretcher, but they could have used a third, and I could have used a fifth. Everything is quieter and more reverent than expected. Principal Daniell follows David after giving me a stern look.

I look to the Terminator for an answer. I want her to tell me how to make things right. Instead, she says, "Don't look at me like that. How dare you! You're not my project. I'm not here to groom you like a lost pet that needs a bath before adoption. Get out of my room!"

In a happy accident, I find David's class ring sitting on the desk. I take the ring and scurry out the door. I wish I knew of an easy and quiet exit, but Vegas casinos are not famous for open-to-the-public secret exits. I run down the hall to catch up with David, but he is already gone. I do not have a hotel room key of any kind so I know there is no place to go, at least not at this hotel. I check my pockets in the elevator on the way down. I have a ten-dollar-bill.

On the ground level, I find an outdoor escalator. I walk toward the Aladdin casino. I think I may go through their Desert Passage market to locate cheap (by Strip standards) clothes. Once inside, an elderly clerk takes one look at me and scoots me out of her stall. She yells, "You skinny rat! Go!"

No clean clothes for me. No food for me. No chicken feed for me.

There is a hoochie that I befriended last week who works here at the Aladdin. She works for a time share company near the main casino floor. She hooks people up with free tickets for things like the Beatles impersonator shows after they tour the time share.

What she does not realize is that when you cart these folks out to the sticks and say, "Look! Our property has real grass," that is the wrong approach. Those people are not coming to Vegas to look at the grass. If they are interested in grass, it is of a different variety.

I stop by her desk to see if she is working. I wave hello to one of her friends that I met once. She says, "Oh, you smell like cat litter, rattlesnakes, and blood. You cannot be here! It's not appropriate."

It is time for my Southern Boy self to turn on the charm. I say, "Oh, beautiful: Why you so uptight 'bout 'tis? I'll take care of myself and you too."

Typically, this tactic works. It has always worked before. Today, it is not working. I am removed immediately by armed guards. At least they helped me find an ungraceful exit quickly as I start to slink down the street toward the MGM Grand to see if I can pop into a crapper to change clothes. But, first, I have to find clean clothes. If I were thinking clearly, I would have done it earlier in the Desert Passage and haggled.

The dampness outside that follows the rain makes for an unusually humid day. I have not had humidity like this since I left Georgia five years ago. I blame the rain and Principal Daniell for destroying my mojo. But, if I think about, this city has it in for me. It does not want me here.

The sounds of steelpans fill the air as I continue walking. I do not know what direction I am going but happen on the Hawaiian Village after a few minutes. A sign reads, *What happens in Vegas happens here.* There is a sign for a show featuring Joe Krathwohl but only on Friday, Saturday, and Sunday. I am not sure what today is, but it was Monday through Thursday. I do not know what Joe did Monday through Thursday, but he was probably off somewhere doing it right now.

Hot damn, what it must be like to have not one job but two! There is an open stage area with two young women in plain black string bikini tops and long grass skirts the color of Surge. I want that Joe's job. I will be here for him Monday through Thursday. As much as I am all about redneck cocaine, I am all about pussy too.

One of the kiosks is selling CSI shirts. That score is a quick pick-up. I walk over to the store selling "Christian Designs" and find a pair of generic tourist shorts. Unfortunately, the cashiers see me. I have to pay for those stupid things. Even on clearance, the shorts are more than half of my ten. While walking by an overstuffed baby stroller without a baby, I grab a handful of random items out of the open diaper bag. Finders keepers, right?

Fortunately for me, there is a lot of construction behind the Aladdin. The Marriott is building a massive time-share complex called the Grand Chateau. I move back from the Hawaiian village toward the time-shares where I know security will be questionable. I should be able to find a bathroom. My plan is to double-back on my route and head to the Krave nightclub at the Aladdin. I know a dancer in there that likes kissing when she was drinking. And, she likes keeping her money in her boots and she likes taking her boots off for me. All I have to do is offer to rub her achy feet. Dancers have ugly feet, tiny titties, flat abs, and hot asses. All dancers are saving up for boob jobs; gnarly feet be damned.

The best that I can do is a porta-potty. It smells like a 'visiting team' locker room and a dairy farm. I am scared to touch anything because I know there is no place to wash my hands. I take off my damp hoodie and leave it on the bright green floor. I thought that I was wearing a tee shirt, but I am not. I do not know how that happened. I pull my shorts down and see that my boxers were more than a few days old. Shit covers me from my waist to knees. Oh, man. I am shamefaced, and I am the only one here.

What happened to me? When I was living at Mom's, she always made sure I had clean clothes to wear to school. I ate pop-tarts on the way out the door. I would love a strawberry pop-tart and orange juice. And, what is this feeling? What is that feeling my chest? I touch my sternum. Do I miss home? What is wrong with me? I swore that I would never miss Douglas County, Georgia. Hell, no! My lips are involuntarily smacking again.

I place the stolen items on top of my least dirty possession: the black hoodie. I have a small box of prune juice with a sippy straw, pack of white wet wipes, a soiled diaper, something pink and rectangle shaped with vomit on it, and a red rubber circle with raised dots on it. I am looking through the items when someone bangs on the door, "Open up! It's the PO-leece!"

Like lightening, I put on the clean but stolen tee, clearance basketball type shorts, and empty my pockets. Another knock comes with the same ominous verbal announcement. I am sweating and throw the hoodie, undies, oversized pants, stupid baseball cap, and baby crap into the now too-small toilet.

I try to act calm when I come out. I slow down and say, "Whoa, man! Wait your turn."

In my moment of trouble, I try to flash a grin. It almost always works, but when I see a reflection of myself in the building's new windows, the reflection does not look like me. One of my front teeth is gone. The other is crooked now. It was not like that the last time I looked in a mirror. I do not know when or where that was. Why did David not tell me? I am, officially, a meth head. Most of my teeth are black near my gums and rotting inside my mouth. My skin looks sunburned and is peeling. A traitor inhabits my body and soul.

"Aw, I'm just messin' with ya, dude! CSI and stuff. Love your shirt, dude. We saw you go in. Hey, is this shitter free now? I gotta go." A slick-looking man says. He had been flipping X-rated cards at the street corner.

Card Man is in his mid-fifties and scares me. He reminds me of a Western version of Principal Daniell. He is tall and foreboding; or, some other word from my English vocabulary list that I never fully learned. So, it takes a hustler to see my hustle. I am in over my head.

Without something better to do, I wait a polite distance outside the porta-potty. Card Man pops out a few minutes later. He says, "Hey, you weasel! What you did in there was wrong! You don't leave easy evidence out there like that! What are you? Stupid? Or a cop in training? Are you trying to entrap me? What is your problem? There's a chemical reaction going on in that toilet. What were you carrying?"

My head feels scalded from the addiction and lies that are burning onto my forehead. There is a gnawing in my stomach. I feel the full weight of my shame for the first time.

I beg, "Please. I'm young. I'm stupid. But, I need a job. I have to get my life together. I have to do something. I almost killed my best friend this morning."

"What? What did he do to you?"

"Nothin'. He was dumb enough to come see me out here."

"You're stupid, and I can't do stupid. You would be a liability to me. And, besides, you're addict."

I protest, "No, I'm clean. I've turned my life around. I promise."

"How long have you been clean?"

"About five hours. I'm pretty sure that I haven't had anything since seven this morning."

"Crap, boy. I can't do anything with you. You would be lucky if the Vegas PD picked you up. They may try to rehabilitate you or something. Nah, they're not going to help either. You need some religion, boy. What are you?"

"Uh, I'm white. I guess," I reply without understanding the question. What did Card Man mean *what am I*? "Fine. I'm part Cherokee, okay?"

"No, boy. That's not gonna work. Okay, listen. Did you have any Catholic friends growing up?"

"Yeah, man. There were these twins in my class and-"

"And, I don't give a damn. Here's what you're going do, Hombre. You are going to walk all the way down the Strip; past Wynn. You're going to go to the Las Vegas Catholic Diocese. You're going to ask them for help. Tell them you're a Catholic that has seen the light. Tell them you want to go back home. Tell 'em you saw a saint if you have to, dude. You do what you need to do to get clean. This place is not a friendly town to outsiders who are not tourists with money, and you are an outsider. And, you don't have no money!"

On that note, Card Man moves into his position on the street corner; flicking cards at tourists that looked like they had money as he went. He is looking at their hair, shoes, and purses. He is out chasing the almighty dollar. I start walking back toward the strip. I can walk across the dirt lot, next to the Aladdin, or keep walking down the Strip. I could follow my original plan and go into Krave and hit up a girl for money.

I look like a meth addict. How could this happen? I could not stop thinking about David and the Principal. Then, I wonder, did I dream the whole thing up? Did I leave him there in bed and walk away? How many days ago was that? If I am dreaming, I imagined a very scary female terminator disguised as a hot chick. I wish I could talk to Alicia or Tommy. They would be right here with me. I would not be walking the longest strip in the world alone. This must be my walk of shame. A holy dread fills my body.

It feels like my walk consumes most of my day. Hours later, I am at a small Chinese fast food restaurant near Fashion Show, on the other side of Venetian and past Treasure Island. I sit at a little iron table underneath a red tent. I have to do something. I have to do that something right now. I am desperate. Can I still call collect? I have not seen a 1-800-Collect commercial in half a lifetime.

Out of the corner of my eye, I spot an old sun-faded receipt. The receipt flaps trapped between Styrofoam Chinese food containers in a trash can. Some minimum-wage worker will empty the cans any moment. I snatch it. I aggressively march into a coffee shop at the Fashion Show. The mid-afternoon line is short. I borrow a pen from a barista and write down Amanda's hospital contact information in Atlanta.

With my usual grin, I plead my case to the baristas. I explain how my friend had been taken by ambulance this morning. I ask them to ask Amanda to please get in contact with everyone's family. The baristas think I am tripping. I can see them looking into my soul. After a minute, one nods her head in agreement. She will contact the hospital.

I lean forward and softly say, "Please, if you do talk to Amanda, tell her that I'll reemerge after I'm sober. Ask her to tell my mom. I haven't talked to anyone back home in Douglas County for years. I don't know if they know I'm alive. It's Douglas County, Georgia, not Colorado."

"Sir, are you going to the Cathedral across the street? You've missed midday mass." The barista says, scooting off to the side. Her manager has her eye on us. The entire store is attentively watching me, ready to pounce on me and devour me whole. They know that I am not right. I know that I am not right.

"Yes, I'm going right now." I concede. "It's a long story, but my senior English teacher predicted today would happen. She did not foresee my redemption. Good thing she did not finish reading all the way to the end of my life story."

"I will pray for you. If no one is there right now, stay at the church until someone comes. Someone will find you and help you. They will tell you what to do." The barista reassures me.

Knowing that I cannot go backward, I move forward. I want to talk to Amanda to tell her what happened. There is this metaphysical energy pulling me back into the store. I could pop into their bathroom and use so easily. All my will power focuses on my feet moving one step at a time further down the Strip.

I want to use the small tattoo on my shoulder like a telecommunication device and call Amanda myself. I want to tell her to tell my family that I am sorry and that I am a terrible person. I never want my destiny to be dependent on others ever again. I never want anyone else to clean up the messes that I have made; ever. Never! I want, always, to have my own money, my own stash, my own clothes, and my own damn phone. Wait. I cannot have a stash. The days of having a stash are over. It is now or never. I need to rule my stately kingdom again.

Eight: Melissa

October 31, 1997 11:15AM
Douglas County High School

If someone had interviewed me on my first day of high school, I would have said that I envisioned my entire secondary education career as a rebooted *Grease* mini-series. Then, my family moved to Villa Rica, Georgia on the western edge of Douglas County, Georgia. This place is a dump compared to Florida.

The commuter traffic is horrible, and I never see my dad anymore. My mother has spent an agonizing eighteen months trying to ingratiate herself into the inner social circles of this backward place. The high school here is the epitome of cronyism, political favoritism, and ignorance. I abhor it. But, here I am holding a crock pot of fondue cheese walking toward Mrs. Couch's CL English class on Homecoming day.

"When someone says *period costume*, Melissa, they need to be more specific." Stephanie snaps at me while wearing a crimson Regency-period dress. "My senior thesis is on Austen so, of course, I'm going to show up as Elizabeth Bennet."

"Blame the cheap costume shop that you rented the dress from, Steph! It's not my problem that you are wearing a Georgian dress pattern with Renaissance colors. It looks like you sacrificed a raven to achieve that color." I yell back at her.

"I made this dress by hand, thank you very much. Nacho cheese dip isn't a period food either. No one ever heard of nachos in the moors of Great Britain. You're not doing a good job of setting up this class party. I am already juggling too many proverbial meatballs on my foam plate, between organizing Homecoming and Prom. I was glad when the class voted for you to throw the party today; but, you're failing." Stephanie says as her black Mary Jane's squeak across the recently polished laminate floors in the Lower Banks building.

"We haven't even walked into the classroom yet, calm down." I snap at Stephanie.

"And, it's raining, Melissa! Did you schedule that on purpose?" She barks back at me.

"Well, you all trusted me to organize it, so you don't get a say, do you? Let's just see if Homecoming and Prom go off without a hitch. And, how in the world did the ladies at Hancock Fabric let you walk out of there with crimson taffeta without scoffing? They took you for a fool, and it's your fault. I bet your meatballs give someone food poisoning." I snipe back at her while using my elbow to open the door to the classroom.

Mrs. Couch is standing a few inches inside the classroom door. Her eyes fix on us with our two slow cookers of food. She looks as though she was going to chastise us. Her face distorts in shock.

"Girls! What have you done?" Mrs. Couch says with a gasp.

I am rendered almost speechless and see Tommy standing just behind Mrs. Couch. I try to make eye contact with him, but my mouth is open. My eyes are quickly filling with water. Tommy is becoming blurry. I feel like a sailboat that has had the wind stop blowing through its sails. I cannot find any words that are willing to come out of my mouth. I think very highly of Mrs. Couch, as we all do, and her opinion matters a lot to me.

"It's okay, Mrs. C, Mel was being authentic by bringing us all something that we could eat with our hands," Tommy says. "See. She had me bring in her plate of fruit for her, like a Greek goddess."

Tommy makes an excuse for me in a hurry and giggles. An expensive membership to the Chapel Hills Golf Club and Tommy are part of my mother's grand plans for elbowing our way into Douglas County society. Preeti rushes around Tommy and Mrs. Couch to take the still-warm appliance out of my hands. If I had been thinking, I would have rubber-banded the lid to the base.

"You smell like a Mexican restaurant's buffet on Sunday after a week of Cinco de Mayo parties," Mrs. Couch takes the meatballs from Stephanie while still gawking at me. "What are you supposed to be, dear?"

"I'm a maiden fair," I say to excuse my appearance.

"You, Miss Ayers, are the opposite of a fair maiden. You look like someone just dragged you out of bed in a whorehouse! Where are the rest of your clothes?" Mrs. Couch chastises me. Stephanie looks pleased.

"She's Ophelia, you know, *after* she drowns!" Jeremy says while smiling ear to ear.

"You're in a corset, in my classroom." Mrs. Couch scolds. "I'm going to have to start chanting a prayer in a Latin. Please cover your cleavage, mademoiselle. What would Principal Daniell say if he walked in on this? He would think that I was running a teenage brothel! You've given free peeks to us all."

"Principal Daniell may want some garlic bread and cheese for his meatballs," Justin says. He is smiling with a mouthful of food. Justin may Dipsy dumpster-dive for most of his meals.

Justin goes back to the utensil table. He and Jeremy are the only boys not looking at my buxom. Michael almost choked on one of Stephanie's meatballs after Justin's snide comment. My social climbing mother could have whipped up something better than cheese dip if she wanted me to star in her personal rendition of *Vanity Fair*. Sandra, the woman who gave birth to me, was thinking about pleasing the boys in the class and not the woman who was in charge of the grade on my permanent academic record.

"People will think you're a can-can dancer, my dear. Cover yourself! Today's party is not a French class." Mrs. Couch says. She looks toward the windows facing the football field.

A stray custodian has stopped to look in on the class. I cannot tell if he is eyeing the food or me. He is probably concerned about how much he will have to clean up following a party full of high school students. I know enough about organizing parties to know that janitorial services are arranged in advance. My mother has had me in wedding planning training since I was fourteen.

"I'm Marie Antoinette," I say, setting down my backpack and pulling out my white cardigan. "See? I am wearing sacrificial white. Can I get an A, please? The party is going. People are eating."

"Marie Antoinette wasn't British. You have to be British." Mrs. Couch corrects me.

"She can be Emily Dickinson. She is wearing white," Preeti propositions with a tooth-picked meatball at her mouth. "That is, if you don't tally her time with Tommy. That would preclude her from wearing white here, or at her wedding."

"Congratulations, Preeti! You're my first senior of the year that will be serving detention with me. I will need you to help me with some horribly boring yet intricate task. I will invent your torture later. But, you're mostly serving detention for saying that Emily Dickinson is British; only partially for implying that Melissa is a woman with low moral character." Mrs. Couch clarifies.

"I'm not a woman of low moral character," I defend myself. "I didn't plan on it raining."

"Then, let's go with Tommy's suggestion of Ophelia, shall we?" Mrs. Couch compromises. She does not want to ruin our period party day.

We are staying in the classroom to eat through our lunch break. It is pouring rain outside. I do, in fact, feel like a drowned rat. I walked outside between buildings to get to the classroom faster. It is a mistake that I cannot correct.

"Seniors!" Mrs. Couch claps her hands together. "This was to be a period party day. In the event that Melissa did not make it plain to you, the period that we were talking about was Shakespeare."

Amanda, who is wearing a nun costume, looks over at me. She says, "I thought we were in the *Canterbury Tales*."

"What? No one told you to be the Virgin Mary, okay? That's your fault. We started in the middle ages and then moved into the Renaissance last week." I quip.

"I wasn't here to hear that," Amanda says while adjusting her habit's sleeves to stay out of the cheese.

"Goodness gracious! This is a beautiful trifle. Look at the sharp layers. A loving hand freshly cut the fruit. Who brought the trifle?" Mrs. Couch comments.

"I did, of course," says Tommy. Tommy is donning an eye-patch and playing pirate; as long as his pirate is a subject of the British Empire.

"Your instructions were to make it yourself. It's part of your assignment. Who made this trifle for you, Tommy? There is a strawberry on top of it." Mrs. Couch says accusingly while scooping out the strawberry. The poor berry is about to pay for its transgressions in the jaws of Mrs. Couch's discerning mouth.

"I used my mother's recipe, Mrs. Couch. She oversaw everything that I did." Tommy answers.

"Well, then, what is the bottom layer, Tommy?"

"Cherry pie filling," Tommy says while glancing out of the corner of his eye.

"You're telling me that your perfectionist mother lets you come to class with her crystal trifle bowl, from her second wedding, with cherries on the bottom and a strawberry on top?"

"There is a red fruit on the bottom. It may be strawberries." He admits sheepishly.

"Canned?" Mrs. Couch asks with her eyebrows lowering in small increments.

"Yes?" Tommy answers with a cringe.

"No. Look at the white, plush heart of these strawberries. They were cut no earlier than second period today. Did you dissect them in Physics, Tommy? Or did the trifle mysteriously show up at the attendance desk on your walk to the Banks Building?"

"I put the whipped cream on top," Tommy says. He is trying to stand his ground.

"No, sir, you did not. I'm a working mom. I know the difference between homemade whipped cream and artificial factory-made whipped topping that contains no actual cream!"

Mrs. Couch is interrogating him. I cannot rescue him. Besides, I am drowning. I am Ophelia now.

"Of course, he whipped the cows to whip the cream, Mrs. Couch!" Will says snidely with a quick witted *Charlie and the Chocolate Factory* reference.

"Brilliant, Mr. Eason. At least it was a British author." Mrs. Couch admits. She moves on to fill her Styrofoam bowl and heavy-duty Chinet plate.

The food sticks uneasily in my mouth. I am not certain if I should trust my classmates. Maybe it would have been better, and safer, if we all bought our dishes at the grocery store. I brought my nacho cheese in my mom's Crock-Pot and left it in the science lab in Warren-Dorris until just before class. Stephanie negotiated a similar arrangement with the Social Studies department upstairs. The boys brought in pre-packaged dishes that were, generally, much easier.

At this moment it feels very unfair to be a female. I cannot even eat half a mouth of food with the judgmental stares coming from my classmates. Will, Matt, Justin, and Jeremy boldly boast their regular school clothes. But, they received credit for their store bought crescent rolls and chocolate pudding cups. Why did they get a pass? I at least cubed the fake ultra-processed cheese myself and let it melt all morning in the crock.

It seems an undue burden to expect the female CL English seniors to cook while the males simply had to bring in food; except for Tommy. Tommy's mother did all of his work for him. If she could birth her own grandchildren, I am certain she would. If Mrs. Hood were my mom, my nipples would have been bandaged in the event of an embarrassing emergency, like rain on period costume luncheon day.

Preeti is a gypsy, of course. She flows easily all around the classroom like a breeze. She has a long, sheer lavender skirt coupled with a white shirt. She is wearing hoop earrings and a tied scarf around her head. While almost effortless, Preeti has tried harder than any of the boys in our class.

Anne has on some flowing gown that makes her look like an angel. I cannot tell if she rented her costume or if it was a Halloween one. But, again, Anne is a girl. She tried to participate even if she may not have been as Globe Theater worthy as Mrs. Couch would have preferred. Mrs. Couch gives Anne a lot of breaks. It is not fair, but we all understand the reason why. I am certain I am even supposed to know about that business.

Michael dons a Highland Scot-inspired kilt in the spirit of either Mel Gibson in *Braveheart* or Christopher Lambert in *Highlander*.

If Michael were a girl, he would be the prettiest in our class. It is a shame that nature wasted his symmetrical features on a boy who lives in a county where pretty boys are tormented. I hope he moves away as soon as he graduates. He deserves better than DCHS can offer, and that is hard for me to admit that about a preacher's child. They are often arrogant spoiled brats.

Seth is trying to work the room as a very short Othello in a shabby cape with a drapery cord. Sadly, Seth does not live with his mother. But, Seth has his personal money. His cape tells me that although he did complete the assignment himself, without parental intervention, he did not think enough about the period costume party to drop a significant sum of money on it. He spent less than four dollars on his assignment while many of the girls rented costumes for at least twenty dollars, which does not include the cost of food. My superlative for Seth would be: Most likely to succeed despite short stature and receding hairline.

Sweatshirt-clad Matt is lying all over his corner desk, which is where he hides in every class that we have ever had together. Tommy told me that their mutual friend, Ryan, has not been in the gifted classes since tenth grade. Matt misses him most of all, according to Tommy. Today, Matt is awake to eat and is consuming more ten girls. He brought in two two-liters of Mountain Dew; which, of course, are Shakespearian somehow because he is a guy. For someone who sleeps through his classes, I do not know how or why Mrs. Couch tolerates him. I think he is friends with her son, Brian.

Justin is wearing tattered clothes, as always. None of us have ever had the poor taste to say anything to him. The girls in the class will discreetly wrap foil around the leftovers and send them home with him. Even though Justin has not said anything publically, we think he is with a different foster family this year. That may be for the best right now, which is sad to admit. I have heard at least five different versions of his short life's sad tale. I did not know social services or foster homes existed until I overheard the Nicole and Heather gossiping about him last year. None of us know if he is black or white. He has olive colored skin and keeps his hair short. We do not want to ask, even though Stephanie tried to goad me into doing it my first week here; that witch!

Mrs. Couch opens a dusty back costume closet for Justin to look through quickly and pick out something to put on. He chooses a ridiculous bard hat with a feather, but it was better than the faux Indian headdress from former Am Lit students. I had my money on Mrs. Couch's back wardrobes brimming with the bodies of former students rather than decaying costumes like a specialized theater department within the school. I wonder what Mrs. Couch did to earn the nickname Lady Macbeth. Surely blood must have been involved, or the name would not have stuck.

Brittany's ensemble rests on a hanger wrapped in a clear plastic garbage bag beside her. She's still sweating from the second block and in her track clothes. At least she is wearing a black velvet flap cap with neon-colored feathers over her short blonde pixie hair. I imagine the hat will smell lovely later. She will not get her costume deposit back from the shop in Carrollton if that is where she rented it.

There is no way to change into Lycra clothing, while sweating, in a high school restroom, especially without assistance. With her tall height, short hair, unkempt nails, and athletic clothes, she looks butch. I skip volunteering to help her peel off her used clothes. Brittany shows the Robin Hood type outfit to Mrs. Couch for credit. I loathe how Mrs. Couch shows favoritism. You would think that she could grant a queen's pardon to my cheese with how much leeway she is giving all the other students.

Will is wearing all black, per usual, and moping in the corner. He is the moodiest nefelibata in our graduating class. He is socially awkward and tries to put on airs. Today, he is claiming that his black turtleneck makes him Hamlet. Oh, I hope not.

How can Will be Hamlet if I am Ophelia? That is worse than murder most foul. He just wants to be in an old black and white movie. He thinks he is Sir Laurence Olivier. Unlike some of the other boys in our class, at least he showers and does not smell. Douglas County teenage boys reek of hormones and self-importance. The element of false self-importance could be generational or a leftover remnant of the devastating population losses the county suffered during the Civil War. I do not care either way. I only care because it affects Tommy.

David must not have understood the directions. He arrives in a bed sheet pinned into a toga. At least he was wearing an undershirt. I am not certain how much David knows about routine grooming practices. I thought that is what guys' locker rooms were for these days. Georgia boys are less groomed than Florida boys, even though they wear more clothing. Maybe David did listen. He could be Julius Cesar although Brutus would suit him better.

Jennifer is sitting near David. She is in a pink juvenile Halloween princess costume, complete with a cardboard cone hat and attached white veil. She looks a little bit like *I Dream of Jeannie*. Jennifer is rough around the edges, which comes from having a working mom.

At least half of my personal education comes from my mother. She wants me to pledge her sorority, Chi Omega, when I go to college. She has been meticulously polishing me for years. Unlike Jennifer, I know what type of brassiere to wear for what occasion; or, at least to wear one! The element about Jennifer that bothers me the most is her, now, two-year high school commitment to straddling the line between girlhood and womanhood. I frequently notice that she is lax in shaving her armpits when she wears tank tops during the winter months.

We all belong on the Isle of Misfit Toys. Shakespeare must be rolling in his grave. I have no idea what Michelle is trying to be. She looks like she might be a bar wench or female pirate. She is laughing and falling all over Tommy; pretending to be drunk. I saw her pick out her outfit at the costume shop off Marietta square. I happened to be there at the same time; but, I was already in a dressing room behind a curtain when I saw her. Her entire presence is obscene; batteries and fashion ensemble not required.

An ill-fitting costume-quality under-bust corset clads Michelle's abdomen. She wears the plastic corset on top of a thin white peasant blouse. I can see the outlines of her nipples, and they are pointing in different directions; east and west. We are three minutes from a circa 1993 MTV Panama City Beach Spring Break style wet tee shirt contest. I am just waiting for RuPaul to burst through the doors and award a 'whitest of the white trash' sash to Michelle. That tramp is not wearing a bra. Her daring move to rent a corset inspired me to buy a real one for today. Mine has steel bones. I am sporting wedding lingerie. It was quite the investment. My mother approved the purchase.

If Michelle and Tommy want to be matchy-matchy, then let them. I would rather not deal with Tommy. He is rude, crass, and cuts corners in his school work. I feel sorry for whatever girl he marries. She will be destined for misery with his slacker, philandering butt. I wonder if his mother can compensate for that with her crystal trifle bowl.

I can picture Mrs. Hood saying, "Would you like a cherry on top of your scoop of self-contempt? Or, on the side, with eternal bitterness cut with a dash of rancor?"

Mrs. Couch is without a doubt trying to channel Elizabeth Taylor's Katherina from *The Taming of the Shrew*. She wears the same costume every year, which probably fits her teaching salary. She has a decently made circlet for her head and long, gaudy gold earrings that scream 1983. Her dress is entirely emerald green with a modest but fitted bodice that accommodates a more matronly figure than what she might have had when she first purchased it. She probably made that getup for herself in 1983 as well.

Holding students to her stylistic standards of fashion would not be reasonable of Mrs. Couch. None of us have a hundred dollars to drop on a costume that we will only wear for one school day. I wish Crystal were still in school. I would love to see what she would have come up with today. She is an Amazon but a well-dressed, tasteful one. Many of the other girls do not like Crystal because she is blunt, but I like her at least as much as anyone else that I have met in this forsaken hole.

Heather and Nicole are the last to join the party. They return late from running administrative errands for Mrs. Couch. The two suck-ups disgust me. Heather is wearing a traditional gothic period dress with sleeves that touch the dusty floor of the classroom. Her horned headdress seemed to suit her. The additional height from the plump crown-like feature makes Heather seem more haughty than usual. She is the Wife of Bath in very way imaginable.

Not to be outdone, Nicole is wearing an actual snood; and, it is ivory white. You can buy hand-woven snoods at the Renaissance Festival, but I have never seen anyone wear one outside of the festival. The snood is very striking against her long, dark hair. Although her dress looks a little bit like a garb from a civil war movie, Nicole comes across as British enough to be Victorian. She has a parasol in one hand, which would not do her any good today. It is too delicate for the deluge outside. The most useful thing that she could do with it would be to stand in the center of the football field and act as a lightning rod. I think lightning may indeed strike this classroom today. There is an odd, almost polrumptious, electricity in the room.

Nicole surveys the classroom as Heather updates Mrs. Couch on her completed errands. Condemnatory eyes fall on my white cardigan. With a swish of her massive skirt, Nicole flutters over to me and paws at me with her laced-gloved hands.

Nicole says, "Oh, dear, what is this? Your everyday sweater for a period party? You're not acting like a good hostess, now, are you? Aren't you going to offer me some refreshment?"

"Have some cheese, Nicole, before the guys eat all of it," I say looking down at my plate.

Everything tastes like cardboard today. American high school girls are mean and have been known to be that way for generations. It is prototypical behavior and society has come to accept it. There is an explicit rudeness unique to Douglas County that I cannot explain or excuse. The thoughtless and provocative behaviors come from a century of hating outsiders. It is bred into their blood. The teachers reinforce it while the school administration tolerates it. I cannot wait to get out of this place. I abhor high school. The guys are bad, but the girls are worse.

"Oh, but you're my hostess, won't you be a dear and help me?" Nicole says as she grabs my hands. I resist. I do not like have people moving me without permission.

"Look at the beautiful food! Nicole, I have a plate for you." Heather says. Heather motions with her head for Nicole to join her.

The crystal trifle bowl entrances Mrs. Couch, Heather, and Nicole. It is as though they are examining a museum-quality rare gem. Mrs. Couch is holding Nicole's plate for her. The trifle is already down to the bottom layer when Heather splats a big pile of strawberry-cherries onto their plates. Bar none, the trifle is the best food that anyone brought today. It will be Tommy's saving grace. His mother has cooked up another good grade for him; or, at least, layered a higher grade with her great attention to detail.

Sensing what could happen next, I move my plate forward on top of my desk. I have skipped any liquid food, like the cheese, and only had a bit of bread with a few grapes. Nothing is sitting right today. I wonder if my corset is too tight. If anything plunges to the floor, I will have a hard time bending at the waist to pick it up.

I brace my heeled boots against the frame of my desk. I prepare, once more, for Nicole to start tugging at me like an indolent child. Nicole chides me a little more, but I ignore her. Finally, she grabs both of my hands with her gloved hands. I hold on to the desk with my legs and feet. I hold on to the delicate lace of her gloves. Between me and the lace, the lace gives first.

Nicole screams with a high-pitched unladylike squawk. She flies backward, out of her ripping lace gloves, and into Heather who is holding a plate full of strawberry-cherry trifle. Bearing the countenance of someone more foreboding than her typical self, Heather drops her Styrofoam plate to tilt it forward instead of backward. The trifle lands on Nicole's head and her ivory snood. The trifle splashes off Nicole's snood and onto her parasol, dress, and Mrs. Couch's emerald green silk.

Hiking my skirt up had been a key advantage. My Doc Marten lace-up combat boots bear the brunt of the trifle splash-down in front of me. I am able to get up and step back from the mess in one smooth and swift motion. I do not offer to help when Nicole starts yelling at me. In contrast to Nicole, my cardigan and I are unblemished.

After having a good laugh, Tommy and Matt use their brute strength to hold Nicole back from me. The mess vexes Heather to the point of tears. She goes to the restroom to change her clothes, maybe so she can help clean up. Rather than take responsibility for their actions, I have a feel that it is time to play the classroom blame game again. I am preparing myself to receive it on all sides now. But, I am glad that I refused to budge; I have nothing else to lose today.

Heather is practical enough to wear her street clothes under her regular clothes. Nothing quite screams, "Beat me up" like wearing gothic clothing a school bus. Heather is faddish enough to get rides home from friends, but she never wanted anyone to know where she lives. She says it is because she does not want her fellow cheerleaders to toilet paper her house. Sure. I imagine Tommy will be toilet papering my house tonight. My mother will croon about how it is because he likes me. He does not. His mother may like me, but love does not translate through generations like a crystal trifle dish.

Mrs. Couch starts crying that we are the absolute worst class ever in the history of forever. She yells that we can spoil anything special that she organizes for us. She uses words like *ungrateful*, *childish*, *immature*, and *infantile*. She goes on and on about how glad she is that she had moved her gradebook right before the party.

Preeti packs up the leftovers with aluminum foil. She slips them into paper grocery bags and hands them to Justin. He nods and hides his face. There is no shame in being poor. But, here, there is shame in admitting that you are poverty-stricken in front of your peers. Everyone else's families are benefitting from the county's booming growth. Justin feels guilty for having to live off those tax dollars in foster care.

Tommy catches my arm on the way out of the classroom. He says, "Hey, Little Miss Badass, that was pretty slick. Whatcha up to later?"

"It was unintentional, Tommy. Nicole shouldn't have grabbed me. She got what she deserved. Newton's Laws of Motion applies to her and everyone else on the planet too. It was science. Speaking of grabbing boots, how did you make out with Michelle? I suspect you stole third base before her stale cinnamon buns were finished reheating in the faculty lounge. Leave me out of it! Love triangles are not part of trigonometry."

Nine: Michelle

December 3, 1997 7:00 AM
Perry, Georgia

The street I am watching looks like it should be busy, but it is not yet. Part of me wants to go out the front doors of the motel lobby and keep walking until I hit an ocean. I do not care which ocean. I would walk down a nameless road and become a nameless person. Any identity other than Michelle Lynn Worthan would be fine. I hate my first name. My parents named me after a sad Beatles song. I hate my middle name even more. Almost every girl in Douglas County has the middle name Lynn; it is drab.

This morning, I feel trapped inside my body in ways I cannot explain. I look down at my almost cold coffee which I poured at six-fifteen. Coffee turns bitter after forty-five minutes. I too have become bitter in the same amount of time. The sun is not up yet; even the sun is afraid to come out today. I am restless and caged.

I had not bothered to knock on Mrs. Couch's door this morning. I walked across the pothole-ridden parking lot to the lobby without permission. I have never understood our county's Board of Education policy on students staying overnight in motels. The motel rooms are required to open to the outside. Once we are secure in the rooms for the night, the teachers are supposed to place duct tape on the door to see if we have left the room overnight. I have always wondered: What if we do? What are the consequences? Will they send us back to Douglas County by airmail? Call parents who would not drive a few hours to retrieve us? Anne's parents would come and get her.

When I first woke up this morning, I was very careful not to disturb Anne. Anne and I were friends for a very long time but everyone changes in high school; except, of course, for Anne. She is a sweet creature. She is perpetually twelve-years old. She is easy to startle and slow to judge. She was sleeping so soundly that I would have felt like a Brutal Betty if I woke her.

"Michelle, let's torture the front desk clerk and speak to her in a French accent," Will orders me in a smug tone. "It would amuse me. And, I know it would amuse you too. Have a little fun before we start the day. How often do we get out of Douglas County? It's Perry, after all."

I am glad that Anne and I are not partners this year. Will and I are a better-matched team in debates. Anne could be paired with anyone and do fine. But, I want to do more than fine. I want to dominate the state-level debate team competition today. At some point, I became a wolf and Anne remained a lamb.

Will can tease and torture a soul for fun, even strangers. I do not have that level of contempt in me. Thank goodness Will was never violent; at least, I do not think he is. What we have in common is that we are latchkey kid survivors. We both have abandonment issues.

Neither of us trusts anyone over the age of twenty-five. We are Gen Y kids and are often suspicious of Gen X'ers too. We like listening to radio show hosts Barnes, Leslie, and Jimmy on my Walkman on the bus ride to school. But, even they do not get us. In both of our situations, our sundry of parents left us to raise ourselves.

A waft of wind blows an empty cigarette soft pack through the parking lot. Perry feels immaculate compared to Douglasville, and white. Houston County has a military base, Warner Robins, and I do not imagine military people tolerate disorder too well. I need order too so I welcome it. I appreciate the cleanliness. Even though our hotel lobby is severely outdated with late eighties décor, it is clean. I look in the corners for mold, like our hotel in St. Augustine had when we traveled there in seventh grade. The lobby is, surprisingly, mold-free. The St. Augustine field trip was the first time I traveled out of state. If it were not for school trips and academic competitions, I would never leave home.

"Will, leave the motel clerk alone. Don't be ghetto. You're not the pimp that you imagine you are." I snipe at him. If I ever let him get away with anything, he would smell weakness, and that simply will not do. I must constantly remain vigilant and defensive.

There were four girls in our room last night, but I did not catch the name of the other two seniors who were with us. I glance out the lobby window, and one girl walks across the parking lot. She is looking around. There is nowhere to eat. We are subsisting on coffee, creamer, and sugar substitute.

As a varsity team member, I have been in this situation before. There is something horrifying about waking up hungry and far away from home with a twenty-dollar-bill to last the weekend. I packed pre-made peanut butter and honey sandwiches in my carry-on sized suitcase, but I want to save them for later when I am truly hungry. The wanderer was too polite to look; or, too scared. Will and I try to make a game of keeping others away. Our game isolates us more than I originally calculated.

"I would never want to be a pimp, Chelle. What have you been reading? Clearly, it was something horrid and not worth the paper that it was printed on." Will says.

The notes for today's debate cover my copy of *Angela's Ashes*. I move my crumpled notes to the side. What I would not give for the ability to edit our notes and reprint them coherently for today. The teams that live close to Houston County High School will have a distinct advantage. The locals will have slept in their beds, eaten warm breakfasts, and printed fresh notes from late night revisions.

"You assume too much, Will, and you know what they say about people who assume. You make an ass of you and me. Have you seen anyone from the junior varsity team this morning? One is walking over here now. I think I see Anne too. I don't have my contacts in yet."

"If you can't see, four eyes, how do you know you're not drinking liquid dog feces?"

"Because your mother spent last night in the Douglasville location of her chain of whorehouse, Will, and took a dump on your forefather's grave. That would be a long walk for my morning cup of joe."

My chipped black nail polish reveals my bad habit of nail-gnawing. I wish I could be like Anne. She was never bitter, or unkind. She is perpetually clean and perfect. She went to sleep with beautiful skin and woke up with it. She does not bother to bring an acne masque with her, or special lotions to keep her skin calm. I have to travel with those burdensome modern potions. Anne radiates sunshine wherever she goes. I hate her. I do not hate her. How do I feel about Anne? I do not know.

"Michelle, you're dirty and smell like the oil refinery off Bankhead Highway," Will says in a harsh tone. "You haven't brushed your teeth this morning. You didn't use eye makeup remover last night either. Your liner is caked on like you're hosting a drag queen's birthday party. If you can't love yourself, who will? Please tell me you are wearing clean panties."

"I'm not wearing any panties, Willy. Your dad's crabs needed a pair for the passport photo to book a Transatlantic passage back to the motherland. Eat shit and die."

Will is too blunt. He is acting inexcusably rude. I have a scorched earth policy with him. Descendants of Greek immigrants do not play. Will is a baby and not a coffee drinker. He does not understand the constant battle against coffee stained teeth.

Glug, glug, glug goes my coffee creamer into my next hot cup. I have been drinking coffee alone in the morning for years. I started when I was eleven because it felt like the grown-up thing to do, but now it takes four or more cups before I feel awake. I need to be awake for the competition. I think my father longs for his morning cup like I do mine, but his cups did not swish with coffee alone. He needs something stronger to make it through eighteen-hour work-days. I think he is screwing his secretary too.

One of my unnamed roommates pops in, "I found a snack machine but it's broken. It doesn't make sense to have a motel where there is no food. Why is Mrs. Couch not awake? We have to register and be in our rooms by eight o'clock."

Will says, "Thus, the nature of pre-registration. I pre-regis-tered our team at the beginning of the year, months ago. The high school is only a little ways down the road. Mrs. Couch will eventu-ally wake-up. She sleeps in, ye of little faith. Go back to your play-pen and wait for the adults to tell you what to do."

If anyone were to squeal Mrs. Couch's secret, it was not going to be me. Mrs. Couch is not a bad person, but she is not a good one either. If I had to place her in the novel, she would not be a hero or a villain; neither protagonist nor antagonist. She is something in-between the two forces of black and white. She seems to have not fully made it into adulthood even though her only child is in our class. She once verbally warned our class and called herself Lady Macbeth; but, it did not suit her. I have not known her to have blood on her hands.

Mrs. Couch did not wake-up early or support our competitions. She wants to get away from her empty house and her son, Brian, as much as everyone in our class. I do not imagine she wanted to be a mother but somehow felt obligated to some previous husband to have a child. They are at the beginning of a very messy divorce right now. Everyone is talking about Mr. Couch and how he has shame-faced Mrs. Couch for years, but nothing is final until the Sentinel prints it.

As much as we have been in English classes these past few years, with teachers grooming us for some glorious but yet-named college career, I have not seen Brian set a toe in Mrs. Couch's hall-way. He avoids her at all cost. He was on the gifted education track with us for ninth and tenth grade but then dropped out. Several of the boys dropped out. They knew that Mrs. Couch would not toler-ate their insubordination, cheating, or lies. Thankfully, Tommy is smart enough to have made it all four years.

I pour myself a fifth cup of coffee. I place the right side of my face against the cool glass window. I am still not waking up. I feel hazy. I am bored, so I am starting to overthink things. Anne is rubbing off on me in a bad way. I have been half looking at the window for her, but she has not turned up in the motel lobby yet. We lost Anne. I am not going to leave my cup to look for her stupid butt.

My dream jarred me last night. In the dream, I was in an old city somewhere on the East Coast. I was wearing a hefty jacket. Despite the jacket, I was freezing. I was looking for something. I am almost half-walking in last night's dreams and this morning's reality. In my limited experience in life, I have found tip-toeing on the edge of what is real and what is imagine to be a very precarious place to be; and, not for the faint of heart.

"I know what you're thinking. I won't tell the trite quasi-jocks our little secret." Will says.

"Oh, Captain, my Captain, tell me what stupid little secret you think you know," I answer.

"That everyone thinks we're in love, and we're not. We're not even dating. We only mutually hate other humans so much that we choose to be selectively anti-social. You know I won't take you to the prom. I know you're not going. You never will. You think it's beneath you. You've missed Homecoming every year too."

"You're a wicked little-" I start but am interrupted by Will.

"What are you going to say, Michelle, 'fart-knocker' like you're cool enough to watch MTV?"

Will is a snake that is going to wrap around my soul like a boa constrictor. He will kill me. His death grip grows tighter with each breath that I exhale.

"Your family doesn't have cable television. Oh, please! I'm not even entertained." Will says.

"I don't give a crap what everyone else thinks. We had a deal. We're not branching out and having a pretend break-up for this pretend relationship. We're just going to keep going until the end of the year, until college. I'll keep your secrets, and you keep mine. We'll never see any of these people ever again. What do you think life is going to be like afterward? Are we going to send Christmas cards to each other's houses in the care of our parents? No, thank you. Go to weddings and baby showers? What vulgarity!"

My version of prom happened a little more than three years ago; in the eighth grade. I went to the middle school graduation dance with the one boy that I had always liked. His name was Tommy. My pulse races when I think about Tommy. It sends tingly electricity down to my fingertips. I look at my notes to make sure that my tingles have not accidentally ignited.

I adore Tommy and have since Kindergarten. He is the most suave, magnificent boy that I have ever seen. He is perfect in every sport. He is perfect in everything he does. He is perfect at the science fair; although very few people even knew that he competed in that. He is first place in all things, including my heart. I need to get through these awkward years and then re-emerge with a college degree in four and half years. I know his parents will not allow him to marry until he has at least a bachelor's degree.

Tommy's parents have a detailed plan for his life. If Tommy were friends with someone that his parents did not approve of, the friend was gone; like Ryan. If Tommy were to date someone that his parents did not approve of, the girl was gone; like me.

I will work to make myself fit into their plan again. I had even begged Mom to continue to stay in the same social groups as Tommy's mother after Mom went back to work at the end of our eighth-grade year. But, few people knew about Tommy. Anne knew about Tommy because she was there. But Anne is a quiet saint that would never reveal my secret. I do not even have to ask.

Anne gawkily stumbles through the motel's front lobby doors. Will and I look at her because we are not certain how she got to the lobby doors without us seeing her. She looks wide-eyed and sweaty despite the cold.

She stutters, "I wanted to go for a morning walk to clear my thoughts. But my stroll did not make it far before I realized I was alone."

Will immediately leaves. It is as though he is allergic to Anne's presence; as if he is a vampire burned by her light. I try to smile, but I do not think anything connected my brain to my face. I cannot move my facial muscles to make a smile. I do not remember the last time I smiled; before high school, maybe?

"There is a doughnut shop just across the way. It made me think of David. He cannot pass a doughnut place without at least looking in the window. I wish he had joined the team this year. Michelle, did you find some coffee? There is some across the street, with the doughnuts."

"You found food? Did you get us anything?"

"Well, sure. But, I don't think we should eat doughnuts right before a debate. It could mess with our glucose levels. A banana would be much more practical. Well, an apple would be better than a banana. Why? What did you eat?" Anne says innocently.

The skin around Anne's fingertips is slightly blue. I wonder how cold she is. She is not wearing a jacket. Her hair is almost soaking wet. We cannot take her anywhere.

"We haven't eaten anything. We're starving. Aren't you hungry? Do you even know how to tell if you are hungry? I'm about to start screaming. I hate it when you make me explain the obvious to you."

"Don't be mean, Michelle. I don't know. I didn't wake up hungry. So, I guess I wasn't thinking about it. But, yes, I should eat. You should eat too."

Anne is like a doll to me. She is like a human doll that I used to dress-up and play with but have grown tired of in my teen years. I do not hate her. I am tired of her. I do not want her to remind me of my youth. I guess I was young once. I was as young as her; actually, I was younger.

"You have to eat something in the morning. You can't skip breakfast. You're going to have to be independent and learn how to take care of yourself. See, here's the thing: my mom works so she can't remind me to eat three times a day, take a shower, and do my homework every single day. Did you go across the street by yourself?"

I try to bite my tongue, but I can feel my natural acrimony foaming in my mouth. It tastes bitter. I am bitter.

"Well, sure. I didn't want to wake up Brittany or Amanda's replacement. What is her name? Preeti?" Anne says, lost in her thoughts. I wonder what was happening in the world inside her head.

I flatten my right hand and slam it on the table immediately in front of her, and centimeters out away from our precious notes. I start to breathe heavy. I cannot control my anger any longer.

"You CANNOT go off by yourself, Anne. It isn't safe. I know that no one has probably ever told you, but people kill girls our age. They kidnap us and do bad things and then our families never find us again. Oh, Anne! My goodness. I couldn't stand it if that hap-pened to you. You have to learn how to take care of yourself. You can start by eating breakfast and not running off. Have you had your insulin? Did Mrs. Couch see you leave? Did you have permission to leave the property? What if you had gotten lost and not found your way back."

Anne quietly contemplates, "No. She accidentally left the curtains to her room open. She's laying face-down on the bed in her slip. I don't think anything will wake her up. Do you think she's depressed about Brian and all the trouble he gets into outside of school? Are the rumors true? You know, about the thing that no one is supposed to know about or talk about."

I cannot help but let my head go straight down into the notes. Anne is rather sheltered. She is callow. How did she make it to our senior year without accidentally harming herself? I would not be surprised if she breaks a finger or toe in a mouse trap this trip. She seems like the kind of girl who should not be allowed to go on school trips without good adult supervision. Anne needs guidance; at least a little while longer. I am so glad that I took the only copy of the room key with me. Anne would have locked us out. What was her plan? Whittle a backup copy out of a bar of motel soap? No. She had no plan. She floats through life ignorant of the real world and without a plan. She has always had responsible parents with modest money.

Will bursts through the old glass doors with a bag of doughnuts. He is also carrying several cups of water in a drink carrier. My eyes flash over to the clock just behind the clerk. It is half past seven.

Breathless, Will says, "Look. Don't any of you ever tell anyone that I did this; ever! I will say that you all are liars!"

"Thank you, Will," I say without hesitation because I am truly grateful. "You're a pimp."

"I bought as many doughnuts as I could for ten dollars. When I told the sales clerk that we were over here, she gave us two extra doughnuts from yesterday that were not thrown out with the others last night. I think we should save those for Mrs. Couch. We need to start walking if we're going to make it in time. How far was it, Michelle? Do you remember from last year?"

"I don't know exactly. It was a ten-minute drive, probably six miles." I try to calculate.

"We can run six miles in an hour if we run the same rate that we ran in PE our freshman year," Anne adds, being useful.

The two junior varsity teammates emerged from the side hallway behind my table. At least one has been listening for a few minutes. The Listener is wearing a relatively new hooded sweatshirt with matching pants from the school's athletic department. The navy and gold clothing make her seem older, even though she already looks serious. Her name is embroidered in gold: Brittany.

"That street isn't safe to run on. There's going to be too much traffic in the next hours, and we can't carry our boxes of materials that far. I'm hot-wiring Mrs. Couch's car." Brittany says.

Will drops the bag of doughnuts on the floor near the door. He is stunned. Alpine Brittany swoops in to pick the bag up. The five of us sit at a table meant for two. We huddle. Brittany and the other JV girl chow down into the doughnuts. I elbow my way in to retrieve one. My left hand emerges with a coconut. I despise coconut.

I state the obvious, "You're right. We have to carry those big boxes of articles. I mean, Anne is doing her Lincoln-Douglas style independent of us. The affirmative and negative teams, both varsity and JV, need the boxes to do the best job possible. Anne needs a few pages of her notes. It's not fair to send us into competition intellectually naked. Besides, Anne can't walk that far. Brittany can play teenage girl *Frogger* out on the roads and go withdraw us from competition."

Anne smiles at me. She leans against my shoulder. She feels as light as a bony feather. Her skull feels as though all of her fluff was stripped away long ago and the spine is all that is left; half-skeletal and half-angelic. For a moment, we fall silent with our mouths full of food.

Will is eating his second of the two blueberry doughnuts. We will need to finish in a hurry at this point. The junior varsity girls beat us all. The two indelicate girls are licking artificial powders and sweeteners off their fingertips like ravenous pups. I wish that I could eat quickly in emergencies without getting nauseous.

"Yeah, we just ate. I'm not running right now. I'll just upchuck on the side of the road." Brittany says.

The other JV girl sneers at me and says, "Oh, get off your high-horse, Michelle. I know you know me. You and Tommy went to some dance together in middle school. Tommy and I volunteer with Special Olympics together. Stephanie and I sit at the end of Mrs. Couch's class; for Am Lit and now Brit Lit. Don't act like you haven't been in the trenches with the rest of us. That broom riding witch has been insufferable. I can't wait to graduate!"

"Yeah, Ho, I know you." I smart off. "And almost all of the men in Douglas County know your momma too. Yes, I mean in the biblical sense."

The girls' thick fingers wrap around my turtleneck in less than a second. She is immediately in front of my face, nose-to-nose. Everyone in class calls her Gypsy Girl, but I have not paid attention to her. She has a short temper and strong hands. I try to swallow but cannot. Her two thumbs are in the sweet spot of my windpipe. Of all people, Anne intervenes.

"Preeti, we love you. We have to look after each other right now. Mrs. Couch is out. We can't count on her. I know you're upset that I'm Amanda's alternate for this trip now. Please help me do a good job for her, you know, for her slot. She worked so hard to get the school to this level." Anne condoles.

"Brittany," Preeti says as she releases my throat. "Let's try to wake up Mrs. Couch one last time. What would you do if this was one of your coaches? Isn't there supposed to be an even number of us? Who is missing?"

"There were six passengers in the van yesterday. Mrs. Couch drove. Anne sat in the far back with Michelle and I. You two," Will says while pointing to Brittany and Preeti. "Girls were in the middle, in the captain chairs in front of us. Who was sitting in the front with Mrs. Couch?"

The five of us stare at each other. I think for a moment. I start counting on my fingers.

"Did you share a bedroom with anyone last night?" I ask Will.

Will shakes his head 'no' and says, "One of us is missing. But everyone who registered for the debate is here: affirmative JV, negative varsity, and Lincoln-Douglas."

The full weight of the responsibility of losing one of my classmates hits me hard. I drop everything and run back to our room. I can sense the burning stares of the others in the back of my head. I never ran in public, even in emergencies, until now. The brusque air fills my lungs, and the cups of coffee start catching up with me. Now I have to go to crap. Where is the nearest toilet?

My worst nightmare is that we end up on WSB-TV trying to explain to Monica Kaufman how we lost a fellow student. I hope the lost kid is not as stupid as Anne. They could be in a ditch somewhere.

I look around the girls' room again and go to the bathroom. I want to cry, but I cannot muster it. I am not one to cry over my circumstances, but I do silently fear the repercussions. I run back out the hotel and toward Mrs. Couch's room.

The wind is so loud in my ears that I do not hear Brian say my name at first. He is closing the door to his mother's room and holding his finger up to his mouth to indicate that I should be quiet. I try to slow my heart, but it keeps racing. I attempt, in vain, to listen to what he is saying, but it is all garbled in my brain.

Brian shows me the van keys in his hands while he continues to talk. I continue not to be able to hear him. I wonder if this sensation happens to anyone else during emergencies. Brian helps me to their family van nearby. He opens the back. He has already packed our boxes. Handwritten directions to Houston County High School are in his hands.

Anne is walking behind me and steadying my shoulders. Brittany and Preeti are looking inside the thirty-nine dollars per night room and shaking their heads. The television is still on from last night. The flickering static is the only sign of life in the room. Mrs. Couch is still in the bed. I think I hear the sound of her snoring as I walk away.

Twinkling brown eyes meet mine. For a moment the world stops as I look into Brian's eyes. He is sober, sober as a judge. He is soberer than me with my caffeine jitters and jolts. I am shaking.

The rumors about Brian are horrendous. Mrs. Couch never speaks of him. I had assumed that with a well-established, although not well-respected, mother that Brian has always been the dud in the complicated mother-son relationship. I have never considered his point of view.

I never expected him to help us. I did not ask for his help; yet, here he was, turning the key in the van. He must favor his father more than his mother. Maybe that is why Mr. Couch was leaving Mrs. Couch. She must be the lay-about that has driven her husband to seek homely comforts elsewhere.

Ouch! I bang my knee on the middle row's captain chairs' armrests. I limp to the back row, tucked in a corner. Anne is holding onto me like I am her doll now. I am not certain who needs who more. A throbbing pain wraps around my body like a stadium blanket.

This entire morning was one hundred percent Anne. Things worked out. We are on our way to the state debate. Even the armrests are padded enough that my knee is not bleeding; only bruised. This one time, this one big thing worked out. Things work out because of chance, not because we were blessed. It is not like today was not our turn in the universe to have something work out like this. It is more like winning the life lottery. This one time, this one lucky thing is happening, and it is happening to us.

Ten: Seth

"We're not going to die, Seth. Don't do anything stupid, bro. Don't write a freakin' letter like to your girl some jackhole in a bodice ripper. Don't go all drama queen on me like a whiny lil' girl. I'm surrounded by enough estrogen, bro. Man up!" Tommy says while shaking my shoulders.

But, what Tommy does not understand is that this is an emergency. We could die. Panic seems appropriate. We have miscalculated everything. A pop-up blizzard caught us in the North Georgia wilderness. Matt, Michael, Tommy, and I have made it back to the Methodist church van that our scout troop was borrowing for our annual Appalachian Trail camping trip.

No one predicted snow this weekend, despite the foot of snow that we have to wade through to reach the van. It is the largest accumulation that any of us had ever seen. All of us are Georgia boys and had not planned on snow; ever. Our scoutmaster and the other two parts of our troop have not made it back to the van, or any of the adult volunteers. We are on our own to survive.

"I'm so cold, I can't think straight. Tommy, you have to find a way to stay warm without panicking. I can't feel my fingers. Who can still feel their fingers? We're going to have to light a match?" I say with chattering teeth.

Each of us is, thankfully, wearing a head lamp. It is a scout essential. Now I see why. I occasionally hold my fingers up to the lamp to warm them. I wish the light bulb in the lamp emitted a little more heat. I had not packed gloves. It was not forecasted to be this cold, or to snow.

"Aren't there park rangers or something? They'll find us, right?" Matt says.

Between the four of us, Matt is closest to Tommy. Matt will always take Tommy's side, even if it meant freezing to death. Michael is a pansy and fence straddle. The preacher's son is always a good person to know. I will need a college recommendation letter from his father in about three years stating that I have good moral character. Preacher Dan will not recommend me for anything if I let his son die.

Michael says, "There are park rangers back at Amicalola. There's none here on Springer Mountain. We were supposed to go to Noontootla. I think. I saw a sign saying that we're on a forest service road, but I don't know the number. Do forest service roads have names? Even if we could contact a ranger, how would we tell them where we are?"

"I wish we had done the East Ridge trail like last year and just gone home. Who thought this was a good idea? Why did we pull camp again? We were set up. Everything was fine. Did someone

get bored and think, 'Hey, let's kill the boys? It'll be great for fund-

raising.'" I lash out.

I do not want to die out in the wilderness with these three

dorks. I want to die an old man in a lavish bed full of hot tanned

women in bikinis. No. I want to die an old, old man with Heather,

in a bikini, in my bed. Just Heather.

"Didn't one of the dads keep a car phone or cellular phone in

the glove compartment for emergencies? This is an emergency! We

should call 9-1-1. It's ten o'clock and pitch black. This isn't going to

get any better. We accidentally found the van as it was. If Michael

didn't have a key – by ACCIDENT – I don't know what we would

have done." Matt adds.

My stomach growls and there is a twisting pain. Trying to hold

back in extra drama in my voice, I say, "Let's go ahead and eat the

granola bars. We'll think better. Lunch wasn't very good today. I

was looking forward to chicken and rice for dinner. My dad doesn't

cook."

Michael moves from the front passenger seat to the back with

us. He has the cellular telephone and turns it on. The screen is

orange. Michael extends the antenna. I do not know what to do next

because my family does not have one. We are not well-to-do like

Tommy's family or politically well-connected like Michael's. Matt's

mom is a young widow but does not work because she has money. I feel like an outsider because I have nothing of value, like a cellular phone, to offer these boys. I can only offer my survival skills, and those are rusty at best.

Matt takes the phone from Michael and presses 9-1-1. There is a peculiar shiver in my spine. We all hold our breaths to see if it somehow makes the gadget work better. There is no dial tone. It does not work. Nothing rings and then there is a fatal beep. This is only the second cellular phone I have ever seen. I have no idea how to work it.

"Lunch at school was crap today. I mean, I was all looking forward to high school and stuff thinking that there was going to be hot high school chicks and awesome cafeteria food. Hamburgers and pizza were supposed to be flowing every day. But those mean cafeteria ladies, man. They give me the evil eye. High school sucks." Matt says while looking at the small phone.

Trying to make conversation, Tommy nudges me. "Seth: so, do you miss living with your mom? I miss her. She makes the best mac n' cheese. Her brownies are always awesome. I want chips right now."

I smile a little thinking of Mom. I wish I had all the gold in Fort Knox to help take care of her. She left my father when I was in fifth grade. I thought my life was going to be fine because I made it to the end of elementary school with my original family intact. Other people's parents had started getting divorced here and there.

At least two-thirds of our high school has their original two parents still married and living together, except for people like Matt.

Most of my friends have stay-at-home moms, but my mom had to go back to work. Unfortunately, mom went back to work in her native North Carolina. She wants what is best for all three of us. Dad not yelling at us every day was best. Then, Dad cleaned up. The judge let me choose who I wanted to live with this school year. I wanted to stay with my friends and go to the same high school. I wanted to keep going to the same church and remain in the scouts. I wanted to sleep in the bedroom where I grew up. I would give up all of this crap for mom right now.

I miss mom so bad. A fat tear rolls out. I quickly wipe it away. I do not want to be the drama queen. I have had to make choices in my life that these other boys have never considered. Screw them!

"Stupid, she made everything out of a box. It was Kraft!" I say.

The three guys see right through me. They love my mom too. She had kissed their boo-boo's too; back when we were growing up. She worked with their moms to sew on badges and fundraise. Then, all of their moms turned on her when she left my dad. They judged her and were afraid that she was going to take their husbands. It was the harshest of life sentences.

Matt starts tearing through his pack. He is up to something. Matt is the best actual scout in the entire troop. He is resourceful and can think in emergencies. He is probably going to end up being

President one day, or an Army Ranger. Yeah, I would sleep much better at night if guys like Matt end up protecting our country. I feel like I do not have anything to offer in that category. I am still short for my age. I am jealous that the other guys have started getting chest hair.

"Listen up, jackholes!" Matt says. "We're going to make a fire in the camp cook set in the back of the van. We're going to need to move any extra equipment out of the back to the front seats. Move it close to the windows to keep us insulated. We're going to have to crack a window somewhere."

Blonde angel boy Michael has dark circles around his eyes. He looks blue, exactly Carolina blue, in the face. Tommy and I move torn rucksacks, equipment, maps, sleeping bags, and some extra coats around. *Oh.* A bag of Butterfinger BBs. Those are going inside my jacket. I will share if I must.

Michael whispers, "It's okay. I think I'm warm again. Go ahead. I'm going to give my eyes a break for a minute. I don't think the church would be mad if we broke a window, though, to let in some fresh air. I can't feel a thing."

Matt leaps from the bench seat he is on. He sits in front of Michael and shakes him violently by the shoulders. Matt says, "You're freezing to death, you asshole! I'm not going to screw up my chance of going to Heaven by letting the preacher's son die on me.

What am I going say? 'Oh, Michael was such a good boy until Matt let him die on the AT!' *Nuh, uh.* No, sir, I'll kill you first!"

Michael is very startled. I grab Matt by the knees to pull him off. He is both mad and self-righteous at the same time. Michael is accustomed to being babied by throngs of church ladies. We are not church ladies. We are foul-mouthed brats according to Miss Michigan Face.

I say, "Don't you guys remember that Jack London short story *To Build a Fire*? Our situation is like that. We're going to freeze to death if we don't build a fire."

Tommy sits. He is waiting in the back like he is waiting on instructions from his coach as to what to do next. He is impotent in every situation in life where there is not an adult telling him exactly what to do to succeed.

Do not ask Tommy what his science fair project is this year. His mom will complete it for him. I cannot wait to see how that mess will play out at the fair. I bet he wins first place. He wins everything. Adults are so enamored with him that they cannot see what is plain to the rest of us: Tommy is a tool.

I knock Tommy on the shoulder as I go by. I try to follow Matt's plan, but organizing in a cramped space is difficult. I help Matt remove the two bench seats closest to the back. We could have used an RV or trailer for this outing, but the rig would never have made it through the incline and narrow, winding roads.

We have more purse-size bags than the senior citizens group at church. All sorts of crap fill the cotton bags that we will never need. I shove a blue speckled enamel kettle to the side and a cast iron popcorn popper from the fifties. Finally, I slam my hand into a Dutch oven. *Shit*! That thing is more like a cauldron. I do not know much about Dutch ovens except that they can be used for anything, and hurt like Hades. My hand throbs with pain. I happen on a copy of a scouting manual.

"Tommy," I question him harshly. "How much acid rain is in Georgia? Like, if we were in the middle of nowhere and had to melt snow to get water, would it kill us? Do we need to throw an iodine tablet in there or something? Or, is it okay because it's snow?"

Michael meekly replies for Tommy. "Crystal is the one that did a project on acid rain. Tommy did something on recycling. Right, Tommy?"

Tommy turns from the window. "Uh, I think that's what my project's on. I'm not sure. Ask Mom."

"You're a tool, dumbass!" Matt starts on Tommy. "You're like the Georgia version of Forrest Gump. If you were in a Jack London story, you would be the guy that pissed on himself and froze to death. How did you make it into gifted classes for ninth-grade, *huh*? You don't even know how to write your own name. Now, wake up! We all need to take off our wet shoes and put our extra pair of socks on. Take the old socks off first and then put the dirty ones on top of the news ones. Our feet will be warm and dry, as long as you all followed directions and are wearing wool!"

I open up my granola bar and start eating it while changing socks. I lay out a small tarp in the back of the van. I place our thirty-degree rated sleeping bags in a square around the popcorn popper that was at a diagonal. Next, I put the Dutch oven on top and started looking for paper to burn. There is a large collection of random trail maps from over a decade of assorted scouting adventures.

Next, I press the cigarette lighter in to get it well-heated. I crank open one of the side windows. Compacted snow trickles through the crack and hits my freshly socked feet. In an effort to move around the van more easily, I had not put my dry hiking boots back on.

My feet are instant blocks of ice. The cold travels straight up my legs and into my stomach muscles. I am shivering. Everything starts to hurt, even exhaling my icy breath hurts. There is an ache traveling through the blood vessels in my body.

To stay awake I whisper, "Do you all hear that? The loud thumping? Is someone outside?"

Not realizing that I had stopped moving, Matt pulls me away from the window. He sits me down on one of the sleeping bags. He briskly rubs my arms and folds me into a burrito in a fleece blanket. He takes off my wet socks and throws them to the side. He is scared and a little mad at my stupidity.

"C'mon, Seth. You can't be stupid like that. You hear your heartbeat. Quick, Michael, hang another tarp or waterproof bag between the open window and the bags."

Matt takes off his socks and puts them on my feet. I think my feet a still attached. I cannot feel them, and the numbness is traveling so fast. I am warming up, though. I am humiliated that Matt has to take care of Michael and me.

Tommy was not helpful. We would have to tell Tommy when he had to stand, eat, sleep, or take a dump. He was useless. I do not want to be useless. I want to be able to take care of myself, if not my brother scouts.

I am weary and drowsy. I am very sleepy, and the sleeping bag is warm. I think I remember my mom fussing over the temperature rating on the bag. Mom forced my Dad to buy a lower temperature rating than the minimum requirement; in case it got super-cold sometime. Some of the other guys have borrowed their equipment from big brothers, cousins, or neighbors. At least my stuff is new and will keep me warm. I hold my head up for a moment to see barefoot Matt lighting maps on fire in the Dutch oven.

"My mom sent juice boxes," I whisper. "We don't have a pot to piss in, but we have juice."

Michael is in his bag and asleep. Tommy is awake, but his consciousness is not in the same van as the rest of us. He is checked-out. He is very much like a possum. I remember the same blank look on his face when we were in Vacation Bible School together, when we were quite young, and he pooped in his Underoos.

Having already gone through our packs, Matt throws a juice box at me. It hits me in the head. I sit up. I am confused but okay. I do not remember lying down.

I say, "I thought I just laid down for a second, man. Calm down."

"You didn't lie down for a second, Seth. You have hypothermia. That was almost four hours ago. Nothing has happened, but we've been back here awhile. Michael has slept through the whole thing. He's scared to death but not scared enough to stay awake and take turns watching the fire."

Thoroughly embarrassed, I sit up quickly. I say, "You don't have to take care of me. Let me take a turn and I'll watch the fire. You and Tommy need a break. Where are your shoes?"

Matt is rubbing his toes, but they are an eerie purple. I see the cover of one of our ninth-grade required reading books burning. Good. It was perfect tender. We are ahead of Jack London's narrator that we were thinking about earlier. Maybe we will live to read, and do homework, another day. Tonight is the longest night.

There is a little heat traveling through the cast iron from the Dutch oven to the popcorn popper, but not enough to keep toes warm. The traces of warmth that are oscillating through the van seem to murmur ominous predictions. I immediately pray that we live, do not get lung cancer from burning books, and survive frostbite. Poor Matt, I am wearing his socks. I take off the double layer of socks and toss his socks to him.

"Here. I warmed your socks up for you," I say, feeling remorseful.

"What about your toes? You're smaller than me. No offense, but, you are."

"I'm in my bag. I'll sit up with the bag still zipped up. I'm fine. You know what I should have done? Taken someone else's gloves or hat, or something, and put them on my feet."

"Shut up. I already thought of that. The rest of the troop took the good stuff. We just have the leftovers to work with tonight. If anything could be easily packed, or taken down the trail, it was. Everyone left the things that were too cumbersome, or impractical to carry, behind."

The fire is hypnotizing. The small novels and maps are burning faster than traditional wood fires. We truly were surviving in the backcountry. I am desperate to know what time it is. In our struggle to return to the van, a falling branch smashed my wrist and digital watch.

"Hey, Seth. I need to tell you something. It's important." Matt says.

"What? Something more important than surviving a pop-up blizzard in the North Georgia mountains? Remember, you wouldn't let me write a note to Heather. And, dude, she's hotter than you."

"Something happened while you and Michael were asleep," Matt says with a solemn glance.

"We're in a church van. What happened? Did a bear rub his butt against the window? What?" I tease.

"Do you know what grass is?"

"Yeah, Matt, I know what grass is. I've done all the same service project as you. We're Boy Scouts. We help old ladies with yards. What?" I say. "Just say whatever it is. Don't make me guess."

"No, Seth; like, the other kind of grass. Think: Weed. Mary Jane. Marijuana?"

"What? Oh. *Um*," I stumble over my words. "Well, I remember watching *Cartoon All-Stars to the Rescue* in fifth grade in Mrs. Beasley's class. And, of course, the frying pan commercial where the lady took the egg and was like, 'This is your brain, and this is your brain on drugs' before smashing the second egg."

"Tommy smokes weed. That's why he doesn't give a crap about anything. He's blazed; like, most of the time. I don't know how he does everything he does: soccer, scouts, baseball, basketball, football, and band. It's nuts! But, think about it, Seth, how does he get it all done and remain super-calm? How does he still get straight A's? He was on Ritalin in elementary school."

Little Tetris pieces of random information start to fit together in my brain. Tommy does do it all. He also has a brother who is ten-years older than him. Tommy and his brother have different moms, so they did not grow up together. But, we all live in the same town and go to the same church, so I know who is brother is. He is big and aggressive. I have heard people call him *Hulk Face* before.

Something unpleasant happened to Hulk Face, but I cannot remember what it was. He traveled across country, or something, and has not been around since we were in seventh-grade or so. Maybe Hulk Face started doing drugs, and Tommy did too?

Tommy's parents are all over him, how could they not know? They have to know. They do all of Tommy's schoolwork for him. Tommy is such a star for the school and is in the Douglas County Sentinel's sports section, here and there. Do all the adults know and not care?

"Seth? Did you hear what I said? Do you understand?"

"I believe you. I didn't see it before, Matt, but I see it now. Did Tommy smoke in here?" I say alarmed. "Is that the funny smell?"

"Yes. That's it," Matt says pushing his lips tightly together.

"Oh, I thought it was the old socks or the maps burning. That's pretty foul. Isn't he going to die or something? Do we know a drug addict?"

"I don't know what makes a person an addict. But, I'm not crazy about ratting on our brother scout either. I don't know what to do. He was just so brazen about it. He wanted me to try some, but I said 'no.'"

Matt has his legs crossed. His hands tuck into armpits. He is rocking back and forth. I stare at the burning maps. The novels are ashes. My naivety about Tommy's activities is going up in the tiny floating cinders.

"There is one small container of kindling. I was saving it for the coldest part of the night. But, I'm going to trust you and leave you in charge, Seth. We have to keep the fire going. We need to plan on no one else coming here to help us until after sunrise, around seven at least. Remember, we can't kill the preacher's son. But, if we take a vote and throw Tommy out into the snow, I can probably live with that."

"Yeah, man, I got this. Get some rest. We don't know what is going down tomorrow," I say in a false yet reassuring manner.

If Matt stayed awake and kept the fire going up until now, then I should be able to as well. I want to be the kind of person that other people can rely on in emergencies. But, truly, there is only one person that I want to depend on me: Mom.

After a few minutes of listening to the fire, Matt falls asleep next to me, on top of the tarp. I worry that he will get too cold, so I creep on top of Tommy's bag to bring Matt's bag over to my side. There is no way that I can put him inside the bag, so I unzip it and wrap it around him. My toes quickly freeze from the brief excursion out of my bag. I hop back in and zip half-way up. My heart races to pump more blood to my hands and feet.

The guys are going to make such fun of me, but I have got to do it. In case something happens, I cannot let another minute go by without at least writing a note. I find a trail map piece that is not burning well. It cools in my lap for a moment.

I am thinking about Heather. I have known Heather since her family moved to Douglas County when we were in the second grade. She had the most beautiful blonde curls back then. She smiled all day, even when we had to practice handwriting or other tedious tasks. Her favorite book was *Black Beauty*. Her favorite thing to do on the playground was ride the tire swing.

Back then, Heather was afraid of wasps and her mother dying. Her mother is dying right now; she has cancer. I hope Heather never gets cancer. She was the only reason I went to confirmation class at Michael's dad's church. I owe my salvation to her and Jesus.

Not knowing when we will be rescued, or if we will survive, I focus on writing one note. It is the most important note. In pencil, I write on a Neels Gap trail map: *Mom. I love you. I want to come home. Love, Seth.*

I hold it tight and watch the fire. Like a dunce, I sit like a scared child and rethink my actions. I cling to the note on the map. Even now, in the blizzard, I can feel her fiery spirit. Her spirit calls out to me, "Seth, come home. Stay awake or you'll freeze. Come home to me. Come home to North Carolina."

Eleven: Jennifer

March 6, 2009 5:12 AM
Atlanta, Georgia

"Just push, Jennifer! You're moments away from being a mommy!" a room full of nurses, an obstetrician, and my husband coax.

What do they think I'm doing here? Painting my nails and calling for a cocktail? I am horizontally squatting and pushing as hard as I can, despite the fact that I cannot feel anything. I regret the epidural. The baby is not coming out.

"That's easy for you to say, Andrew! You're not the one PUSSSHIINNGG!" I scream.

Andrew is the most intolerable partner that I could have ever imagined. There is nothing romantic, graceful, or virtuous about giving birth. My hip bones separate and my daughter's head finally makes it most of the way out. She is stuck in a horrible position. I look over to my former classmate, Amanda, who is at my side. She is a labor and delivery nurse. If things go wrong with Annie, I need Amanda here. I require at least one person with common sense to be with me throughout this ordeal.

"You've got do this. Focus on the next contraction and get her out of there. The Pitocin is not doing you any favors right now. The minute she's out we can stop the epidural. Then you can get you back to normal, okay? But, Jen, you have to give me a good five minutes of hard labor now. Get ready. GO!" Amanda says.

I push my husband away instead of wrapping my fists around his balls like I want. I grab the bed's side rails and inhale as deep as possible. I am on the tall side, so the hospital bed feels very confining. My feet are in the stirrups at the end of the bed, which makes my knees fold in an almost cartoonish position. I push another time. *Pop*. Anneewakee Elizabeth Kowalski is out.

Oh, that was wretched. Why do people do give birth more than once? I start counting to ten and close my eyes to the random dot on the ceiling that was my focal point for the past three hours. I look down between my legs to see the OB and nurses gathering around. There is no baby on my belly.

I immediately worry because I cannot hear the baby cry. What is wrong? Babies cry the minute they come out of the mother in the all the TV shows and movies? Why is my baby not crying? Of course, many of those babies are infants, not newborns.

Amanda takes my hand, "Okay, Jen. Here's the thing: Little Annie is blue. Now, it's okay. They're going to get her breathing. But, you see, she was born in the posterior position. That's not ideal. But, the good news is that she's out. I know it was a little hairy there for a while but, honestly, I'm glad the forceps didn't work. I'm not your doctor, obviously. I'm just sayin' that it's not what I would have wanted for my birth."

"You said *hairy*," I mutter to Amanda, instantly remembering my *au naturel* crotch.

"No judgment, girlfriend. You just brought another human into the world. You don't have time for a skin infection from improper or dirty waxing. You won't believe what I see on-the-job."

Wah, wah, wah. Annie's sweet cries breathe life back into me. I am so glad she is breathing, but it took a minute to get her started. The blue fades and she pinks up.

The nurses and OB give me a strange look as they place my baby on my belly. Annie is full of blood, but I know it is my blood, so it is okay. Little Annie looks exactly like my mom, and maybe a little like Jeremy. Her toes are tiny. I have eaten turtle tracks in ice cream that are bigger than her toes. And, her head is such an awkward shape; poor angel.

Crying, I say, "We've had a terrible night, but it's all worth it."

Andrew comes back over to us. He extends his arm around me and Little Annie. I am glad I did not remove his testicles a few minutes ago.

"My sweet Southern ladies. My girls. Oh, Annie, Daddy loves you. Daddy's been very impatient for you to get here. And, you were too patient, too. You're a little late, my darling." Andrew says.

The brand-new daddy caresses his little girl's face. It is strange to say, but I feel like I am interrupting them. Annie will be a daddy's girl. I can tell. Andrew will fuss over her boyfriends and pretend to clean shotguns when they come to visit. He will spoil her at college graduation and give her a car, or something ridiculously expensive. He will take her prom dress shopping at the finest boutiques in Europe. His family has the money. He will spoil her, even though he never spoiled me. I was just a bride for a day then an indentured servant for a lifetime.

"We're going to take the baby, clean her up, and let you get stitched up." A nurse says.

In one swift movement, Annie is off my tummy, out of our arms, and screaming again. The room feels very frosty now. I want her back. How can I miss her already?

Andrew turns to Amanda, "My goodness. Jennifer and I can't thank you enough for being here. We had not expected to have to deliver on this side of Atlanta. If I had thought Jen would go into labor early, I would have voted against coming to Lennox for baby shopping. But, it happened. Babe, we're a real now family. We have a teeny little human that has both of our DNA. Maybe Annie will be witty like you, Jen."

"You don't know the half of it! I sat catty-corner from her for three years in high school English." Amanda says.

"When you say 'high school English,' you diminish the grisly boot-camp style classroom environ that was Mrs. Couch's program." I chide. "I'll have to start mentoring Annie now for her to survive the program in fifteen years."

My mouth is parched. I sip on ice water. With a nod from the nurse, I motion for Andrew to follow Anneewakee. Our little Annie will not be left unattended.

I expected a boy for the first half of the pregnancy. Discovering the baby was a girl was quite the surprise. All of the old wives' tales could not have prepared me for her. She was a very active pregnancy. I had some bleeding early on. Andrew fell in love in the minute he saw her on the ultrasound at twenty-weeks. He worshiped the amniotic fluid that she bounced in.

"Shit!" I yelp. "Feel free to be gentle. It's my first time having a needle in my spine!"

My epidural is out now. Amanda sits next to me and holds my hand. She is the perfect person to be here. I labored for almost twenty-four hours. I do not feel like being a stranger in a strange land again and having to explain everything right now. I cannot stand explaining myself. I am thirty seconds from being Mrs. Couch's surrogate daughter and yelling, "Because I damn well said so, you little assholes!"

Amanda is sensitive and intuitive. She pats my hand harder as she feels my blood pressure rise. I am sick of medical staff quibbling over details as though they have never delivered a baby before. Why can people not just do their jobs these days? They had one little task: deliver the baby. Asking me whether I wanted to save the baby this, or whatever about the heartbeat that; it did not amount to a hill of beans. I only want Annie.

During elementary and middle school, students were assigned class seats alphabetically. Kelly and Strickland are not close alphabetically, so Amanda and I did not get to know each other until high school when faculty stopped alphabetizing us. Sitting with someone with a last name that began with the letter S felt rebellious. Also, I was tired of sitting next to Jeremy. Some schools separate twins in classes; but, what do you do if both twins are in the gifted program? You are together all day and night. The least that Jeremy could have done was pretend to be stupid and let me spend precious years enjoying Anne.

"I have a regret," I confess to Amanda. "I am sorry that you were absent the day Crystal performed *The Song of the Chattahoochee*. Crystal was bumptious. She and Mrs. Cough never conciliated."

Amanda smiles thinking about Crystal. She says, "Fancy words for a fancy lady. I miss my Crystal Pistol. I had hoped she would join the social media world, but government employees rarely do. Did you ever see her on stage?"

"No. That's another regret I have. Anne said Crystal was sonorous and would have made a skilled voice artist. Please, never tell Crystal I said that."

I feel like a sweaty mess, which was how I felt for most of high school. But, Amanda looks like she did not mind too much. I am glad she did not linger at my vag when Annie was being born. It was messy.

There was something about being a nurse that gave Amanda a strange fortitude. I could not believe that Amanda came to my January baby shower. I did not know who Andrew had invited off my Facebook friends list. The whole event was a surprise. Seeing friends from high school was probably the greatest comfort and astonishment; of course, there was a fair amount of drama.

"You know, my regret," Amanda parrots back to me. "Was that I never found out what happened at the alternate reunion last year. I wanted to ask Melissa. I mean, the last time I checked we had hung out and got tattoos together in memory of Tommy. I shouldn't criticize how someone else handles a trauma, but I could never sit down with her and talk about it either. What happened to Justin? Or Michael? Or Michelle? You were closer to David. I'm glad we saw him at the reunion. He lost so much weight."

Amanda holds my hand tighter. The stitching is taking a long time. What are they doing? Sewing a cross stitch of a kitten with the phrase *hang in there*? I am grateful for the distraction.

My placenta had to be sent off for biopsy. Even Amanda looks confused, but we accept it. There are so many things that are happening that are not in any of the parenting books. I studied for this labor harder than I had studied for my CL English exam or even my graduate thesis. Who gives two shits about unreliable narrators in Virginia Wolf's novels? Not this girl.

"It's so strange how the unexpected keeps happening," I say. "I think I'm learning to expect the unexpected. I was there the day that Melissa turned. She and I were both in Savannah for a year and a half or so before I graduated. We were walking along the river and something happened to her. I have no idea what snapped, but it frightened me. I thought she was going to go full Ophelia on me, like Tommy had said that she would that one day in class. But, she dug out some extra strength from somewhere. She's not like the rest of us anymore. But you, Amanda, you weren't quite like the rest of us either."

"Well, that's borderline racist; just kidding. Kinda kidding and kinda saying it is racist, okay? I know what you mean. What happened to Melissa? I want to know more. Make my break worthwhile. I have less than a half hour before I'm needed."

"Oh, please, girl. I don't think of you like that. You're a Southern gal like the rest of us. The thing with Melissa: It was almost a year after Tommy died. Now, please remember, I never liked Tommy. I was never Team Tommy."

I inhale with a sharp gasp as the OB finishes. She nods to me. They will want me to walk to the bathroom soon. I am too tired to go to the bathroom. Can I not just pee on myself? Nevermind: I cannot pee in front of Amanda.

"Oh, c'mon. You're Team Jacob, but you're not Team Tommy. That sounds like a load of cow manure. Me thinks you a hypocrite, Goody Jennifer." Amanda says in a fake Puritan accent.

I appreciate her *Crucible* reference and laugh for a moment. I see her point. Both Tommy and the fictional Jacob from *Twilight* are slightly wild, red-blooded American boys very much from the late part of the twentieth century. Metrosexuals they are not.

"Amanda, are you confessing that you've read *Twilight*? Oh, my! I thought that was beneath you. When we were in Mrs. Couch's class, you always chose the most sensitive topics and books to analyze. When we had to choose a Shakespeare play to review, you chose *Titus Andronicus*. When you presented in class, I thought for certain that you were going to drink blood out of goblet or something. I'm dark. I like dark. But, you, my friend; you have an ancient soul. There is no reason for you to be reading paranormal crap. You should be reading real literature, or teaching it."

In a hysterical fit, Amanda lets go of my hand and laughs hard. I have known her for fifteen years or so, but I cannot recall hearing her laugh before. She was the student that would take the teachers to task for not doing their jobs. Amanda was the smartest person in our class; but, not the most popular. Her raw intelligence and ambition made her intimidating. Tommy was one of the few boys that had a fondness for her. But, I think he was just keeping her in his back pocket for when he went to college and needed help writing papers. Tommy was an odd one. He respected the girls that did not like him or fall for his artificial charm.

"Whatever. I saw *Twilight* on your Goodreads page too. That's what gave me the idea. The bookstore at whatever airport I was in – maybe Fort Lauderdale – was lacking good literature but I chose it despite the limited selection. I wanted to read that crock of teenage angst before the movie came out on DVD this week. I don't have time for movie theaters anymore." Amanda says.

All of a sudden, I think back nostalgically to an untold number of Friday and Saturday nights at the dollar movies on both Douglas Boulevard at the Carmike and on Fairburn Road near the Big Lots. Amanda did not hang out in my same low-brow circle of friends. I think Jeremy, Anne, David, and I dropped hundreds of dollars at those places over the years. I try to edit my thoughts when it comes to David because I know that Amanda and David's wife struck up a personal and professional relationship after the ten-year reunion last year.

"Talking about movies makes me think about Justin working at the theater. We used to go and see him there from time to time. When I say 'we' I mean David, Anne, Jeremy, and myself. David was good the last time I saw him; but, you know, that was at the reunion. We're older now. We're at that awkward age when not everyone is a parent yet and..."

Shit! I messed up big time. I took for granted that Amanda is not a mom yet. She does not seem to have anyone special in her life either. Oh, crap. And, she has been very generous to my family. How can I keep my foot out of my mouth? Bad foot!

"Don't worry about me. I'm tough. I thought I might marry sometime; have a three bedroom, two bath home with a white picket fence in the suburbs. You know, like you. But, it's not my time yet. I'm having too much fun. I'm married to my work, and my work gets jealous if I spend too much time dating. We're in our late-twenties. Being a parent is too big of a commitment for me right now. I think we were raised too traditionally for me to just go off and have a baby without having a church-worthy big wedding and marriage like you and Andrew."

Amanda side steps the child discussion with a smooth tactfulness. She lacked that in high school, so it is an acquired skill. She is a grown-up now and, yet, I still feel like a legal adult that has existed in a prolonged state of teen 'hood.

Amanda's cheeks lower on her face. She is thinking deep thoughts about something. I am uncertain what to do. She looks like her brain is on a different continent. I do not want to pry. I know Andrew will look after Annie, but I do want to spend time with Amanda. I am not sure how to bring her back to the moment. At a loss for alternatives, I take her hand and squeeze it gently.

"Oh, I was thinking about something awful." Amanda starts. "In a moment, it feels as though we were back in high school. Our senior year, I was scheduled to go on this field trip with Mrs. Couch. I think it was for debate. But, hindsight being twenty-twenty, that was about the time she found out Alicia and Brian were pregnant. I mean, Alicia's bun was half-baked. A size two was only hiding a small pumpkin!

"Alicia and Brian were not the first couple to get pregnant, but they were the first in our little pod of people. They were the first ones to own up to the pregnancy openly and say, 'Hey! We're young. We're going to be teen parents but, you know what, support us or screw off.' Anneewakee was so happy for them."

An inferno races through my soul. I have an unnatural anger come over me. I suck my breath deep in as though I am about to breathe fire. Instead of spewing fire, I am barely managing the pain in my crotch.

"Screw Mrs. Couch and her pretenses! She was a bitch on fire and a hot mess herself too! She sat at her little desk in the front of the classroom holding court with us like we were her personal lackeys. Anne was just a little girl, and Mrs. Couch was awful to her. Anne was ignorant to the in-progress political chess game.

"Anne was just thinking, 'Oh! I know people that are having a baby. Here, let me hold it and squeeze and play dress up.' She wasn't playing political games. We were eighteen-years old but so much younger than other generations at the same age. Goodness, me! I miss Anneewakee. Anne!"

"You're going to bleed out like that, Jennifer. I heard the medical team say that the placenta is unusual. They're sending it off for biopsy. You have to calm down. You don't want a hemorrhage. What happened with Mrs. Couch? I left for college the week after graduation. I couldn't wait to get out of Douglas County. I wanted to be gone. But, now I regret not keeping up with everyone. Besides, no one talks to me. If anything, they speak to my voicemail."

Calmly inhaling and exhaling deep, I try to recall the exact series of events. My mind is feeling fuzzy from lack of food and sleep. There are few people that I can discuss the abusive Mrs. Couch with these days. She is a local legend and retiring soon. I do not want to defame her, but few understand what it was really like living within the four walls of the English gifted program.

I start, "Anne worked at Stephanie's family's floral shop for most of high school. Goodness! Is Beautiful Lee-Dunn still open? Anne didn't want to work there after high school, no matter what. She became a waitress at that steakhouse near Hospital Drive, right? What was its name? We called it the B-and-D for Bite and Die."

"I don't remember. Hospital Drive near Chapel Hill, or where Hospital Drive is near the hospital? Georgia State Bank was there. They were bought out last year." Amanda says. "I liked that place. Melissa's mom was the branch manager there after we graduated."

Amanda has started to forget the names of the roads in the county. Good for her for being away so long. I want to let these things slip from my memory too. I wish that I could memory dump everything that I know about Anne's murder and leave a permanent bookmark in her story that stops at graduation. Her tale is too sad and does not have a happy ending. I am not an optimist, but I still prefer a fairy tale ending.

"The grill was off Hospital Drive near the old Sears Outlet store. It was across from where Kroger used to be. Anyway. Anne knew that college was not going to work out for her, so she dropped out after the first couple of weeks and went from waitressing part-time to full-time. Right before Christmas, she took the morning off and went to a funeral.

"A friend of hers from Lithia was killed in a car accident. It had something to do with illegal racing. Anne shouldn't have gone. She should not have taken a few hours off. She was so sensitive and tender-hearted!

"The DCHS English department was having a Christmas luncheon at the B-and-D right after the funeral as Anne was coming into work. She waited on their table. There were eight teachers there. Mrs. Couch was a class-A bitch on a good day but was repulsive when she was drinking. She pulled Anne over to the side and ripped into her. I'll never forgive Couch for that!" I say.

"Lickskillet Junction," Amanda says. She remembers everything.

"Your brain will melt like mine one day," I say sarcastically.

The anger burns in my too-empty belly. I touch the excess skin on my stomach and try my best to calm down. I can feel my blood pressure rising. I am ready to snap like a taut rubber band.

"That is so weird," Amanda says as she looks at her phone. "What did Mrs. Couch have to rip into Anne for anyway? Anne wasn't one of her little teacher's pets, like Heather and Nicole. But, Anne wasn't on the outs with Mrs. Couch around graduation either. What the heck?"

Amanda feels a pull-back in time to rush to Anne's defense as well. I wonder how Amanda feels about Anne. Mrs. Couch had appointed Anne as Amanda's replacement at some high-level state debate competition. I think Amanda has let go of all the pettiness from high school. Annie's baby shower reminded me that not all of us are in that place just yet.

Big tears filled my eyes. I say, "Anne told me that Mrs. Couch had pulled her to the side and told her that she was disappointed in her for leaving college. She said that education was a lifelong commitment not to be thrown away. She thought that she needed to grow up, go back to school, and work it out.

"It was completely opposite of all of that stuff that happened February of our senior year. Anne had called me crying on Christmas, but I couldn't spend too much time with her on the phone because we had family calling in and wanting to talk to our parents. Looking back, doesn't that sound stupid? I didn't spend time talking to my best friend the day before she was murdered because people were calling my parents' phone line? Why didn't I have a cell phone? I could drown in my regret."

"You have a good excuse today. It's your hormones. You just had a beautiful, perfect baby girl. Enjoy her. We'll talk later about Anne and why you're not Team Edward."

A cry involuntarily coughs out of my throat when I saw Andrew at the door. I quickly finish, "How anyone could hurt Anne like that, I'll never comprehend. She was just a snippet of nothing. I mean, I know that she wasn't physically tiny, but her soul was...emergent... or something. I can't even think of the right word. She was having a bad day and then to have a former teacher rip you a new one like that. If I had been there, I would have been arrested for breaking open a can of whoop-ass. I'm still pissed."

Amanda looks surprised, "Well, I'll let you get back to your baby. But, I didn't know that had happened. We have a new Annie in the group now!"

Andrew lays our Anneewakee in my arms. It is time to see if the breastfeeding classes paid off. We have the last class scheduled for tomorrow night because I am a procrastinator and chronically under-prepared if not unprepared.

I wave goodbye to Amanda. I see her looking at her phone. She probably has to start a shift soon. Northside is not her hospital. She will need time to drive and change. It was bighearted of her to stay with me through the worst of labor. I wonder what has happened to her over the past eleven years that has tempered her soul. She has a calmness that I crave.

Cradling Annie in my arms, I cannot help but think about Anne. Anyone from our class would clearly understand that I named my Anneewakee after our Anneewakee. But, I do not want to share my Anneewakee with everyone, so she is "Little Annie" right now. She is beautiful. Her eyes are tiny sparkling blue. Her hair is dark like Andrew's; at least for now. I involuntarily start humming.

"Jennifer, you're humming," Andrew calls me out. "What is that? *The Imperial March*? Are you humming Star Wars stuff to Annie? I'm calling Jeremy. You're not yourself."

"Don't bother him, it's only five in the morning," I say.

I try to place what I am humming, but nothing comes up. Anne was the Star Wars fan and overall sci-fi geek. Maybe I had started humming something, but I do not know for sure what it is. I feel self-conscious having been scrutinized and put on the spot by my lesser half.

Andrew is watching us with caution as Annie is trying to latch. I do not feel like the expert in the room right now. I will have to teach him how to be a better husband, yet again.

Then, something flips in my brain. This lovely creature in my arms is my Anneewakee. I am here to protect and defend her against all. I will yell at every teacher that ever says anything remotely considered to be cruel or callous. I will push for her to have the best opportunities but I am going to raise her to be independent and vigorous too. Just because she shares a first name with my friend does not mean that she will grow to be weak. I love Anne, but she was never fully of this Earth either. There was a remoteness to her; a quiet. I do not want my daughter to be quiet.

Carpe Diem, I think. I will get a pillow for the sofa with the Latin phrase on it or tattoo it on my ass. I will teach my Annie to go out into the world and get what she wants. I want her to have an ardor about her soul, like me. I want to correct all the mistakes that I ever made in not being a perfect and supportive friend to Anne.

I want to right all my wrongs. I want Amanda to finish calling whoever she is calling and say, "Yes, Jen. You're up for the job. You'll make a great mom at age twenty-eight."

"She latched!" Andrew cheers.

"Andy, thank you for your support and everything. But, you know, I've got this. I've got this whole motherhood thing. You don't have to stand over us. I'm not going to drop her," I say while staring him down.

"I know. It's just when we started this journey and everything, well, I know it was me more than you that wanted to have a baby. I know it's a lot of work. I don't want you to grow resentful. I want to be right here for you in every possible way. What can I do?" He says. He is red-cheeked with enthusiasm.

"You need to go take a nap. We'll take care of Annie in shifts until your parents can drive here. We'll call them at a decent hour; maybe eight o'clock or so." I say with authority.

Andrew nods his head. He lies down on the little sofa for dads. He is too excited to sleep. I can see him flip over and smile every few minutes. All is well, and I have not dropped my little bundle of love. She is nursing and snuggling into me. Her newborn lips curl back now and then. She has a crooked smile, like Jeremy's. My somber, but silent, prayer is that I will do a better job protecting my Annie than I had with Anne. May her soul rest in peace.

Twelve: Emma

November 20, 2012 10:57 AM
Douglasville, Georgia

The school secretary writes my first name in bubble letters on a nametag with a purple marker. It reads *Em Ma*, as if my Christian name needs added exotic street flare in my native county. Next, the secretary scribbles *Julian's Mom* underneath it. My nametag looks like a tired preschooler scribbled it. I give the secretary a dirty look, but she is immune to it. I have lost my touch.

The marker the millennial-aged secretary uses is grape scented and reminds me of third-grade. The scent is a stark contrast to the rest of the office, which smells like old soup can labels, laminated paper, and isopropyl alcohol. The competing fragrances overwhelm me. I walk out to the main hallway.

My ears sense the almost inaudible *splish, splash* of lukewarm late-autumn rain drops as they drip from the aging covered walkway near the entrance to my child's school. *His school* I think to myself as I sit down on a colorfully painted bench. The bench touches the back of my calves instead of my knees like regular benches. Everything here is built around the young; and, I am so glad that it is the way that it is because he is only three-years old.

One quandary I face when talking to acquaintances about my child's school is how I do I refer to the school. What do I call it? It is a public elementary school; but, it is not a typical Douglas County preschool through fifth-grade elementary school. There are two small classrooms set aside for preschool special needs students.

While my friends from college blab to me all about the costly private preschools that their children, who are the same age, attend; I am stuck. Online and in real life, where your child attends preschool is a big deal. It is a larger indicator of what you can forecast for that child later in life. What can I expect for Julian?

In almost every OB-GYN office there are recommended pregnancy books. *What to Expect When You're Expecting* is one of those must-read books. I glanced through the book during my pregnancy with Julian. There was nothing in the book about how to handle fellow preschool moms. Julian was not my first pregnancy, or my last, but he followed a painful miscarriage. I had been particularly careful with that little bun in my oven. I ate whole foods and strictly followed my orders for bed rest when I almost lost him at seven weeks gestation. Not many people expect a special needs child. I think I knew before anyone else.

I am mulling over the idea of what *special needs* truly means when a fellow mom sits down next to me on the miniature bench. We share a glance but do not smile. We are guilelessly waiting to hear our children scream while they go through a typical morning routine ahead of a class party. We hover like hawks ready to swoop in with sign language and deep pressure hugs. I nervously fidget with the ribbed cuffs on my sweatshirt. I am only semi-aware of my bench neighbor as I focus all my energy on listening out for my child.

"He was doing fine when I was in there a few minutes ago." The other mom says. "Don't get your knickers in a knot."

The woman wheels her stroller and infant to the side of the bench with deft precision. She retrieves her Starbucks coffee from an attached cup holder. Her manicured nails, highlighted blonde hair, and iPhone draw the attention of students walking to the office. We are sitting in the lobby of a Title One school, but my bench neighbor does not appear to care. She clicks away at her phone with her thumbs. I cannot remember what a manicure feels like anymore.

"How do you know my son?" I ask, trying to calm my voice. "Do they not teach stranger danger anymore? Or, do they save McGruff the Crime Dog for the older kids?"

I look down the cream colored painted cement block hallway toward a door that opens to the soccer fields and playground. The main entrance double doors and the field doors create a pleasant draft of cool, humid air. I try to change my mindset from being automatically defensive to being cordial, maybe even pleasant.

"Yeah, I'm friends with the teaching assistant, Nicole, so I know your son. I'm Jennifer."

Jennifer skips eye contact and continues on her phone. I have seen iPhones in stores but never known anyone that actually has one. My first instinct is that she must still be working, at least part-time, but then she picks up her infant to nurse. Her youngest is a bald-headed little girl with shiny micro-earrings. She finally takes off her gold-rimmed aviator sunglasses to look at me. She grimaces.

"Yes, of course, Jennifer," I say. "I don't know if we've officially met, but you know my husband. You gifted us an afghan for our wedding. Thank you, again."

Jennifer does not say anything. She stares outside. Some fifth-grade boys giggle at her half-exposed left breast. She does not want to be here with me, or the boys, or her infant. But, she is too immodest to cover herself either. We both suffer the giggles and glares.

After a long silence, I stumble over my words. "I haven't met Annie, but she has a lovely name and, how lucky, she has an adorable little sister too."

"Well, I used to be a speech-language pathologist, if you can believe it. I hated working with autistic kids. When I saw one on my schedule, I cringed. One time I called in sick. Well, there's no calling in now. My daughter's autistic. Julian is too, isn't he? I bet your whole family is trying to keep that mess a secret."

Now I recognize the shrew better. I see the dark circles of worry around her eyes. Her skin looks a little dry. She is dehydrated from not drinking enough water. Her lack of sleep has made her conversation blunt and bold. I immediately try to forgive her. It is not for me, or her, but for Julian. Julian and Annie could be classmates for the next fifteen years. A decade-and-a-half is a long time to hate this crass woman. I do not know if I will have the energy for it.

"Julian hasn't been fully diagnosed yet. His ped has said that if early intervention didn't work, then he will have an autism diagnosis at his next well-check. His check-up will be this spring. We're working hard against the diagnosis. I guess if your son isn't talking by age four then they don't exactly offer you grace, do they?"

I reflect on Julian's two-year appointment where I had to explain that Julian was not merely having a bad day, or week. He had not said a solid word in a year. The pediatrician became flustered, and his face turned red. Julian had passed his one-year autism screening because he was walking and talking. Then, Julian stopped. He regressed. It has been an exhaustive fight ever since.

"What the hell does that mean? Either you have autism, or you don't." Jennifer yells. She becomes confrontational. A vein pops out on her forehead. She winces and readjusts her nameless infant.

"At our pediatrician's office, they don't want to diagnose children until they turn four. Julian isn't four yet. If they feel like he does have autism, then we'll go on a waitlist for a neurologist for testing. It's a long process. How did your daughter get diagnosed? Does she have autism?"

My heart rate increases as I move into a more defensive posture. I am sick of people yelling at me: the therapists, the school officials, the teachers, fellow parents, church officials, and even random fellow shoppers at the local mall. They can all kiss my ass. When one member of your family has autism, it feels like the entire family does. We are all ridiculed and cast out.

"Annie got her diagnosis at a developmental pediatrician in Atlanta. My husband was working there, but not as a doctor. Is it different where you go? I don't know if free clinics would work for us. We're used to the health care system we have. I would die if we were on an HMO. Isn't that what you have? It seems like the county workers have health care but not much, right?"

"Our health care is none of your business, Jennifer. Everyone's always told me that you're a rude broom-riding witch with no tact, but I had to see it to believe it. Julian's case is complicated. I would talk to you about it but you're not a doctor, are you? You're just the county know-it-all. I'm glad that Annie's was more straightforward for you."

"You have a doctor in your family, but she ain't gonna help you. I know her better than you."

"Sod off, you termagant." I rasp a little from both my emotional state and my dry mouth.

I clench the book in my lap. Out of habit, I had carried a book with me to read today. I planned to wait alone and enjoy my five minutes of free time. Seeing Jennifer, and finding out that she also has a child on the autism spectrum, was not in my top one hundred things that could have happened today. Meeting her was a shock to my system. I become acutely aware that I am now inadvertently curling up the pages on the long end of the book.

My copy of Temple Grandin's book *The Way I See It: A Personal Look at Autism and Asperger's* is part-book and part-talisman against the unknown territory that lay before me. Fortuitously, the publication date is the year Julian was born. It is dog-eared, full of highlights, and well-loved already. I cling to it for hope.

"You sound like her, you know, even though you're not blood. Anyways. I've seen him. Julian has autism all right. Our kids' brains are a mystery. Annie never talked. She doesn't grunt or make any vocations. She's never laughed. Even if she said, she'd probably save that little gift for her father; not me. Does Julian laugh?"

Jennifer straps her daughter back into the infant car seat attached to the stroller. Her daughter does not make a sound but goes immediately back to sleep. I have never seen a child this quiet. I stare at the infant like she is a unicorn. I have heard of good, docile babies but have not had one myself.

"Julian laughs. It sounds like angels tickling his feet. There was a little melody to it when he was a newborn. I hadn't thought about it until you mentioned it. I guess it's been a few years now since I heard him laugh like that. Every child is different. Every laugh is unique. But, I did get to hear it and those moments were a gift. I think I even have some on video somewhere. I'm sorry that you haven't heard Annie laugh yet. They're both still so young. Maybe it'll..."

I stop my sentence short. Jennifer's eyes become enlarged. Her pupils dilate starkly against her green eyes. She is livid.

"Shut up, Pollyanna! Don't say that. Everybody says that. At least moms like us should be honest with each other. My kid's autistic! She's not going to laugh, talk, or cure juvenile diabetes, okay?" Jennifer's lips are quivering with rage.

There is an assumed and silent grief to parenting special needs children, especially within the first months and years of their diagnosis. Some parents manage their pain well, like my husband and I. Jennifer is not managing today. I know all about grief. You have to address it, quietly, on a moment-to-moment basis at first. Then, you ride it like an ocean wave until you can get back to shore. You steady yourself in reality, on shore, and then wait for the next wave to sweep you back out into the depths. I have offended Jennifer. Having not met Annie, it is now safe to assume that her functioning level is lower than Julian's.

"Calm down! I didn't mean to hurt your feelings, but I'm still holding onto hope for my child. Julian has regressive autism. He learns a skill and then it can, but not always, disappear then he has to relearn that skill; again and again! We have to work hard to re-meet the milestones. We never know when one is going to go away. He's woken up in the morning and lost another skill. It scares the poop out of him and us, as parents."

All of Douglas County knows that Jennifer has a bombastic temper and is prone to impulsive and destructive behavior. I try to take pity on Jennifer and her plight; that is what my sister would do. I want to hear Jennifer's story, but I also want her to hear mine. A hopeless place is no place to be for either of us. I cannot let her destroy Julian's uncertain future by judging him in such a rash fashion.

"What the hell, Emma? What do you mean he can learn a skill, and then it disappears? Annie's not like that. She just never learns the skills to begin with." Jennifer says. She cocks her head to the side. Her lips are still half parted like a duck-face posing porn star.

I quickly fire back at her, "There are different types of autism, Jennifer. Julian has the regressive type. I teach him every single day at every single meal how to hold a spoon, somewhere between meals that skill evaporates. I have to re-teach him skills every day. Yes, it's exhausting and frustrating. He ate sweet potatoes for two years and then just stopped. No amount of feeding therapy, love, or money has been able to get him to eat a new food in over two years. I offered him a million dollars once just to see if he'd take a bite; not a single bite!"

I pause. I fake a laugh a little to lighten the mood. I slow down and say, "Not that I have a million dollars to offer him. The autism therapy will break us as it is. Once you're officially diagnosed in Georgia, your insurance company doesn't have to cover any treatments for your child or any diagnostic tests for your child. Well, I mean, adults with autism for that matter too. It's not like they're covered on regular insurance. There's Medicaid, but that process is a hot mess."

"That's stupid. We have great insurance because my husband works for the hospital system. But, Annie has classical autism. If you said autism a decade ago, in a clinical setting, she has what you would have thought of as autism back then. There was none of this *autism spectrum* business. Maybe Julian doesn't have autism at all. You're not a doctor either. How does your dad feel about that, by the way?"

Jennifer bites the corners of her lips and purses them together tightly. She is used to using her words to hurt and slice a fellow woman. She must have been in a sorority. Having patience with her is exhausting. I am over-extending grace as a favor to my dear husband. We cannot afford to have me arrested today. My father would tell me that he raised me better. There would be no acceptable excuses in his eyes. My stepmother would judge not-so-silently from a lawn chair.

"There are a lot of disorders on the autism spectrum right now, Jennifer. Fragile X is on the autism spectrum, for goodness sake. And, that's a genetic disorder. I'm shocked they're on the spectrum, but they are; at least for now. There are a lot of us on the spectrum now." My words come out quickly and passionately.

After thinking about Jennifer and her husband, I reflect on all of the challenges that we have faced inside the medical system as outsiders. We have medical insurance, but we are not preferred clients. We are not easy. Jennifer and her family are part of a medical care system that is built against children like ours. Both of Annie's parents were medical care providers before becoming parents. They judge children like ours. People like them think that special needs children are less-than-worthy of basic medical care and therapies. I sigh inside but try not to cry or become sad. They are now rowing in their own boat going down the same shit creek as me.

The teaching assistant, Miss Thigpen, comes into the hallway. She gives both of us a gentle smile and shows us into the classroom for the Thanksgiving party. I wonder if she heard our raised voices. I do not make eye contact with either woman and swiftly move beyond Jennifer and her stroller. Etiquette would dictate that it would be more polite to wait and go in together, but this has not been a polite day for either of us.

On entering the classroom, I immediately spot my darling sitting at a little table with five other children. There is a table behind him with six more children. Many of the little ones are smiling and seem to be having a good time together. Julian is rocking back and forth. He is excited.

The classroom is colorful and calm. I sit on my knees near Julian. He is happy but calm. If Julian becomes agitated, he turns pink and sweaty; but he is fine right now. He sits calmly in his blue Thomas the Train shirt and brown corduroy pants. I am happy that he is happy.

A fifth-grade helper visiting for the party swooshes by me and places a single piece of paper towel in front of each student. Miss Thigpen follows with a leaf-shaped construction paper cutout. Julian's neighbor jumps up and down in his chair. I focus intently on the child to see what could be wrong. The student's leaves fall the wrong direction. I quickly move my hand to correct it.

The lead teacher, Mrs. Moore, admonishes me like a child, "He'll have to get used to not having his way. It's part of life."

I bite my tongue and try to humble myself because this is not my classroom. My parents are always very defensive of their classrooms and assorted harebrained methodologies. Teachers rule their classrooms as small, autonomous kingdoms at this school and most others in the county.

Although we are living in the metro Atlanta suburbs, our children are at a Title One school. We may as well be inner city or rural Georgia. The suburbs are not an automatic defense against poverty. Title One schools are those identified where most of the student population lives in poverty. There are four Title One elementary schools in Douglas County.

Our particular school, North Douglas Elementary, has a higher percent of the students living below the poverty line. Every day children are showing up underfed and without enough school supplies to manage a full day of learning. My parents spent most of their careers teaching in Douglas County but never taught at Title One schools. Both sets of our parents expressed grave concerns over Julian attending one of the lowest ranked schools in the county. The teachers are firm, but seem qualified. It is like a little family here.

I wish I could ask Julian if his teacher is kind when I am not here; when foreign eyes are not on the ultra-organized classroom. I wish my child could even give me a thumbs up or down as to how his day as been. I wish he could tell me if he has to potty. I pull up the back of his long-sleeve tee shirt. His *Cars* pull-up training pants are showing.

Oh, no. There is a design near Mater on the training pants indicating that he is wet. I whisk Julian off to change him in the classroom washroom.

The unisex classroom washroom is quiet. It is the quiet that comes from thick concrete walls and a solid wood door that are hard to find in public places these days. I snuggle Julian for a moment on top of the changing table to make sure that he is okay. He stares at some unknown point behind my head and to the left. He does not acknowledge the tiny commode behind me. It sits there like a challenge to us both.

I whisper, "Lovey, do you have to go again? Tell Mama before I change you. Don't wee on me."

Julian does not make any signs but allows me to slip a new pull-up on him. I wish he had not outgrown the size-six diapers. They were so much more absorbent. If he is not potty-trained by age four, our church will not let him continue to go to Sunday School with the other kids. It is hard to believe that I was married there five years ago. It seems like a different life. Julian has changed everything for us. Julian's toilet training is on a long list of milestones that we are racing to meet.

I once joked with our geneticist, "I'm potty-trained. You don't have to teach me. We have to teach him. He also needs to re-learn how to walk, to run, to go up and down stairs, and talk. If you have a solution, doc, let me know, we're in the market for one."

As I open the door to exit, Jennifer is shoving her daughter into the single commode washroom before we can exit. "Hurry it up! She has to go! I never imagined pissing could take so long."

A little blonde girl, who must be Annie, rushes to the tiny toilet. She urinates without hesitation. I try not to stare, but I am so shocked by how easily it all transpired that I do not know what to say. Annie is toilet trained, and she made it all look easy. I continue to carry Julian out of the washroom. It feels like he gained twenty pounds in less than a minute. I cannot breathe. The whole classroom smells like generic dollar store brand Pine Sol. I want to run away, but only if Julian can come too.

"I didn't know anyone was waiting. Good for Annie for being potty-trained." I say.

Despite my flood of emotions, I try not to focus my anger on the high-functioning child. I want to acknowledge the mother in some way. Maybe Annie will cure diabetes after all. I do not want to talk to Jennifer, or be her best friend, but feel some strange social obligation to connect with her since we find ourselves in a similar situation.

"Of course, Annie's potty-trained! She's not stupid. I'm not stupid." Jennifer quips as she gives a Valley Girl eye roll.

I look at Julian's *Thomas the Train* shirt and start to feel like a steam engine myself. I feel hot steam boiling up in my stomach and moving to my lungs. Suddenly, the steam focuses and comes out my mouth instead of a whistle.

"How dare you! How dare you imply in a room full of young people with developmental disabilities that any one of these children is stupid, or that their parents are stupid, for not being potty-trained, you presumptuous witch! Ride your trite ass broom somewhere else, Grendel's Mother, you trifflin' gold digging hag-beast!"

Mrs. Moore rushes to the aide of her false idol, Jennifer. Harsh words volley among us all. I wave goodbye to Julian as Miss Thigpen hands me a Kleenex tissue from a box shaped like a school bus. I find myself escorted to the principal's office by Miss Thigpen.

"Good for you, Emma. You said what the rest of us couldn't. Keep advocating for Julian. Advocate for more children. Keep pushing back. I've known Jennifer since high school. We went through the College Level classes together. She's had that coming for about two decades. I can't believe that you called her Grendel's Mother. That is very Mrs. Couch. She would approve."

"You were one of her students? What do you think Judy Couch would say about all of this today?" I ponder aloud walking very slowly toward the school entrance.

"Jennifer and I are Class of 1998. You are Class of 2000, right? I can't imagine that Mrs. Couch changed her stripes too much in those two years. I think she would make Jennifer responsible for her words. Your father would too."

"I went to Alexander. I never had the old Couch as a teacher, but I do wonder what she was like the classroom. I don't know her well."

"Jennifer couldn't control herself in school and was always in trouble. But, you know Jennifer is still hurting from everything that happened in 1998. Annie's legal name is Anneewakee. When I saw the student roster I knew right away who she was even though I didn't recognize the last name."

"I didn't realize."

"Did the Sheriff's Office ever solve?"

"No. It was Cobb County jurisdiction anyway."

"Did Mrs. Couch retire? I thought I saw something in the Sentinel. When you see her at the Mercantile, give her my love. I don't know if she'll remember my last name. Tell her that Nicole from 1998 says hello. I think of her every Burns Night. Does she still have the dinners? I don't imagine so if she's retired. How is the family farm?"

"The farm is good. We still sell eggs and honey through Waldrop Mercantile in Winston."

"That's a drive from here. Why stay up here in North Douglas when your family is south and west? It's a new school but an impoverished one. I mean, the county dump is just up Cedar Mountain Road, you know. We're so far away from everything. This is almost Paulding County."

"When we were first married, we moved north of the railroad tracks to be closer to the Sheriff's Office on Highway 78. We didn't need to be near Daddy in Winston back then. Then the housing market crashed. Now the Douglas County Detention and Law Enforcement Center has moved down Highway 92 toward Interstate-20. Inmates start relocating in a few days, probably before Christmas."

"You haven't been married that long, four, maybe five, years?"

"A lot has happened in five years. I miss the farm now. Do you have any favorites I can bring in for you? I have to make the drive anyway. The mercantile will be slowing down for the winter soon."

"Since you asked, sorghum syrup if they have it. I want the good country stuff. I need it to make my granny's cookies at Christmas. Let me know how much it is and I'll pay you right away in cash."

"Julian can give it to you as a Christmas present. You'll need high-quality syrup for any cookies submitted for any elementary school cookie exchanges in Douglas County. We have high expectations. What do you think Mrs. Moore would like?"

"You mean Mrs. Bore? I tried to get her to participate in a faculty book exchange and she wouldn't do it. She's as dull as dishwater. I don't think she reads, cooks, or travels. I don't know what to recommend. She's not from around here, so we don't have much to say to each other."

"I used to have customers like her when I was working at the restaurant. If I were still bartending, I think I would say that she needs bitters with a side of truth and a dash of personality. She needs to be careful where she makes her bed."

"I know what you mean. Mrs. Moore doesn't know Jennifer or her history. She just sees the bling, the hair, the phone, and assumes that she's rich. But, I say that once you're trailer trash, you're always trailer trash."

"No, Nicole. That's not true. Jennifer is white trash, and she never needed to slide down a pole to prove it. But, it didn't have to do anything with her family or where they lived. Respectable people live in trailers too. Trash can be grown anywhere."

"True. That reminds me of Tommy Hood and that hussy Melissa. Now, that is a tragic tale."

"I will consider myself a good mother if Julian, Sammy, Robert, and Giles don't grow up to be like Tommy. I've heard my father talk about him, and not fondly."

"Wait. What am I missing? Who are Robert and Giles? I figured your mother-in-law was watching Sammy this morning."

"Twin McWhorter boys arriving in 2013."

"No! When exactly?"

"This summer. It's too early for an ultrasound, but there is extra testing because of Julian's medical history."

"Congratulations, but you won't sleep until 2030, Emma!"

"Don't I know it! Have a happy Thanksgiving, Nicole. Good luck with the food truck this holiday and stay safe. I hope your carry and conceal permit is current."

"Yes. If you get bored on Thanksgiving morning, come and see us at the race. Does anyone else know the news?"

Telling Nicole will be as good as telling the entire county. Although she has many redeeming qualities, Nicole is a gossip.

Maybe the holiday or syrup bribe will slow her mouth down. But, really, who will care that we are having our third and fourth sons? We do not have any reason to suspect that they will be on the autism spectrum as well. Sammy has been fine so far.

The air is crisp outside. A wave of nausea and grief greet me when I place my hand on my car door. I ride the wave and let it pass. Right now, I miss Mom. Her memory inspires me to try harder as a mother, especially around the holidays. She always remembered gifts for my teachers during the holidays. She was the ultimate diplomat and would have handled today very differently. My memories, desires, and woe take me back out into the sea of grief. At this rate, I should be a world class grief surfer. Now, I need to find a wave to ride back to the shore.

Thirteen: Nicole

◆━━━━━━━━━━━━━━━━━━━━◆

January 25, 1995 6:35 PM
Douglasville, Georgia

Heather and I shiver on the front steps to Mrs. Couch's house. While walking here along Campbellton Street, we passed our high school. I want to live in historic downtown Douglasville when I grow up. In the meantime, Heather and I act like children as we poke at each other to ring the doorbell, but neither of us can bring ourselves to do it.

Tonight is Burns Night. We are invited to a special dinner this evening, although neither of us knows what Burns Night is. The intricate handwritten invitation on thick paper explicitly stated not to be late. Unfortunately, we are five minutes late. Neither Heather nor I want to suffer the natural consequences. We were fortunate to receive an invitation as two of Mrs. Couch's favorite students, or informants, depending on how you viewed our situation.

Both of us gasp as a shadow figure leaps in front of us towards the doorbell. Heather clutches my arm. I trip backward off the step in the dark. The shadow grabs my opposite elbow to save me and my granny's spiced sorghum cookies. The doorbell never rang. I am shaking when we see a figure coming toward the front door. My grandmother's ceramic serving platter clatters against my bracelet. I am frozen in time and do not know what to do.

"Quick! Come over here, Justin, Heather, and Nicole." Brian whispers from the side of his house.

"Hey, man. Sorry, I'm late. My parents wanted to go to dinner at church first to drop off food. I can hardly wait until I'm sixteen and can drive myself. Thank you for the invitation, Brian." Justin says as we scurry around the side of the house.

"I'm glad there isn't a fence!" Heather says to me as we try to keep up with the boys while wearing tights and Sunday shoes.

"Girls, mind the bricks along the path. They're old and out of place. Justin's been here before in the daylight, but y'all haven't." Brian says. "I'll tell Mom that we were on the back porch, and some-one was going to ding-dong-ditch."

The back porch of the Couch family home is almost as large as the house itself. I cannot tell how large the yard is or what the flowers may or may not be like in the dark. Long white sheers flutter around the exterior of the porch like ghosts caught in the icy winter wind. We ascend several sets of steps before we are at the back door. A man sits off a side porch smoking a cigar.

"What did you bring? I'm starving, Justin, and Mom won't let us eat early." Brian says. He reaches into Justin's cookie tin.

"It's my grandmother's pecan lace cookies," Justin says, but he does not smile.

"How is your grandmother, Justin? She told the best stories on Grandparents' Day at school." I say.

"She can't get out of bed anymore. She's awake enough to tell us not to take her to a doctor. I don't want to talk about it."

"Justin's grandmother doesn't trust modern medicine," Brian explains through a mouth full of cookie.

"I'm sorry," Heather says. "My mom has been sick this year too. It's hard. You have to act normal for everyone when your whole world is falling apart."

"Exactly," Justin says and nods in agreement.

Brian and I stare at each other for an uncomfortable moment. He looks like he wants to tell me something but I do not know what it is. His lips are moving, but I cannot make out what he is saying. I offer him a cookie from my plate. Brian declines. Justin and Heather talk about caring for their loved ones. Brian and I do not know what to say. I help with my younger brother and sisters, but that is different than caring for an adult who will never be able to care for themselves again.

"I never knew your nickname was Nickajack. That's cool." Justin says. I smile.

"Nicole's mom is the best," Heather says. "Her parents have done so much for my family since my mom's sickness. Miss Brenda helped me make shortbread cookies for tonight. She said it was Scottish, but I don't know why she wanted me to make Scottish cookies."

"Oh, gawd. Do you not know?" Brian scoffs.

Justin, Heather, and I look at each other but do not know what he is talking. We hear heavy boots hit the wood porch. Cigar Man walks over towards the back door and out of the shadows. The white sheers flutter away from him. The sheers are scared of him as well.

Cigar Man has thick, dark hair with a receding hairline and partial comb over. There are a few gray hairs near his temple. His mustache is old-fashioned and connects to his sideburns through his beard. If he looked like a president, he could have been one between Lincoln and McKinley, but I am not certain which one. He has plump lips and beady eyes hidden in rolls of tough, fatty skin. He licks his lips and looks at Heather. He clumps into the middle of our small group.

"Why, my little Georgia peaches, tonight is Burns Night to celebrate Scottish poet Robert Burns. That's why your most exalted teacher is playing her cassette of bagpipe music again. The tape is stretched out a little around *Are Ye Sleeping Maggie* but, then again, Judy is a little stretched out too."

"Dad, that's nasty." Brian admonishes Cigar Man, who we now know is Mr. Couch.

"What? These young ladies will find out about life soon enough? You both look lovely this evening, by the way. Brian, why haven't you complimented your dates?"

"They're not our dates." Justin clarifies. "We're in class together, though."

226

"What? Are they not seniors? Oh, my, my, I thought for sure these lassies were eighteen. The best drink to go with shortbread is whiskey. I won't tell your parents if you take a little sip tonight. Cross my heart." Mr. Couch says with a forced grin.

"Hey, guys, I will take you on a quick tour inside. Mom won't let Dad smoke inside the house."

Grateful for the graceful exit, Heather and I hurry behind Brian and Justin. Justin knocks his head on the back door. He drops his tin, but Mrs. Couch is at the door to greet us and catch the rogue cookies. She peers around the corner at her husband. Her eyebrows furrow together.

"Don't worry, sweets. Your heavy-booted lover was just greeting the guests." Mr. Couch says.

"We hired a piper for that!" Mrs. Couch quips. "I am about to give my speech."

"In that case, I'll have another whiskey, Brian. Send Hal outside to have a cigar. Ladies, would anyone like to join my cousin, Hal, and I for a breather on the porch? We've successfully not lit anything on fire yet."

"The night's young. There's plenty of time for the Douglas County Fire Department to be called in yet. It's happened before." Brian says.

"Well, if your damn mother didn't insist on lighting the porch up like a Viking funeral then we wouldn't have to call them!"

"Language, Joe! Don't embarrass me tonight. Not everyone is used to your misbehavior and antics. Heather and Nicole, please forgive my horrid husband. The more he drinks, the more he forgets himself. And, Joe, this is your mother's house. Don't burn your family home to the ground out of stubbornness!"

Mrs. Couch ushers the four of us further into the house. She is wearing a peach colored brocade two-piece skirt suit. The suit would be polished and professional if it were not half an inch too small in the bust. Her nude heels and oversized pearls make her the epitome of Southern grace this evening. Ten years ago she might have also had charm, but I can see that Mr. Couch has worn it out of her.

"Thank you all for your cookie contributions." Mrs. Couch says to us moving into the massive open kitchen near the back door.

Justin is wearing a white button down shirt, tie, and black silk vest. He looks as though he was decked out in a full suit earlier tonight but left the jacket in his parents' car. I have made mistakes like that as well. He will be our graduating class's best-dressed male. His grandmother is a seamstress and makes most of his clothes. None of us can compete with tailored clothing.

The three of us are better dressed than Brian who is wearing an untucked plaid wrinkled Abercrombie and Fitch button down shirt. My mother will not let me see the Abercrombie catalog. I have always wondered what their clothes represented. Brian's most noticeable accessory tonight is a large deep brown leather belt. I doubt the belt is his but rather a hand-me-down from his dapper father.

Guests begin to gather in the kitchen, following their host's lead. Mrs. Couch gives a well-paced and brief welcoming. A gifted English teacher from another high school recites the Covenanters' Grace. As the four youngest teenagers, we slide toward the end of the self-serve buffet line along Mrs. Couch's long countertop.

"The kitchen is the only room that isn't red. Rumor has it that the interiors walls are painted with the blood of failed students. I assure you that it's plain ole paint from the local hardware store." Brian says. He shares a light chuckle with the three of us.

"Your house is intriguing. How old is it?" I ask.

"My great-grandparents built it in 1930. It's a little older than the original Mashburn Hall, before it burned of course. They gave my grandmother the house in 1950 right before Dad started school. He's lived here almost his entire life. There are only two bedrooms. My grandmother died a few years ago, so I grew up sharing a room with her."

"Did your Mom redecorate it after your grandmother died?" Justin asks.

"Yes. My mom took part of my grandmother's estate and restored the house. She loved doing it. The candelabras and red paint are her special touches. The built-in bookcases are hers, of course. My dad doesn't read. The fireplaces are bricked over but she wants to restore them to coal burning. I feel like I'm living in an episode of *This Old House.*"

"What has life been like without your grandmother?" Justin asks. He looks desperately sad.

"When I walk home from school, I expect to see her on the porch. I can smell her ginger lemonade sometimes. It's strange. I can feel her here. Mom and I don't talk about it much anymore. Dad never talked about her."

"You didn't move on, Brian. You kept living, though. I think that's okay." Heather says.

Heather has the benefit of being a natural curly blonde, husky-voiced, and brilliant. Boys always look over me and towards Heather. Teachers prefer her to me. Sometimes I think my mom prefers Heather to me. But, Heather's family has been through a lot this school year. Her mom was diagnosed with breast cancer over the summer. The treatments have made Mrs. Thornton lose all of her hair, even her eyebrows and eyelashes. There has been no time for shopping or social niceties.

People find Heather vulnerable, innocent, and relatable. She has enough cleavage to necessitate a bra. Her hips are much wider than last year even though her waist is still skinny enough. She can wear cheap discount store clothes and still look sophisticated. Tonight Heather is wearing her mother's ivory cable knit sweater with a black skirt, black tights, and clogs. I am hunter green with envy. At least, I am wearing a hunter green colored jumper dress with an ivory turtleneck. I feel like a toddler compared to Heather.

Justin hands me a white coffee mug of soup. Brian shows us how to balance our disposable plates on top of the mug and still be able to eat. Now I understand why Mrs. Couch spelled out to us that the desserts should be cookies. We are eating with school cafeteria sporks and toothpicks tonight.

A teacher I recognize places a small amount of ground beef on my plate. She smiles and tells us to wait for the haggis to be addressed. Potatoes and turnips are plopped on our plates as well. Small block cheeses, sausages, and crescent rolls line the counter-top. Justin and Brian fill their plates quickly, but Heather and I hold back. Heather is wearing ivory and does not want to ruin her mother's favorite sweater with sauces, gravy, or liquid. The soup is a clear chicken broth that looks harmless enough.

Brian, Justin, Heather, and I find a corner to stand in while Mrs. Couch fast forwards the cassette tape to a specific song. Her stereo system's speakers are like furniture. Several guests have to move away from the speakers for the song to be heard. After the song, an unknown gentleman stands up on the chair and recites a long dialogue.

Without sufficient tables and chairs, there is nowhere to sit down. Retired teachers and other elderly people are sitting on the family sofa, fainting couch, and love seat. The cigar smoking men stay outside. We hear glasses clinking on the porch. The walls are thin. Well-dressed women saunter while their husbands mingle.

"Do you know what you're eating?" A woman in velvet asks while looking at my plate.

"Don't tell her!" Brian begs.

"It's sheep organs. It's full of Vitamin A so have another helping. Growing children need their vitamins." The woman says while walking away.

"Who was that?" I mumble with a mouth half-full of ground beef. "This is ground beef, right?"

"Yeah. Probably. Cooking sheep organs for thirty people is expensive on a teacher's salary." Brian shares as if he is excusing the lack of attention to important details.

"That was Stephanie's mom, the former Mrs. Douglas Lee." Justin murmurs to me.

"I didn't know Stephanie's parents were divorced." I admit.

"Rumor is that it had something to do with my dad. My grandmother was a business partner with Stephanie's mom, Belle. Belle was going to assume ownership of the florist shop that they ran together. But, things went sour. Stephanie's father got into the mix. He must have found something that caused him to file for divorce. Stephanie lives with her father." Brian shares.

Mrs. Lee does not look like Stephanie. Stephanie has a ballerina's athletic body and pale skin. Mrs. Lee looks almost like a cheetah with spots on her orange skin. Her hair has been bleached until it is almost white. Her hair has been teased repeatedly, and she has the split ends to prove it. She is wearing the highest high heels that I have ever seen, but that is not shocking when compared to her fur stole. She is grotesque.

"They tell us to play fair, follow the rules, share, be kind, respect the elders, and whatever else when all they do is act in the opposite manner. Actions speak louder than words." Heather says.

"Adults get themselves into trouble," Justin offers as though he is the county's resident sage.

"I can't wait to be an adult," I say.

We hear the heavy step of Mr. Couch and his boots walking across the creaking wood floor. The thought of Mr. Couch referring to himself as Mrs. Couch's lover earlier made me vomit a little in my mouth. I am not used to teachers and other adults behaving like high school seniors.

Mr. Couch offers small punch glasses to both Heather and I. The punch looks like ginger ale mixed with rainbow sherbet. The punch was gorgeous an hour ago but has now turned a single shade of brown. The coloration favors baby poop.

"Be my guest, ladies. The boys can retrieve their own punch." Mr. Couch says.

Heather smiles politely and then takes a sip. She grimaces. Mr. Couch coaxes her to drink the cup. I hold my cup close to my lips but cannot bear to sample it. It smells horrendous.

"Why does it taste strange?" Heather asks.

"The soda went flat. Drink up unless you're afraid of store brand ginger ale. Or, is it too fancy for country girls like you?" Mr. Couch goads both of us but only looks at Heather.

"It smells. I can't." I say.

Mr. Couch interrupts me, "Now don't be petty. Don't be rude. Didn't your mother raise you right, girl? If a man offers you a drink, you accept it, drink it, and say thank you."

Brian stares at his father and places his hand over the top of my drink so I cannot sample it. He presses the punch cup down so it is almost at my waist level. Mr. Couch watches Heather drink some more. Justin pretends to knock into Heather so she cannot finish anymore. Mr. Couch sneers at Justin.

"Be careful, boy! You're in the presence of a lady. You don't want to ruin her dainty sweater."

"I am in the presence of a number of ladies every day, including your wife. Shall I call her over here?" Justin says defensively.

"No. She's listening to her ex-lover wail *A Red, Red Rose* on the porch. That will keep her eyes and ears occupied tonight. But, I find it boring. Blondie, do you want to see the garden by candlelight? There's a tree swing in the back."

"No, thank you, Mr. Couch. I feel warm. I'm not myself." Heather says.

Justin steadies Heather. Brian loops Heather's right arm over his shoulder. We shuffle out of the corner where Mr. Couch had backed us in. He looked hungrily at my untouched cup of punch. I was trying to think of something to say, but my mouth went dry. I could not even stammer. All I could see were his evil eyes. The only sound that I could hear was a deep Southern drawl on the porch talking about a rose.

"Now, Peaches, you haven't touched your drink." Mr. Couch says with a smoky breath.

"I think I'm allergic to the sherbet." I fib.

"Don't lie to me. Good guests will try anything and everything that their hosts offer them." He says as I try to follow Brian, Justin, and Heather.

Suddenly, I walk backward into a dark room and the door slams shut. I hear a bolt latching. I am not certain whether to scream, cry, or attempt an escape. I hear others breathing in the room. As my eyes adjust to the darkness, I can distinguish indirect light cascading in from underneath the door. There are four pairs of occupied shoes. One set is horizontal. Heather!

We hear a snort and the heavy boots walk away. I am still holding my cup of punch. The room smells like my little brother's but not as pungent. There is an aroma of a year's worth of dirty socks hiding under the bed but also camphor. We must be in Brian's bedroom. The punch seems to have a stronger stench in here.

Brian clicks on a small Tiffany style table lamp. The room is small compared to those in modern houses. There is a twin bed, chest of drawers, dresser, and wardrobe. There is no closet. There are no posters on the wall. The room looks more like a guest room rather than a teenage boy's room. A few books lie around the bed. There are no toys or electronics. There is no television, stereo system, ceiling fan, or air vent.

I set the punch on the dresser. Heather is lying asleep on the floor. We only had the lights off for a minute or two before Brian turned his lamp on. It took her almost no time to fall asleep. I thought she had been well-rested. She did not seem tired when we were eating. I cannot wait until she wakes up so I can tell her all about how she embarrassed me.

"Nicole, when will your parents come pick you up?" Brian asks.

"I said that we would call them before walking home. It's only a mile away. There wasn't an end time on the invitation."

"That's not going to work out. You have to get a ride from Justin's dad when he comes back from church. He'll be here any minute. You can exit through my window."

"I'm in a dress. I couldn't possibly exit through-"

"Yes, you can! My dad fooled Heather into drinking at least a full shot of whiskey. He was trying to trick you too."

"Do your parents drink, Nicole? Do you know what alcohol smells like?" Justin asks me, looking concerned.

"No. We're Baptist. I don't know anything except to stay away from alcohol." I admit.

Heather's cheeks are rosy. She lies asleep and unaware on Brian's bed. While unmade, his bed wasn't dirty. I thought all boys had dirty rooms until they got married and then they had their wives to make their beds for them. Brian does not seem like a typical Douglas County boy. I cannot put my finger on what is wrong with him, but something is not right.

Brian opens the plantation shutters on his window. He takes two screws out of the window and opens it. The window opens onto the front porch. Justin and Brian work to move Heather through the large opening. I take a large step, lean forward a little, and step out of the window without any trouble. Justin offers his hand to steady me, but it is not needed. I accept his assistance to be polite.

A car moves slowly around the corner coming towards us. It must be Justin's father. Justin goes to the passenger side window to talk to his dad. He runs back to us with bad news.

"I'm sorry guys. We have to go straight to Douglas General. It's my grandmother. Good luck, okay?"

"Thanks for asking, Justin. We'll see you tomorrow. I'll get your grandmother's cookie tin back to you. I promise." Brian says.

"We'll pray for her, Justin." I offer, but it seems like too little too late. He is gone.

Brian and I pick Heather up underneath her shoulders. She is starting to come around. She smells like a fruitcake and is snoring while walking. This was not how I planned on Burns Night going. What I had originally viewed as an opportunity to meet college girls and make contacts turned into some sordid and disgusting.

In the street lights close to the high school I can see a dot of whiskey on Heather's sweater. I do not know how I will launder that out. If I tell my mother, she will have my hide for having gone to a party with alcohol. But, I did not know there would be alcohol there. I do not know if Mrs. Couch knew either. I have never seen anyone drunk before.

"Did your mom know there would be whiskey?" I ask Brian.

"Probably. You would have to ask Mom. My dad has been drinking for as long as I can remember. Last year she ended up reciting Amy Lowell's poem *Patterns* from memory on the back porch while wearing a whalebone brocade corset, pantaloons, and lace-up boots. Dad put some moonshine in her punch. It was deeply embarrassing for both her and me. But, that was his point. He wanted to shame her in front of her closest friends and colleagues."

"What a monster."

"Please don't tell anyone at school. Mom wouldn't have invited you if she didn't trust you."

"Of course."

"If my father invites you or Heather to work on his next campaign for office, decline. Be firm."

"Whatever you say, Brian. I'm in no position to argue."

"Dad is already collecting people to work on his 1996 campaign. I don't even know what he's running for yet. But, he wants pretty, young girls to work in his office, and the more naïve, the better. You're naïve, Nicole. You've been brought up very sheltered. You didn't even know what whiskey smelled like tonight."

"We're fourteen, Brian!"

"I know you're religious. I respect that. Everyone at school knows how devout you are. You will probably end up being president of the Fellowship of Christian Athletes or something, okay? But, now is not the time to turn a blind eye. I'm trying to save you and Heather. My dad has taken a shine to Heather tonight for whatever reason. He won't let go so easily."

As we approach my home, additional lights turn on inside. There is a figure standing at the screen door. It is Mommy. She rushes out the door to help Brian and I carry Heather.

"What happened, Nicole? I thought you were going to a party at your teacher's house! Heather smells like an 1885 saloon."

"My apologies, Mrs. Thigpen. There was a former student, who is now in college, who spiked the punch with something. My mother was so sickened by the ordeal that she had to take her migraine medicine and go to bed. She will call you with full apologies in the morning." Brian says. He is a cool liar.

"Who are you? Aren't you too young to host the party?"

"I'm short for my age, I know. I'm Brian Couch, Mrs. Couch's son. She told me to see that Heather and Nicole got back home safely. I trust that they have. I should go and be with my mother now. She'll need to be looked after tonight."

"Mommy, I didn't know what to do so we came home early. All of the grown-ups are still at the party."

"Why didn't one of them drive you home? We may have to take Heather to the hospital, Nicole. This is serious. You three are still children."

"We thought the fresh air would be best for Heather. Didn't we, Nicole?"

"Yes."

"Heather only had a sip of punch. We didn't want to waste any-one's time. My father is campaigning for office and meeting with some important people. I didn't know if I should-"

"Yes. You always *should*, Brian. You should always interrupt adults at a party when children are in danger. What were you thinking?"

"Yes, ma'am, I understand. But, we are young adults. Heather did drink on her own free will. Nicole didn't. Nicole smelled something in the punch. Right, Nicole?"

"Yes." I contend.

My mom helps Heather into the house. I stand on the sidewalk for a moment. I do not know what to say to Brian. I have more questions than statements. I am more curious than judgmental against the Couch Clan. Brian looks at me. He moves towards me as though he is going to kiss me. I step back. My parents will be watching.

"You can't come to another party unless it's at the school. It's not safe, Nickajack."

"I would like to come to another. Your parents seem engrossing."

"They're both sick. The parties are a fundraising gimmick. You don't belong there. Your family is admirable, but not rich. You're a smart girl, but not well-connected."

"I'm not a girl. I'm a woman."

"You're a girl, and I mean that as a compliment."

"How is that a compliment?"

"It means that I respect you enough to not want to see you grow up to be a woman who dresses in brocade in her forties lusting after long lost loves on her dead mother-in-law's dilapidated back porch. I want you to grow up to see love blossom in its own time. I don't want you to grow fearful of heavy footsteps belonging to wild men. Enjoy the spring."

"But, it's winter."

"One day you'll figure out what I mean. Just remember this conversation for that time. Good night, Nickajack."

Brian nods at me and walks away. It takes less a minute before his figure is out of sight. I was not ready for him to kiss me when he leaned in earlier. I am not certain that was even his intention. But, right now, standing on this cold sidewalk in my scuffed up shoes, I regret not kissing Brian.

I wanted my first kiss to be about me, not rescuing Heather. Now, I wonder if I was too selfish or greedy. Was Brian simply trying to charm me? Were his intentions sincere? If so, he will ask again. He will be patient. I will be patient.

Fourteen: Justin

March 1, 2010 6:01 AM

Lithia Springs, Georgia

There is a series of harsh bangs on my studio apartment door. I look at the composite wood door vibrate from my couch. I thought that I had fallen asleep watching the local news, but there is only static on the television now. The dull roar from the screen competes for my attention with shouts from the breezeway.

"Justin! Juuussstin! Where are you?" a familiar male voice cries.

"Leave me alone!" I answer back to the disembodied voice. "This is a private residence. I am fine. Now go away."

"I'm going to call the Sheriff's Office for a wellness check!" The voice threatens.

"Go ahead!" I say as I pull my grandmother's quilt over my head.

Phew! I wonder if you are supposed to wash quilts every once in a while. Mine stinks of burned grilled cheese sandwiches, a pungent fire, and spent gunpowder. I wish it smelled different. I long for my entire life to be scented differently. My life was not destined to be this way. I am certain of it. I bought an expensive scented candle to cover up the stench, but it did not work. I can still inhale the aroma of my self-alienation and depravity.

When I started renting this studio apartment, years ago, I lived alone. But, the ghosts live here with me too. They smell like dead

243

leaves and campfire ashes. I remember the voice on the other side of the door. The voice resonates with the sounds of falsehoods. A whiff of a knockoff version of Calvin Klein's Obsession cologne wafts through the one-inch door crack.

The door pops open suddenly, and all-too-easily. I eye my sidearm on the coffee table but do not bother to get up. It is only Michael and Brian. I had not been able to tell from the shouts that there were two different voices. I am losing my professional edge. I should have been more alert. They had used a simple credit card to pop the door's privacy twist lock. The lock was designed for parents trying to keep snooping children out of their rooms, not grown men carrying a piece.

"Robert called and said that you missed a lot of work. What's going on? Why are you hiding under your old quilt on the sofa? Didn't that thing used to be white on the edges? It's looking brown." Brian says while taking a couple of sniffs around the apartment.

Okay, fine, he will probably smell that someone in here was smoking pot in the past few hours. Too bad no one else has been here for the past few hours; at least, no one with lungs to smoke with me. Come to think of it, that in an incredibly romantic thought. I would love to sit on my couch and smoke pot with the dead. I have a multitude of questions for them. My grandmother knew people who could commune with the dead.

"When was the last time you shaved?" Michael says with folded arms. He's leering at me from a distance like I'm a sick puppy in the county's animal shelter.

"2003!" I bark at him and dive back underneath the quilt. "You're not my mother!"

I mull over how angry I am at the world when I feel two sets of weak arms struggle to pull my thin frame off the couch. I struggle a little as they pull me into the bathroom but feel too tired and laden.

Turning the corner, Michael accidentally knocks over my bathroom copy of *The Walking Dead: Compendium One*. I am livid now. I love that book. Brian seizes my legs and puts me in the filthy bathtub. At the same time, Michael holds me down for a moment and tries to peel my shirt off. Brian starts the water. It is icy.

"I'll freeze my balls off, dumbass!" I say while trying to get up.

In jest, Michael makes the sign of a cross as me squirts body wash on me. I showered a few days, but do not remember when. Maybe it was last week, or the week before. I am afraid that they will try to reason with me about my behavior. I do not want them to that. I only want to stay here in my apartment. I am not bothering anybody.

"Hey, Michael, is that shower stuff or dishwasher detergent you just used?" Brian looks alarmed. He grabs the bottle.

"It doesn't matter, does it?" Michael says.

Michael is a real boy scout. He tugs to get my wet shorts off. Brian and Michael have come in here to salvage me. Michael has barely been able to rescue himself after Alicia's death. The entire county knows that he has been to counseling and is on antidepressants. When the Class of 1998 was growing up, we never knew anyone that had been to counseling. Counseling was for city folk.

The fluorescent lights flicker in a strange pattern my bathroom. I feel like I should see a pattern in the flickers but know that there is none. I would worry about the coming zombie apocalypse except the apocalypse seems to have already come and gone from West Georgia, including Douglas County. There were no zombies. I would have preferred zombies to the flood waters.

The Great Flood of 2009, and its subsequent death and destruction, has rendered me completely unable to care for myself or others. In a field that requires me to protect and defend others all the time, I have a growing disdain for everything about myself. I resent that my body needs to be fed three times a day, bathed regularly, and requires water to survive.

I hate my body. I hate my job. I hate my life. I hate everything and everyone. I merely want to go to sleep and stay asleep forever. I wish the lights flickered answers to life's most important questions in Morse code. But, I know Morse code and cannot see a pattern. The ghosts live in the lights. They are talking.

"Man up!" Brian says. He throws a washcloth at me.

"We're on the verge of calling 9-1-1, Justin. We are worried about you, Dude. Your landlady said that you hadn't paid for last month's rent. She was trying to be patient because she knows how hard you had to work last fall. Everyone is trying to be patient with you, but it's not working out. You're not getting any better." Michael says with his hand on my shoulder.

Normally, Michael's hand on my shoulder would be awkward since I am naked and in a bathtub. But, I see that he is trying to help. He feels like slime. He smells like fluffy white bread; his hair is about the same color. I loathe feeling helpless like this.

"Screw you! Screw both of you. Brian, you cannot fathom what it was like last year. You don't know what I've seen. Not just during the Flood; but, the before and after. Oh, the infinite and impossible figure eight of crap that I have to skate through day in, day out.

"I don't have a supportive family to see me through the hard times. I don't have a great love in my life. I don't even love myself. I can barely tolerate myself. I just sit here on the sofa and watch the damn news!

"All I can see is dead bodies. Care for other people has over-taxed me. I'm tired of taking care of myself. I'm exhausted. All of this has been consuming. I can't look after another single living thing. Nothing. I don't even want a fish to feed. I don't want a houseplant to water."

Anger grows hot inside my cheekbones. I feel exposed in my nakedness. I hate that the boys have seen my apartment. Nothing could survive in this place. There is a single window in this furnished above-garage studio. It lets in enough light to see by for only an hour or two a day. Otherwise, the walls are complacent in keeping the grime inside. The filth festers here.

"What about a fish? You used to love fish, Justin. You always had aquariums and stuff. Whatever happened to your passion for aquatic life? What happened to your passion for living? Didn't Anne interview you for a piece in the school newspaper? You were like an expert, dude!" Brian says as he sits scrunched next to the tub.

"Anne? *Ugh.* Anne. She was awful. Stupid girl messed up all of the information. Proper nouns lacked capitalization. Anne practically eloped with comma splices after ninth grade English. She was a terrible writer and ugly too. I could not stand listening to her in class. We always seemed to have English classes together. Everyone thought so highly of her because she was so social and always talking to people; why? Don't talk about her here. We stand in my apartment. I have a say. I say that I don't want to hear anything about that wench." I blurt out.

"Dude! Oh, gawd! What was that? She's, like, dead and stuff. You don't have to talk about her. But, for goodness sake, don't go off on her like that. That's not fair. She's not here to defend herself or anything. If there were grammatical errors or whatever, then her newspaper editor or sponsoring teacher should have caught 'em. I'm sorry the universe hasn't always gone your way." Brian says. "Quit being a cry baby. You're worse than a little girl!"

"What!?! Being dead doesn't give her a reprieve from all of the bad stuff that she did in life. I wasn't The Pardoner in class. That was Meth Head Matt. And, he shouldn't have gotten a second chance either. Why do people always go around thinking that they're going to get second chances? I haven't!" I vomit my words on the two ex-friends.

"You're full of wrath and resentment. You need to clean up your heart, Justin. I can't help you with that. The only soap that you need is Jesus. He can wash that dirty heart of yours. We all need second chances now and then. We all need grace. It takes my breath away that you would go after Anne like that. She was murdered, when? Ten years ago? Twelve years ago? I don't think she conspired to mess up your fish story. She was just a student like the rest of us; perfect imperfection." Michael preaches at me.

"Get out here. It would serve you right if I drowned right here in this bathtub, you jerks! You presume that I can't manage myself, my life? I was doing just fine. Things were peachy perfect until you walked in here and reminded me of all of this crap. I hated school. I hate Douglas County. I hate it all." I yell.

My downstairs neighbors bang on my floor to indicate that I have been too loud. I scream at them too. I wish I could bellow in

Ukrainian like my landlady. I howl in some primal voice that comes from a mournful, oppressed part of my psyche. My life's goal has been to avoid feeling as though my circumstances have imprisoned me. I have failed. I always pitied the prisoners that I watched over.

Brian puts his right index finger to his lip and says, "Do you remember Robert's wedding? Do you remember going to get Robert for help when his bride fainted? You cared then. It reminded me of when everyone was talking about being in Brit Lit together our senior year. I always felt left out of the gifted and CL circles because I had not been in my mother's class with you all. I was not gifted. I was not one of the specially selected either."

"You should have been in there, Brian. That was a crime, dude." Michael says.

Michael does not know the half of it. There was a crime. There were multiple crimes. I know because I helped burn some evidence. I have smelled ash around the clock every day since that night. I hear heavy footsteps on my apartment's exterior metal staircase. Someone is wearing boots. I hate hearing the sound of heavy boot steps.

"You were there, Justin." Brian begins. "I remember that you chose to write an essay from The Franklin's viewpoint. Remember? From *Canterbury Tales*. You are being frank with us now, and I appreciate that. I want to honor your wishes; but, you're in no shape to be left alone right now. I am being frank with you. I don't want to control your life. But, I don't feel comfortable leaving you here alone in your apartment with zombie comic books and a loaded side arm carelessly left on the coffee table. The safety isn't engaged. Are you thinking about killing yourself?"

Deflecting Brian's bluntness, I look at Michael. "Yeah, I was The Franklin. And, pretty boy Michael here was The Parson. Tell me, Parson, what do you have to say? How will I pay for my human crimes? They already haunt me. They gnaw at my belly like zombies. My sins consume me."

"Yes, I was The Parson," Michael says interlacing his fingers together as he is carefully considering what he was going to say next. "You were The Franklin. But, that was long ago. I have nothing to say about crime and punishment; that is your specialty, deputy. I don't think you need to be a deputy anymore, though. Admit that the Great Flood was too much to handle, for any of us to handle. The truth comes with a shame-free guarantee."

"So, may I please excuse myself from this interrogation, Parson?" I say in a mocking tone.

"If you don't like who you are, Justin: change. Start over and evolve. Backtrack to the last point in time that you were happy, and then change. Have you not been happy since a fellow ninth-grader screwed up a feature on aquariums? Whatever. Change it all. Change everything that has happened since you were fourteen years old. Forget it all. Pretend like it never happened." Brian says.

"You were never an academic, so there is not much to lose concerning formal schooling. You always told everyone that you had gone to the *School of Hard Knocks*. So, pretend that you didn't go to the *School of Hard Knocks*. Go and do something different. Go and be someone different. If you don't like yourself, let Justin die right here in the bathtub." Michael says.

"But, I want him to get out of the bathtub, Michael. Justin, I want you to emerge as someone different. Change everything. Leave this place and never look back. You're already behind on rent. Settle your debts and walk away from it all. Start with throwing away the rags that you have been toting around with you from rented room to rented room. Just leave everything here in your studio apartment and donate it. Walk away from this and I don't think you'll regret it." Brian says.

I inhale and submerge myself under the bath water. For a moment, I think about being a *Betta splendens*. When visiting pet stores as a child, I used to notice the Betta fish seemed to have more, or less, vibrant colors based on how well people were taking care of them. I want to take care of myself and become vibrant again. Horrible things have happened to me. I have done shameful things as well. I want to stop the cycle. I want to be vibrant.

What do I do next? I come up from the water. I have to be cautious otherwise Michael will think that he has baptized me again. I am not confident that Methodist preachers do that, but he would love to take credit for an artificial miracle. My name will be in the weekly church newsletter if I am not careful.

"I'll get you some clean clothes," Michael offers. Brian hands a towel to me.

"I don't have any clean clothes. I haven't had clean clothes for a month." I admit. I should feel ashamed, but I do not.

"Do you keep a set of clean emergency clothes in your car?" Michael asks.

I nod in answer. When Michael exits, Brian and I are left alone together. I do not want to force conversation. I have nothing to say. I stare at the hot and cold knobs in the tub. They are rusty and seem contaminated somehow. I have not kept this place as clean as I should, and it shows. I can see that now.

Brian shakes a threadbare Homer Simpson beach towel at me. I stand up, take the dingy towel, and start drying off. At some point in time, my hair got wet. It is longer than normal. I do not know how to ask, so I simply hand scissors to Brian. I do not care how he cuts me.

Without a word between us, Brian starts cutting my hair. It is so long that the ends have a gentle curl. If I had been to the station recently, a supervisor would have said something to me about my hair. I wonder how long I have been inside the apartment.

"Penny remembers you, from our vacation in Charleston. When I told her that I was coming over here to help you, she was happy." Brian says. I see now that some of my hair has started to turn white around my temples.

"How is little Penny?" I ask trying to think outside of myself.

I pull the towel tighter. The towel probably was not very clean. It smells like the chlorine from the neighboring apartment complex's swimming pool. What worries me most is that the pool has been closed for at least the past seven months. I am glad that I am not a father. I would not be able to take care of kids right now. Douglas County Division of Family and Children Services would be all over me to do better.

"Penny isn't a little girl anymore. She'll be twelve in a few months. Can you believe it? Next year she'll be a teenager. I need to start saving for her to get a used car of some kind. Remember how important it was us to drive to school as teenagers? It was like the whole county was new money and we thought only poor kids took the bus. Thank goodness things are not like that now. But, it seems like we have more residents living in poverty than ever." Brian lectures me.

"You're an ass and sound like your ass father. I was one of those poor kids that rode the yellow twinkie up through my senior year. I didn't have a choice!" I snarl through gritted teeth.

Brian stares at me through the reflection in the large glass mirror in my disgusting bathroom. The mercury is wearing off the back the mirrors like an irrevocable darkness is enclosing our frame. There is nothing left to say.

"After this morning, I'm not going to be Justin anymore. None of it matters. Pretend like I'm dead, okay?" I mutter.

"How close were you to my dad? I remember you volunteering for some of his campaigns in high school." Brian says while staring at my head with scissors. It would serve me right if he took the scissors and plunged them into my skull right now.

"Why do you ask?"

"It's just that the way you're talking right now reminds me of him. Old Joe always felt like he didn't have a choice. He wanted to be someone. But, for him, that usually meant have a different girl on his arm. He would change everything about himself to make his latest obsession-victim comfortable enough to prey on."

I breathe deeply. Brian has no idea what I have done. He has no clue about how much his dad had asked me to do all those years ago. He could not have known for all of these years. If he does, he is the biggest fraud of us all.

"Did he ask you to do anything illegal, Justin?" Brian digs in.

"You know your father," I say while trying to focus on not being murdered in my bathtub. "He's evil."

"No, man, I need to know if you know something that I should know too. Like, for example, do you remember anything about the girls, or whatever?" He asks and sets the scissors down.

Brian either intentionally or unintentionally gave me the hair cut that I had the later part of high school. I guess this is how I will always look to him, like 1998 yearbook Justin. I look stage ready for a Kid 'n Play video.

"Yeah, he liked the girls alright," I confess. "Or, he hated them. Stolen kisses, illicit grabs, and all other forms of harassment were a game to him. He never saw it as a crime. He didn't see his actions as causing offense. Honestly, it probably never occurred to him that any female would legitimately not want to be with him. His self-grandeur didn't make his crimes any less reprehensible."

Michael comes to the doorway just as I see Brian's hands move in the mirror. He uses his arms and grabs me in a choke hold. The blood simultaneously squishes into and away from my brain. I know that I only have a few seconds to do something before I lose consciousness.

Since I am so much taller than Brian, I pick him up off his feet and carry him on my back a few inches to the bathroom door. I slam him into the door. The slam knocks Brian away from my back and throat. Michael starts screaming in protest. I hear people in my doorway shouting in Ukrainian or Russian.

Turning my head to the left, I see my landlady coming toward me with a large, black cast iron frying pan. She is wearing a blue gingham apron and holding her arm perpendicular to her body. She is holding off her oversized grandson who is walking my way.

Brian and Michael had gone to my landlady first. They told her that they were checking on me. Or, was it the other way around? Had I accidentally named them as my emergency contacts at some point in time? Did my landlady call them to check on me? Some friends they have turned out to be! I will choose better friends in my next life. I knock the wind out of Brian as I slam him against the door.

"*Hamno*! Take your things and get out." The landlady's grandson yells at me.

"Hey, racist bigot, go back to your native continent! I've probably tasted more white sugar than your communist-lovin' ass. You don't know all the great things that I've done." I say in my defense as I start to put on the clothes that were, until recently, in Michael's outstretched arms.

The landlady will survive and thrive. If she has had sons or grandsons, I am sure she has not seen anything new today. I did not give her an education or anything. Maybe Brian is right. I do sound like his father.

"Do me a favor," Brian says looking at me with a bloody nose. "Robert is waiting outside to take you to wherever you need to go next. Your landlady is evicting you. She's apparently already given you notice. Just don't mention to Robert how much you hated his big sister. He's doing you a huge favor by giving you a ride. You don't get to ask anything out of me. You don't get to ask anything of me ever again. Stay away from my family. Stay away from Penny!"

"You heard the man!" The grandson yells with his fingers pointed at me. "Your cop friend is doing you a favor. Grab your things and go. We're keeping the security deposit so we can disinfect this place. There are cockroaches now! You're three months behind. My grandmother has already said no more renting to cops. You've turned out to be a deadbeat!"

"Look!" Michael starts an apology. "We're sorry for our friend's behavior. But, you see, he's sick. Not all police officers are like this. Justin has been an officer for over a decade, and he's done a lot for our community. He just hasn't done a lot the past three months. Please forgive him. His friends have pitched in to cover his back rent too."

I survey my furnished apartment one more time as I exit. I look at the rag my grandmother's quilt has become. Silently, I eye the empty pantry and sink full of mismatched dirty dishes. I had collected them at garage sales over time.

There is a lone well-read book on the floor. I do not have a computer to take with me, only my phone. The television, coffee table, and futon couch were part of the rental agreement. There is nothing to take with me other than memories, if I chose to keep the good with the bad. Today is not the first day that I have lost all of my Earthly possessions and had to start over again.

What I would not give to time-travel back six months; to before the Great Flood. For me, the Great Flood of 2009 is when everything went downhill. Or, maybe it was earlier. Maybe things started in rapid decline in 1998.

Michael hands a cash-stuffed envelope to the grandson. My landlady kicks up her chin at me and walks out of the studio apartment with her grandson-turned-bodyguard. I could have used that money to start a new life; and, who knows? Maybe that is what they had intended the big bucks to go.

How did Michael restart after Alicia's death? She has been dead less than six months. Michael, Brian, and Penny all seem to be doing fine. How can they grieve so quickly and move on like nothing happened? How can anyone in this sick, pathetic county move on after this disaster? We divert traffic around washed out bridges but how can we drive around the pressing sadness? I am the only sane survivor in the bunch.

If I had gone quietly, they might not have used the cash to pay the back-rent. I barely remember how much my studio apartment was. Two hundred and fifty dollars a month? Two hundred dollars bi-monthly? I have lived in this studio for years, and the rent kept going up over time. So much for the recession hitting Georgia; land owners are still making a pretty penny. Preachers, teachers, landowners, teenage girls, and politicians always come out on top, but never me.

Fifteen: Tommy

◆━━━━━━━━━━━━━━━━━━━━━━━━◆

October 18, 1996 6:50 PM
Fairplay, Georgia

My candy apple red Ford F-150 is the best looking in this make-shift field parking lot. I wish the gravel roads had not gotten dust on her. I turn the ignition off. My truck rumbles and I take the keys out. My parents adore me and buy me whatever I want, and I wanted this truck. I needed customized plates that read "TOMMY79" too.

A badass truck is incomplete without a hot girl in the passenger seat. I smile at Alicia sitting next to me as we are ready to party crash Camp Blood in nearby Carrollton. She grimaces in return as an Oasis song that was just playing on 99X is cut short. Everyone has a different version of partying hard; but, this is our junior year. I am mostly throwing caution to the wind. I intentionally drove the back roads to get here tonight because the newspaper nerds are in the truck bed. That is a long story and not worth publishing.

"I would tell you to kiss me, but I don't know where those lips have been today," I say to Alicia.

"Isn't that what your mom says to your dad? Or, does she say objects in the mirror are smaller than they appear?" Alicia verbally counters with an unlit cigarette in her mouth.

"Girl, you're going to have to up your game from yo momma jokes if you want to hang with the big dogs tonight. Some of these bitches out here are college girls. They will eat you alive."

"You mean you want them to eat you, Tommy. You think college panties are fluffier than high school panties. Be my guest! Go forth and investigate. Pretend you're at the science fair and see what your swabs say on Monday. Gonorrhea? Chlamydia? You'll be able to get a job at the Center for Disease Control as a human petri dish."

"No, I'll leave the porta-potty blowjobs to you. Are you going to wear a shirt? It's going to get cold. I don't want to run through the woods with you and have your bra popping off."

"*Aw.* Tommy, I didn't know you cared. You don't want my tits distracting anyone from you. That's what the rub is." Alicia says as she exits my truck.

Alicia grabs one of my dirty flannel shirts. She buttons it up and reaches underneath to pull off her strapless bikini top. Alicia has two walk-in closets full of designer and vintage clothes in a home with seven bedrooms. The way that she is acting, it is like she opposed to wearing clothing. Part of me likes that she is wearing my shirt without a bra. But, part of me is nauseated. She is wearing my lucky fishing shirt. I want to go fishing tomorrow afternoon. It was over seventy degrees today. The weather is terrific for bass. Alicia tosses her bra into the back of my truck. The bra almost hits Stephanie's head. Stephanie fakes a childish vomit.

"Feel free not to act like you are barnyard born and raised, Alicia," Stephanie yells from the truck bed.

Each year, the seniors do all of these bonding activities together. They meet in the gym parking lot of Douglas County High School and the people who have cars and can drive and take as many people as they can. Sometimes our friends at the two other high schools in the county, Lithia and Alexander, unofficially join in too. I am not a graduating senior this academic year, but I do have a truck, which makes me an asset.

I volunteered to haul two people in addition to myself. Someone had to take the newspaper nerds. Alicia was already with me. People have been riding carefree in the beds of trucks for years. "I'm free to decide" as they say.

I am crashing the crap out of this senior trip. Besides, the newspaper girls needed an escort. If I am their ride, I stand a good chance of ending up in school newspaper pictures with the seniors. This year will be my best school year ever; at least, until next year.

Alicia is not my girl, but she jumped in the truck as I was leaving our neighborhood. She is always up for trouble. I have known her since preschool. We get along like Bonnie and Clyde. She is too wild to give a crap about me; and I kind of like that.

Everyone else's moms have them lining up to try to get me to ask their daughters anywhere or anything. I want to be able put my hand in my pocket without a girl trying to intercept and hold it. Nothing will ever impress Alicia though. She wants the ultimate bad boy. I am a stereotypical decent gent that happens to be a badass. But, I am good at pretending to be good; which, when I think about, probably makes me a poser to the upperclassmen who know me best.

I strike my zippo and offer it to Alicia. She lights her cigarette like I imagine a Playboy bunny would. We love flirting with each other, and it is become quite the game. The game distracts me from the pain. She only does it to make potential beaus jealous. I do it because the game makes me happy.

That is to say that Alicia's fake chase makes me happy for a few minutes. Then I am onto the next new thing. I always seem to need something new and exciting to do. I think that is the reason I love playing sports. I love being on the court or the field. If there were hockey in the Deep South, I would play hockey too. I am on the wrestling team but only when I am not busy with another sport. There is not enough attention on wrestling, so it is my lowest priority.

Walking around to the back of my truck, I lower the tailgate and help Stephanie and Anne out. Anne is the class doll. Everybody loves her. I help her down like a gentleman. I avoid cursing around Anne because she is genteel.

Anneewakee was sick when we were in fourth grade. Everyone at our elementary school went back to their churches and added her to their prayer lists. She is the living embodiment of innocence and piety. People universally love Annie. I hate her for that. I want to be universally loved for who I am. She was forcefully born into saint-hood in an unfortunate way. Anne is shaking and, since she is more than a foot shorter than me, I hold her for a second. She trembles like a kicked puppy. I secure her a little longer.

"Annie, can I lift you down?" I ask in a gentle tone.

"Thank you. I am robust enough." Anne says. She pushes a weak smile through to reassure me, but I know it is a fake.

"Ride in the front with me on the way home, okay?" I say. Anne acquiesces with a nod.

Stephanie clears her throat for me to help her down. Speaking of sainthood, Stephanie is not a saint, but works every moment of every hour of every day to see if she can achieve that status and drag the rest of us along with her. Skank-phanie rubs my nerves raw; but, I want her to go home and tell her Daddy that she had a ride in the back of my truck. Let us see what trouble this quick ride gets me into tonight. I look forward to it. She will be the perfect mother someday. She is always trying to make the rest of us grow-up. I imagine her becoming a female preacher; since Methodists are apparently okay with that now.

Alicia and Stephanie are very different from each other and, yet, lifelong friends. Alicia was close to Anne growing up too. Anne and Alicia spent a lot of time together as children. There were five school days a week, ballet on Saturday, and church on Sunday. All of us frequented youth group on Sunday nights. The three girls are the closest thing to sisters that I will have, but my mom only likes Stephanie and Anne. Mom invites Alicia and her family to our annual Independence Day party but does not approve of how Alicia has turned out this year. She caught us popping pills in the guest bathroom at the party this year.

Stephanie is a generic Douglas County prima ballerina. The only ballet that I have seen is *The Nutcracker*. In the fifth grade, the gifted students went on a field trip to the Alliance Theatre to see the classic. I do not remember much about the ballet performance except for the Sugar Plum Fairy. Stephanie is Douglas County High School's Sugar Plum Fairy. Alicia is a dark nymph or demon. She is like that girl dancing in her underwear in Stabbing Westward's music video *Shame*.

"Smile, Tommy. Tonight's interactive haunted trail is your thang." Alicia says.

Anne takes a few Polaroid pictures as I greet the senior football players. Some cheerleaders wave at me while the Homecoming Queen blows a kiss at me. I am a Homecoming Court escort this year but hope to be King next year. I love seeing the seniors. All of Alicia's bad titty vibes melt away when I see my classmates and friends from across the county. I even acknowledge some rivals from Carroll County with a well-timed nod, but we do not shake hands.

Before I can even say hello to everyone, we are standing in line under a covered shelter heading down toward the haunted trail's entrance. I look in my wallet and find five twenty-dollar bills. My cigarette burns out. I toss it down into the hay and smudge it out the best I can. I like partying, but I do not want to burn this place down.

I tap Anne gently on the shoulder. My lips contort as I try not to blow my last puff of smoke in her face. I say, "Hey. I got this. You can tell everyone we went on a real date and that I paid like a gentleman."

"No, Mr. Hood. Thank you all the same. The newspaper staff account is paying for us to be here. They're also paying for the film and for its development too. Stephanie has the low speed thirty-five millimeter. We'll have to head back to the school later and scan it, though."

"What the heck is a scanner?" I wonder aloud.

I try to think of what a scanner would be and why it is not in a hospital. I think Anne is smarter than I give her credit for these days. We have only had one College Level class together so far, and she sits silent. I almost always forget that she is in there until I am looking right at her, like now.

"Well, we can't tape or glue the pictures into the large section formatting paper like we did last year. We have to use this thing called a scanner to take a computer picture of a real picture. Oh,

Tommy, it is the coolest thing ever. You should stop by the newspaper room sometime during fourth-period and take a look."

"That sounds stupid. I mean, like a waste of time. Why would a newspaper nerd take a picture of a picture?"

The truth is that I do not know what to say to Anne. I make conversation with some basketball friends as we are about to purchase our tickets. The four of us plop into a group of strangers. I need to grab Stephanie, Alicia, or Anne's hand to make certain I stay in the same group with them. Not knowing who to pick, I grab Anne's hand. She holds it and does not act like it is consequential. I have held her hand before, but not since the first grade.

I can hear the radio near the main desk. I start hopping up and down and becoming distracted. It is the end of the "I love you always forever" song that I despise. There is a reason why sports teams avoid playing pop music before games. I try to psyche myself up to start seeing fake blood and dismembered plastic dummies.

Anne stretches onto her tippy toes and leans towards my ear, "Well, you have to have something to turn the printed picture into a digital image on the computer. That way you can edit it. It's just like the cropping we did for the middle school yearbooks but instead of using rectangles, edges, and Exact-O blades, we use computer software. It's the latest and greatest stuff, Tommy. You don't have to broadcast to anyone that you came by to see the staff. You never know if it might be something you want to do in college."

While bouncing up and down to the Red Hot Chili Peppers, I think a moment and confess to her, "I didn't do jack crap for the yearbook. My mom is responsible for the majority of anything I did at Stewart."

"She's been very supportive of you." Anne sides with my mother. Great.

"And, you know what, Anne? Your father has been very supportive of you. I know no one in the social studies department gives a crap about the student paper. Your parents want newspaper staff on your college resume, and they gave you the tools to lend to the school to get it done. My parents buy my sports equipment, so I get it. But, don't pretend like what you're doing is exciting." I say in a fit of anger.

I do not know why Anne exasperates me. My words fall out of my mouth without a filter. The words cannot be unsaid, and I immediately regret it. Anne drops my hand. I was looking forward to talking to her without her childhood sweetheart eavesdropping. My angry words crush us both.

Anne looks equally devastated as we start along the trail with our tour guide. Alicia slips a half-smoked joint into my back pocket for later. She is paying me back for something, but I forget what it is. I obsess over the idea that I hurt Anne. It could not have been at a worse time. We hear chainsaws and start running through the trail from scene to scene.

Our eight-person group walks into a scene where chains restrain a woman to a wrought-iron bed. Her nightgown is blood red from her breasts down from a staged childbirth. Alicia screams with glee. Stephanie takes a picture since the Bloody Girl actress is DCHS alum. Bloody Girl winks at me and blows a kiss. It makes me nauseous. I think everything out here smells like chicken shit. Stars and bars, I am so glad I am not a girl.

The thirty-minute experience is over too fast. I wish we could have stayed in that forest all night. I want to stay here, at this moment, until I can finally get things right. A random college fresh-meat girl hits me with silly string as we accidentally run into the group in front of us. I smile at the girl, and Anne catches me with her Polaroid. I feel guilty.

Anne is staying two steps ahead of me. I was hoping she would get scared and reach for me. She never did. Now the trail is over. Anne's boyfriend, Chase, was killed in a car accident earlier this month. She should not be here. It is too much for her. She will go home and cry tonight. I have heard my mom cry on nights like this. She waits until she thinks no one can hear but the walls in our new house are thin. I can hear the wails and the pain etch my bones.

Alicia snatches my hand. She loops my fingers through the belt loops on her blue jean cut off shorts. She smiles like the demon that she is. She shouts for all to hear, "Oh, you bad boy!"

I grab my hand away faster than lightning but one of my bas-ketball teammates boo's and says, "Get a room. Everyone else already has."

It is too late. A girl with a head full of big 1992 spiral perm hair cups her hands near her mouth. She yells, "And, wear a condom, you freak! She's like Waffle House. She's open twenty-four-seven."

Stephanie is mortified and grabs my elbow as we are walking to the dirt lot. She says, "If you want the newspaper staff to pay for gas, you need to take Anne and me back to school right now. This scene is ghastly."

Alicia looks hurt, and I did not know that she had an ego to bruise. I think they are all on the rag. For a moment I consider get-ting lit just to make it through the forty-five-minute trip back but cannot with Anne in the truck. It is past twilight now. I ship Alicia to back with Stephanie. The forces of light and dark can battle it out where I cannot hear it. I need to say something to Anne. She pulls herself up and into the passenger side seat.

Anne whimpers, "You don't have to apologize even though you should. You don't have to like me. You don't have to like the newspaper. You don't have to respect our school. Most of the Eye of The Tiger staff and DOCOHAN staff don't go to the pep rallies because we know that the jocks don't support our efforts to docu-ment the school year. It's a bit turgid to you all. But, what you all do for the school is boring to us. It's not like we want you to lose; then we would have nothing to write about that month. We just want to be free to pursue something different. Just because what I enjoy is poles apart from what you love doesn't make it any less splendid to me. Okay?"

My heart sinks and there is a lump right above my lungs. It is like the feeling I get after a coach yells at me for doing something stupid or self-serving on the field. I am not sure how to label this feeling. I feel like I am not acting like a good team player right now. Anne and I are on the same team. I am sure she has to ask, fight, and fundraise for her little clubs too.

"Annie, what do people say about me? What do they think?" I ask the expert while leaning to turn on the heat a little. I am chilled all of a sudden. My fingertips go numb first. I am frightened of what Anne will say.

"Tommy, it doesn't matter what other people say about you or think about you. It's what you believe about yourself. Maybe that's why we've been going through some thought-provoking literature this year in Am Lit with Mrs. Couch. I suppose she's on this kick to get us to discover ourselves. That's why she tells us she's treating us like college students."

"The only college student I ever knew was my big brother. Well, half-brother. He hates me. He thinks I'm a pee-on, on a good day," I say and quickly add. "But let's not put that in the paper, okay?"

Gazing out the window thoughtfully, Anne folds her arms and tells me, "I think you need to think about what will happen after graduation. High school has not been kind to all of us. Middle school was a challenge for me, but high school has been exceptionally hard. I know that everyone is still treating me like I'm a delicate little doll, but I'm not. It's hard to stay me when other people are growing up. It seems so effortless and natural for everyone to grow up but me. I just care enough about you as a person to want to see you keep growing up. It doesn't all happen overnight."

When Anne says *overnight*, I picture us discussing Arthur Miller's *The Crucible* in class earlier this week. I am only thinking about football right now even though basketball practice has started. Mrs. Couch asked a question after we had just read the first section out loud in class. My plan was to wait for the movie to come out Thanksgiving weekend and catch-up then; after football. Mrs. Couch's question almost sunk me when Anne had said something mind-blowing. I do not remember what Mrs. Couch's question was, or what we were talking about, but I remember what Anne said.

To be truthful, I remember how I felt about what Anne said more than what she said. She said something about it never occurring to Abigail that she was going to be responsible for other people's lives and death. Anne knew all of this stuff about Abigail and said that her behavior was that of a girl younger than seventeen. I think Abigail was meant to be our age, and that was why the state of Georgia decided that it was a good idea to make us read the book our junior year.

Maybe, my college years will be a little bit like high school and the real world. I had assumed that college was just going to be like high school but with more alcohol, girls, parties, and pot. But, what if I am like Abigail? What if my thinking is younger than what it should be, and people could live or die because of how I act and what I decide to do? That is how Anne's guy died.

The impactful realization hits me right before our turn onto Selman Drive. I have a hard time breathing while stopped at the red light near the new church. Things get blurry, and I hear a roar in my ear.

The roar in my ear is Alicia yelling at me with her head stuck through the rear window, "Tommy, I said, 'Do you want to go to the Stewart Mill shopping center parking lot or across the railroad tracks?'"

I park parallel to the covered sidewalk near the gymnasium. Anne and Stephanie have already headed towards Upper Banks. The hum of the heater adds to everything being too loud in my head. I look down and see the blunt in my left hand. I do not remember lighting it. I see myself exhaling smoke in the rear view mirror.

I look at Alicia, "I hurt Anne. I messed up."

"Crap-on-toast, Tommy, forget her! You play with all the girls too much. You need to focus on what you want and go after it. You don't need all the girls to love you, just one."

Alicia is spiteful and full of aggravation after her gauntlet of insults. Her woes will soon be gone. She just lit up too. At the rate we are smoking, Alicia and I should buy marijuana in bulk for a discount.

"You think the universe is like chess: black and white. The universe is like Battleship. We're all bombing each other and losing left and right. You took a hit but I just took a bigger one," she says making light of the fact that I am smoking.

My actions wounded me tonight. I want to forget them. I distract Alicia with an additional insult, "People totally think you live in Corn Crib."

Alicia and I know that she is upper-middle-class, and her parents are not *nouveau riche*. They come from an old founding family in the county. Actually, the Kennedys and Keatons are from Campbell County.

The land where we stand was Campbell County before the Yankees messed with the county lines and renamed it during reconstruction. She should be a debutante; that is, if Douglas County had fancy balls. All of that antebellum nonsense washed away with the blood spilled on this ground during the Civil War. No one in

Douglas County gives a shit about noble gentlemen and their ladies. We have been in survival mode for over a century.

"As if, Tommy! School is gross. I'm dropping out." Alicia says.

Her dilated eyes reflect the moonlight a little too much. The bright fluorescent lights in the parking lot near the main gym make me feel like I am on center stage. I should say something inspirational or meaningful. But, instead, I sit here and get high.

Thinking back to a stay-in-school pep talk from a basketball coach years ago, I say, "What are you going to do? Become a stripper? End up on Jerry Springer or Maury? Screw it! Just become a prostitute. It's the oldest profession, right? You're going to end up like a black hole. Your darkness is going to suck up everything around you."

"You are a misogynist tool," Alicia mumbles as she clops more black lipstick on her mouth. "You're a stupid, immature high school boy who thinks that he's so special and the center of the universe. You want everything to revolve around you. You don't even know what a black hole is. Have you even thought about taking a class in Physics or Astronomy? No, because you don't even know what science block you want to take next year after Chemistry.

"You have a whole team of coaches to tell you exactly what to do, Tommy, and when to do it. I'm surprised you could even drive us back to school. You're used to sitting on a bus and letting everyone else take you places! You are not even sitting in the driver's seat of your own life. You let your mom buy your clothes, do your home-work, compete for you, and be your agent like you're a jacked-up movie star."

An involuntary gasp comes out of my mouth. It feels like Alicia has clawed at my heart. She had already painted her nails black with a Sharpie marker while traveling back to school. Now, she is out for blood. She was holding a mirror up to my face, and I do not like what I am seeing through her. But, I cannot sit here and take it another minute. If we are going to have a scorched earth policy, then she will burn with me.

Writhing with anger, I say, "You want everyone to think you're such a rebel, a hot little piece of ass whore! But, you're not. No one noticed you until you started wearing black tar on your face and cursing. What do you have to be so angry at, Miss Priss? You don't like being your parents' favorite? You don't like being spoiled with hundreds of thousands of dollars a year? Going to an island every time you bat an eyelash? I know all about you. I know all about your sorry ass. You're probably still a virgin. I've never seen you commit to staying with a single guy long enough to get past second base. You're a tease, Alicia."

Alicia snickers. She snorts hard. But, it is not a little girl's laugh. She knows something that I do not. I cannot stand it! In my rage, I miscalculated something. I got something wrong. What was it? She shrugs her shoulders and extinguishes her join in my truck's ashtray.

Without warning, Alicia leans over and whispers in my ear, "I am spoiled, but not by my parents. I have a man; a real man. And, he takes care of me. I'm his little Lolita. Have you read it? *Lolita*? Douglas County probably banned it. A Russian man wrote it while living in France. My man likes it when I read it out loud, in French, naked on his bed. It's the highest form of art in his opinion. Then, we make love. And, he takes care of me all day and all night,"

The bitch grabs my chin with her right hand and jerks it towards her. Without warning, she licks the right side of my face like a snail and leaves a slime trail in her wake. I lean back and fumble to open the driver's side door with my left hand. I am horrified. I am sick. I am in disbelief. Alicia grabs my crotch as she slides over me to fall out the driver's side.

Even after a tricky landing on the pavement in her four-inch platform Mary Jane's, she is still laughing like a maniac and flashes her tits at me as she walks away. She is crazy. I have never heard anyone belch out spite and hate like that. She has changed. Alicia is manifesting herself into what all of our parents feared for each of us. She is going to end up dead on some street corner with AIDS. I can practically see the future track marks on her arms as she walks away toward Campbellton Street.

There she walks away with my lucky fishing shirt. I assume that she will be headed toward the railroad tracks next. I will drive the opposite direction. I need to stop by a gas station and get rid of her nasty bikini top. I predict the Douglasville Police will roll through my neighborhood tonight. They may even stop at the Kennedys to inform them of their daughter's untimely death.

Pfft. Whore. Addict. Bitch.

Sixteen: Alicia

"You know what, Tommy, this cute blue dolphin motel room is perfect for our little so-called summer break," I say and pinch his arm. "You wanna light up before the slag in your bed wakes up?"

Tommy does not move. I try again, "C'mon, Tommy. Wake-up. It's Alicia. I'm your favorite girl now that your girl ain't yo' girl no more."

Something is not right. Just to be mean, I walk over to the ice bucket and grab an almost empty bottle of Smirnoff. I open the dusty curtains on the west-facing window. It is bright outside. It has to be afternoon. I hold the cold, empty bottle to the tender part of Tommy's neck. He does not move. I rub my eyes.

Maybe I am still high or still dreaming. Oh, please do not let me have to call 911 on this dumbass. I do not know the actual name of the hotel where we are staying, but I think there is a dolphin somewhere on the sign. It was glowing when we drove here; whenever that was.

"Tah-ahh-Mm-ee," I say as I tickle his feet.

The feet are icy cold. The room is hot because the air never kicked back on. We left the balcony door open last night. The hotel had had a situation before where kids like us had left doors open to try to air condition the entire Gulf of Mexico.

When I drink, my senses become distorted. Sometimes I cannot talk or walk. Other times, things feel cold when they should feel hot. I have had too many icy showers that way. I try not to linger on that thought too much. I try Tommy's feet again. They are cold. They are blue. No. Not now, Tommy. How can he leave me here? I am high and in Florida. His mother will be livid.

I throw my body on top of him screaming. I start hitting him trying to get him to wake-up. His body is hard. I cannot move it. A girl is lying in bed next to him. Who is it? Is that Michelle? *Wow.* She has changed since high school. I did not even recognize her. She looks like I did in high school. Tommy was the one that wanted to come down to Florida and see her. She is not stationed at Eglin but works at a nearby airport. If she has any medical skills, I need to wake her up now.

Shaking, I start jumping up and down on Michelle. She startles awake. The half of her face that was on the pillow is sweaty. Her makeup is melting off her face. Her personal pool of indignation puddles on the hotel pillow. Her hair is sticky. She is disoriented. Michelle groans and says, "What? What?"

"Bring him back to me," I cry.

"Who?" She says after looking at Tommy for a moment. She clears her throat and takes a sip of a clear liquid that was next to her bed. *Oops.* She thought her drink was water. It is cheap rum.

"Tom, dearest, wake up. Alicia needs you." Michelle says with a smile.

"He's not waking up, Michelle," I state. I feel like a balloon floating into outer space.

"Last night was wild, honey. I've never experienced anything like that. You and Jason are the best. Are you together? Or did he just come along? What happened to Matt? Where are we headed tonight?"

Tommy is not moving or breathing. Michelle does not comprehend the situation. She had been an academic jackrabbit in high school. I am livid that she has chosen now as the time to go stupid on me. Our two-bed motel room seems large now. I feel like I run in slow-motion to get to Jason out of the bathroom. He may have fallen asleep in there after vomiting. He cannot hold his liquor.

Jason is not the devil, but he is a hobgoblin in his own right. He is smaller than average, like me, and has bright ginger hair. To his credit, Jason has mad medical skills. He is a trained paramedic.

"Jay!" I cry and bang on the bathroom door. I force it open.

My not-quite-a-boyfriend graduated two years before the rest of us. Jason has an actual career; whereas, Tommy is a social status away from being homeless. I do not know how Tommy paid for his quarter of the trip, but he had made it happen. He has always had money; or, rather, his parents have.

Blinking for what felt like a moment, I open my eyes to see that Jason is putting on his shoes near the ocean-view balcony. Even the waves of the crystal clear ocean seem extra blue today. I think they know that Tommy is gone. I try to find words to tell Jason what is going on, but it feels like I have cotton in my mouth. Not being a mind reader, Jason looks at me and knows that something is wrong.

"Where's Matt? Are what's-her-face and Tommy okay? That was quite the little fender bender that he had yesterday. He may feel achy today. I'm achy from last night too, but he's really gonna feel lit. Did I say lit? I meant to say, 'He's gonna feel it.' He's twenty-one years old, and it's Tommy. I bet he took harder knocks in football. He bit my lip when he kissed me. I don't know, but I think I liked it. It didn't feel right to kiss a married man, though. How are you feeling, baby? You were on fire. You tore us all up."

I shake my head *no* as the room starts swirling. Jason moves quickly to the other room. Michelle has been silent up until this point. I keep staring south at the ocean as I hear the commotion behind me. A large glass bottle shatters on the kitchenette's tile. Pill bottles shake furiously.

My ears register a fleshy thud and crunch on the floor. Next, I notice Michelle's screams. Jason had moved Tommy's body off the bed and into the floor. I think he will probably start CPR any moment. Jason has been teaching me what to do. Now that there is an opportunity to do it, I cannot. I do not think I can even walk over to the room phone and put my finger on the rotary dial. I sit on the floor and wait.

Michelle stumbles out to me. A sex-stained sheet wraps her boyish body. She sits next to me and hugs me. "Alicia, I am sorry. I've killed our Tom."

I think to myself, "Bitch, please. You were just another hole for him to poke."

Tommy absorbed phony fandom like a dry sponge. When Melissa stopped worshiping the toilet he pissed on, he revisited old territory. In that sense, Michelle was an ancient desert that every nomadic herder in Asia has roamed. I do not know how she thought things were going to go with Tommy.

Everyone in Tommy's life had been trying to baby him and cheer him up for almost two years now. He had glorious sex with two girls and a guy while drunk and high. Is he happy now? I will never know. I hope Matt did not film it. Matt likes to document life experiences. Unfortunately, those life experiences may be admissible in a murder trial. I do not want a Florida jury secondhand witnessing what happened in my vagina overnight.

"I've loved him for so long. I've loved him since at least the fourth grade. This can't be happening! This isn't happening!" Michelle cries. She vomits on her sheet.

I pick Michelle up a little by the elbow and half-drag her to the bathroom. I am not cleaning up Michelle's vomit. There will be people in uniforms who want to talk to all of us. She needs to let the vomit out now. It may sober her up.

We hear Jason put the phone receiver down. He rushes over to us holding pencils and pads from the end-tables dotting the suite. Jason says, "You both need to remember as much as you can. You must write it down. Write down absolutely everything you can remember. It will help the EMTs when they arrive."

"What? All of it?" Michelle says in a surprisingly deep voice.

"Completely uncensored! Write very single detail. The doctors at the hospital are going to try to figure out what happened. We need to help them as much as possible. If we're dishonest or shady, then they can't help. I don't say this to scare you. But, I feel like we owe it to Tommy and his family. We need to think about everything that we did yesterday. We need to think about everything that he ate and drank."

"*Uh*, last night? We ate pizza. It was plain. No, it had pepperoni." I start. "But, what do we say Jason? He did heroin, screwed Michelle, drank vodka, and screwed some more? His poor mom will whittle every detail out of us. I don't want her to know. All the decent families of Douglas County shun me already."

"Okay, let's keep going. That was around midnight, right? And we took vodka shots here. But, before that, we went somewhere and had Jell-O shots and something else. Then, Matt left. We had lunch at a metal-sided diner near Gulf World. What was that something else?"

We are twits. The three of us are sitting on the floor trying to piece together the past few days. It is as though we are working on a school project that was due four hours ago.

Last night, Tommy rambled, "How many peanuts does President Carter have to plant if he wants to harvest them before the Greek month of Ethos when the lunar eclipse surpasses the circumference of France? The answer is that the number nine feels like the color orange except on Tuesdays when Mrs. Couch has a nervous breakdown."

We were all high, but Tommy was especially tripping. He talked about Anne. He covered Michelle's face with a pillow and cried while he was having sex with her. He kept calling her Anne. Michelle was too stoned to care. I did her a solid and moved the pillow off her face after she fell asleep but before Tommy finished. Tommy finished himself this time.

"Did we eat dinner after the accident? Or did we just have the Jell-O?" Michelle asks us.

She actually may have a point. I looked at her when I noticed that Jason was no longer with us. He was in the room with Tommy and opening the door for fellow paramedics. He explained how he had moved the body because Tommy was a friend. Jason said he wanted to be able to tell Tommy's one night stand, wife, and mom that he had at least tried CPR. I do not think Jason had given mouth-to-mouth but had only attempted palpitations.

Jason is strong for his size and exceedingly athletic. He has a presence about him that brings me great comfort. Even though we have only been together this weekend, I like the feel of him. I love that he completely ignored Michelle last night too.

Unlike Tommy, Jason and I entered into our relationship still hurt and bleeding from our pasts. We both have done things that we are not proud of as adults. Our families disowned both of us. We knew each other from church as children but became reacquainted earlier this year. We will probably move in together later this year since we are already outcast sinners.

When I first saw Jason again, I was upside down spread-eagle on a chair. He saw me at a buddy's bachelor's party last year. I was private dancing that night in Paulding County. Fine, I was stripping and giving lap dances. But, the money was outrageous. I love being able to skip asking Brian or his family for money.

The Couch Family is reluctantly generous, but I want everything for my little girl. Jason practically tried to take me out of the bachelor's party. We struck up a conversation. I did not care what he thought of my career. The last time I saw him was when he bought something from the floral shop years ago when I was working there after school with Anne. I think his grandmother died. He never talks about her, or his parents.

Jason was right; the men that I came across while stripping were stronger than me. They were mean. They were meaner than the former mean men that I had had in my life.

One night, I was shaving with KY jelly and saw that I had a bruise from my hip to my calf. That was it. Some guy affected part of money-maker, and that was not kosher. I do not even know which guy did it. It was probably a group of them. The bouncers are very lax when working private parties because the pay for the girls is so high; but, they still have a job. If I am helping people get paid and they are not doing their jobs, then that is a problem.

Looking at Michelle, I am grossed out and angry. She never really had to work for money. She does not have to work like me. She does not take any pride in herself. She had been the requisite prude all through our sophomore year. In eleventh-grade, she put on a black turtleneck and labeled herself a tortured artist.

That wench tormented me with unkind words and untrue rumors when I started wearing black towards the end of eighth-grade. We had a friend that was going through something. The friend said, "If you support and still support me and accept me, then wear black on Fridays."

We wore black on Fridays for at least a year, but then the black became part of everyday life. I had been a rat and told the counselor about him. He said that he wanted to kill himself. The friend drew little dash marks on his wrist. He then sketched a miniature pair of scissors at the end like he was going to cut his wrist open. He obsessed over his homemade coupon-cutting wrist marker tattoos.

A friend's suicide threat was the most insane, intense thing that I had ever experienced. In a side conversation with the school counselor, I had told her about it. She asked me to find out why Jeremy wanted to kill himself. So, I did. I played detective. Jeremy was a closeted gay. The counselor did not want to help him after that.

What would have happened if I had played detective with Tommy? In all honesty, he would have tried to turn it into a game. But, what if I had been a better friend to him and tried to figure out what was wrong? The thing is: I do not think he wanted to die.

All of this is an accident. Everything that happened yesterday was an atrocious accident. Our day was perfectly normal and then, while leaving a tacky tourist gift shop, Tommy decided to drive my car out onto the strip. Hundreds of people lined the main street. Cars blew past the speed limit. Tommy tried to turn left out of the shop and onto Front Beach Road. A drunk fifty-something mom with a car full of young teenagers hit us on the driver's side.

Michelle and I were on the passenger's side during the accident. I was in the back with Jason. Michelle was in the front with Tommy. Tommy had taken the most direct hit. But, he walked it off just fine and we never called the paramedics. I do not have full-coverage car insurance. I have a mountain of regrets, and Tommy's death has just climbed to the pinnacle of this crap mountain that I call my life.

"Girls, the coroner will be here in a few minutes. It's time to say goodbye. They're going to have to do an autopsy so Tommy's family probably won't want an open casket funeral. Right now is your last chance," Jason says in a very professional voice.

Michelle looks like a little bird falling backward out of a nest and not able to fly just yet. She says, "What? But, I'm naked. I'm dirty. I can't. I'm not ready. Right now can't be it. We were going to fly to Mexico together. We had all of these plans. We were-",

"Well, then, ma'am," one of the paramedics says in a judgmental but professional tone. "Perhaps the two of you should have thought about that before not getting checked out for internal injuries after an accident. Have you been seen?"

"No, I'm fine," Michelle says. She pulls some hair away from her face and behind her ear like she did in high school. She would do that when one of the science teachers would call on her, but she was too shy to give a full answer.

Michelle was awful in every academic subject other than English. She is too far in shock to understand what is happening. She cannot see the obvious. The paramedics want to get her to the hospital to do a blood draw. They want to compare what is in her blood and Tommy's blood.

"Here's the thing, Michelle," I say holding her left hand with my two hands. I try to comfort her and give her a little pat but comforting a fellow female is not one of my strengths. "We were in a car accident and then drank a lot of alcohol. I mean, we drank an unusual amount of alcohol. And, other things happened after that. You need to be looked at, Michelle, even though your hit was more indirect. You were in my VW Beetle. I am telling you to do this. I don't want your dead, banged-up body on my conscious. Besides, your naked body reeks of discount Alabama state line liquor."

We had had my bug towed back to the hotel. It is not drivable. The plan had been to wait until today, which is already here, and rent a car to drive back while leaving mine here in an auto shop for repairs. Or, alternately, to tow it to a nearby larger city and have the parts replaced out of pocket and away from insurance claims.

But, I think reality is marching into my life like the Big Bad Wolf. It is blowing my straw house apart. Jason and I will be lucky if we dodge a murder or wrongful death charge. Tommy certainly must have ruptured something. His mother will never let this go. I do not think I ever could if it were my Penny. I am glad she's with Brian this weekend.

Paramedics examine Michelle. I scoot to the side. Jason comes over to hold me. The two of us are not as dirty as Michelle and Tommy. Jason has already showered this morning. He is ready for whatever happened today; although, I am certain he did not plan on this.

I showered late last night with Tommy after Jason went to sleep. Matt was getting high in Tommy's bed. He was messing around with Michelle. I do not know what they did. Matt's semen might be lurking in the motel room. Michelle's hair smolders. The burns could be from Matt because it was not Jason or Tommy last night.

At the last minute, Tommy decided that he wanted me in the shower. I let him, and we did not use a condom. We have been having sex with each other, when we are bored, for years. He was my first sex partner, although I lied to him and told him he was not. I hope the medical people do not find out about last night because they will tell Jason.

The one thing I promised Jason is that I would not let the guys have vaginal sex with me. He would tolerate other sex acts. I was all right with even more things. I need to find a douche right away. *Lord, help me if Tommy gave me anything I cannot give back, like a child or a sexually transmitted disease.*

My long hair is in pigtails. At this moment, I want to cut them off. Last month, I started eating better and dressing more modestly. Most of the Southeast's lowlifes could be my gynecologist at this point. I am fortunate that Jason does not mind my profession; at least, not yet.

There is simply no way that Tommy is not here. I get up, walk to his room, and look at him on the stretcher. He is gone. He does not look like himself. His features echo one of those Halloween actors that we had encountered at Camp Blood so long ago.

I had not been there for Tommy and Melissa's wedding. I was working. I heard from Michael that Tommy resembled a distended caricature of himself during the ceremony. With all of the drugs and alcohol, it was probably a miracle that he had remained alive this long. He had just turned twenty-one. He is young. He was young.

"He'll always be a childless adolescent punk," I whisper to Jason with the ocean breeze whisking through the open door.

Thankfully, no one is paying too much attention to the ambulance in the parking lot. Check-out time must have come and gone. We should have already left too, but we needed the extra day to get the rental car situated. Michelle does not have the long drive back to metro Atlanta. The parking lot is empty. I see one housekeeper on the lower floor, but she seems undeterred by our quiet drama.

"No, he'll always be dead, Alicia," Jason says holding my wrist tightly. He wrenches my wrist up and towards his shoulders so that I have to face him.

My boyfriend does not mean to be this brutish; I know. But, I know that if I so much as breathe wrong that he will snap my wrist like a twig. I cannot work with a broken wrist. My body brings home the bacon. I have to navigate this moment carefully.

Jason continues his speech, "I don't want you to romanticize or fanaticize about Tommy. His body is already rotting. He was rotting when he was alive, and he'll rot faster now that he's dead. He did this to himself. He was a big boy, and he made big boy decisions. He bought his own alcohol and brought his own drugs. We used condoms, right?"

"Yes. I mean, I think so." I say. "I did. I don't know about Michelle."

"Well, I assume Tommy knew how to get what he wanted. If I had known that he had hard drugs on him, I wouldn't have let him ride in your car on the way down here. I feel like a culpable idiot too!" Jason says.

Jason releases me. He closes fists and starts hitting his fore-head in quick succession. I have a math problem formulating in my head.

"I don't think Tommy brought drugs with him. We picked him up at his parents' house. His mom had packed a bag for him. She, of course, wouldn't have packed that. Think about it. He was quite shaky but doing okay on the way down here. Are you thinking what I'm thinking?"

"Michelle," Jason connects the dots faster than me. "That's why Tommy wanted to see her. He knew that she'd give him any-thing and that she would be off his parents' radar. He didn't want his parents to know that we were meeting Michelle. He said it was because he was embarrassed that he had screwed things up with Melissa not that long ago. I mean, goodness, they haven't even been properly divorced yet. He said it had to do with that."

"But, of course, it wasn't," I say as I flame with rage. I feel like I could almost combust on the hotel room threshold.

"Tommy didn't want us to know that Michelle had a stash waiting on him. That's why Michelle is so torn up. She's not only drunk, but she's coming down from a high. What do you think it was? It was certainly not marijuana. Pot would take the edge of the pain and nausea, granted. Something else killed him. I had some. You had some. But, we're not torn all the hell up like Michelle. She had something dirty." Jason says.

Jason rushes back inside. I see his hot ass in the corner of my vision talking to the paramedics. Jason directs Michelle out of the bathroom and toward the balcony. I do not know what to say to her. I remain uncomfortably mute.

I am not certain what is happening until the police pull into the parking lot behind the coroner's van. Slowly moving inside, I stand casually next to Tommy's body. I start smoking a cigarette like it is the most natural thing that I have ever done. My false façade of fake emotion is one of the few positive traits from stripping.

"Good afternoon, gentlemen," I say in a calm voice. I exhale down toward the ground but away from Tommy and his stretcher. "We are having a bad day here."

"We're here to…" One of the officers starts. He comes into the room and looks around. The disgust on his face is evident.

"You will be looking for Michelle. She's out on the balcony, but all of her drugs, alcohol, and sex toys are out here on the table. Please take excellent care of my best friend, Tommy." Jason says giving the stretcher a little kick.

"He has a great right throwing arm that we'll want to be careful with that so he can show off at this year's homecoming game when there's an alumni tribute. In the seventh-grade, he cried at the end of *Where the Red Fern Grows*. His wife will not want to know about the girlfriend, of course. I'm assuming that I'll need to be the one to call his mom, the preacher, and scoutmaster." I say.

"We can," offers one of the officers. The police officer steadies my shoulder, but I burst into tears. I cannot hold it together. I am not ready to say goodbye.

While locked in a mist of gray emotion, I hear the coroner tell Jason, "He probably died from a hematoma of some kind. Could be epidural, subdural, or even a cerebral contusion. It would be hard to tell without a you-know-what. I don't want to speculate further until we notify the family. But, I think the drugs complicated whatever type of internal bleeding he had. Now, the naked girl won't tell us what it may have been. Do you know? It will give us an idea of what to test for and make it go faster."

Without too much hesitation, my mind floods with thoughts of Melissa, Tommy's mom, and even Mrs. Couch. I say, "I think you should test for heroin, cocaine, prescription painkillers, and all other narcotics. He had a script for something, but I don't know what it was. His pills will be in his toiletry bag inside his suitcase. He never wanted the rest of us to see it."

Now, I feel the burden of my biggest mistake. My biggest mistake was assuming that Tommy was right and knew everything. My second biggest mistake and regret was that he was wrong. I never took any action to counteract his plummet of self-destruction.

I will never forgive myself for accepting a hit of pot the first time he offered it. I should have called him a nerd and shunned him. I should have spread rumors that he had a new type of STD that could be transmitted just by listening to his silver tongue. I should not have had sex with him on and off for the past five years. He called our sexual escapades practice, but it feels painfully intimate. Now my heart is breaking into a million tiny pieces.

In hindsight, I should not have driven him down here. I want to rewind the past twenty-four hours. I should have told Tommy that we were too old for a trip like this. I should have told him to get a job, get a car, and get a life. I should have told him to stay with his wife and honor his commitment. But, no, he was channeling Old Joe.

The heavy steps of the officers walking toward Michelle give me chills. I had thought for the longest time that Joe was the devil himself. Old Joe was evil. Joe was bold, aggressive, dominating, and controlling. But, no, it was Tommy.

Tommy was the devil in my life that had haunted me for far too long. His one kindness was letting Michelle be his partner-in-crime for this venture instead of me. Now she can be responsible for the leftover wave of crap from Tommy's decisions instead of me.

Goodbye, Tommy. I promise that one day I will sit back and let my mind drift back through the years. But, I cannot do it today. I will be Little Ann. You can be Old Dan. We will run through the fields. I will see you there. No. That is not right. I will not run through the fields with you. I was never Little Ann, was I? You are already running through the fields with your Little Anne.

Seventeen: Anne

April 17, 1998 8:08 AM
Jekyll Island, Georgia

A stifling sadness looms over me. I should be happy today. I am not packed away like a sardine in a classroom learning about something that I will never have to know again. I have the luxury of enjoying the beach on a field trip. Our hotel is oceanfront and the nicest place we have ever stayed on a field trip. I have a thousand little things that I should be grateful for this morning. I ate fresh cantaloupe for breakfast. The one exception to my happiness is that I had a dream about Tommy last night.

As I am exiting my shared hotel room, Amanda and Preeti greet me on the other side of the door. They look tense, sad, and concerned. Each grabs one of my hands and starts to rush towards the Holiday Inn Resort lobby. I wish they had given me another minute to finish French braiding my hair.

State Beta Club conventions happen once a year, and this is the last one of my academic career. Mrs. Couch is our sponsor. After traveling with Mrs. Couch for debate team earlier this year, I had wondered if I should come on this field trip. I could not resist the island's call. The state convention is my third trip here in three years but first on Jekyll Island. Plans fell through for our usual facility in

Macon, and I am grateful. Preeti and Amanda are acting weirder than ever this convention, and 1996 one was pretty freaky.

Preeti says, "Sweet Anne, something terrible has happened. Paul McCartney died. Amanda just stepped out to get something from the drink machine, and she saw the headline on the newspaper in the dispenser over there. I have some quarters if you want to buy one. We know how much you love The Beatles. I'm sorry, Anne."

Skeptical, I suggest that we go to visit the girls from Lithia or Alexander to see if we can watch one of their televisions for a minute or two. We discovered a broken television on check-in yesterday afternoon. Combining all the students from the three county high schools resulted in a mere twenty students for this field trip. But, of course, we had to divide rooms somewhat based on school and gender. We do not know the other girls very well. They did not seem overly friendly.

"Are you going to cry?" Amanda says as though she is interrogating me. Maybe she feels that I am an inauthentic fan if I do not fall face forward and wail like a professional mourner.

It is spring of our senior year. I have been saving my part-time job money to get away from Douglas County. I only work weekends now that Valentine's rush is over, so school trips are perfect; at least until Mother's Day. I do not know what I will do after high school. I wanted to spend time this field trip unearthing what everyone else is doing. My plans have changed significantly since February. I am not confident that I should still go to Georgia Tech even though I was accepted.

I hope starting college is not as traumatic as all the adults say it will be. I feel like a death row inmate who should carefully order his final meal. I would love to eat seafood while we are here. There is no fresh seafood in Douglas County. I want to live somewhere where I can eat fresh seafood every day if I wanted. I am flat out resentful of Jennifer going to Armstrong Atlantic this fall.

The three of us knock on the Alexander and Lithia girls' suites, but no one answers. We walk by the boys' rooms too. I pause for a moment and then catch up with Preeti and Amanda. They are blathering about Brian and Alicia, Tommy and Melissa, Seth and Heather, and other prom couples. To the best of my knowledge, neither girl has a date. I do not either. I have to go because I am on the newspaper staff, but I do not want to go. I cannot think a worse prom situation than having to work it by conducting student interviews.

"Has Will ordered a corsage for Michelle, Anne?" Amanda asks.

"I don't think so. If Will has, he didn't order it from Beautiful Lee-Dunn." I gossip.

"Is Jennifer going with anyone? Who would take her?" Preeti says.

"If Alicia wants to go she'll have to wear a tablecloth." Amanda chides.

"Ladies, prom night is not the unofficial night to lose your virginity. Have some self-respect. We can go without dates. It is not a problem. Do you know of a boy in Douglas County that makes enough on his own to pitch in to rent a limo? No, and neither do I. The girls work and go to school too. The boys party and waste their time. Besides, we should be saving ourselves for marriage." Amanda says in a scathing tone.

"Your parents are, like, missionaries or something, right? Don't judge the rest of us." Preeti pipes in.

We start walking toward the room where we think Mrs. Couch is staying to see if we may ask permission to see the other girls. Preeti and Amanda keep talking about prom. I am desperate to make a phone call. I want to talk to someone, anyone, who is a little more grounded. I am mad at Jennifer, but I could call David if he were not in school right now. Crystal is working.

"Anne, are you still upset about Paul? Was he your Beatle? Is that why you look so dower?" Preeti says.

No. Besides, George is my Beatle. Is it so misguided of me to not care if Paul McCartney died? What kind of fan am I? I guess I should care. But, I am here in this beautiful place for such a short duration. I do not want to think about death. I do not want problems from the real world to chase me down here.

I have a half-hearted idea to walk down the sidewalk towards the convention center and eat at Blackbeard's. Not there; maybe

Zachry's that is in the same little shopping center as the Jekyll Island Pharmacy? I wonder if I can shake the chatterboxes.

In an odd turn of events, we rap and tap on Mrs. Couch's sliding glass door. Her suite opens to both a pool view and ocean view. The sun rose hours ago, and it is still beautiful. I cannot neglect this opportunity to stare out at the Atlantic Ocean. I let Preeti and Amanda raffle around outside the room knocking and peeking like little anxious children. Amanda wants everything on a schedule and to know exactly where we are supposed to be and at what time. She wants things running like clockwork. I wonder what college she is going to in a few months.

"What is going on?" Preeti says rhetorically.

"I'll tell you exactly what's going on," Amanda hisses like an angry pit viper. "Mrs. Couch has gone and done it again, that cantankerous bludger. What a sponsor. I mean, any one of the five or six teachers could have come with us on this trip, but she was the first to jump on it since she had tenure and status priority."

"She pulled this same stunt when we were on our debate trip earlier this year. I don't know if she is just allergic to mornings or if she is not capable of travel or what. She seems so on top of things by the time we get to her class in the early afternoon. What's up?" I say.

"What happened? Why didn't I hear about this? I was supposed to be on that trip. What was I doing again? Who went in my place?" Amanda said swirling her wire frame sunglasses in a circle.

"I went in your place and ended up placing second in the state. You're welcome. It is just another medal for the school to take credit for, right?" I say in my defense.

"Anne is spot-on," Preeti says. "Mrs. Couch did emotionally check-out on us while we were there. But, Brian was there too, and he drove us back and forth to the event. He also raffled through her purse and found money to take us all out to eat at this delicious place-"

"You, WHAT?" Amanda screams.

An ill-wind blows outside the suite. Amanda's eyes shrink to the size of peas. She puckers her lips together like an irate donkey in the cartoon-like books that we all learned how to read out of long ago. It does not take too much to make Amanda angry. Preeti pretends to be more relaxed. It is part of her gypsy act.

"I did a damn good job too," I say while channeling my work-self instead of my school-self.

Amanda was not going to pass me over like she always did. Her eye was on the prize, and she had torched many school relationships in the wake. The only thing is that I never knew, exactly, what she thought the prize was. Does the trophy go to whoever escapes Douglas County? There are kinder ways to achieve that end. Amanda is burning relational bridges like it was going out of fashion. We start walking toward the ocean.

"What happened to Mrs. Couch? Your faculty sponsor always has to show up at each event and check-in with the school if you are absent on school days and so much more. She couldn't just vanish." Amanda says. She is dumbfounded.

"She didn't vanish, Amanda," Preeti adds. "She was there, but she was unconscious in the hotel room. We all swore to Brian not to talk about it. So, you can't say anything. We don't want her to get fired. We just want to be able to find her if we need her. But, girls, c'mon. We're eighteen! We're legal adults, except for Anne. We don't need Mrs. Couch to make it through the day. Practically everyone staying at the hotel this half of the week is here for the Beta convention too. It's not a big deal."

"Disgraceful! Was she drunk? I didn't know she drank. I would have heard rumors." Amanda says while inadvertently looking a little bit like Vivien Leigh in *Gone with the Wind*.

"No one said anything about being drunk. We shouldn't assume or speculate either." Preeti adds. She was doing damage control now because she had promised Brian too.

"Well," Amanda said in a matter-of-fact tone while sitting gracefully on the sand. "I heard that she is peeved to no end that Brian and Alicia are having a baby together."

"What do you want her to do? Have Alicia and the baby killed? Press Alicia's hand and impose an abortion sentence. She has no legal claim to Alicia's uterus." I say. I feel so hurt by Amanda's bluntness.

"Alicia could pretend to be ashamed. She flaunts her sin. It will come back to haunt her." Amanda retorts.

"No, duh! Amanda, that's not news," I say. "Everyone can look at Alicia's belly and see that she's like ten months pregnant. Mrs. Couch doesn't want us to talk about it. And, she's right. It's unprofessional of us. She probably takes it personal because it's going to be her grandbaby. If there is a grandchild, then she is a grandma. Becoming a young grandparent is a mid-life crisis waiting to happen."

"She's too old for a mid-life crisis." Amanda snaps back at me.

"Don't act all highfalutin because you have a job, Anne," Preeti says. "We don't have to be professional. We're not working girls like you and Alicia."

"Working part-time in high school is not the same being a prostitute, Preeti." Amanda answers.

"There are kids at school that don't know about Alicia because she dropped out: out of sight, out of mind. But, how could she not drop out? I think it's bold of Brian to stay. You would think that if he was so interested in the baby that he would go out and get a job somewhere. He's still a butt muncher." Preeti says.

"Who peed in your porridge, Preeti? Stop being such a judgmental hard-nosed bitch. You're not the child of an enlightened Yankee that you claim to be. Just wait until you grow up and fall in love." I say in a raised voice.

"All I can think about is the videos that we watched in Sex Ed starting in middle school and how we all thought that human reproduction was so mysterious. We would ask questions, and then no one would answer. But, they had to have known, right? I mean, a lot of the teachers were parents too. Obviously, they figured it out at some point in time. Then, those idiots, they kind of sprung AIDS education on us in high school. Uh, thanks, people. If we have sex, we die." Preeti says.

"Anne," Amanda said turning to me. "You do know that's why Mrs. Couch flipped out on you during your Hemingway discussion, right? That was a solid argument and, I think, in a college environment would have been very appropriate. It was just too soon, dear."

"I'm not your dear!" I say in explosive anger.

"Hemingway? Oh, crap! When did that happen? I don't remember Hemingway." Preeti says.

"It was ridiculous," I start. "We read that Hemingway short story, right? It was, um, what was it? It was *Hills like White Elephants*. I think that's right. So, the whole basis of the story is that the events take place while the characters are waiting for a train in Spain."

"Oh, and then the rain on the plain; yeah, yeah, yeah," Preeti mocks.

"No! Not at all!" yelps Amanda, deeply offended. "This is not *Pygmalion* that we're discussing. It's a short story. Oh, goodness, how will you ever pass the CL exam? All of this work will be for nothing, Preeti. Goodness. My heart hurts. Stop breakin' my heart."

"Okay, so," I say with big hand gestures to get their attention. "There is a forty-minute wait for the train. Hello? Forty minutes? Forty is the same number of weeks of a healthy pregnancy."

"It's disgusting that you know that," Preeti says with cruel judgment.

"Look, I live in the real world," I defend myself but try to remain calm. "I volunteer in my church nursery. There are hordes of women out there birthing babies. Forty appears to be the magic number of weeks that everyone wants for a healthy baby. There is this whole March of Dimes thing that tries to get women to take steps to get their pregnancies to full-term. There is nothing gross about growing up, getting married, and having kids. I think that's what a lot of people want, Preeti. I want to grow-up, get married, and have children. Unlike Alicia, I hope to do everything in the right order. If not, my parents will kill me and it won't be an issue. Didn't you have that mandatory health class our freshman year?"

"I think I exempted it and took weight lifting instead," Preeti taunts me.

"Well, you may need to know this for the CL exam. Take notes, Preeti." Amanda snorts a little.

I continue, trying to sound smarter than I truly am. "We all know that the term *white elephant* is used when something obvious has happened, but no one wants to talk about it, right? It's the so-called white elephant in the room."

"Shut up, Anne!" Amanda interjects. "You are thinking about *an elephant in the room*. We do white elephant gift exchanges on the DOCOHAN Staff. I'm going to have a stroke. I'm going to die here on the beach. The waves will sweep me out. Oh, for pity's sake. You both are making me sick."

Amanda walks away and goes up the stairs. I think about our last gift exchange when she ended up with a keychain from Spencer's Gifts that had faux plastic poop on the end. It was hilarious. Amanda thoroughly deserved it. I knew she would not touch it. I bet she put it directly into the trash. But, it was worth it for a moment. I wish I had had a camera. There are so many events that I can picture in my mind. I pray that I could capture them all, catalog them, and save them for later. Amanda's face while holding a keychain of fake poop would be in there forever.

"The beach will disappear by afternoon," Preeti says as she rises and dusts the sand off her shorts. "I thought for sure that Amanda was going to tell us the tide schedule and give us a history of the shells that will wash up after. Why is she here? Why didn't she just go directly to college and get some credit that way? Let the rest of us enjoy our senior year."

"She doesn't know as much as she thinks," I add looking out as far as my eyes can stretch. "I'm sure Paul McCartney isn't dead. They would have had something on MTV this morning."

"Hey, airhead, our television set was broken this morning," Preeti says in a sarcastic tone.

"I saw some of the boys watching it as we were walking by to get to Mrs. Couch's room. It must have been his wife, Linda. She had cancer or something. I mean, it's still sad, but she's a person. People die. I can't imagine all the remarkable phenomena that she must have seen in her life. The few interviews that I saw on Oprah make it seem like they were so in love. And, of course, it's tragic when love dies. But, there are different types of loves and losses."

"You looked in the boys' room?" Preeti says with a gasp. "You're a slut, Anne. Amanda was right. Alicia's transgressions are rubbing off on you."

Behind my sunglasses, I roll my eyes. "Preeti, I have a brother. There was nothing in there to write home about, like in a little camp letter. Boys are gross until after college. They're ill-mannered, perpetually famished, and full of hormones."

Preeti storms off. My temporary roommates have taken a different route in high school than some of the rest of us. They may babysit, but they do not earn a paycheck and pay taxes. I have been working at Beautiful Lee-Dunn for most of high school. I must admit, it is different than I thought but not as scary as I had imagined.

By working after school, I get to dip in a toe and then retreat each night back home. Almost everyone who wants to work is working right now. We have no background or experience and the employers often skip asking for a resume. Of course, I only started working at the florist because Stephanie's family owns it. Alicia worked there too when she was keeping out of trouble.

Several of our classmates volunteer for Mrs. Couch's husband's political campaigns. Brian, Tommy, Justin, and Matt have all volunteered for him; Alicia and Stephanie too. The only reason I was able to be hired at the floral shop was because Stephanie decided that she would rather volunteer for Mr. Couch instead of volunteering at her family business. If I have a choice of volunteering or earning a paycheck, the paycheck wins. Crystal taught me that.

David started bagging groceries. Jennifer is learning how to con people at tarot card readings. I think the work experience has been good for me so far. I can see a stark difference arising between myself and some of the other girls in my class. They are looking for others to care for them rather than caring for themselves. Maybe they want MRS degrees and to be stay-at-home moms. I do not. I want more.

Amanda will go off to some nameless, expensive private college. She will shun her HOPE Scholarship and go wherever she wants just for the sake of leaving Georgia. I think that is foolish if Little Miss Perfect does not have another scholarship in place. She just wants to go to school and not work or volunteer. All the teachers love Amanda, but they do not see her impracticality or lack of real world knowledge as a deficit. Preeti is not much better.

Floral assistants sometimes see things that other people do not see or, rather, want to shield their eyes from seeing. I see the vans driving to the back of the shop to sell "recycled" goods. It worries me. None of it sits right in the pit of my stomach.

I know the floral shop charges customers for new items when, sometimes, those items are not new. I am not sure where the recycled vases, pots, wire, wreaths, foam, and trinkets originate. But, recently, I have developed a pretty good idea. That idea makes me nauseous, so I try not to think about it. I am looking forward to quitting when I leave for college this summer, wherever that may be.

Amanda and Preeti think they know everything, but they only see one part of a story. Their limited life experience cripples them into not making the right inferences at the right time. It frustrates the daylights out of Mrs. Couch. I know why Mrs. Couch is face-down in her bed and does not want to wake up.

Alicia and her geriatric boyfriend come into the shop once a month or so. I know Alicia sees me. She knows me but acts like she does not around him. And, that is okay. But, I get riled when the man that she is seeing does not treat her well either. I feel like you can tell so much about a person when they take you out. The man that is with Alicia comes in, talks to the manager, and leaves with an envelope. Alicia keeps her eyes down and stays quiet. That is not like her.

The man that brings Alicia is very possessive of her. He literally cannot keep his hands off. He does not want to stop touching her long enough for her to look at flowers. When he talks to the manager, he does not take his eyes off of her. I have missed seeing Alicia at school and church. She seems like a stranger now, and I want to tell someone about it. I want to yell, "Hey, Alicia, this creepy dude isn't right."

But, who am I going to tell? There is no one to listen; at least, not to me. So, I will keep writing in my journal. I have it with me all of the time. I try to write in it every break. If I did not, I would go insane. It is in my purse right now. My new purse has a narrow cord-like strap that attaches to the multi-color woven bag which I can wear slung-over-the-shoulder. The advantage to it is that there is a thick zipper on the top. The disadvantage is that I have to remember to watch out for wear on the strap.

Outsiders look at me and judge me. They think I have only had one boyfriend. I never offer to correct them. I value my privacy. I honor my heart's quiet brokenness. I have had some life experience now, and read enough books, to know something is suspicious when it looks suspicious. Amanda and Preeti would not know if something was fishy if they were lost inside a fish market.

The man with Alicia bothers me. He rubs her belly. He keeps an arm around her walking in and out. It is almost like he owns her. I cannot believe that a spoiled girl as beautiful and smart as Alicia is so lonely that she feels she cannot do better. I hope the tables turn soon; for her sake. Alicia and Crystal both should be graduating with us. I do not know Brian well. I wonder how he feels about Alicia having a boyfriend. I am uncertain if Brian knows about the man. I am not comfortable approaching Brian and outing Alicia's private jailer.

Alicia does not look like the pregnant moms at church. She is still small and wears regular clothes instead of maternity clothes. I think she still gets her clothes from Hot Topic at Town Center Mall but just buys a slightly bigger size. Her black hair is streaked blue on one side. She still wears a lot of makeup. Amanda would say that she was covering her immorality with makeup.

My heart smiles when I think of the old Alicia. The new Alicia wears more makeup now than she did when she was doing the pageant circuit as a child. I think she may still go to Little Five Points to that boutique shop to buy Urban Decay. It is next to a head shop. A secret that I know that few others do is that Alicia has extremely sensitive porcelain skin. She can break out in a rash from the slightest change in her makeup or, sometimes, even from drinking orange juice.

Just like when I work the floral counter, I try to set my thoughts aside and live in the moment. But, the habit does not come naturally. I want to soak in the sun and ocean. My skin feels thirsty for it. While other girls in my class have hours of free time to go to tanning beds, I am mostly stuck indoors, day and night. I walk back toward the pool alone. Amanda and Preeti wandered off long ago while I lost myself in my innermost thoughts.

While approaching the pool, I see Mrs. Couch. She is wearing a draped black lamé strapless bikini. Massive Elizabeth Taylor style sunglasses shade her eyes. *What the hell!* Lady Macbeth cut and dyed her hair this morning. Her curly mullet is gone and in its place is a refined Betty Grable style.

Instead of bottled dirty blonde, Mrs. Couch is now a redhead. Maybe Paul McCartney did die! I am stunned for a moment. I am not positive whether or not I should acknowledge her. I look at her in disgust and awe. She is laying belly-down on an old Budweiser beach towel swathed on a hotel fully-reclined chaise lounge. The beach towel is so threadbare that she might as well recline on nothing. I can see the 'Bud' frog of the Budweiser frog trying to escape the clutches of her thighs as she bounces her lower legs back and forth like a 1950s teenager.

Mrs. Couch is sunbathing and reading Toni Morrison's *Paradise*. Who is that? I have never heard of that author. He is probably old, British, and dead. I wonder if they have his work at

Douglasville Books. Maybe Mrs. Couch had to go out to Oxford Books in Atlanta right before it closed.

"Hi, um, Mrs. Couch. We tried to come see you earlier this morning and," I say, but she cuts me short.

"Anne, you're eighteen, right? And, you're at the ocean for the first time, no? Okay, go and do something. I'm not here to entertain you. I'm not going to tell you girls what to wear, or when to come back. I'm not going to tattle that your bathing suits are not school dress code. I won't remind you to watch your bathing suit strap ties around the boys. I simply don't care. I'm reading. But, I'm a teacher. I don't have a lot of money. So, please, don't do anything that will require bail."

What's bail?

Eighteen: Michael

◆————————————————————————◆

December 18, 1999 5:15 PM
Douglasville, Georgia

"I do not think that being the son of the preacher qualifies me to give you any pre-marriage counseling," I confess to Melissa.

Dad is inside the sanctuary waiting with Melissa's groom, Tommy. Melissa is the most nervous bride I have seen in my entire life. That declarative carries a lot of weight coming from a preacher's kid. She paces up and down the room like a caged animal in a white dress three times her size. I know that I should think that she is beautiful. I should say something to her, but I can barely open my mouth.

My heart's one true desire is that I would be the one marrying tonight. Instead of Melissa, I want Alicia. No matter how far Alicia has fallen, I still love her. Tommy blows through girls like a nor'easter through a pile of fresh leaves. He will stick his dick in anything for five minutes or less; nevermind the damaged reputations he leaves in his wake. I would not want Alicia to feel about me the way that Melissa is feeling about Tommy right now.

"Maybe Tommy should marry someone else? Would you, Michael? Would you marry someone that you didn't want to for the sake of being married? I need to talk to Preacher Dan. If I write a note on a piece of paper, would you take it to your dad?" Melissa asks me. Oh, no. The situation is a no-win scenario.

"Melissa, you're a dear friend. I love you and Tommy. Equally, I should add. I love you both, equally. But, I'm not certain that half an hour before your wedding in the bride's room is the right time to start writing notes. I think Preeti and Stephanie would both kill me if they thought I had brought any ink anywhere near you."

"Tommy is like Heathcliff, Michael," Melissa shrieks. "He can't quite commit to anything. He thinks he's good at everything which makes him good at nothing. He's neither a complete rogue nor farmer, or he's both. Tommy is neither a husband nor a lover. I don't want to be either Cathy or Isabella. I don't want to be in this book."

We are in a small classroom in the Methodist church's education building. Melissa's eyes are huge and red. The contents of the bride's emergency box are all over the floor. She sent Stephanie to get clear nail polish for some odd reason. Preeti is getting ice chips. I thought ice chips were for people in hospitals but, evidently, Melissa needs that right now.

"Well, maybe *Wuthering Heights* isn't the right story analysis for your situation? Could you be Scarlett and Rhett instead?" I ask.

"Rhett was Scarlett's third husband. The first two died; one young and one old."

"Well, let's keep thinking of other literary characters. Where is know-it-all Mrs. Couch when you need her? I'm certain she would have the perfect answer." I say. I try not to sound mean, but I do.

"Mrs. Couch is probably sitting in a pew with her new husband. I guess she's not Mrs. Couch anymore. Will God forgive me if I'm making a mistake? I mean, I didn't know what to say to Tommy. In all the movies and books and whatever, all the girls say 'yes' when men ask for their hand in marriage. Whoever heard of someone saying 'no.' And, besides, no one has ever declined Tommy. My mom acted crazy when I told her that he had asked." Melissa says at breakneck speed.

"Crazy? How?" I ask.

I did not know what else to express. I feel obligated to come up with something. It would almost be more comfortable trying to pull a bouquet of flowers from my sleeves like a street magician. This entire conversation is awkward. My palms are sweaty.

"Mom was elated! She was over the top excited. I was finally excited after I saw that she was excited. People act like Tommy is a space shuttle and he's going to the moon. And, for some stupid reason, he asked me to be his, like, um, what is it called? Co-pilot? What is that even called, Michael?" Melissa orders.

"Oh, *uh.* I think it might be a mission specialist. Okay, Mel, you're a mission specialist, and Tommy is the pilot, and you both are going to jet off into the future together. Congratulations." I say.

Melissa is so emotional that I am thinking about reaching into my pocket for that personalized flask all the groomsmen just got. Then, I remember, I am not a groomsman. I am here as an unofficial church representative, which is how I got locked away with the bride. I was wandering the halls herding lost guests. The bottom line is that my dad wanted me to be certain our high school friends were not roaming the halls looking for the reception before the ceremony began. They may be combing for alcohol. There is no alcohol here tonight; but, the guests may not know that.

"Tommy asked me to marry him while he was high. He was high, Michael! Tommy was spiraling down in a blaze of glory. He must have thought, 'Well, might as well ask Mel. I don't have anything better to screw up, now that I quit college.' I'll sit on this gigantic pillow naked, playing guitar, and ask my girlfriend for her hand in marriage. Gotta have a wife because that's what Mommy Dearest says." Melissa lashes out.

I could have been anyone in that room at that moment. She needed to vent, and I just needed to hang on a little while longer. I looked out the window to see if I could get the attention of a girl to help me out. I do not have any experience in girl territory. I have two little sisters, but that does not make me an expert. Maybe Jessica or Ginger are drifting through the hall right now. I should try to find them. They would know what to say to a despondent bride.

"I'm sorry he's not your Mr. Darcy, Melissa. I know that's what my sisters want in a guy," I say.

"I think he felt obligated to get married because his parents still want to keep riding the high from high school graduation last year. I mean, everyone else is completing their sophomore year at college. I'm here about to be chained to domestic servitude. He's a drug addict, Michael. I don't want to marry a drug addict. I want Tommy to grow up and be responsible."

Thankfully, Stephanie blasts into the room with clear nail polish. I feel saved. Stephanie lifts up layers and layers of fabric. Tommy once called Stephanie *The Sugar Plum Fairy* while we were at a freshman wrestling event. Well, not our real freshman year. It was ninth-grade. That seems like so long ago but, really, it was not.

"Stephanie, Melissa is having a hard time right now. Please help her." I ask in a quiet tone as I walk toward the unhappy bride.

Stephanie stops clear polish shellacking Melissa's legs. She is staring at me as Preeti is coming in the room with icy water. Preeti holds Melissa's hand as Melissa chomps hard on the ice. She sounds like bunny eating carrots. The three girls stop and look at me. Knowing the pain that Melissa is in, I am at a loss for what to say.

"Here's the thing, Melissa. I like you. I like you a lot. I like Tommy a lot. I don't want to feel an obligation to take sides. You, Dad, and Tommy should have ironed these things out ahead of time. You don't have to be here. Tommy is an addict; yes. Of course, he is. He's been smoking pot since about the summer before ninth grade. He's the first person who asked me to keep a secret. And, his secrets have not done me any favors. Those secrets burden my soul. You didn't know him before high school. You went to a different middle school. Where were you? Chapel Hill? Chestnut Log? Look, Tommy's an addict just like he's a football player, basketball all-star, and whatever else. It's part of who he is. He can never change it."

Preeti walks over to me and slaps me. *Ow*! My ears pop and faint sounds roar like thunder around me. I think the fact that it was an angry slap made it more unpredictable. The suddenness of the damage makes it worse. Preeti is part gypsy and part Yankee, or something, and has no qualms about being rude and violent. I am shocked that she allowed her college to accept her quitter status. Her life has not been the rosy path that she expected; but, she had no reason to hit me.

"How dare you, asshole! You don't get to yell at the bride. You don't get to unload on her and add to her burden right before what should be the most special day of her life. I work with sorry insurance sales agents like you all day. I see your slick tricks and smooth appearance covering up a pox-marked soul. Don't spread your disease on her." Preeti screams at me while pointing at Melissa.

Melissa stands silent. She looks at the floor. Her shoulders slump toward her waist. Her wedding gown looks as though it will slip off her body, like a sad doll.

"And, by the way, Tommy is an EX-football player and an EX-basketball all-star. Tommy could be an EX-addict if he wanted to. But, Tommy doesn't want to, now does he? And, why would he? Everyone in his life enables his bull crap." Melissa says.

"Here's the deal," Stephanie says to diffuse the situation. "No one knows that this is happening but us. Mel, if something happens, we have all witnessed the same conversation. If you need help making Tommy an ex-husband, you let us know. I know that no one wants to talk about divorce on their wedding day. And, sincerely, I hope it's not going to bring bad luck. But, my love, I don't want you to feel stuck. And, you know what, Michael? I don't want you to be racked with guilt if something bad does happen between Mel and Tommy. We're all adults here, and we will behave as such."

Melissa crumples to the floor like a closing umbrella. She starts crying. Stephanie looks sternly at me. I feel the daggers. But, then, Preeti goes one further and throws the leftover ice water on me. *Brrr.*

The ice water takes my breath away. It is already an exceedingly cold December. The heat is also not turned on in the dressing rooms for the wedding. We would save the electricity and turn it on in the morning right before the children got here for Sunday School. *Wow, wee!* That is cold. I am freezing.

All the girls are laughing. Melissa stops crying. Rather than doing anything that I would regret later, like name-call or worse, I decide to go ahead and leave. I am halfway out the door when Melissa grabs the back of my tuxedo jacket.

"Oh, Michael, I'm sorry. I know I shouldn't have laughed. But, you'll freeze. I want you to stay with us. I'll need to get used to having a boy around during girl time." Melissa says.

"Well, I feel used," I say and grab a chair to sit down. The wedding wait will only be a few more minutes. It would not be honorable to leave these three in an unfamiliar church in such a state. At the very least, I should be an overly-gracious host. Everything I do seems to reflect not only on me but also my family and church. "But, I'll stay despite my feelings. Let's try to distract ourselves."

"Oh, I have a question. And, it's a question that only you can answer, Michael," Melissa says gathering great composure.

I'm thinking that Melissa is going to relate this conversation back to our English classes. She will quiz me like Mrs. Couch. I will fail miserably. Do I know the proper family tree of the Earnshaw family? Heck, no. I think everyone died in the end. Brothers, sisters, cats, and dogs; I have no idea.

"What did you say to Robert in the few minutes before his only sister's funeral? You are the unofficial spiritual leader of our class.

You defied school administration and quoted scripture during our baccalaureate's inspirational reading. I want to know what comfort you have for me. I need emotional strength right now. Tonight is my hour of need. I think you're here for a reason. Tell me. Show me."

"You can't ask me that. You have no right." I say almost speechless. The memory of that day floods back into my mind. I am drowning in emotions. Melissa should not have asked this; not now, not ever.

With the emotions swirling in my head, and thoughts of *Wuthering Heights*, I go off on a tangent, "This is not nineteenth century England, girls. You are not in some twisted romantic relationship. Things are so much simpler than all that. Don't make this situation more dramatic than it needs to be. If you don't want to be here, walk away. It truly is that simple. Well, that may not be entirely accurate. You will need a car ride from someone. But, you're not Cathy. He's not Heathcliff or Edgar. On a good day, he's just Tommy."

Preeti takes the last dribbles of the ice water and pours them slowly over my head. It is time to leave. Stephanie looks longingly and scuffles to me. I did not know what she wanted to say. For me, there was nothing left to say or add. There is nothing else that my brain can formulate that may bring comfort or joy to this gaggle of girls. They are off in some imaginary land comparing the tangible, but flawed, men in their lives to some idiotic romantic notion that Mrs. Couch conjured up for them in class. Mrs. Couch has been peddling this crap for decades.

"As class president, I hereby nominate you our class chaplain." Stephanie declares.

"Stephanie, that's a bunch crap because we all know that our student council doesn't exist anymore. None of it made a flip of difference." I reply.

Right now, these three girls look like they are the *Austin Powers* femme-bots. Refined and deadly with machine gun parts ready to explode out of their dresses and demolish me on a whim. I want to leave. I cannot muster another ounce of decorum or chivalry.

"There were six of us. Three are here. We have a quorum. There is a nomination. Do I hear a motion to make Michael the permanent chaplain for the Douglas County High School Class of 1998?" Stephanie says.

I detest parliamentary proceedings. I can walk down the hall. The unnecessary drama does not have to continue. I am in control of my life. I have no obligation to my high school class.

"So moved," Preeti says to my amazement.

"I second," Melissa says smiling.

"Can I decline nomination?" I ask. Resistance seems pointless.

"No. You're now in charge of all of our spiritual affairs, as a class representative, between now and the end of time. You can sleep when you're dead. Now, go and see if they're ready. You're our gopher now," Stephanie says authoritatively.

Stephanie is rubbing my normally calm nerves raw. She just steamrolled me! This winter break cannot be over soon enough. Anne's murder tragically clouded last winter break. Now, this winter break is all about Melissa and Tommy's wedding. Next year I'm going to ask for more hours at work that will keep me busy and away from unnecessary drama.

The door closes quietly in my face. I hear the girls yelling back and forth at each other for a moment. I think about walking down the hall, but I am too resentful of being called a gopher. I had helped, a little, during one of the drama productions at school. But, to call me a gopher was unfair. I had seen the *Mystery of Edwin Drood* that the school did and agreed to help, when the Drama Club asked, for *Nunsense*.

Dad and I are too busy at church during the Christmas season for me to help with the Boar's Head Festival. But, I did go one year. Mashburn Hall looked like an entirely different building. I felt transported. I want to feel transported now. Melissa's family has decorated the fellowship hall to resemble a Bronte novel scene. It looks like a dump truck of rose petals were thrown everywhere. I hope the food is good.

"You shouldn't have asked about Anne's funeral." Stephanie chastises Melissa.

"I'm a wreck. What do you want? I can barely speak coherently, and no one has gone to get water yet! My corset is suffocating me."

"Well, I was mad and threw it at Michael; remember?" Preeti says.

"Poor, Michael. We ask so much of him. He's not like the other boys. He's always calm and, ladies, we take that for granted. He's one of the few boys that doesn't think he's on *Beavis and Butthead.* We shouldn't mistake his kind soul. He's very mature. I think he'll go back to college and do great things." Stephanie says.

"How can Anne not be here? She was here this time last year." Melissa says.

The girls open the door from the dressing room and into the hallway. Stephanie is shocked to see me only a few feet away. She is holding the ice bucket. I cringe. I don't want to have another drop dumped on me. I see Preeti sitting on the floor with Melissa when the door closes again.

Stephanie leans over to whisper in my ear. "I have a confession. I had sex with Tommy."

"What? Like, recently?" I say. My mouth goes dry. I'm in shock.

"Earlier this year," Stephanie whispers. "Will I burn in Hell for comforting his white, virginal bride?"

"Since they were engaged? Oh, Steph, how could you sleep with Tommy?"

"We didn't sleep. It was just a quickie. I don't think it should even count."

"The Lord sees everything. It counts. Have you told Melissa?"

"No. I don't want to burden the bride."

"You should burden her. It speaks to her to-be husband's character. Putting Melissa in a situation where she could unknowingly acquire a permanent sexually transmitted disease is abuse, Stephanie. You have to tell her. You are perpetuating violence against her body. Melissa is going to have sex tonight with a man of very questionable moral judgment."

"Tommy was traumatized. I was just helping out a friend. You weren't worried when he was just an addict. Why are you worried about his bodily fluids now? I'm sure Melissa knows. She must."

"He used you. You're not the kind of girl that Tommy should use as a whack-rag. You come from a respectable family. You shouldn't be sleeping with anyone. Sexual liaisons, outside of marriage, are adultery." I admonish her. I know I sound like Preacher Dan now.

Not knowing what will happen now, I shift away from the girls. I hear some sobbing noises. A man that I do not know comes to the door to queue the girls. Stephanie joins them. Tommy's family has gone all out for the wedding ceremony. There is a small team of wedding planners. I need to get between the helper dude and Melissa, right now, before anything proceeds.

Tonight was meant to be the social highlight of the Christmas season. But, Tommy and Melissa should not be getting married at all. Tommy should not have asked. I do wonder if Tommy asked Melissa, or if it was his mother. Can parents propose on behalf of their children? Is that an arranged marriage? Can people do that in Georgia today? It does not seem legal.

If a Christmas miracle were to happen this year, this moment would be a perfect time. I stayed late at work earlier this month so I could see the lighting of Rich's Department Store's Great Tree at Underground Atlanta. I think most of Atlanta stayed to see that. I stood around with a couple of co-workers that I do not know very well to enjoy the moment.

I love where I work. I love working where I go to school. I love working with all types of people. This month, I learned what Muslims believe when a co-worker decided to share with me. I appreciated the conversation. A woman who works in a row of cubicles diagonal to my desk is Taoist.

My co-workers are like family to me and have no spiritual expectations of me. They just know me as Michael who answers the phone. I do not think I even have a nickname. I am certainly not known as 'the preacher's son.' I feel like no one expects anything out of me except to just be Michael and to show up and do the best job that I can every day.

A long time ago, I was on a scout camping trip where we all nearly died. The troop split into fragments up and down part of the Appalachian Trail. I was with Tommy, Matt, and Seth. Matt was obsessed with not letting me die since I was the preacher's son. I feel guilty for that. Matt should have saved himself first. He ended up with some painful frostbite injuries.

Matt has been a massive failure since high school. Matt, David, and Ryan are always in trouble. Preeti knows more about that than she should. The way things are going Stephanie will be in trouble here soon too. The sad fact is that Stephanie's family has the money to get her out of trouble.

Tommy has floundered. He has nosedived for the past year since Anne died. He is not going to school, and he is unemployed. I did not even know what unemployment was until Tommy told me. He has never worked. He has only volunteered for this one corrupt politician.

Somehow, Tommy and Melissa are going to have an apartment not far from Arbor Station. I think she is working at Parisian at Arbor Place. Melissa is fashionable and tasteful, so maybe it is a good job for her. I will always remember the way that she looked when wearing a soaking wet white dress with a white bridal corset underneath. Tommy should have married her that day. She will never be as lovely as she was when she was fighting with Nicole. She is full of fiery passion. Tommy does not deserve her. It is ridiculous that

Melissa has been saving herself for Tommy when he has been loose with all of his decisions. Those decisions will affect her now too.

My mom had had a conversation with me about women working. Mom had not worked when I was growing up. She said that it was hard for women to make enough money to work outside the home after they had children because childcare was so expensive. Childcare used to be difficult to find. Most 1980s moms stayed at home with small children. I am proud of Melissa for working and going to school like me. But, I do not know how the girls of my generation are going to make it on mall jobs.

It is Y2K time. Almost all the boys I know are employed. Most of us in the tech field are making very decent money. Melissa will be the sole breadwinner of her family. I do not think that is what my mom had in mind when she talked about women working outside the home. I worry about how she will afford childcare. I imagine Tommy will stay at home, but I doubt he would want to watch a baby as he lies about on a couch smoking weed.

If Anne had not tutored me in Microsoft Office and formatting documents, I would not have the job that I have now. Anne gifted me useful skills, which is an amazing gift that I can never give back. I miss her dearly. There is so much I want to tell her. There was only a scant bit left unsaid between the two of us before she died.

Anne and I were not terribly close. We grew up together. I knew her from school and church. I wish I could talk to her right now. She would know what to do and say about tonight and I could go back to just being Michael. She could be the spiritual leader.

"Melissa? I need a word." I say as the wedding planner rushes her down the hall.

Stephanie stands between Melissa and me. She mouths the word 'no.' Preeti stops the planner and closes the interior door leading to the sanctuary. Melissa nods at me.

"Do you know about Tommy?" I ask.

"Yes." She says.

"I mean, do you know about Tommy and his exploits? About *all* of his exploits? He has been engaging in some, um, thing that, uh-"

"I know about all of, Michael. Thank you. You've been great tonight." Melissa says.

The cumbersome sanctuary doors open. Music plays. The pre-chosen, and parental unit approved, bridesmaids and groomsmen flank the church altar. My father nods at me and the wedding planner. Preeti and Stephanie flare Melissa's long train.

Tommy stands near my father. Tommy is looking at the side of the sanctuary where the Christmas tree stands. The evergreen giant is covered in foam ornaments and does not have artificial lights on it. The insurance company said that they would be a fire hazard. Tommy seems especially enthralled with the tree. I wonder if he knows where he is.

With Melissa halfway down the aisle, Tommy stumbles backward for a moment. Groomsmen Matt and Ryan steady him. It feels like five-minutes ago that we were being confirmed together in this same sanctuary; except, Tommy was sober in 1992. I will take a wedding, confirmation, or baptism in this sanctuary any day under any circumstances. The worst types of events here are funerals. May Anne rest in peace.

Nineteen: Jason

◆————————————————————◆

March 1, 1992 4:57 PM
Douglasville, Georgia

"Son, I say, why are you in here? Aren't you an eighth grader?" Preacher Dan scolds me as I sit down in an empty classroom at church. "Are you here for confirmation class?"

Last week's weekly church newsletter held an open call for all students to attend confirmation class today, here in this classroom, at this time. We are missing the youth group's potluck downstairs, so this dang well better be worth it. I am giving my life to the Lord, but I also want a hamburger. I am ravenous. My stomach is a bottomless pit. Tommy said the grub would be worth it. A few more boys walk in the room.

"The little 'Youth' box in the church newsletter that my grandmother gets every Wednesday said 'anyone.' So, here I am. I'm anyone. Okay?" I defend my attendance.

"What's your name? I'll write it down with the others," an assisting parent asks.

"I'm Jason. I'm Ida's grandson, okay? And, yes, I'm in eighthgrade." I say blandly.

My grandmother does not care for Preacher Dan Vansant or his family. Dan is the new preacher. I do not like him either. He acts like a politician. Grandma does not like Dan insisting the congregation call him by his Christian name. She wants her preachers in robes at eleven o'clock every Sunday morning. Grandma would also prefer an older pastor, a mature congregation, sermons strictly based on scripture, and a building that has stood strong since the Civil War.

"Good for you for being here." Preacher Dan's son, Michael, says.

Confirmation class is not an elite club; it is a class that happens once a year. I was still living with my dad in the sixth grade. I did not have an opportunity to go to the classes two years ago because there was no one to bring me. Now that I live with my grandmother, I can walk to church. I may have become the most active youth in the past year. Granny's house is small but full of love.

I am not as familiar with the sixth graders yet, so the preacher makes them go around and introduce themselves. What is the big deal about being an eighth-grader? I was in Kindergarten while they were still potty-training; whatever. The girls walk in as a group as Preacher Dan introduces himself. The parent volunteers leave to prepare food downstairs for us to eat at the end of the class. I feel guilty because I do not have any parents volunteering.

The class consists of Tommy, Heather, Crystal, Anneewakee, Michael, and Seth. Alicia and Matt are signed up for the class but absent today. Hold up. Anneewakee has changed her mind; she is now Anne. Okay, Anne: You are trying to pretend like you are a grown woman. That is fine. You still look like a little brown mouse.

"Children, we are not going to delve into anything too deep in this class. We're just going to hit the surface of what our denomination of Christianity is. Then, we'll have dinner downstairs in the fellowship hall. Okay? We will perform a sketch at the Easter sunrise service. Later in the day, you'll be confirmed with your family and friends as witnesses. Now, who needs to baptized in addition to being confirmed?" Preacher Dan says.

"What does that mean, Preacher Dan?" the mouse squeaks.

"Well, Anneewakee, that means that some children didn't have their parents bring them to church when they were little. The babies get sprinkled with water while the parents and congregation recite vows. Did you get baptized? Remember, I wasn't at this location when you all were little. I think you probably were. I doubt your parents overlooked that. Now, who else?"

"I'm only here because my parents promised me a gold medallion to Turtles Record Store," Tommy says. He is a little too honest.

"What?" questions Seth. "I'm jealous of your good fortune, dude. Are you going to the Highway 5 store near the Chinese Pagoda or the one in Mableton?"

"I want Chinese food," Crystal says.

Heather, turning from starring out at the playground says, "I've never had Chinese. Does it taste like American food? Are they open on Easter?"

"Oh, there is this amazing cheesecake there." Crystal starts but Preacher Dan clears his throat.

"Children, we're not talking about Chinese food. Let's get back to salvation. Now, I'm not going to be here every session, so you all need to focus on while I'm here." Preacher Dan stops and looks over at Anne who has her hand raised.

"Well, you did ask if we have questions and I want to know if we can go to the Chinese Pagoda when Tommy goes to Turtles. It could be like a class field trip." Anne the mouse negotiates.

"I think I may go to Mableton because the store's bigger," Tommy adds.

"You jerk! How can you say that to Heather? She wants to try Chinese food." Crystal scolds.

"Can we use the church van? We're old enough to be considered youth now." Anne says.

"Are there seatbelts? There's that new law." Heather says.

Preacher Dan interrupts, "Thank you for that, girls. We will consider a field trip at a later date. We need to get started today because you all will be expected to attend Ash Wednesday service this week. I want for you all to know the importance and solemnity of-"

"Wait! How did my twenty-dollars get to be about Heather wanting Chinese food and Anne going on an Irish field trip with Scarlett?" Tommy looks puzzled, even though it is a valid question.

Lacking any clear direction, I say, in a deeper voice than the rest, "Preacher Dan, can we talk about Chinese food later and do what we need to do? Let's all agree to get Heather some Chinese food before this is all over."

"Go home and ask your parents if they baptized you as a baby. If not, come back and let me know. We'll make arrangements, okay? Now, we are moving onto the history of Methodism. John Wesley was born in 1703."

"Who is John Wesley? I don't remember him from the Bible. I thought we were talking about Jesus and Easter." Heather says flipping her blonde hair.

Heather is a self-centered mess. I think I saw her try out for cheerleading this past August. She lied about her grade. The other cheerleaders kicked her out. Our middle school athletic field is mostly dirt and the cheerleaders practice off to one side while the football players try to scrimmage on three-quarters of the field, so none of the girls get hit. She is annoying like a cheerleader. She is chewing gum which draws attention to her buck teeth.

Preacher Dan answers, "John Wesley is the founder of Methodism, so it's important that we-"

"Why was he only born in 1703? Why wasn't he born before Jesus? Didn't he flip in Cousin Elizabeth's womb or something?" Crystal asks.

Crystal is contemplative about her question. Maybe taking a class with eleven and twelve-year-olds was not a good idea. Tommy flips a bird at the girls when they are not looking.

"You're thinking of John the Baptist, Crystal." Preacher Dan corrects with great patience.

"*Um*, Crystal," Michael whispers. "John Wesley was an Anglican minister. The Anglican Church is a branch of Protestantism. So, Methodism isn't, in truth, that old."

"Well, son, I'm proud of you," Preacher Dan says.

"What is Protestantism? Is that like Chinese? Is there an opposite of Chinese food, like Japanese? Or, is Japanese food a sister food to Chinese since they both use chopsticks." Seth asks. He is either slow or hungry.

"No. We're not talking about Chinese food anymore, or their cheesecake," Preacher Dan starts raising his voice.

"Okay, so cheesecake is Chinese but not Methodist? I thought cheesecake was a New York thing. Are there Methodists in New York? Do Methodists eat cheesecake? Is that allowed after we're confirmed? If not, we should go on our field trip before sunrise on Easter morning." Anne says while looking confused.

"Oh, Anne," Preacher Dan says intentionally rocking and knocking the back of his head against the classroom wall. "Cheesecake isn't Chinese or Methodist. A cheesecake can't be Methodist because it doesn't have a soul."

The girl with pigtails, Crystal, is offended. "Excuse me, preacher man: My grandmother's cheesecake has soul."

"Crystal, I didn't mean to hurt your or your grandmother's feelings. I was not talking about soul food. As a matter of fact, I don't know why we're talking about food. We're supposed to be talking about John Wesley tonight."

Preacher Dan is a fount of patience, but this is getting old. The girls continue to chat about misplaced geography, international food, and field trips. Preacher Dan takes off his eyeglasses and rubs the top of his nose where his glasses' nose pads have rubbed his skin raw. Michael remains in silent support of his father.

Before Preacher Dan runs out of fortitude, I ask a question. "What happens when we die? Does everybody go to the same place? Or, are there like different rooms?"

"Well, Jason, I think I know why you ask and, let me say: I'm sorry. I think all Christian denominations go to the same place when we die. But, don't tell a Baptist that."

Preacher Dan quietly chuckles to himself as he repeats the word 'Baptist.' After a moment, Dan starts rolling in laughter. The laughter grows. It becomes contagious. We all start laughing with him even though we do not know why. The joke is over our heads.

"They think they'll be up there all alone. The Baptists believe in predestination. I'm sorry. I can't stop laughing." Preacher Dan explains.

"I don't think any of us will aloft to Heaven on the bodies and souls that we trampled on the way there," Seth says thoughtfully. "But not everyone agrees with me."

"What about Cath-o-dists? Do they go to Heaven? They're not Protestants." Tommy says while trying to look smart. He is not smart. I think he has had too many hits to the head.

"Son, they're not Cath-o-dists. They're called Catholics. And, I think most denominations believe that other denominations go to Heaven. Even, for example, the Orthodox and what not. So, yeah," Preacher says sounding more grounded. "Moving on..."

"I was in the locker room with Jeremy one day, and he said that the reason that he and Jennifer didn't die in the tornado that hit their trailer park was because they thought the man upstairs might be giving them another chance to repent, go to church, confess, and straighten out their lives," Tommy says in a matter-of-fact tone.

Preacher Dan answers, "Well, I don't know Jeremy or his family so I can't speak to their beliefs."

"Oh, you don't know them because they're Catholic. And, my grandmother says that all of them think that the rest of us are going to go to hell. They worship idols and speak in tongues. Do they handle snakes? Maybe they do. I'll ask my grandmother." Crystal says and sits back thoughtfully.

"Please don't. Please don't ask your grandmother. There appears to be some generational confusion about the finer details of Methodism." Preacher Dan says as he shakes his hands in the air.

The room grows quiet. We have broken the preacher. His face is turning bright red.

"Kids, I would surely like the honor of being your spiritual guide on this journey. I would like for all of us to come to some agreement that this class is important for these very reasons. Catholics have different beliefs than we do but they don't speak in tongues. Sometimes they have masses in Latin, which is an old language. Oh, my goodness, I want to answer all your questions. But, I'm going to have to take a walk. I need some air." Preacher Dan says as he exits the room.

With the preacher's exit, we're left to our own wiles. I can hear Preacher Dan's fine leather shoes walking down the hallway with the slightest heel click. Michael shrugs his shoulders to excuse his father's departure. Tommy makes an obscene gesture behind Anne's head, but the finger bobs in Seth's direction. Anne sees it out of the corner of her eye and scowls at Tommy.

Heather looks around like someone abandoned her at a bus depot. "Did he just leave? He can't just leave. What's wrong? Is class over? What are we supposed to do?"

"Sit down," I yell at the unruly group.

Because I am much older, at least to them, they listen immediately. Heather's eyes open and she crosses her ankle to assume a default lady-like position. Anne looks like she could be floating on a pink cloud somewhere. Crystal is thinking about food. The boys are glaring at me like I am their coach.

"Something that you all are going to have to learn in middle school is how to control what you're thinking on the inside of your heads and learn to keep it in there. Preacher Dan seems like a nice guy. I don't know him that well. But, we can't ask more of him than we would of any other teacher. Would you all talk like this in Miss Mead's class? No. Would you be this unfocused in Miss Shipp's class? Don't answer that." I say and laugh a little.

Seth speaks up, "Maybe if we had a chalkboard, you know? We have this board that we for scouts down the hall. Can we go get it?"

Michael, Tommy, and Seth burst out of the room. They leave me with the three girls. When I first sat down tonight, all the girls looked alike and sounded alike. Now I am starting to be able to tell them apart. I am emerging from a rough couple of years. I do not feel connected to this group, but want to feel that way. I feel older and more detached. I want to say something teacher-like to the girls, but I am uncertain what to say. The girls look young; almost like toddlers.

Clasping my hands together, I start, "I don't mean to yell at you three. But, we need to get through this class. I don't want Preacher

Dan to quit being a preacher because we couldn't work together as a group."

"We usually don't work with the boys," Heather says. "I mean, we're not allowed to play with them too much. The boys were really rough on the playground last year. Some girl got a bloody nose. The teachers keep us separated."

"Okay, Heather," I say as I start to see the issues coming together. "You are in a class with boys. You are not on a playground. Now that you fine ladies in middle school, you have a separate boy and girl teams for sports. So, you have to share the athletic field, but you don't have to play immediately around them if you don't want to fully integrate.

"But, you do have to work with them in class. When you're in class at school, you have to work with them then too, right? When you grow-up and go to college, you'll have to be in the same classes as boys. Unless you go to an all-girls school, which would be weird and I'm not sure if there are any in the state of Georgia anyway."

"There's Brenau up north, Wesleyan around Macon, and Agnes Scott in Atlanta, Mr. Know-it-all" Heather calls me out. She is all-cheerleader even if she did not know it yet. "And, besides, you're wrong."

"Oh, Catherine Marshall went to Agnes Scott," Anne peeps.

Anne is a fan of Catherine Marshall and the book *Christy*. My grandmother is too. Maybe Anne is just a young version of my grandmother. I hope Anne has better luck in her life than my grand-mother has had. My grandmother is fifty-one years old and raising a grandchild. I know it is hard on her, but she is my only family right now. Hopefully, Anne will not always be a little brown mouse.

"Excuse me, people," Crystal says. "There is also Spelman College. My mama went there. It is geographically the closest one to Douglas County of all of the ones y'all just mentioned. But, Heather's right. The teachers still separate out the boys and girls for almost all class projects. So, big man on campus, does that change next school year or what? Because I would look forward to something a little less academically challenging; you know, if we get to mingle with the boys and have to keep it simple so they can play along too."

Oh, that girl! She is a pistol, as my grandmother would say. I am madder than a hatter at each one of them. The system is culti-vating them into a 'separate is better' mentality. They will be ren-dered incapable of teamwork with the opposite sex. I blame the teachers. The teachers probably did not want to hear complaints from the parents because middle school boys are notoriously...well, whatever we are. *Dang it*! I hate being wrong but they are going to have to learn.

"I'll give the same speech to the boys, but we're all going to have to do the same work at the same time. So, we're not going to be throwing balls around every class. But, you know what? We're not going to be knitting either. It's going to be somewhere in between." I say. I feel flushed myself.

"It's a stereotype that girls knit," Heather says a moment before popping her gum.

"Well, actually, Heather, you do knit," says the innocuous Anne. Heather tries to kick a leg out from underneath Anne's chair. Instead, Heather hurts her foot on the antique solid wood student chair.

With that, I make a graceful exit to muddle around the church's hallways. After some time to cool down, I make my way to the scout storage room where I find the preacher and three boys hiding. They pat me on the back and thank me. Apparently, my voice echoed to the floor below through the vents. They heard some of what had just happened. But, hiding out in the scout room was not a strategy. How did pulling this team together land on my shoulders?

"Get back in there, team," I say jokingly. "There is church lady potluck food at the finish line."

"Well, hot shot, the high-schoolers already ate all the hamburgers. I think we're stuck with hot dogs." Michael says full of remorse.

Tommy speaks up, "I want to ask something serious of you all."

We look around the room and wait for Tommy to say something stupid. Maybe his brain works like a lightning flash. His words could be brilliant or pitiful.

"If we all die, then that means that someday I'll die too," Tommy says in a meek tone.

"Yes, son," Preacher Dan says. "You will unless the Lord comes first."

"Well, if I die, and you guys are around, tell my mom. I would hate for her to get a call from someone that didn't know me, like a nurse or something. And, I want someone to tell all my teachers and coaches, so they aren't looking for me." Tommy says tearfully.

"Bless you, Tommy. Have you ever known anyone that died?" Preacher Dan says and puts an arm gently around his shoulder. The preacher had taken for granted that his son, Michael, had grown up knowing about life and death a little bit more. Tommy has been sheltered or had a lucky family.

"No. I heard that my dad's first wife died a long time ago, but I never knew her. She had cancer or something. He doesn't talk about her; or, if he does, it's not when I'm around." Tommy says as he looks at some scabs on his knees.

I feel older and more responsible than I did five minutes ago. So I make the impossible offer. "Tommy, I'll do it if I'm still alive. I'll call your mom and tell everybody at school. But, I think you'll probably outlive us all. You are younger than me. Maybe we'll end up in the same old folks home? *Hmm*?"

"Speaking of old folks home," Preacher Dan says. "We need to come up with a service project for you all. Who wants to go see the nice elderly folks at Wesley Woods before Easter?"

With that, the boys and girls teams were back in the same classroom and coming up with ideas to entertain the sick and elderly. The group decided that we would all go to a Chinese restaurant in Atlanta on the way back. That way, Heather could have Chinese food and cheesecake if the restaurant had it. We set out which roles to assume in the middle school version of the Story of the Crucifixion; or, alternatively named, Stations of the Cross if we wanted to invite our Catholic friends, Jennifer and Jeremy.

Anne's parents bring food up to our classroom. They set aside hamburgers and bags of chips for us. Michael's mother follows with a pitcher of sweet tea. Plans start to hash out. We make a commitment to the next seven weeks of confirmation classes. Commitment is not my strong suit, so this feels like a big deal for me.

Crystal volunteers to play the role of Mary. Preacher Dan assigns the role of Angel in the Garden to Anne. The little brown mouse will be perfect. Heather gets to play Mary Magdalene. Absent Matt draws the short stick and has to play Pontius Pilate. He will have the most dialogue to memorize.

Seth will play Peter. Tommy will play Jesus. I would have liked to play Jesus, but I will be a Roman soldier. Michael will be Julian the Baptist because Crystal says that he should. Alicia will be Judas because she did not show up today. I sorry bad for her, and I have never met Alicia.

Thankfully, my role also means memorizing fewer lines than the others. We will recruit the fourth and fifth graders to be extras; that is if they wake-up on time and made it to the sunrise service. I hope we can pull this together as a class and get through confirmation without a hitch.

"Preacher Dan, I'm here. My parents dropped me off. I guess I'm supposed to do stuff here, but the pageant ran long." A tiny girl with a flat face and red lips says as she enters the classroom door.

The red-lipped girl captures my attention. She is still wearing her pageant sash on top of her everyday clothes. She is wearing stage makeup and has big hair. I have never seen someone our age wear bright red lipstick. She looks all wrong because her body makes her look like she's in first grade. When she sits down, I hear Heather tell her that her right eyelashes are falling. How can eyelashes be loose? Is that contagious?

"I have stuff for you to do," Tommy says in an annoying fashion.

"Shut up your mouth before I make you shut it!" The girl says. She is tougher than she looks.

Anne's mother leans over to Preacher Dan, "That's Alicia Kennedy."

"Alicia, you'll be playing the role of Judas." Preacher Dan declares.

"I don't want to," Alicia says in a smug tone. "I'll be Mary."

"No. Crystal is Mary. Crystal was also on time. Judas is what was left over." Preacher Dan says in a firm voice.

"Was anyone else late?" Alicia asks.

"Matt hasn't made it here yet." Preacher Dan says. His face is turning red again.

"Well, what was Matt assigned?"

"Pontius Pilate." The girls tell Alicia.

"I'll be Pilate. I don't have a problem with having real or fake blood on my hands. I've had some acting classes." Alicia says. She sits up straight in her seat after declining a hamburger.

"That's not for you to decide, Alicia." Preacher Dan says. She's too defiant.

"Think about it, Dan. Do you want someone reliable to memorize the longest speaking role in the sketch or not?" Alicia says tersely.

"Yes, that is why I'm assigning Matt to that part."

"Matt's probably busy hanging out with Ryan or some other non-church going folk. The company you keep, y'all." Crystal says.

"Matt is a natural leader and honorable scout. I trust him." Preacher Dan says, and his ruling is final.

Alicia scoffs and rolls her eyes. There is no satisfying that one. My grandmother would slap the crap out of her without batting an eyelash. I thought the other girls were irritating, but Alicia is the worst. I am so glad that I do not have to repeat sixth-grade again. I forgot how tedious sixth grade girls were.

There is a bitter cattiness to middle school girls. Maybe the teachers are right after all. In keeping the genders separated, they are sincerely protecting us boys. Girls in my class have started to pull back a little because they're ready to start dating boys. They think they can fool us into overlooking what we've been through the past two to three years. *Nuh, uh*: I am not forgetting.

Easter is going to be new and different this year. If all goes to plan, we will be baptized, and commit our lives to the Lord. Then, one day, we will go to Heaven and see each other again after we die. Preacher Dan will be there. My grandmother will be there. My parents will be there. It will be like a church picnic where there are enough seats for everyone, but no extras are necessary because everyone we know will be there.

Wait a minute: That means that the girls will be there too. Well, that is okay. If we all die at the same age, like we were all born in about the same years or grades, then I will have two years of quiet out of all eternity because these girls are two years younger than me.

Twenty: Ryan

◆————————————————————◆

September 9, 1996 9:09 AM
Douglas County High School

My fall schedule is messed up. I do not know which old biddy does the scheduling for students these days. Our scheduler may be a stupid computer in some random administrator's office. Nineteen ninety-six is the year of change. Standing in a line, with my hat in my hand, is not the way that I wanted to start my junior year.

Since last school year, the county schools have transitioned to block scheduling. For the 1996-1997 academic year, students attend eight classes, or blocks, a year instead of seven. Now, after spending two years in the extra hard English classes, I am not registered for gifted American Literature with everyone else this fall.

Missing gifted American Literature has to be an oversight. I thought starting the school year late due to the Olympics would have given them more time to iron out the kinks. My knickers are in a knot today for sure, as Mrs. Couch would say.

"Ryan, is that you?" Tommy says with a pat on my back. "I didn't recognize you with the whiskers, man. You know the ladies prefer a man with a clean face. They don't want scratchy kisses or other oral delights. *Ha!* Why weren't you in class this morning? I planned on you taking notes and me copying them later. You're going to have to fight for a textbook, man. I didn't see any extra on Couch's desk."

"I didn't realize that Am Lit had already happened. I'm in weight lifting for the first block. What did you talk about?" I ask.

"No, man. You have to show up before school to get your textbook. Mrs. Couch doesn't want to waste time on that during the first day of school. Did you not get a note over the summer? Did your mom get a phone call? I don't know how it all works. I'm living for four twenty this afternoon, if you catch my drift." Tommy says with a half-baked smile.

Block scheduling was not the only walloping change over summer 1996. My parents split up, unofficially, over the summer. I think my mom caught my dad cheating. He went to some fancy soiree and misbehaved. That happens to old men sometimes when they are outside their old lady's immediate supervision. Old folks are worse than neutered yard dogs. They make bad decisions that ruin everyone's lives.

Now, Dad will not let Mom have the house because he likes his rose garden too much. But she is too stubborn to move out and lose her chance at maintaining her status in old society. Mom and Dad hate each other but will not do anything about their sour marriage. It is like *War of the Roses* or *Madam Bovary*.

"See you at practice this afternoon? You know you can't show up to practice high, right? The coach will know and take it out on all of us. He has a zero-tolerance policy or something. I wouldn't cross the lines this year, dude. You know you have to be discreet, right?" I ask knowing the answer.

"Always. Don't let the office trolls hassle you too much." Tommy says. He waves and exits the school's front office.

Douglas County High School's front office has two sections: attendance and everything else. I am next in line for the 'everything else' side when one of the office ladies escorts a fellow junior, Stephanie Lee, behind the counter. I hate that she has cut in line in front of me. I have been waiting for almost thirty minutes and missing my first class of the day.

"Miss Lee, you are not starting off the school year on the right foot." A woman admonishes Stephanie.

"Can I start on the left foot then? I'm wearing wedges on both." Stephanie smart mouths back.

Office ladies do not reward patience. In this school, students who succeed are those who elbow their way up to the big kids' table. If our local newspaper still had society pages, you would find Stephanie there: front and center. She knows how to elbow and get her way. That is what comes of having parents with generations of steadfast affluence, as opposed to my situation, which is having parents who spent generations of solid capital. That has left me and my brothers high and dry.

"You shouldn't play with your reputation, Miss Lee. People will think you're a tart. Tarts don't go to college. Just because wedges, short shorts, and camisoles are in fashion doesn't mean that they are allowed at school. You're causing a distraction!" The office lady says while flipping through some cards.

"In your personal experience, what happens to a tart?" Stephanie says. She rolls her eyes.

"I have no personal experience with tarts because they're not allowed at Douglas County High School. If you have that attitude, you can transfer to Lithia or Alexander. I hear Lithia has a unique in-school daycare program for teen moms. That's straight where you're headed if you don't adhere to school dress code."

My anger gets the better of me. I shove my arms into my jacket pockets so hard that my fists break through the worn fabric. The office lady throws a glance in my direction and puts her forefinger up for me to wait another moment. My first-grade teacher had the same habit. We must all look like whiny babies to them.

"Trust me. Douglas County boys aren't seeing anything that the international community didn't already bring to Atlanta over the summer. The swimmers, runners, and other athletes wore far less than me." Stephanie complains to unsympathetic ears.

"And, where are they now? Scuttled back to their countries of origin, yes? Under the thumbs of their dictators and kings? Wearing what they're told when they're told. And, not smart mouthing to their elders. When I was your age, the school staff measured our skirt length using yard sticks and chairs in this very office." The office lady says with a stern face.

Stephanie has the thick Prentice Hall American Experience Literature Book under her arm. It is blood red and has a pioneer touching a Sequoia tree on the cover. I hate that Stephanie is in gifted Am Lit. It is the end of the first period of the first day, and she has already started. I am behind.

"Whatever." Stephanie retorts with too much attitude.

"That's it, Little Miss Sassafrass! I'm calling your parents to come pick you up. It will be counted as an unexcused absence. You could have saved that some time for Homecoming dress shopping, but, no. You had to waste one today proving you're headed for social ruin."

The office lady picks up the telephone handset up off the switch hooks. She references a blue parental contact card and presses seven numbers with the end of a pencil. Stephanie sits down in a chair next to the office lady's desk. The desk plate reads, "Miss G. Clinton." Good luck to Stephanie. Old Lady Clinton used to rock on her front porch holding a shotgun daring anyone to challenge her.

Miss Clinton clears her throat. She speaks slowly into an over-sized transmitter, "Mr. Lee, this is Douglas County High School. We're going to need you to come and get your daughter, Stephanie. Her denim cutoffs are so short we can see her religion. Shorts, dresses, and skirts must be knee-length. There are no exceptions. She's in violation of school dress code and cannot return to class."

After a brief commotion on the other end of the phone, the office lady looks at Stephanie and says, "Well, you apparently have a get-out-of-jail free card. Your father says you can leave school in your car. He says to go to Cumberland Mall and buy some longer pants. I will tell you that you will be tardy upon your return, Miss Lee. You are a junior and knew the school dress code before you showed up this morning. You are not setting a good example for the freshmen and sophomores, for shame. You are the first student to earn detention this school year. Congratulations."

Stephanie smiles smugly. She snatches her backpack from her lap. She slings it over one shoulder and exits the front office with her Mustang keys out. You can do that when you parents can afford to buy you a car and let you drive it to school. I had to suffer in silence while riding the bus this morning. It is rare for junior or seniors to ride the school bus here. It indicates that you are poor, both of your parents work full-time, or your parents do not want to take the time to drop you off at school. Those three situations are each a badge of shame.

The commotion over her nasty shorts thrills Stephanie. She thrives on being the center of attention. There are convicts in the county jail with a stronger moral backbone than her. Once she was out the door, I become on the so-called student chopping block.

Miss Clinton sneers at me, "Sir, are you homeless? You can't just walk into the high school."

My school clothes are hand-me-downs from my older brother, Rick. Rick stole them from our oldest brother, Chris. The rags are humiliating, but I have to keep them in decent condition for my younger brother, Josh. They are Tommy Hilfiger, but well-worn and out of fashion. I hate being a middle child.

Swallowing my pride, I answer, "Yes, ma'am. I'm a student. I'm a junior. I need to talk about my schedule. I'm a gifted student. I need to be placed in my gifted classes like I do every year. There should be no exceptions this year."

"Oh, no. Another one of Mrs. Couch's students has made the pilgrimage to the front office to complain. Let me guess. You want into Am Lit." Miss Clinton says.

"Yes, ma'am," I reply. My stomach is full of butterflies.

"Due to block scheduling, not all of the gifted students can take every single class together anymore. Sorry, kiddo."

"That's not fair. I never registered for weight lifting. What am I going to do with a class in weightlifting? I'm going to be a writer. Mrs. Couch loves my writing."

"She says that to all the underperforming ones. Don't worry. I'm sure there is a bright future for you in weight lifting. Most of the other classes are full. Are you eligible to take CL Calculus?"

"What? No. I'm a junior. I still need Trigonometry. I won't be able to take that until next semester: Spring 1997."

"Do you want a student slot in Russian? Drafting? Maybe a typing class?"

"No. I'm going to be a writer. What will I do with those? I need to take American Literature from the best teacher on campus. I deserve that."

"Oh? So now you're entitled, and your classmates are not. Every teacher here thinks that they're the best teacher on campus. I can assure you that the teacher that you have in the spring semester will still be challenging and quite exceptional. He or she will think they're the best teacher on campus too."

"Okay, fine. Is the spring semester teaching the exceptional kids as well? Teaching a gifted class requires extra training and certifications. I am exceptional in every way. I want my class schedule and transcript to reflect the challenge level of the classes I'm taking."

"I don't think you understand how our school system defines exceptional. You are thinking about the label gifted. But, if you want an exceptional education teacher, I can arrange something. It will require a parent-teacher conference and some testing. You'll fit right in, I'm sure."

"Yeah. You probably don't want my dad showing up here. He owns-"

"I don't care who your father works for, son. I work for Douglas County High School. I'm sorry to be the one to tell you that you can't always get what you want. You cannot be in Mrs. Couch's gifted American Literature class this fall. Case closed."

"But, then how will I ever find a job as a writer?"

"You can always find a way to pursue your dreams. Be creative."

"But, you don't understand. Clearly, if you understood then we wouldn't be having this conversation. Anyone worth hiring in this county as a writer has to go through all four years of Mrs. Couch's gifted program or she won't recommend them. She doesn't write recommendations for just anyone. You have to be in the program and score a four or higher on the College Level test. Block scheduling is insane. You're trying to mess up my entire future!"

"What's your name?"

"Ryan Bearden."

"Ryan, you're not getting into Mrs. Couch's class. She handpicks the students that she wants each year. You didn't make the list."

"What? What list?"

"Not everyone who goes through the first two years of gifted English is allowed into the third and fourth years. Do you understand now?"

"What? That's insane. You can't tell me that this has all been a waste of time?"

"It hasn't. I'm confident that you've learned valuable skills. There is a line behind you."

"But, what do I do?"

"Go to your next class, Ryan." Miss Clinton says. She looks over my shoulder and yells, "Next!"

"No," I mutter.

"Ryan, I will call the school resource officer in here."

"What's a resource officer?"

"Oh? You haven't had the pleasure. Let me help you with that."

I stand here, in the front office, like a docile idiot. I do not know who to appeal to, or call. A white-haired man dressed in a generic police uniform comes to the front office's window and knocks on it. I nod and walk out. The officer keeps his hands on his belt. He puffs up his chest like a cartoonishly bloated blowfish.

My feet should have taken me through the cafeteria and down to the Warren-Dorris building for Chemistry. But, as my feet keep taking steps, I realize that I am walking through Mashburn Hall and towards the Banks building. In a blur, I realize I am walking down the stairs to Lower Banks and the English department.

Before I can take a breath, I realize that I am standing in Mrs. Couch's classroom. Her senior English students are sitting down.

My mouth is open and dry. I do not know what to say. All I can manage is a wide-eyed stare. She has betrayed me and my family's trust.

"Get out of here, Ryan, unless by some miracle you're suddenly a senior. You don't want to cause a scene. I will talk to you and your father later about what has happened." Mrs. Couch says.

Mrs. Couch is wearing the same dress that she always wears on the first day of school. She continues to wear dresses with shoulder pads even though my mom stopped wearing clothes with them long ago. There are tiny needlepoint chalkboard earrings in Mrs. Couch's ears. She only wears those on the first day of school. Her entire wardrobe revolves around the academic year. She has been wearing the same wardrobe since before I was born. I heard my father talk about that once. Mrs. Couch and I are cousins by marriage once removed.

"No, Mrs. Couch. Please. I just want to ask why. I thought that I was a good enough writer to be in your gifted Am Lit class. I want to take CL English with you next year. Why?"

Mrs. Couch shuffles me to the hallway. I feel like she is banishing me from the Garden of Eden. I look down at her. I must have grown over the summer but did not notice until now.

She places a hand on my shoulder and says, "This is what's best for you right now. I purposefully had the back office scheduler alter your class enrollment so that you would be able to take journalism both this fall and spring as your electives. My colleague, Mr.

Boatright, is an exceptional writer himself, outside of teaching. Mr. Boatright teaches as both a practitioner and expert."

"But, I won't be eligible for College Level English next year. What will I do?"

"There are different routes to take to get you where you need to go. Trusting that your teachers know what is best for you right now is the first step. Now, please excuse me."

"Why don't you believe in me?"

"It's not that I don't believe in you, Ryan." Mrs. Couch says with a face full of scorn. "Can you give me an example of an adverb? Right here, right now. Give me a single adverb."

"I don't know what an adverb is."

"That's second or third grade English at most schools across the country. Give me a subordinate clause."

"I have no clue about subordinate clauses, Mrs. Couch. Why does this make any difference to me? I want you to help me be the best writer that I can be."

"You are young. You can't see the wood for the trees. You don't know how much you don't know. Do you even know what's on the College Level test?"

"Senior English? British Literature? I know all about that. I've read Shakespeare this summer."

"No. Not at all, Ryan. It is English language and composition. Now, get to whatever class you need to be in. I've given you a much longer leash than I ever have any of my other students."

"I will hit on a path to get into a gifted American Literature program. If not Douglas County, then I'll transfer high schools."

"You would transfer into a sub-par program to prove me wrong? How? Are you moving?"

"My dad owns properties and houses all over this stupid ass county. I can say that I live wherever I want to, Mrs. Couch. But I would rather be here in class with you."

"That's not happening this year, Ryan. I should give you detention for using foul language, but you're not one of my students this semester. You're not anyone's English student this semester. You need to leave this hallway. Deal with your disappointment, however you see fit."

"I'll talk to my dad."

"Please do and give him my regards."

"He could pull his financial support from Mr. Couch's campaign."

"My job as department chair has nothing to do with my husband's politics. How you choose to communicate with your father is your business. I do not allow students to threaten me. Good day."

Mrs. Couch retreats into her classroom only to slam the door in my face. With deft precision, she calls the class to order and starts issuing textbooks. I gawk at the class longer than I should. Within sixty seconds of calling the class to order, Mrs. Couch is administering a quiz on her summer reading assignments. It is *Madam Bovary*.

A rage is burning inside me. It feels like a nuclear reactor of hormones, emotions, anger, frustration, and disappointment in myself. The circumstances have melted together into a whirlpool of melancholy. Now I know part of what the Smashing Pumpkins were describing in *Mellon Collie and the Infinite Sadness*.

A heavy weight falls on my shoulders as I walk from the Banks building through the cul-de-sac and towards Warren-Dorris. I love this high school. I do not want to transfer. But, I will be damned if that witch gets the better of me. I do not want her keeping me from my dreams. I do not want teachers telling me that, at age sixteen, I cannot be a writer. I do not want any adults telling me what to do at all. I am an adult.

Stopping in the school's cul-de-sac, I look toward the junior parking lot, across the weight lifting room, football field, and behind the gymnasium. My family has attended Douglas County High School for four generations. I cannot imagine going anywhere else. It makes me sick at my stomach.

"Hey, man. What's up? Where are you headed to?" Matt says as he crisscrosses the cul-de-sac.

"Chemistry. I'm late." I admit. Matt will not squeal.

"I didn't see you at book pick-up this morning for Couch's class."

"Screw, Couch. She's a bitch. You know how these women get when they get a little bit of power. She's riding her power trip on her red rag of glory right now, dude."

Matt says, "What? But your dad is..."

"I know, man. It's not fair. But, I don't give a shit. I'm thinking about skipping Chemistry right now anyway."

What would my father do if this were him? He would find a method to get his way. If he did not get his way, he would seek out revenge. He would take bribes and gain strategic political allies. That is what he had done with his cousin and Mrs. Couch's husband, Old Joe. Old Joe is dirty.

Joe has his fingers in everyone else's pies. He has a long memory and a detailed catalog of the entire county's gossip and sin for three or more generations. That is how Joe gets what he wants. Brian has shunned his parents' ways, but I have a feeling he will stop judging us and get with the program soon.

Joe and my dad are real men to me. They do not want to be puppets with some know-nothing teacher pulling their strings; telling them when to dance and when to be quiet. No! If they were in my situation, they would become the puppet master and buy the whole sideshow carnival while they were at it. They would own and control the situation. Even though I feel helpless and out of control now, I will not be by the end of tonight.

"I'm blowing this place, man. Wanna come with me?" I ask Matt.

Matt nods for a moment, thinking. "Nah, dude. Thanks. I think the teachers and administrators would figure it out if both you and I were missing at the same time. That could be bad news. Where are you headed?"

"Home." I lie.

"Do you mean your mom's place? That's a walk. Do you have a car this year? Did something work out?"

"*Nah.* I'm going to walk to my parents' old house. I know where they have hidden a key." I say. At least that sentence is mostly true.

"*Wow.* I didn't know your parents still owned your old house. That place brings back memories. We buried a pet back there, right?"

"Miss Nutterbutterworth," I say with a smile.

"Yeah, that was crazy. Who knew that squirrel would climb a bird feeder."

"I don't want to talk about it." I say. I look down at my grungy shoes.

"If you leave, dude, make sure that you're not the next Nutterbutterworth, okay?"

"What does that mean!?!" I yell at Matt. He's not making any sense.

"I'm only saying not to forget that teachers will miss you. When you don't show up for your classes, one of the office ladies will call your parents and stuff." Matt says.

"I'm not in the gifted classes anymore, Matt. No one will miss me. The regular teachers have no idea who we are. Plus, my parents won't care. They're busy with their new lives. That's the advantage of being child number three."

"Oh, dude. I would love to know that feeling. My mom is all over me. But, I'm her only child, you know? No brothers or sisters to distract her. She's constantly in my business. No matter where I hole up in the house, she is always following me and asking questions. I love her to death, but I need to breathe a little. She's always pretending to put my clothes away and going through my drawers and stuff."

"You're lucky, dude. My mom is burned out. She doesn't want to have anything to do with her Bearden boys anymore." I say. It hurts to speak the truth aloud.

"What's going on?" Matt questions. He thinks my parents are having a typical divorce.

"Nothing. My mom just wants us all to grow up, you know?"

"Well, you can't quit being a mother, right? She'll come around." Matt says. He is thinking about his mom, Ms. Miranda. Ms. Miranda would not give up.

"I don't care if my mom does or doesn't. Later! I have a date with Mary Jane."

"C'mon, Ryan. Go to class and we'll meet up after school."

"F-it, dude. I'm over this place." I say.

Without bothering to wave goodbye to Matt, I leave the campus as quickly as possible. I pass the Shehane Gym. I walk down Selman Drive. I am off campus in less than a minute.

I am leaving. I am not telling anyone. I am going to be a man about it. I am walking off this campus and never coming back. If they want my textbook from my first-period class returned, they can come knocking on my door with their hats in their hands.

Stephanie has it going on. She has learned how to work the system in her favor. She even got out of jail for free today; well, almost free. I am going to be like Stephanie. I am going to take advantage of coming from a family with money and education. I am going to work the system, so the system does not end up working me. I am not going to be anyone's stooge. I am going to forge my writing career through gritted teeth.

Stupid junior class president Stephanie can manufacture her floral shit bouquet of soirees and pep rallies. I do not want to participate. She thinks that she speaks for the class when she only speaks for herself and her cronies. Her greatest concern this fall will be dress shopping for Homecoming because it is a foregone conclusion that she will be representing the Class of 1998 in the Homecoming court. I know exactly where the money to pay for her dress will come from, that materialistic slut. I know what her head looks like from behind when she is bobbing for apples.

My mother was Homecoming queen here, on this exact football field, decades ago. Look where that dumbass title got her! Nowhere. Douglas County is full of former Homecoming Queens and their all-too-common husbands. In an effort to replicate the social structure of high school, they join golf clubs and sleep with each other's wives. Phony ass pricks. My dealer is more loyal than my father.

Mrs. Couch thinks that I am Madam Bovary. She is underestimating me. She has placed me in the same category as my mother: subordinate. I am not going to be like her, or like my mom. I am not going to pine away my life dreaming about something better. I am going out into the world getting it. I am taking the initiative. I will not be a victim of my circumstances. I will not be the one with arsenic in my mouth at the end of the day.

Twenty-One: Stephanie

The ten-year high school reunion will be the death of me. Like a scalding desert wind, I must face the burning flames of my youth. Instead of building friendships, I acquired useful people to stuff into a virtual curio cabinet. People came and went from my life as I deemed them useful. It was all for not. Today is the day to pay the piper, and I must learn how to tweedle in the next five minutes, or fail.

My mother slowly revealed her ambitions for my life over time. Through my college graduation, she was the driver. I was a backseat passenger to my destiny. She wanted me to marry anyone from anywhere other than Douglas County, Georgia. Without batting an eyelash, she would have twisted her Southern morals for me to engage in a strategic sexual partnership with a wealthy California lesbian. She told me that you could love the money. Her plan was always for me to be a prosperous man's trophy wife.

Like a rose slowly blooming from spring into summer, I always assumed that I would continue to blossom throughout the summer of my life and into the fall and winter. But, tonight, I realize that my mother's devious plots for me stopped on my first day of summer. Now, I am here. My husband assumed the driver seat on the day that we were married. Now, he's gone; if not technically then emotionally. I am left to wilt and die in the garden where I was planted.

Michael, a high school acquaintance, is speaking to me over my cell's speakerphone as I stand half-dressed and sweating on an empty ballroom floor. There is a cold sweat dotting my forehead as I hear his words slur into my ears.

"What do you mean there is another reunion, shithead!" I scream into my LG Chocolate.

Michael hangs up on me. He'll have to learn the art of forgiveness. Why did I appoint him the spiritual leader of the class? Oh, I was not thinking the night of Melissa and Tommy's wedding. I would say something horrible about Michael this moment, but everyone else here loves him.

I stop clicking along in my Ted Baker silver platform heels, pause, and spin on the left heel to face Heather and Nicole. "Ladies, it is show time. We're going to set out a few fewer tables than we thought we needed. Actually, let's just set up eight. People don't have to sit on their butts to socialize. We'll make it look like we never planned on a hundred people showing up. They can have their drinks and moan without the rest of us."

"Stephanie, what are you not telling us?" Heather asks sharply with her eyebrows scrunched.

"Well, then, I'll be blunt. There is dissension in the ranks. Michael, Melissa, and friends abandoned ship. It appears that one of our peeps may have organized a surrogate reunion." I grit my teeth so hard that I am certain they will break. I am glad they're veneers.

"What? Why? Is it the healthy food? The lack of free alcohol?" Heather says and looks disheartened.

"No, it can't be the healthy food," I say. "Melissa, Preeti, Michael, and Matt are all at the alternate reunion. Melissa is a lipstick lesbian vegan that doesn't drink alcohol. Preeti is a high-strung uneducated slut, but that wouldn't cause her miss an opportunity to wear a push-up bra and flash a business card. Michael is not in his right mind, evidently. I don't know how he's still living in Douglasville. He's been flying under the radar for a while. Matt is a jailbird meth head, so I know why he's not here. I saw that his address is his family's old address from high school. He's probably homeless. *Ew.* It's hard to imagine that some of us grew up to be homeless people."

"You've certainly kept track of everyone," Nicole says with a concerned look. "Do you know who has HIV, rides dirty, or sleeps with a nightlight? You're police, judge, and jury all in one."

"It's a little creepy, Stephanie," Heather admits.

"I'm simply organized. I want to have enough food for the guests present. People in Douglas County don't know what RSVP means." I say in a frustrated voice.

"I know what RSVP means, Stephanie, and I live in Douglas County. Don't get mad at us. Maybe this isn't a personal slight against you." Heather says with a calm voice of reason.

Touching my closed phone to my lips, I look around the room at the empty chairs knowing that the optimal situation would be for them to be full. At this point, each person that attends lowers the cost per person price and increases any financial gains that the girls may have.

The new information makes me itch. I was already itching from the oppressive humidity, but it is markedly worse now. Sweat soaks through my silk slip. I would give anything for a towel to sit on. Right now I regret skipping sensible cotton briefs.

David and Carrie walk through the door all smiles. I hate them. I loathe their happiness. I despise their sunshine farts and dope addict unicorn eyes. I roll my eyes and sulk off the dance floor. They can revel in a grotesque display of emotion without my oversight.

"Heather! Nicole! How are my favorite wedding caterers?" David says hugging Nicole.

Carrie adds, "Well, our only wedding caterers, David. That is until we have an anniversary party one day. Right, David?"

I close my eyes to try to think of what to do. I posted all of the information on MySpace, Facebook, Classmates.Com, and asked someone to post something on Twitter. I even paid out-of-pocket to advertise in the Douglas County Sentinel, in print and online.

What was I thinking? This expensive little soiree is a disaster. I figured it was a clear 'yes' when Heather and Nicole mentioned it to me. But, now that it is an hour before the reunion and the ballroom is vacant, I estimate that the presale of tickets will just cover my out-of-pocket expenses. My husband can afford this folly, thank goodness. His purse strings are looser than Alicia's ethics.

Pulling a chair over, I say, "What was that saying that I saw somewhere on the World Wide Web while putting all of our reunion information out there? Something about, 'When I die, I want my classmates to be my pallbearers so they can let me down one last time.'"

Nicole laughs out loud, but Heather is not amused. Heather starts calculating. She has grown-up. She is not the same Heather that I knew in school. The Heather and Nicole that I grew up with would have never settled on being food truck operators. I do not even know what Nicole meant when she said people were driving dirty cars. Nicole is so behind the times. The girls roll like rejected cafeteria hags on wheels. David is not judging them since his mother was a lunch lady, but everyone else will. How will I tell them that this is all their faults?

Heather says, "It's an hour until food service. We can divide the food in half and save the other half and offer it tomorrow at a park or something. I had calculated enough food for all presale and estimated an additional fifty percent more would attend at the last minute. So the difference is serving seventy people verses one hundred, give or take. It's not terrible. We will manage."

"What? Did you plan on fellow students not attending? Because I was counting on all three hundred and four of us, or whatever, being here tonight. That's why I booked a big facility!" I scream waving my arms in the air of the large banquet room where we are standing.

"I thought some of your classmates passed away," Carrie says.

"There are no excuses for skipping the ten-year reunion!" I answer.

Ever the shrewd businesswoman, Heather says, "That's nice, Stephanie, but it's not good business. I would never plan for a number like that. On the one hand, I don't want anyone to go hungry; but, on the contrary, I'm not feeding people for free. Everyone can have a polite amount of food. You know what? In a few cases, people can have an impolite amount of food. But, I never planned on everyone being here. I told you that we would cater based on numbers and we will."

My head is spinning. I hear Third Eye Blind's "Semi-Charmed Life" swirling around like I am in a tornado. For a moment I wonder if I am the only one that can hear it. David and Heather steady me a little. I see Nicole trying to talk to me, but I choose not to hear her.

I can only hear nineties alternative music in my brain right now. Next, I close my eyes and start seeing pierced eyebrows,

Abercrombie and Fitch plaid shirts, and halter tops with high-waisted jeans. My feet almost feel as though they are walking in a parade along Campbellton Street. There are swirly visions of Tommy Lee Jones in *Men in Black*. It all competes for my attention when I finally sit down.

Nicole is standing next to me. She blurts out, "Stephanie is going through fertility treatments right now. We need to keep an eye on her."

"Traitor," I cry and kick off my heels in her direction. "That was confidential."

"Stephanie, we need to know that. We want to take care of you, okay? Let us help you through this. If you're trying to get pregnant, you cannot stress out about this. It's not optimal for you or the baby." Carrie says soothingly. She rubs her bursting belly.

Who is she? *Ack.* I do not want her here. Why does Professor Carrie have to be so nice? Does she not know we come from Douglas County? We have arisen from a highly competitive and suddenly affluent area just outside of the Interstate-285 perimeter. I do not want her to bring tidings of comfort and joy to this show. I want her to bring in classmates, and she does not know anyone else. *Agh.* Your Rolodex will make or break you, and she does not have one.

"Carrie, Stephanie isn't really like that. She, more, um, well, what's the word?" Nicole says diplomatically.

"Amanda Wingfield!" David says, wearing a wicked grin. "She's the meddling mom from *The Glass Menagerie* that drove the narrator away. Tim? Tom? Whoever."

"Shut your pie hole, fatty!" I bark at David. "I am not a shadow of a former Southern debutante. I have drive. None of you know me at all. I have connections that you would piss in your pants to know. I want everything a certain way. I want to bring refined sensibility to our little celebration here. I want things to be tasteful instead of us all acting like we've taken two steps out of public housing squalor. This reunion would be in a dilapidated county gazebo near the train tracks if the majority ruled. I want..."

"You want to pretend that we went to McEachern instead of Douglas County. I know. I get it." Heather says. "We started high school in a rural Georgia suburb and graduated four years later from a suburban metropolitan high school whose faculty had not quite caught up with the times. But, Stephanie, maybe you need to give some credit to other people for evolving into cultured and sentient adults. Not everyone is like you; but, you know what? Not everyone wants to be like you either."

Wench. Heather nailed it. I would rather eat broken glass than tell her she is right, though. Heather knows nothing of the pain that today is causing me. Yet, I know some of her deep-rooted agonies, and Nicole's too. Brian Couch will be here. He is a knife that twists in all of our backs.

"Heather, aren't you supposed to be working? Nicole? Cat got your tongue? Get to work, ladies. The food won't walk itself out here and look presentable." I say sharply. I check the time on my Chocolate.

Brian will show up with his iTouch full of electronica music looking too cool for school. Brian used to have a thing for the prude Nicole, but she was married to her religion. My parents raised me without religion. My mother, Belle, planned for me to convert to whatever my husband's preference was. Right now, I am on the books as a Catholic, but that had not put Jesus any more in my heart now than it did in high school when Nicole popped off her impassionate sermons.

In the meantime, three or four girls walk into the ballroom. They look around the space as though they missed prom a decade ago. They were nobodies in high school. They are nobodies now. I still do not know them; even though I may be friends with them on MySpace. They approach me for hugs when I realize that I am still not wearing my gown over my lingerie. I decide to warm to them following a group compliment on my elegant dress. My dress is not a dress at all but, instead, a Victoria's Secret blush pink slip with contrasting lace detailing,

"These are tiny pieces of art," I say, looking at the pile of name tags. "I spent a lot of time on the name tags. My stepdaughter loathes me. But, I made her scan, copy, and paste the formal pictures from the yearbook onto the name tags. We had at least twenty-five class-mates move or drop out. I had to go back into even older yearbooks to find photos of them."

I had such attention to detail that no one else would appreci-ate. Do The Nobodies know how long that took? What about the newspaper staff? That took forever. Anne would have appreciated it. She would have seen the details and thanked me. No. She would not have thanked me. I would have delegated the task to her. I start riding a wave of tears.

"Can we get a picture together?" One fat girl asks.

"Certainly, dear. Do your dates want a picture with me too? I don't mind."

"Most of our husbands are watching our kids since you speci-fied that this was a child-free event."

"Well, let's all gather in and have a husband take the picture," I say with a plan in mind.

I start in the back of the five-person group. I turn around for a moment, tweak my nipples hard and turn back around. My nipples have a tendency to fall flat with my breast implants. I am a natural B cup but have worked my way up to a DD over the past six years. I try hard to keep my husband entertained with my body. He loves good under-aged breasts on a legal adult. I am not even wearing panties this evening, you know, in his honor.

"Ladies, say, 'Fromage.'" I utter through locked teeth.

The boyfriend-husband photographer blushes vermillion as I poke through the back of the line. The edges of my slip are barely covering my breasts and lady bits at the same time. I open my mouth and wink at him right as the camera flash fires. He licks his lips while taking a few more photos. In less than a minute, I hear the whir of the camera film auto-rewinding. I love it when I hog someone else's film. If one of the fatties gets a poke tonight, I want her boyfriend fantasizing about me.

As the girls disperse, the amateur photographer's eyes remain on me. I fake a listless look. I put a finger on the edge of my mouth. I pull my lingerie down just a little to expose my nipples. He gets off on seeing me. I get off on wasting his time. It is an old habit.

Heather walks up to me with a grimace on her face. She places a translucent bubbly concoction in my hand. She indiscreetly whispers, "Don't get too flushed. It's only gin. I would have thrown in some extra pills from people's pocketbooks if I could have gotten into them without being seen."

"Gin is my favorite. Oh, I don't do drugs. But, if the bartender is here, I would love a White Lady. A White Lady with two lines of cocaine would be amaze-balls. I think a pot brownie later would do wonders. But, when will that be? Sunrise? Probably." I say.

I slurp more loudly than I intended. My eyes cut around to see if anyone can hear us. Photographer boy is still staring at my nipples.

"Of course, not, Stephanie. You are a drug dog that sniffs out other people's crotch stashes and then consumes whatever you can before being discovered by your master."

"I would die for some x, Heather. Can you find some?" I whimper.

"No. What would Elizabeth Bennet do?"

"I am only asking if you saw anything while toiling in the kitchen. Lizzy is, like, my childhood hero but those days are long gone, girl. I don't expect you to be my sister wife, but I could use a little boost right now. I need it to compensate for all the hormones I'm on."

"You're a mom, Stephanie. You can't do this at the reunion. What if you decide to run, Mrs. Salvatore Russo, for political office? Your nipples will be on every social media site ever known to man. You're making bad decisions, Stephanie. I'm the friend who tells you to stop."

"You're not a friend. You're an employee."

"I don't have a contract with you, only a verbal agreement. Get off your high horse, Nose Job Barbie!"

"How blare you cobble me Blow Job Barbie!"

"I said *nose job*, Stephanie. You're drunk. You drank the gin too fast."

"I blount have anything on my chin," I say through puffy lips.

David walks over to us, "It's simply too early in the night for you to decide if this is a boom or bust deal. Stephanie, I can see your nipples. Heather, I can see your intentions. It's all good. It's all good, man."

Carrie places a frosty, wet paper towel on the back of my neck. I walk around in circles for what feels like a few minutes before my heels trip over themselves. My slip bunches around my waist, over my large breasts, and above my round butt. The boyfriend photographer appears with his camera and flash. As I lie on the floor, I think he is taking pictures of my lady bits. I do not know. It is all numb.

"Where's Anne?" I say through thick lips. "Where's Anne when I need her? She was my partner in all things related to school."

People would have shown up simply because they loved Anne. I miss her little black shoes with the cute embroidery on them. I would say, "Anne, I like your shoes" and then she would say, "Thank you. They like you too!"

"Is okay for me to say that I don't miss Tommy? Or is it too soon?" David says with sarcasm.

"Oh, no, David! If we're talking about my non-productive ovaries, then we can talk smack about Tommy's sorry ass. Go for it!" I say. I am bearing the burden of Tommy's promiscuity, along with my own.

I try to stand up, but my legs feel giggly. I tumble over the photographer-turn-voyeur. I hum something provocative in the photographer's ear. He steps away from me.

Noticing the question marks in my eyes, the photographer says, "Not tonight. Not ever. I don't want herpes. Thanks for the offer, though. Your c-section scar isn't even half bad. I could ignore that."

Ripples of humiliation touch the edges of my fingertips and then vibrate against the strings of my soul. I do have herpes simplex virus and human papillomavirus. The HPV was a wedding night gift from a thoughtless husband with two previous wives and countless questionable sexual encounters. From that moment forward, I have been living on the edge of summer and fall.

Oh, the shame. As I muddle through my moment of disrepute, I cannot decide if I am more upset that an ugly creeper turned me down for a quickie or that David now knows that I have an incurable sexually transmitted disease. I want to go to the bathroom and cut my wrists.

David walks over a few folding chairs. I sit down gracelessly. Heather appears from the back room with my street clothes instead of my gown. I do not feel like wearing a high-end suit right now, but it will have to do. Nicole slips off my heels. I will be barefoot, but not pregnant, for the night. I want to be pregnant.

Like a mother, Carrie wipes my face and hands with a wet wipe. She tidies my hair as I stare down at my magenta painted toes. Tears leak from my eyes, but I make no sound. Nicole fends off well-meaning classmates as they arrive. David sits next to me.

"Carrie and I saw Amanda at a convention. Carrie, Amanda, and Crystal are in the same field of study, a little bit." David says. He motions with his hands, almost apologetically.

"So, Carrie is a pediatrician? Amanda always wanted to be. That's nice," Nicole says.

"I am not a pediatrician. David, go ahead and tell them." Carrie charges him.

"Well, Amanda is in the nursing field now. And, in a strange way she helped out Matt and I a few years ago." He says. He pauses for a moment. "She works in emotional health."

"Wait. Did you say that Amanda helped you?" I questioned. "Did she, for example, throw you off a cliff, slit your wrists, or feed you poisoned food? Amanda does not help people. Amanda helps herself."

"Amanda saved my life." David defends her. "She helped contact my family after I overdosed in Las Vegas. Matt reached her through some lady at a coffee shop. Shoot, we didn't have coffee shops in Douglas County growing up, remember?

"When I woke up, Principal Daniell and my mom were in my hospital room. They saved my life. For a long time, I thought that Matt had abandoned me. Then I realized that he left so he could let the people that love me help me. We can't be around each other.

We'll use. Amanda and I have had long talks about addiction. She's supported my journey."

Shocked by the revelation that the boy that carried around a flask is an actual addict, I sit back down. He talks about his condition like he is okay with it; almost like he is not ashamed of it. After a minute, I realize that David is spilling his guts out to me because he thinks I am an addict too.

We, the Class of 1998, are the same age group as the degenerates from the PBS Frontline documentary "The Lost Children of Rockdale County." One of the few differences is Douglas County is ten miles west of Atlanta instead of east. Also, if there was a sexually transmitted disease outbreak, Douglas County health officials would remain discreet. My OB-GYN knows too much as it is.

"Look, Stephanie, here's the deal," David says while making a chopping motion with his right hand. "I'm a recovering addict and will always be a recovering addict. I'll always be an addict. But, I'm also a taxpayer, father-to-be, and clean."

Silently, I walk away from the group. The girls keep talking with their happy voices chattering over Carrie and her bump-to-be. It reminds me exactly of how people were giddy about Alicia having a baby. Why do people worship pregnant women? Pregnancy is a temporary condition, not an achievement.

The entire room is glaring me down. At first, it felt like it was just the five of us. But, now I feel like Anne is here too. I can hear the squeak of her shoes on the floor; it sounds so much like her voice when she's startled. I hear Tommy yelling football terminology off in some distant hallway. The room feels like it is moving back and forth. Next, I blink and think I see Mrs. Couch, but her hair is entirely white.

"Mrs. Couch? Welcome. We're so glad you're here," Nicole says hugging my apparition.

"There is something that I want to give to you, Stephanie. I think it is best suited for you to open since you are class president." Mrs. Couch says to me.

Mrs. Couch had a beautiful gift box in her hand. Navy and gold mesh ribbons decorate the rectangle box. To be a figment of my imagination, Mrs. Couch gives me a rather heavy box. Her hands are algid and dry. Magenta nail polish graces her press-on nails.

Lady Macbeth, the infamous Mrs. Couch, cannot be here. Other people keep speaking to her. Has she not retired yet? There is something on her face that I do not recognize at first. I cannot quite put my finger on it. After another moment and awkward silence, I see that she is smiling. We never saw her smile at school.

"Thank you, Mrs. Couch. I'm glad you're here too." I said, feeling seventeen again. I have such great respect for authority figures, even when they are not terribly good at being authority figures.

"Should I open it now?" I ask. I speak in a humble tone which is rare for me.

"No. I wrote it after *that day* in class. Then, I had something else important that needed to go into the box. I just added to it over time. I never told Brian, obviously. I had told my husband that if anything happened to me that he needed to take it to the reunion. But, glory be, I'm still here. So, here: take the box and open it tonight once everyone is here."

"Oh, so, you and your husband got back together," Nicole states shyly.

With grace, Mrs. Couch pauses and turns to me for a moment. She smiles once again before leaving. Shocked at her lack of familial attachment to Brian, I clutch my throat a little. It is like peeking into a vision of my future. I do not want to be like Mrs. Couch. I do not want to live in disappointment with other people. I do not want unhappiness to follow me wherever I go.

I want to love each of my children, no matter what they do or who they are. I think about Zora who is home with my husband. She is there with Salvatore, along with whatever teenage babysitter he is diddling. Zora is two years old now. What will she say when she is old enough to understand what kind of family she has? I made terrible decisions long ago. She is the happiest result that I could have ever expected from that dark chapter of my life.

Next thing I know, I am sitting back down. I feel like a boiling pot of water. I am releasing bubbles of emotions into the atmosphere. Carrie is holding a new towel to my back. Nicole is holding my hand. She feels guilty about being pregnant and pities my plight, which makes me hate her even more. I feel disconnected from the moment.

In a tailspin of emotions, it hits me. All of the people that I went to school with had mothers. Their mothers may not have lived the entirety of their school career, like Heather's. Or, they may have had stepparents.

Tommy's mom, poor soul, whatever became of her? She lived and breathed for him. These mothers had let their wild children loose from their protected habitats. How could a mother, like Mrs. Couch, turn her back on her child? Even if that child was an alcoholic mess, like David, how could a mom abandon her baby? Of course, Mrs. Baggett showed up. Why would she not? A mother would perpetually see the potential in her child. I would do the same for my Zora, if not my adult stepdaughter Melanie.

Looking around, I am jealous of the people I went to school with, especially Heather and Nicole. I envy their deep friendship. David is recovering from his addiction with the help of his pod of people, I assume.

I hear some noises outside the ballroom. I see Robert, Anne's little brother, coming in with his wife. She is pregnant too. Next, Alicia comes in with Matt, Brian, and another man who has the brightest red hair that I have ever seen. They make quite the little family, if not strange bedfellows. I had heard rumors after Tommy died about Alicia, Matt, and Michelle. No one has heard from Michelle for more than five years. She may still be in jail for involuntary manslaughter.

Brian yells, "Is there room for not-official graduates too?"

Without hesitation, I holler back, "Here? Always. Come. Join the glass menagerie of crazy with the rest of us. Let's put the gin in Gen Y, shall we?"

There are faces that I know will be absent tonight. I was not able to contact Ryan or his family. That alone makes me feel like a failure. They had the real estate connections that I needed to find a less expensive venue.

Justin is working a beat to serve and protect our county. Jennifer and Jeremy should be here soon. I do not know if Jennifer still lives in Savannah or not but Melissa may road trip with her. Will Eason works in Charleston. I doubt he will make the trek here for the reunion. Seth will come tonight, even if it is just to see Heather.

Crystal is in the military. No one knows where the Army stationed Crystal; not with the war going on. Amanda may or may not be here. I wonder who is with Michael at the alternative reunion. If Matt is there, I doubt Preeti will be. Brittany may or may not come. I never hear from her.

For what it is worth, I am living up to my 1997 class president campaign promise. When we graduated, we did not know what the next ten years would bring. I still do not know what the next decade will bring. I hope it brings me another baby. Why is a book-sized package on the table? I thought I dreamed that.

Twenty-Two: Brittany

◆————————————————————————◆

December 19, 2000 4:18 PM
Atlanta, Georgia

My hands tremble with nervousness standing outside the tattoo parlor. In the Deep South, only ex-cons and the Confederate mechanized cavalry get tattoos. The five of us are here at Little Five Points to support Melissa as she tries to heal from her late husband's death. I cannot bring myself to say aloud that Tommy is dead.

Melissa, by all accounts, is at widow at peace. We decided to meet in her current neighborhood, not that there are any decent tattoo parlors in Douglasville according to Matt. To my knowledge, Tommy never visited Little Five Points. He would have called the residents commies, or worse: hippies. Melissa is living nearby with friends who are Agnes Scott students. She only has a bicycle for transportation these days.

"What happened to Tommy's truck? Didn't Tommy leave everything to Melissa? Or, wouldn't everything he had go to her with or without a will?" I ask Matt before we enter that parlor to meet Amanda, Jennifer, and Melissa.

"Tommy's parents sold his truck months ago. Melissa got nothing because Tommy didn't own anything. Well, he thought he did, but nothing was in his name. Tommy's parents didn't cover their joint credit card's bill or anything. They had not been living together for a little while. It's complicated." Matt answers with candor opening the turquoise parlor door.

I have not visited Little Five Points before, but I love it! Not knowing how to best help Melissa grieve, I keep asking her if she wants to go shopping. In hindsight, shopping seems to have been a bad idea since she doesn't have money from her family or Tommy's family. Working at a department store makeup counter has aged her. I doubt she still works at Arbor Place Mall in Douglasville since she doesn't have the truck anymore.

"I'm glad we made time to get tats together," I say. I nod and sit down next to Melissa, Matt, Amanda, and Jennifer. None of them say anything. I feel like I interrupted a conversation in progress.

To avoid the awkward silence, I continue, "I sound like such a sap. Mrs. Couch would be disappointed. She would wax poetic about controlling your emotions and your reputation being a piece of glass that once broken can never be repaired. "

"She thought we were delicate figurines in a glass menagerie," Amanda says.

"I'm not a damn unicorn," Melissa says with a hollow terse grimace.

"I feel like a turtle most days," I say looking at my left ankle, which is in a walking cast.

"With your long legs, you're a gazelle, Britt," Matt says and knocks my shoulder a little.

"She would say, 'A reputation once broken may possibly be repaired, but the world will always keep their eyes on the spot where the crack was.' It was some sixteenth-century crap. Let's all crack our reputations and do something socially deviant." Jennifer adds with enthusiasm.

Matt mutters, "That Joseph Hall quote is not relevant today. Welcome to the twenty-first century, ladies. We survived Y2K."

Jennifer and Alicia are the ones that frequented this side of town in high school. Those visits cracked their high school reputations are permanent. But, the adult *me* feels much more comfortable here. I am trying to blend in a little yet still feel a little ill at ease.

Smokers line the sidewalks along Euclid Avenue. Cigarello stench wafts in and out of the parlor as patrons come and go. My coaches never wanted me to be near smokers. The only person that I knew in high school who smoked was Ryan, and that was after he dropped out.

"One of Tommy's big secrets was that he had come over here with Alicia senior year and got a tattoo. I don't reckon anyone else knew about it," Melissa says. She's frowning. "He had his initials worked into a tribal tattoo that went around his upper thigh. Besides his mother, he was his biggest fan."

I could write a list from my wrist to my forearm of who knew about that tattoo. Much to my chagrin, the list did not include me. Tommy respected me as a fellow athlete. He never had his eye on me. Most guys in high school did not have their eye on me. I am tall. I feel like I have big teeth in a big mouth. My small-by-comparison ears make all my facial features look bigger when I wear my hair in a ponytail. I detest the requisite sports ponytail.

"What? Where? You simply have to tell us everything! Does he have any piercings, Melissa?" Jennifer asks as she flips through pictures of previous tattoos.

Jennifer brings life and energy to the dull occasion. She is thrilled to get an actual tattoo. But, I suspect she wants to be part of the group most of all. Jennifer lives in Savannah and fears that she is missing out on the Atlanta highlights during her time away. If I were her, I would be down South soaking up the winter sunshine. It will not last forever. I hope she enjoys it. Unless she marries a Savannah boy, she will be back in Douglas County with the rest of us after college graduation. But, what do I know? I have never been to Savannah.

"Before we leave, I want to go to Psycho Sisters, okay?" Amanda says.

Amanda has dramatically changed since high school. She was always uptight and focused in school. Most of us found her intimidating. Between Amanda and Stephanie, it felt like they ran the school. They received the most academic accolades while Tommy and I received most of the student-athlete attention. Stephanie is at North Georgia College and, dollars to donuts, I know who is running that campus.

Matt forces as a smile as he leans in to tell me something. Before he can utter a syllable, our attention is drawn to the other three girls. Jennifer starts screaming at Amanda. She has her index finger in Amanda's face. While I missed the first part of the conversation, I pick up the later.

"You tortured me in high school, you snooty jackhole!" Jennifer says. "You spread rumors about my family living in a trailer park. We lost our home to a flipping natural disaster, you insensitive slippery subtle knave!"

"You had it coming, girlfriend," Amanda says flatly. "Besides, that was Stephanie. She lives in a self-constructed ivory tower. That has nothing to do with me. High school is shit. Everybody knows it, but you are having a hard time accepting it. If I'm a knave, then you're a lewd minx."

The five of us look outside as an Atlanta Police Department cruiser pulls in front of the shop. We all fall silent. Matt stands the most to lose in this situation. He is probably holding or carrying something illicit.

"Matt, how's business?" I mutter into his left ear. He is not turning around to eye the cop.

"Turn around sit down. Quit gawking like country-come-to-town. Be cool and they'll be cool. If not, I'll tell them that I'm holding for you." Matt says while flipping through a magazine.

"How could you, Matt?" Amanda whispers while keeping her lips almost motionless.

"It's a little something for the pain is all. None of you have ever had tattoos before, huh?"

Matt had anticipated more of Tommy's guy friends showing up. There were several notable friends missing today including Brian, Ryan, Justin, and Stephanie. They had volunteered along with Ryan and Matt. I think Stephanie and Tommy were working together last Spring. I guess North Georgia College was too important to leave on Winter Break. Not growing up with sisters, Matt does not know what to say or do other than to shift awkwardly to the corner chair to feign invisibility.

Matt and his mom may not have received the Hood family's annual Christmas letter where Tommy's mom, Trudy, detailed the people that she blamed for Tommy's untimely death. Melissa was at the top of the list. All people loyal to Tommy and the Hood family were to stay away from Melissa, forever. I am not certain if Matt knows, though. There was something strange and strained between Mrs. Trudy Hood and Miss Miranda Young. For them to both be scout moms, I would love to have been a fly on the wall when that chasm was created back-in-the-day, probably at the dawn of time itself.

"Shut up!" Amanda says to Jennifer. "You are stupid weird. But, it's all your own doing. I thought it was your angle. You were contrary simply for the sake of being contrary. You didn't want to complete the assignments as given. You always wanted to do something new and different. You thought that you knew better and that you were the teacher. You had no respect for the social structure that was in place before you and Jeremy arrived in our county. It was our county! Your family chose to move there; you didn't have to move. You could have picked anywhere. You could have gone over to Conyers or Dunwoody."

Before Jennifer can say anything about Amanda's international adoption, I step in, "Hey! Jennifer's family didn't choose to lose everything in a tornado, Amanda. Shit happens. Some days we're okay and then other days, life is simply too crap-tastic for words. Now, let's focus on being here for Mel. Oh, goodness! The only other thing I need is a coach yelling in my ear and telling me to pull it together. Or, you know, us fighting over who is going to play Othello for Brit Lit because Crystal should have been Othello and she left!"

A freshly tatted patron walks by us while holding fresh gauze on his forearm. He pauses to comment, "*Othello*? You're all white.

Othello's not white. He's a Moor. You must be from the 'burbs. Stupid crackers."

Amanda yells at him as he crosses the street, "We did the best we could."

"Well, I admit that I rise to play and go to bed to work," Matt says while thrusting his hips.

We share a laugh. We share a pause. We were all thinking the same thing. In the end, Mrs. Couch chose quiet Anne to be Othello. Most of us did not think she was going to be a good fit for the part, but she was. She was splendid at acting like someone deceived her about a lover. Anne never had a lover.

Ryan Bearden lost his cool when he found out Anne was Othello. He thought the part should have been his, even though he was no longer in our advanced class. He never got over dropping out. Mrs. Couch had been so impressed with Anne's death scene that she handpicked Anne to replace Amanda at a debate competition that we went to years ago. Looking around, I realize that I was the only one here today that went on the particular trip. We shared secrets there. I wish I could talk about them with someone, anyone.

Anne and Michelle had a falling out on our way back from the debate trip. I do not know what drama befell them, but they did not speak to each other for the rest of our senior year. Even after Mrs. Couch spoke her peace that queer day in English, something was wrong. Michelle had it out for Anne. She was full of resentment.

I think it had to do with Tommy taking Anne to prom junior year. Now, here I am brimming with antipathy for Michelle more than ever for what she did to Tommy. She was an unsubtle whore full of villainous secrets, as Shakespeare would paraphrase.

"I'm going to tell you guys something. I know high school is over, but I have questions. I need to get some answers. So, I'll share if you guys share," I say.

Knowing that Jennifer will appreciate my directness, even if it will horrify Melissa and Amanda, I ask, "Melissa, what killed Tommy? I heard a rumor that Michelle was involved. Jason and Alicia don't talk about it, but they clearly were there too. Matt, what's up?"

"Brittany, that's so crass!" Amanda says. "Melissa will always be Tommy's dear bereaved."

An available artist comes behind the counter to meet with Melissa. He gives Amanda a playful wink. Jennifer becomes antsy. Jennifer moves from her seat to sit next to me but away from Matt. Jennifer locks her arm in mine and opens her mouth to speak.

"I'm getting a Tamagotchi since that was my nickname for Tommy," Amanda shouts.

"That would be something special we would need to sketch ahead of time. It won't be available today, and you'll need to make a deposit like your friend here." An assistant behind the counter tells Amanda.

"I want the Confederate battle flag," Matt says. Jennifer and Amanda gasp. "You're all toads! Doesn't anyone know the motto for the state of Georgia?

"Enlighten us, Eagle Scout Matt," Jennifer throws him a dirty look. She's not impressed.

"It's wisdom, justice, and moderation," I say. "It's on the state seal."

"Wait," Amanda says almost dropping a large tattoo album. "There is a state seal on our state flag that uses the word justice?"

Jennifer screeches back; apparently stuck on the subject. "You're telling me that the word 'justice' appears on an official state symbol alongside the Confederate battle flag? That's crap. What hypocrites we are!"

"We'll probably get a new flag soon. Roy Barnes is governor now, and it seems to be an important issue to him." I say. "We're getting a new flag someday. It has offended everyone since the beginning of time itself. Even the people that support the current flag want everyone else to quit talking about."

"Well, hasn't that been the flag since the Civil War?" Melissa asks sitting back down.

"No," I say remembering overhearing my uncles talking about it. "We had a flag that kind of looked like the Confederate National flag, from way back when; like, from the reconstruction era or something. Then, everybody got angry at the *Brown vs. Board of Education* decision in 1954 and voted in a new flag."

"Everybody didn't get mad at that decision. White 1950s voters got mad." Amanda reproves.

"So, our flag ain't that old, long story short," Matt says. He sips a green liquid out of a flask. Matt is old enough to drink alcohol, but the boys in school had always put Surge in theirs. I ignore it.

Jennifer leans into my ear, "I can't do this right now. I can't be here right now. It's too much. I'm going to browse Junkman's Daughter and try to find something for Jeremy for Christmas."

Jennifer and her bottle-job crimson hair exit without a word to Melissa. I feel a little abandoned. The fight with Amanda threw us all off.

"Where is Jennifer going?" Melissa asks me.

"She said she's Christmas shopping on the other side of Five. I don't know if she's coming back. Sorry." I offer and then bite the inside of my cheek.

"Jennifer didn't care for Tommy," Melissa says apologetically. "There were so many people that worshiped the ground that he walked on but not Jennifer. Jennifer was close to Anne. Anne's death still breaks Jennifer's heart. She has more questions than I do. She may have almost as many as you, Brittany. Sit with me. I'm going first."

An artist motions Melissa to the back. Melissa's tattoo artist is a mature man covered in faded tattoos. He quietly introduces himself to Melissa. She looks nervous. The artist puts Pink Floyd's *The Wall* on the turntable. As the parlor's speakers flicker to life, the man pulls on gloves. He offers me a chair nearby.

Matt and Amanda banter in the cheap plastic waiting room chairs. Someone floats by me to ask if I knew my design yet. I do not know and never will. The pictures are all blurs. I cannot discern anything with potential. My mouth falls open as Melissa takes off her sweater and jeans. She lays down pulling her boy shorts low. The artist draws a curtain between us and reception area.

Matt speaks up, "Hey! Melissa, do you remember Tommy's basketball number? It would look kind of silly with his football number on top of a basketball."

Melissa and I stare at each other, giggle, and shake our heads that we do not. Tommy Hood was known more for his football number than basketball number. A football tattoo is not an option today either. I prefer the basketball. The roundness of the basketball looks more like a circle of life to me. The Class of 1998 has been out of high school for two and a half years, and here we are forgetting the casual details. The things we took for granted were the first to exit the vaults of our memories, never to return.

"What do you remember about Tommy?" Melissa says wincing in pain.

Melissa's tattoo is painful as it is near her bikini line. She does not want anyone to see. I sit near her shoulder and try to look away. The artist's head is behind Melissa's legs. She moans in pain, and he smiles a little. As he whispers words of comfort, her stomach shivers under her camisole.

"Tommy was full of stories. He could charm anyone, ask Mrs. Couch. He seemed to genuinely like people. But, you have to understand that we met in elementary school. He was different back then, you know, before..."

"Becoming a man whore and drug addict. I'm sure he was distinctive in his typical childish way. But, I didn't know that Tommy. So, forgive me if I don't mourn with you. I was married to a different man than the boy you remember. I know you were fond of him."

"I'm so sorry your husband died, Melissa. I didn't think of it that way." I say and cry a little. I hurt for her.

Melissa grits her teeth and says, "He died in between Michelle's legs, okay? In Paradise City Beach, the same place that we went for our honeymoon. But, I still miss him. I'll never forgive him, but I miss him. They had all been in a car accident and didn't go to the hospital. So, there was bleeding in his brain. Then he drank a lot of alcohol, which made it worse. Since we were separated, the toxicology results went to his mom. She never shared those with me. She blames me for Tommy's death. And, that's a lot for me to think about."

"None of that was your fault, Mel. He made a series of choices. You couldn't possibly be expected to stop him. You weren't his mom. For cryin' out loud! Don't carry that around with you. Michelle and Alicia should feel so much worse. From what I hear, Alicia is managing okay." I try to comfort her.

"Alicia doesn't have a soul; she's a slutty stripper. She sells her body like a prostitute, whether it's for drugs or money. I can't blame Brian for not wanting to marry her. Tommy reminds me a little of Othello." Melissa says. "He was trying to smother me like Othello did to Desdemona. He didn't know me at all."

"Or he was Desdemona and someone else was Othello," I mention.

"There is a long list of those that would be jealous enough to kill." She mumbles.

All of the information is swirling around in my head. I flip the record and start the needle. Matt is next. Amanda sits with Melissa during bandaging. Matt pats the seat next to him for me to sit.

"Matt, what happened? Melissa still doesn't have all the facts, like the toxicology report. Do you not think that will torture her? Did you tell her that you were there?" I say.

"The less she knows, the better. I wasn't at the hotel when Tommy died. I was out trying to score some more for him. He had already blown through everything I brought. You know, Paradise City Beach isn't as cool about stuff like that as they were in the '80s.

The MTV Spring Break Live wild party days are over. Michelle had brought most of her stuff with her. I had never seen anything like it. That is, like, my business. There was international high-grade shit. Jason and Alicia ate some cookies together and took some shots, no hard drugs. Michelle freaking filmed some of the stuff they did. I didn't want to be anywhere close to that drama. That's what got her in deeper trouble. She made a record of her sins."

I turn my head to hear the girls laughing. Amanda looks at me blushing. She shouts over towards us, "Hey! Do you guys remember that *Canterbury Tales* bulletin board in the back of the classroom? It was there for over ten years or something. That was insane!"

"Now, they're just laughing at random nonsense. I want to see if Amanda is actually going to get a tattoo. She is all talk and no walk. I don't think she will." Matt says then takes a sip from his flask. "I have a history with her. If she has a chill bone in her body, it's because I slipped it in her."

I laugh and snort, "You and Amanda? For real?"

"For two minutes," Matt says. "It was once. But, lots of things can happen from 'just once.'"

Cackling, I have a flood of happy memories. I remember us all being alive and young. Very few of us had a clear direction as to where we were going, but we were jubilant at the beginning of our senior year. Tonight, we feel like we have accomplished something grand by living to see our twenties. But, I know we are all on the verge of achieving something grander than we can adequately grasp. We only have two and a half years until we graduate from college.

In high school, there were a few who were still just going through the motions while Amanda and Stephanie had their sights set beyond high school. I laugh thinking about Crystal's Sidney Lanier performance. But, my ADD brain races in a diverging direction. I stop laughing. I remember how empty Mrs. Couch's classroom was without Crystal, our true Othello.

Matt yelps in pain for a moment. He says, "I saw something, a long time ago. I told Tommy. Tommy never forgave me. He was mad at me. I was a fifth wheel on the beach trip at the last minute. I wanted to spend some time with him and explain what happened. Can I rely on you? It is a secret to take to the grave?"

"Yes, if the secret is that austere. I want to know what happened. I can't let this go." I admit.

"I was with Anne the day she died." Matt confides. "I wasn't in the building, but I was nearby. Because I was dealing out of my car, I had to go and go in a hurry. I saw someone familiar. Someone that all of us knew. Some money was involved."

"Anne was murdered, Matt. You have to tell someone. Who was it?" I insist.

"No. Look at what happened to the other person I told. David knows part of the story too. You see, it's convoluted. I don't want to get anyone else in trouble." Matt says. He's tearful.

"You owe it to her family. They're never going to give up searching for her killer, Matt."

Before I can finish talking to Matt, his small tattoo is done. He stands up and turns his head to look at his shoulder in the mirror. There is a half-dollar sized basketball on his back with 'Tommy79' write across it. The tat is perfect for Matt. It suits him. I am glad that he avoided a Confederate flag. His artist covers the basketball in petroleum jelly.

Of all people, Amanda finally found the perfect tattoo for me. It's a medieval squire carrying a sword. The art is less about Tommy and more about me. That is why Amanda and Melissa were all giggles over Canterbury Tales. I will remember Tommy, and Anne, in my way.

We started our senior English class with *Canterbury Tales*. We had an essay where we were to match our personalities to one of the characters. We wrote a thousand words from that character's point of view. The assignment was very challenging because the book was toilsome. We could not tell if our character was male or female at first. When we were seventeen, we thought gender and essays mattered. I got over that real quick.

All of the girls wanted to be the Wife of Bath because we at least knew that she was a female. Mrs. Couch insisted that it did not matter. But, I could not imagine writing as a boy. Mrs. Couch's expectations seemed impossibly high. Yet, after all the fuss, I had chosen to be the Squire. I love my father, and I could relate to that point in the Squire's story. Our graduating class had a lot of students with divorced or deceased parents. I was a daddy's girl. I still am.

The new tattoo stings a little. I exhale long, deep breaths of relief. Before I fully get up, Matt lays down. He looks like he is about to go to sleep. The assistants move him to a clean booth. Amanda remains on the other side of the room. She is having her stencil placed. The control freak drew it herself while waiting for the rest of us.

Amanda had written as The Prioress. Melissa was The Cook because Mrs. Couch said that it was rather short. Looking at Matt, I ask, "Which of the Canterbury characters were you?"

"Dude," Matt's mental processor was lethargic. He was thinking deep. "I was absent the day you guys picked out characters. Mrs. Couch assigned me to be The Pardoner."

"You finished the assignment, right? Otherwise, you wouldn't have passed?" Amanda says.

"I know how you passed, even though it disgusts me," Melissa says. She hits Matt with her ugly bucket hat. I recall that the bucket hat was Tommy's fishing hat.

"That was the hard part about us going through high school, no Internet. We were the last generation to suffer the information dark ages. Cheating must be getting easier every year. Soon it won't be cheating anymore. Ladies, I was just ahead of my time." Matt says with a sneaky grin.

"Jennifer and Anne had Geocities websites, but they were the first in our class to do anything like that," I say rubbing my right foot.

Matt confesses, "I still sometimes go to her page. Her brother updated it after Yahoo! bought Geocities out last year. Her website used to be in the Area 51 neighborhood. I thought it was a wicked idea to organize it like that. Jennifer's site was in College Park. That is very her and Jeremy."

"Is Robert updating it?" Amanda says. She slinks over to us.

"No, I don't think so. Robert is just maintaining it a little. I guess, you know, in her memory and everything." Matt says. Matt and Robert were scouts together so he knows better than the rest of us.

"Did he graduate this year?" I ask.

"Yup," Matt said smiling. "I think he's happy that he'll never have to take a foreign language again. Russian did not work out so well for him."

"Good grief, that class was hard. But, the field trip was breathtaking," Amanda adds excitedly. Amanda did not miss an opportunity to remind all of us that she had been a world traveler while the rest of us did not have passports yet. The Russian Club went to Moscow.

"Thanks for yearbook update, Amanda," I say crisply. I turn toward Matt. "If Robert goes to college, then he'll need to take a foreign language, right?"

"He's not going to college. He's going to go work for the Douglas County Sheriff's Department. He'll probably take night classes at West Central Tech, but I doubt he'll have to take anything frivolous there. I know it's good to know a little bit of a foreign language but two years seems to be too much."

"That's nice," I say thinking back. "I would sleep safer when I visit my family in Douglas County, knowing that he's one of the good guys. Robert is streetwise about things. He knows people. I think he gets that savviness from his photography work."

"He never got over his sister's murder. He's not going to stop until he brings the murderer to justice." Matt says. His face turns solemn.

"How can you get over murder?" Melissa says thoughtfully. "I blame Michelle for giving Tommy drugs. If any of you ever see her ever again, let me know. I have something to say to her about why my husband had to have a closed-casket funeral. I can't forgive her for that. Alicia did the right thing and called me from Paradise City. I mean, if a stoned hooker murderesses can be honorable."

What's honorable when it comes to death and losing someone that you love? I try to shut my mind off with the questions. I look at Melissa. She has more questions than I do. I do not intend to burden her with my plot twists. I know that I came out here under the guise that I wanted to be supportive of Melissa, but that was not the case. Now I have a permanent reminder of my ulterior motives. I will have to walk with that forever.

Twenty-Three: Will

April 5, 2003 9:10 AM
Charleston, South Carolina

Today is the Cooper River Bridge Run. I rent a liveaboard yacht docked in a private marina on Charleston Harbor. Thirty thousand people raced overhead on the Ravenel Bridge in the past few hours. Bless them, some of them are still running. Life on the marina stirred extra-early this morning. The resident seagulls are staying away from the bay.

Three of my Georgia high school classmates are racing in the Cooper River Bridge run. They wanted to meet up with me afterward. I stand on my deck with binoculars in hand wondering if I will recognize any of the people crossing the finish line. Some of my students are running this morning as well. The idea of my students and classmates being in the same city at the same time is like fresh water and saltwater mixing; it's unnatural and should not happen.

Justin emailed me weeks ago that he was coming to Charleston for a run. I was not thrilled. In an old town like Charleston being inhospitable would be the greatest of sins. I am at peace with being a sinner, just not by Charleston standards. I don't have email access on the weekends when I am away from my office. I like it that way. I had no reason to expect any changes to Justin's plans until he called me at o'dark thirty last night. Jeremy and Brian would be joining him too.

My cell rings. I listen to "Fat Bottom Girls" for a moment before answering, "Professor Eason."

"Will. It's Brian. *Ha ha*, man, I know you're not a professor. Did you have overnight guests to impress? You are a sly dog. Be sure to invite her to meet us, okay?"

"Good morning, Brian. Everything you just assumed is not happening. That shit is not happening on so many levels. You don't even know. Welcome to Charleston. I trust it was a hard night." I say. Even though Brian cannot see me, I sneer.

"The unexpected has transpired this morning. Do you have a minute?"

"For you, I do. I assume that you brought the things to Charleston with you?"

"We missed the start time and everything. We haven't even left the hotel room this morning. My daughter, Penny, is with us."

I am surprised that they traveled to Charleston for the race and then missed it. Like a hermit crab, I am a happy introvert and dislike entertaining outside my small circle of faculty friends. I almost considered cutting the rope and stealing the boat. Dammit. How much hospitality should I extend to these three boys and the baby?

"Well, how about we meet up at ten o'clock? Where would you all like to eat? Are you in Charleston or Mount Pleasant?" I ask politely.

"We're on the Charleston side of the bridge. We ate a few packets of honey buns from the vending machine. Do you want to meet at the aquarium?" Brian asks.

"There is historic stuff to do on Meeting Street if you want to feel like you've visited Old Charleston. The aquarium will have family and children." I say.

Ugh. Children. The thought of small snotty things around my ankles makes a little bile creep into my mouth. What hideous creatures. My father told me that we were all children once. I must have been ten years old at the time because he left after he imparted that nickel's worth of wisdom on me. How old could this Penny be? If she were very young, her mother would probably be in tow too.

"A child-friendly place is great. Thanks, Will. See you soon." Brian says and disconnects.

More likely than not, Justin told Brian and Jeremy I am working on my Marine Biology Master's degree at the College of Charleston. The guys may try to get a rise out of me by asking me to meet them at the aquarium. Ah, the high school games are afoot.

I should start walking the two miles to the Aquarium if I want to avoid sweating like a tourist in this humidity. I put my ear buds in and listen to White Stripes's new album *Elephant* on my iPod. I look down at my feet and avoid making eye contact.

In a city full of people, I need a moment to gather my thoughts. My plans had not included Brian and Jeremy. I feel nervous when plans change suddenly. None of these boys were explicitly cruel to me. I cannot say the same for Tommy, Matt, and Ryan; among others.

There is a mountain of disappointments, shame, and sorrow that I have surrounding high school. The best way that I knew to escape that mountain was to relocate to the sea. The mountain remains. I can usually see it from Interstate-20 on my way back to Douglas County every Thanksgiving eve.

I did not have space or access to resources to truly be myself in Douglas County. Not having a car, or a person to teach me how to drive, I was very limited in what social events that I was able to attend. I was angry and envious of the other boys in the county. They had the opportunity to meet up at the last minute whereas I always had to submit a form, ask a day in advance, and then beg someone to drive me. It was not fair!

There were no public transportation options. Douglas County did not have sidewalks, except near the high school. There was no bus service, passenger trains, or even taxis. I do not remember ever seeing a taxi after my family moved there, around 1995, just before the Olympics. It is the strangest place. Rolling my eyes at the memory, I sigh and try to think positive thoughts. I have been in counseling for several years.

In the beginning, I went to counseling because I felt like I had not made the transition from high school to college well. There were essential skills that I lacked. I did not have college-appropriate social skills. I did not have a resume. I could not shake hands. I did not know how to introduce myself. Teachers never taught us chit-chat or small talk. I did not know how much I lacked until I was standing on campus my first semester and failing miserably. Thanks be to God, a professor took an interest in my fish-out-of-water freshman self and guided me.

My high school experience had not prepared me for the real world. It had not prepared me for writing emails to instructors, paying taxes, or finding a job. It had not prepared me to balance work and home. I did not launder my clothes. My first roommate hated me because he felt like I could not clean up after myself and was a slob. He asked that I transfer rooms and, indeed, after his complaints, I did not have a choice. I did not know how to live around other men.

While I was managing in academic discussions, I found that my literary analysis skills were not up to par. I had done well on the English College Level test but was not a talented writer. I feel Mrs. Couch's three-block, two academic year program had been a waste of my time. Of course, it was only unofficially organized that way.

Students could technically show up to Mrs. Couch's final class block the Spring of their senior year. However, it was Mrs. Couch that would not let you swim in her academic cesspool of deceit.

Approaching the aquarium, I see the boys and something else. I walk up to them not knowing if I shake hands or hug. Justin hugs me. Jeremy pats me on the back. Jeremy does not smile, but I have never seen him smile. Brian reaches for a side hug as he holds something in his left hand; or, rather, he's holding someone's miniature doll hand in his left hand.

"Will, this is my daughter, Penny. Pensive Kate is the light of my life and the reason I get up in the morning. Or, as you can tell, the reason I don't get up in the morning," Brian smiles.

Brian is beaming with pride for his little snippet. Penny is very proud of herself too because she is smiling at me. Oh, no, it smiles. A switch clicks over in my brain. I smile too.

"Hi. Tank 'ewe for taking me to th' wear-e-yum. It smells like fish in here." Penny mewls softly.

I do not have to ask whose Penny's mother is. Penny is a tiny version of Alicia. She has brown hair and large green eyes. Her nose does not look like Alicia's or Brian's, but that may be to her advantage when she grows up. I was not that close to Alicia in high school. I knew her when we were much younger. We went to elementary school together before my family moved to Florida for a few years.

"Welcome to Charleston, Penny. Let me show you all of the lovely sea creatures that South Carolina has to offer us today." I say. I make the effort to be a good host for her.

Penny looks like a children's catalog model; if there is such a thing anymore. I, myself, appeared in a few K-mart advertisements as a kid. I was the brown skinned boy who was either an unseasonably tanned white child or Hispanic. I am Boricua on my mother's side. Penny is pale. Be still my heart. She is probably a daycare kid. Is she old enough to be in Kindergarten? Where is Alicia?

Brian grabs my shoulder, "Dude. She's almost five years old. Don't breathe a word about my mom. She doesn't know her."

"Wait, I thought that was her granddaughter. She doesn't know Mrs. Couch?" I ask as we are heading to the entrance. "I thought she would be born with a book in her hand and glasses on her nose. She looks nothing like your mother. Penny is bright, beautiful, and charming."

Oh, my heart aches a little. I do not like children, but I could learn to like a carbon copy of Alicia. There is something that reminds me of home in this child's eyes. The child is loved, looked after, and has great eye-contact. She is well-spoken and not shy when meeting new people around her father. Brian has done well for himself. He had discovered his calling before I found mine. His calling was to be a dad. I wish life had been that straightforward for me.

"Did you know Penny was born on our graduation night?" Jeremy asks.

"No. After school, I didn't really hear from anyone. I moved to Charleston the Independence Day after graduation." I answer.

"You didn't keep in contact with Michelle at least? I thought you two would get married or something." Justin says in an accusatory tone.

Not knowing whether or not I should keep up guises from high school, I answer, "It was not meant to be. After graduation, it felt like adulthood was either going to be excruciatingly painful or kill me."

"Wike the Wittle Mermaid?" Penny says, her braided pigtails bobbing up and down.

Leaning to Brian, I whisper, "She is your mother's grandchild."

"My mom remarried five years ago. Mom is not even the ill-famed 'Mrs. Couch' anymore. She got her doctorate and everything. She married Principal Daniell and assumed a new identity. She's some combination of cockroach and chameleon. She's indestructible in her native environment." Brian says as Penny moves towards an exhibit.

"Good for her. But, I have a hard time understanding how she could prioritize a degree over a child. She went on and on about the glories of love and marriage in class. She didn't say much about parenthood. How does she translate that into her schedule of things that we should do with our lives?" I ask.

"We don't talk, Will. The situation is Daedalus in nature. I know you had some family issues in high school, so I'm sure you'll understand. Please be cautious with words around Penny." Brian says.

"You break her heart by accident, Will, and I'll kill you," Justin says and taps my shoulder. I must have looked gobsmacked because he adds, "Oh, I'm just kidding. I'll use my bare hands. They'll never find your body. Give me a smile. I'm only joking until I'm not."

Brian starts, "We arrived yesterday afternoon. The people who organize the run had a thing for kids last night at Hampton Park. Even though she's little, Penny wanted to run like Daddy, so we all came early."

"Wait a sec: you all took off work early so a kid who isn't even Kindergarten could run? That's insane!" I say.

Jeremy chimes in, "JJ was going to come up from Savannah and watch her for us while we ran this morning but she slept in, as always."

"Something happened yesterday," Brian says. "Justin stayed up with Alicia. I mean, Penny, of course. Justin stayed up with Penny all night. I don't know why I do that sometimes."

"Well, where is Alicia? Why *is* a little girl out here with you on a guys' weekend?" I ask.

"Because Brian is a kick-butt dad, Will, that's why. Now, go tell that child something science-y about fish or marine life." Jeremy blurts out.

Brian, Jeremy, and Justin huddle up for a moment. I feel like a fifth wheel, as Matt would say. It was one of his double-meaning words since his family liked to camp in a Fifth Wheel Trailer. Even though I the guys invited me, I feel awkward. I feel as though I could drown in my stinky stress sweat. Thankfully, I am wearing seersucker shorts and a moisture-wicking light pink polo. Moisture-wicking technology would have been helpful in 1998 Douglasville.

"Tell me, Penny," I start. "What do you want to be when you grow-up?"

"I wanna be a mermaid!" Penny says excitedly and starts to dance.

Penny is wearing tights with mismatched leg warmers that remind me of *Rainbow Brite*. She still has all of her baby teeth. She forces her baby doll to pretend to be a mermaid. I gently stop her from throwing the dolly into one of the petting pools.

"What if being a mermaid doesn't work out? What will you do then?" I ask.

"Oh! I want to be a ballerina and princess and fairy and a daddy and a doctor and a big sister!" Penny goes on and on.

"Well, let's make a plan. You start with swimming lessons. None of the Douglas County high schools have swimming pools, but there is one at Hunter Park. I used to go to my swim team there. Make your daddy take you there. I think there is a bigger one at Jessie Davis. Have you visited Jessie Davis? It is on the other side of the railroad tracks." I say.

"Swimming!?!" Penny says excitedly.

"Yes. When you're older, you could always study marine biology like me. Come out to the ocean and see me sometime. I could always use help from a mermaid." I say, teasing.

I can't even remember the last time I laughed. Didn't someone other than me think to tell this child that she could take swimming lessons? Oh, my. I wish someone had indulged me for five minutes when I was this age. My parents ignored me at this age; neither seen nor heard.

"Daddy!" Penny screams running over to Brian. "I gonna be a mermaid. I swim. Imma be like Ariel. I your princess, Daddy!"

Brian sarcastically nags me about getting him on the hook for swimming lessons. I wanted to respond that he had put me on the hook for child-watching duty. But, in all honesty, it had not been that bad. It was only fifteen to twenty minutes. The other boys were never out of sight. I wonder what they were discussing. It may have had something to do with someone missing an alarm. They can work that out amongst themselves.

"Hey, Will! Do you remember that day in English?" Jeremy says with a smug look.

"What day? There were so many miserable days in high school. In all honesty, I thought we were never going to graduate. It felt as though the buildings would just transition into a retirement community right around us." I reply.

After high school, all the days had started to blend like a beach resort bar's mega frozen daiquiri machine. I have forgotten about what people said. I remember how I felt. My heart sinks. Now I know what day Jeremy was referencing. I covered that topic with my counselor long ago. That session's therapeutic homework was to write a letter and never send it. Well, screw it, I did. I sent that hot mess straight to Mrs. Couch care of the Douglas County High School English Department.

"You know the day," Justin says. "You lost a book and were pissed."

"I do recall," I answer. "And, Lady Macbeth knows exactly how I feel about that day. That is, naturally, if she took the time to read the damned letter."

"Language!" Brian barks at me.

Penny was starting to whine about going to the little girls' room. We walk toward the restrooms. Not being able to take her into the men's room, Brian waits outside the women's restroom like a sentinel. Alicia should be here. She may have fallen back into her bad habits.

"Penny's gone. Are you ready, man?" Jeremy says. He appears more poker-faced than usual.

"Ready for what, Jeremy? You were just talking about English class. What?" I am lost and could not follow where the boys were leading me.

"Remember that day when Mrs. Couch lost her crap on us?" Jeremy says.

"What of it? I was glad that it happened. It needed to happen. I felt validated. I felt empowered. I took it to heart. It was life changing for me." I lie.

"There was a reason, Will. How much do you know about post-1998 Douglas County happenings?" Justin asks. He is in no-nonsense cop mode.

"Brian's mom isn't a grandmother at all, Will." Jeremy is imparting something that he feels is vital and not just a secret.

"Okay. That's weird. Is Brian adopted? I wasn't certain if Mrs. Couch had enough goodness in her soul to be a mom in the first place. She was not a very nice person. She called you a skinny twerp, Justin. I would have preferred her not verbally abuse me either. Excuse me. I've been in therapy." I say. If we are all going to open up right now, why not add fuel to the fire?

"Brian's not adopted. Brian never had sex with Alicia, Will." Justin says. "They didn't have artificial insemination, obviously. One of the reasons why Brian didn't marry Alicia is that they were never together. But, Brian did claim Penny on the birth certificate. To Penny, Brian is Daddy. He'll always be Daddy. He changed her diapers in the middle of the night and found a special infant formula for her when she was allergic to the stuff the hospital gave her. He takes off work to go places with her. But, biologically, she's not the fruit of Brian's loins, understand?"

"I'm so confused. Do you want a daytime talk show host to pay for a paternity test? This is insane. Of course, Brian is her daddy. They have the same hair color. I barely remember what Alicia's natural hair color was. The last time I saw Alicia's natural hair color I think Punky Brewster was still in syndication, okay?" I say while cutting my eyes.

"How much do you know about Anne's murder?" Jeremy looks at me with sorrowful eyes.

"What? Anne's dead?" I cry aloud. It echoes through the aquarium.

I fall to the floor. I rock back and forth in the fetal position. I had so much to tell her and so many things that I needed to apologize for; well, at some point in time. I probably needed to apologize for all of high school. But, how could she be dead? She is our age. She's twenty-three like me.

"Tommy's dead too. Michelle did time for involuntary manslaughter. Alicia was a witness. Did you know? Did either of them tell you anything?" Justin asks.

I stumble as my sea legs turn into land legs. I cannot stop heavy sobbing. For a moment I think about Penny. I am glad that she is not with me at this time. What the hell happened to Douglas County?

Jeremy shows no empathy for the newness of this information. For him, Anne's death is old. "Anne bled to death from a knife wound. She was murdered just after Christmas 1998."

Justin sits down on the floor with me, "Her little brother, Robert, remember Robert? Well, he's still asking around about things. We're deputies together. A few of us are trying to assist Robert when we can, on the down low. We need to talk to you about anything and everything that you may remember."

Not understanding where this conversation could be going, I mumble, "Oh, Anne. I'll do anything for her. But, I don't know what help I can be. I'm studying to be a scientist. *Ha!* Sharks with frickin' laser beams and all that. I was here, in Charleston, during that time. I think. Nineteen-ninety-eight was a long time ago. I have not been to Douglas County for Christmas since 1999. My mom always works Christmas, so the moms with young kids don't have to go in."

"Well, most of us were home from college for winter break our freshman year. Anne died the day after Christmas. Let's go sit down. We have a map of ideas," Justin says as Jeremy helps me up.

The boys are right. I was home for winter break that one time. I had stopped going home for winter break since then; but, they hit the nail on the head. Most of the rest of our class and I were home for that first college winter break. Penny would have been around six months old. Trying to think back to our previous conversation, before the shock of Anne's murder, I was trying to connect the dots between Alicia, Anne, Brian, and Penny.

"So, what does Brian's adoption...claim...I mean, what do you call it? What does that have to do with Anne?" I ask.

"We need to figure it out. The four of us are going to work together on this. Half of West Georgia residents are suspects right now. We need to narrow things down." Justin says just as Brian comes back with Penny.

Hard conversations loom on the horizon. My three classmates and I put on brave faces for our little mermaid Penny. Thinking back, I do not remember my parents reading fairytales to me. I raised myself. Penny has a school of adults swimming after her and helping her achieve her dreams. Every child's childhood should be this way.

"Brian, how is your d-a-d these days?" I ask.

"Daddy doesn't have a dad," Penny says sadly. "I don't have any grandparents at all."

If Brian's father is dead, then I am sure Brian is independently wealthy. His father and grandmother dabbled in real estate. The 1996 Olympics made the Couch family rich. The wealth turned into Brian's father running for one political office after another. In his vain attempts to achieve power, I think Mr. Couch forgot that he had a wife and child. As a slap in the face to his father, Brian seems to have invested all of his time and efforts into Penny. Penny is being raised with love even if she was not made with love.

"Alicia's parents are not involved either," Brian says with a sorrowful look.

"Would you like an uncle, Penny?" I ask knowing the full weight of what it means.

"Oh, yes. Daddy doesn't have any butters or sisters." She smiles and wiggles a tooth for me to witness.

"There is this magical thing called friendship. Friendship can fill in the gaps when we don't have blood relatives with us or nearby. I can be your weird uncle that lives on a boat by the sea." I offer.

"And, I can be a mermaid," Penny says. She is bubbling over with joy.

Few people remember that the fairy tale of the *Little Mermaid* has a sad ending. Ariel commits suicide. I will endeavor to help Brian make sure that Alicia's fate does not await Penny in ten years. In ten years, Penny will be fourteen going on fifteen. That is the same age that Alicia started smoking pot with Tommy. I need to help keep Penny away from the Tommys of the world. I cannot stand idly by and watch the cycle continue. There is a bunch of life stuff that I do not have control over. But, I think I can be a mentor. I can handle being a mentor to a lovely little mermaid.

Brian's phone rings. He answers and places his hand over the speaker. "*Shh.* Guys, its Robert.... Something happened to Alicia.... My dad is there...There's a shotgun...Alicia is on an ambulance... Blood is everywhere."

Penny's face twists into a panic. She hugs her dolly tight. After a moment of listening, Penny says, "Where's my baby sister? Is she with Mommy?"

Twenty-Four: Robert

January 1, 1999 5:34 PM
Douglasville, Georgia

Funerals, and the resulting litany of services, are the great lie-detectors of our society. If you want to find out what a person truly believes, observe them in action at a funeral. Sit back, and watch them dizzy themselves into a circle of hysteria. My beloved sister's funeral is not the first in our family, nor will it be our last. However, it is the most difficult to endure because I know that I will have to manage this, and all future grief, without Anneewakee.

"Hey, thanks for coming, Mrs. Daniell," I say shaking the hand of my big sister's high school English teacher. It's my sad job to welcome friends and family to the viewing.

Anneewakee had classes with Mrs. Couch, now Mrs. Daniell, for two years, but was in her program for four years. As a result, I knew better than to take any advanced English classes; ever. Her students, former and current, call her Lady Macbeth. I haven't senior English yet. I don't know anything about the Lady Macbeth reference except it is not a compliment.

Mrs. Daniell wails in a corner. I am afraid that she is going to upset my mother. I search the crowd to see if I can recognize anyone from Anneewakee's class. I wade through adults wearing black and charcoal gray clothes. Do adults keep black clothes in their closets for days like today? I did not have a suit or tie until I had to buy one yesterday. I never had the need.

Many of Anneewakee's classmates came tonight since they were home for college winter break. Others have either left Douglas County or were off somewhere doing something other than paying their respects. Crystal is in basic training. I do not think Crystal knows yet. Some of my friends from school saw it on the news, and now they're here with me at the funeral home.

Local news covered Anneewakee's murder in a respectful manner. My parents' greatest fear is that the crime scene photos will end up on a Friday night news magazine special. The local police are doing everything they can; or, at least I hope they are. Anne died outside of the Austell city in unincorporated Cobb County. Her death is a jurisdictional mess. She was feet away from the Mableton city limits near Butternut Creek. *Dang it*! I wish I had been there.

For the past four months, Anneewakee was a waitress at the Douglasville location of Lickskillet Junction. Previously, she worked at Beautiful-Lee Dunn floral studio. The studio was a typical flower shop with a highfalutin name. As a result, both businesses have shown their love to our family in the form of a small family-only meal this evening and spectacular flowers. I would prefer the company of my sister, even for one more afternoon, in place of free food and flowers. I know I should be grateful, but my heart craves revenge.

Anneewakee worked an extra day, the day after Christmas. On Christmas Eve, she asked for hours at another location, this time in Cobb County. I have no idea why she did that. The Douglasville restaurant was much safer and closer to home. She had not worked at the Austell location before. I find it suspicious.

I can't help but think that if Anneewakee had died in Douglas County that the investigation would be on the district attorney's desk by now. Some hate-filled criminal would be crapping all over himself and having nightmares about the electric chair. The State of Georgia will send a murderer to die in the lap of Old Sparky in a heartbeat. I pity the fool that screws with the law in Douglas County. They are exceedingly fierce about protecting their own.

Anneewakee's coffin is a few feet from my chair. My parents are shaking hands in the adjoining room. From the corner of my eye, I see a young woman in denim. I walk over to her. Her hair is chestnut brown. I wonder if she realizes that she smells like wild lavender. She's not crying or smiling. Her face seems familiar. I need to be with people my age for a moment, so I introduce myself.

"Thank you for coming to see Anneewakee. I'm Robert McWhorter."

"I'm Ms. Daniell. That was my name before my stepmother shanghaied it. I'm sorry about Anne, truly. Death has knocked on my door too. Is there anything a slightly salty Alexander Cougar can do to help? People offer assistance all the time and I'm sure they mean it. But, I am for real. I want to help." she offers.

"I'm sure you're very kind. Since you mentioned it, would you mind comforting, Mrs. Couch? I misspoke, I mean Mrs. Daniell. She's going to start upsetting my mom, and I can't allow that." I say.

"Sure." The girl nods her head. "I don't know her at all. I think she means well. She respects your sister a lot. She showed me some of her writing. She's very talented. I have something to give you later. If I don't see you, I'll leave at the funeral director's desk. Go and offer a shoulder to the crying masses. They think they're mourning harder than you. It's a brother's obligation."

Life is not easy following just two years behind a sister who did well in school. She tried to get me to follow behind her in a lot of the same clubs, but I didn't take to a lot of them. Lucky for me, I didn't have to ride the bus to school, and I was always able to hang with her friends too. I haven't seen too much of her since she started working. The shock of it all is hitting me hard.

Leaving the viewing room where the closed casket sits, I move to the gentlemen's room. We were not planning on this happening. I thought Anneewakee and I would sit on the same front porch together forever and talk about the old days, which were supposed to be happening right now.

Everything is all messed up. I want to go back in time and save her. I want to know who did this. I want to be able to graduate right now. I feel stuck being a junior. I have not even had my driver's license for a year. How will I help when there is so much that I cannot do for myself yet?

If I am going to throw up, I am in the right place. I could hide in here forever, and no one would be any the wiser. A young man in a hoodie pats me on my shoulder. He cannot speak because he is crying so hard. If my friends love me, they will take me to Hudson's Hickory House at the end of the street before this weekend is over. I can drown my sorrows in barbecue.

The interior of the funeral home is spacious and calming. The building is a two-story rectangle and almost new. On the inside, the floor plan is open. You could stare at the second story ceiling for hours. I will just sit on a couch somewhere. I can greet people from a sofa just as well as if I am in the same room.

"Funeral homes smell, Robert. I'm sorry," Alicia says as she bumps into me.

Alicia is holding a vase of carnations from Beautiful Lee-Dunn. Alicia and Anne worked together there. Stephanie Lee's family owns the flower shop. I do not know what happened to the Dunn family. I wonder where Stephanie and the Lee family are tonight.

"Oh, those are cute," I fib. The flowers are hideous and look sad in an otherwise empty vase.

"Thank you. I arranged the red carnations myself. I thought about having one of our BLD co-workers do it, but I think Anne would have liked that I at least tried to do it myself. The shop is empty without her, but it was before. What's the news? How is the investigation going?" Alicia asks.

"We all have more questions than answers, as always, in these cases. It wasn't a botched robbery. A robber didn't burst into a steakhouse midday and steal anything. It was middle of the damn day. The size of the wound and blood loss don't match." I share. Alicia is a trusted friend of the whole family, not just Anneewakee.

"You sound like a seasoned police officer, Robert. Oh, I took a criminal justice class once; I mean, you know, before I quit and had Penny. Most violent crimes are committed by someone you know. More likely than not, they're of the same ethnic group too." Alicia says in an attempt at being helpful. It's not helping.

"Interesting. So we're looking for a one-sixteenth Scotch-Creek Indian. Thanks, Alicia. That helps. Security footage would be better. The steakhouse doesn't have any video share with us. They're relying on multiple eyewitness accounts. The steakhouse parking lot was busy the day after Christmas. The natural lighting, even the afternoon, was terrible. So, nothing was noticed until it was too late." I say.

"Eyewitness accounts? Who? After I had heard from Tommy about the phone tree call from the church, I thought about myself. You know, I was wondering where I was and what I was doing. I had been in class earlier that day and went to a saint's day dinner at

Jennifer and Jeremy's house that evening. I wish that I had forced Anne to go with us. I'm so sorry, Robert. I feel responsible." Alicia says and starts crying.

Alicia's watery eyes look like crocodile tears to me. She's up to something. She either knows too little or too much. I have not known her to take a class since dropping out of high school. I need to make a note of this before I forget it.

Placing the carnation arrangement on the table near a chair just outside of the ladies room waiting area, I give Alicia a hug. We all want to protect people stolen from us. Anneewakee has been, and probably always will be, the most precious thing in my life. I do not get any more siblings. I do not get niece and nephews. Without thinking about just me, so much was taken from her and the world. She could have done anything with her life. There was limitless potential there. My sister could have done anything.

"There wasn't anything special about that day," I say to Alicia. "I think it dipped just below freezing, but the weather was seasonally cloudy by the time Anneewakee left for work. There was no rain, snow, or anything to indicate anything out of the ordinary was about to happen.

"The day had been utterly mundane. The suddenness of it all surprises me. I know that they make us read all of these bizarre books in school about life and death. To me, none of it ever felt real.

Tonight doesn't feel real either. I feel trapped in a prolonged nightmare." I mutter.

An older gentleman wearing an old suit walks up to me. The man says, "We're just so sorry to hear about Anneewakee. I always looked forward to seeing her at the flower shop. She helped them do a real nice job for my wife's funeral several years back. She's a gem. Please let us know if there is anything that we can do, Robert."

Maybe that is something that I need to think about before the funeral tomorrow. How do I feel about how all of these people are acting? Mrs. Couch is acting insane. Alicia feels guilty because Anneewakee did not go to a St. Stephen's feast day meal with the Catholic family. That is all fine. Alicia does not know that Mrs. Kelly is trying to convert her one delicious cherry tart at a time. Jen and Jeremy's mom does make the best tarts.

"Son, how are you holding up?" Coach Daniell says while holding out his hand.

Coach John Daniell was our school principal last year until the Douglas County Board of Education found someone who loved administrative duties more than coaching golf. Coach was perfectly happy to get hitched and semi-retire back to Alexander High School. He taught health classes, coached golf, and oversaw in-school suspensions as needed.

"Robert's a strong one!" an unknown teacher rushes in. She seems kindly but a little flighty.

"Thanks?" I say. All of the teachers that I don't know look the same to me.

"Robert, I'm Mrs. Graham. I'm the college and career counselor. I just loved Anneewakee. I mean, we all adore her. So, I want you to come and see me when you're ready to talk about this. It doesn't make any sense. It's not going to make sense. That's why it's called a senseless crime. But, I want you to know, Sweetheart, that I'm ready to listen when you're willing to talk. When you're ready to go off to college, we'll talk about that too."

Feeling bombarded, I smile and shake a few more hands before escaping outside. The teachers have mistaken this solemn occasion for a pre-graduation prep talk for me. I do not like it. It does not convey respect for my sister. I go to sit in my truck for a minute. I am hiding.

At times like this, I feel like I should have a crutch of some kind. I want to sip Surge out of a flask like David. I want to have a cigarette like Tommy. I want to be able to arrange flowers into a beautiful disaster like Alicia. But, nothing is coming to mind. I flip through the cassettes in my car but do not see anything that I want to listen to right now. The radio stations have just stopped playing Christmas music.

Tap, tap. Someone knocks on my truck window. I do not know this person. I am concerned if I should roll down the window or not.

The man does not look too strange. He is wearing a sheriff's office uniform. I roll down the front driver's side window.

I say, "Good evening, officer. I haven't been drinking. I think I actually may have misplaced my keys since I sat down."

"Robert. It's Justin."

"Oh, *um*. So, how have you been?"

"Well, shit man, I'm doing better than you; aren't I? What happened to Anne was evil. There is no way that anyone on Earth ever deserves that. Hey, I gotta question for ya." Justin speaks fast. He looks over his shoulder once or twice before leaning inside the car a little.

"Shoot. Well, don't shoot." I say with a chuckle.

Speaking in a murmur, Justin says, "Things are going on that you don't know about, buddy. But, I think you need to know about some of this stuff. So, I want you to focus on doing well in school and see me in, what will it be? Eighteen months or so. I'm working at the county jail right now."

"You want me to visit the jail in eighteen months?" I ask. I feel perturbed.

"No, dude. Look. I am building my career from the bottom up by doing the crap work. You need to see HR at the sheriff's office to become a police officer. No one at school ever thinks about talking to us about becoming police officers; but, I'm telling you, the world needs police officers. The county needs police officers. Our county needs you. Now, get to it or something." Justin says while trying to seem older than he is.

"Anneewakee was killed in Cobb County," I say.

The remorse in my voice tastes bitter rolling off my tongue. It feels like every time the words come out of my mouth that they both become truer and more permanent at the same time. It is a little like being at drama club. I feel like I am merely practicing for her actual funeral that will take place sixty-to-eighty years in the future. Tonight is a dress rehearsal.

"I don't want to forget about Anneewakee. Please don't think that is what I am saying. But, you're going to become angry after all of this grieving. No one blames you. We would all be pissed. But, I want you to take that anger and focus hard on becoming a police officer." Justin says sharply. He's passionate about my career, which is strange.

"What good would that do Anneewakee? She's gone." I ask. I start looking at the inside of my truck cab. I tap the hips of the Hawaiian girl sitting on my dashboard. She does not want to dance tonight. Fine. I do not feel like dancing either.

"You're a grieving family. I want to give you your space. But, think about, Robert. What if you could prevent other families from grieving like this? *Huh*? What if you could stop the bad guys? What if, through professional work and excellent training, you could stop crap like this from happening? You could tip the scales of justice in favor of the good, hardworking people of Douglas County. You could do a lot of gratifying work." Justin's eyes light up.

Mulling over all of the information, present circumstances, and the awful events of the last few weeks, I agree. I nod my head. I do not say anything that is a firm commitment. But, I do feel like I have a renewed purpose. I think about Mrs. Graham and her offer to talk to me. I think that will be my first step. I will speak with her.

This good ole' country boy is not going to go to college. At least, I am not going right after high school like everyone else. College is for people who like school and academics. College is for people whose sisters are not murder victims. I like the people at school but not the academics. Sitting passively in a classroom is not for me. I would rather be doing something valuable for my community. I could skip the foreign languages too.

Justin taps the side of my truck near my open window and walks away. I inhale the cold winter air. It makes me feel less claustrophobic. The funeral home should just hang a sign near the casket and family members that states, "Caution. Don't crowd." Our society would follow directional signage for proper behavior around zoo animals but not for humans.

Death makes things feel so backward right now. If Anneewakee were a tiger, all sorts of law enforcement organizations would be all over the place trying to find her killer. But, she was barely a woman and was not married with children. Without grieving children to drag on screen, people are not going to pay attention.

The media will make up rumors and stories and then it will be Anneewakee's life on trial. They will talk about her short-comings. They will talk about how sometimes she stammered in her speeches and assume that she was on drugs when she had been in speech therapy for years and now only stammers when she is nervous. When a teenager dies, people always assume the worst.

Honk. I startle at another tap on my door. I accidentally hit my car horn. It is only Tommy. I know Tommy from the church. Tommy Hood is one of the reasons there were so many negative rumors circulating about Douglasville teenagers.

I nod and say, "Hey, Tommy. Thanks for coming. Mom and Dad are inside crying if you want to pay your respects. Sign the guestbook and stuff."

Trying to stick to the grieving family script that we discussed ahead of time, I try to limit myself to generic statements. I do not trust Tommy. He is always trying to be slick. My parents and I have to be careful not to say too much while the investigation is ongoing. It is an enormous emotional burden.

But, I have noticed that only the nosiest of people will ask the deep, personal questions. They are not asking because they care but because they want to use the information to twist it somehow for their personal gain. At this moment, I cannot imagine what there would be anything non-criminal to gain. I wonder if family members of people who die of natural causes feel this way too.

"Hey, man. I don't know what to say. Funerals suck. Wanna get high with me?" Tommy says with glassy eyes and a horrible smell on his breath.

Tommy has not showered in several days. His eyes are bloodshot. I am leery of Tommy. He seems to be high on something other than just marijuana. He is also drooling.

"No. I guess I should thank you, except what you're offering is illegal. Oh, and a flipping officer of the law was here at my window not two minutes ago! Get it together, Tommy." I say in anger.

"What are you? Some hot shit on campus now that you're a junior? You want to grow-up and be a police officer too? Modeling your future after Justin!?! He's a loser. You're a loser. Go be loser secret agents together!" Tommy shouts. As he's yelling, he starts thrusting his hands at his crotch in a lewd gesture.

Extreme anger flies all over me. I jump out of my car. Running over to Tommy, I shove him to the ground. Even though I am younger than Tommy, I am now bigger and more athletic than Tommy. He never saw it coming. My true advantage was that I am lucid, and he is not. Without looking too carefully what was underneath him, I grab him by his ratty old high school tee shirt. We skitter a few inches, but I let him walk away.

Strolling back inside the funeral home, I see Mrs. Daniell with her son, and Principal Daniell. They are exiting the front entrance. Finally! I am so glad she is leaving. I would like to run into Miss Daniell again. She came across as the complete opposite of her stepmother. She was down-to-Earth and didn't put up any pretenses. She seems honest, perhaps overly so. I would like to hear her thoughts on grief.

Mom keeps trying to emphasize how permanent Anneewakee's death is, but it is too soon for me to feel it. The rational portion of my brain can easily excuse my sister's absence as being away on a school trip or visiting with friends. I do not feel hurt when I walk by her empty bedroom. Everything is the same as it always has been. I just feel that she stepped out to go the work.

My body seems to have a muscle memory of sorts that is preventing me from believing that she will never truly occupy her bedroom again. Her things are there. Her writing is there. Her work is there. All is the same, and yet Death has come to occupy her bedroom for her.

When her boyfriend died in 1996, Anneewakee wrote, "I've been exposed to liquid death now, but it hasn't permeated the membranes of my soul. But, it will, like an invasion. The death's finality is dark incarnate."

Darkness and death have come to Douglas County. The night sky looks like gloomy. It is as though the complete darkness has swallowed all the stars. I stand in the open air with my face pointed toward the black hole of a winter night sky.

After five minutes or so, my eyes adjust from the outdoor lighting. I can see a few stars. If I am ever in a rage in the future, I will remember this moment and come back here. I will find a way to look at the stars and try again. I promise that I will try before I go into a rage again.

Life and death seem to swallow me. Then, I think about Alicia and Penny. I will ask Alicia if she and Penny will talk to the media for us. If she will talk about how Anneewakee was Penny's unofficial fairy godmother and that her death was a loss for Penny too. I do not want to contrive a situation like one of the characters in the thick novels that my sister read; but, Alicia did offer to help. My appearance on television as a crying brother is not going to do much. The public will identify more with a fussy infant.

Once inside the funeral home, I see that many people went for home the night. The funeral service is at ten o'clock in the morning. It is time for me to go back inside the viewing room. Our family does not believe in embalming, so the casket is closed. People find our ways strange, as we do theirs.

The trauma of tonight would be so much worse if I had to provide comfort to friends and family while standing next to my big sister's taxidermied corpse that is on display like a hunting trophy. How twisted is that scenario? Was the killer here tonight? Did he expect to walk through the reception line, greet my parents, and peer over his trophy? Was he going to come forward and claim it? Was Anneewakee the victim of a serial killer? I may never know.

I silently mouth, "Heavenly Father, Please provide me with the means to bring justice to my sister. Please let her death not go unpunished. Bless and support those who work tirelessly to bring justice and peace to this broken world. Amen."

"Were you just praying?" Miss Daniell says. We are alone in the viewing room with Anneewakee.

"Yes. I don't pray out loud always, but my lips move. Does that count?"

"No." Miss Daniell says. She seems concerned. "If you need to talk to your Father, you cry out for Him."

"Dad's in the other room."

"No, I mean your Heavenly Father. What? Do you think you're going to wake him from his sleep? Do you want me to pray with you? I'm a Baptist. We'll pray all day and all night without ceasing. My spiritual gift is exhortation. What's yours?"

"I don't know. Anneewakee would be able to tell you. I'm lost without her."

"This is a wake, not a pity party. What did you pray for?"

"I asked for a means to bring justice to my sister."

"Then He'll give you the means. His timing may not be yours. Your spiritual gift may be mercy. I have something to help you along your way."

The warm, brown-haired girl unfolds some pieces of paper from her pocket. She smiles a little and says, "I ripped these out of my stepmother's old teacher's edition of her senior English literature book. It's a selection from Sir Thomas Malory's 1485 *Le Morte d'Arthur*. I know you won't have Brit Lit until next year. It's the exact book that she taught Anne out of last year. The county got new textbooks this school year."

A blue line ran across the top of the pages. Outsets on historical context scatter across the five loose pages. There is a fresh highlight on one passage:

> "Now leave this mourning and weeping, gentle knight,"
> said the King. "For all this will not avail me. For wit thou well,
> and I might live myself, the death of ~~Sir Lucan~~ Anneewakee
> would grieve me evermore. But my time passeth on fast,"
> said the King.

The name was Sir Lucan in the passage was scratched out. Miss Daniell wrote 'Anneewakee' in its place. Miss Daniell touches my hand for a moment. We pause before she leaves the room.

I have decided. I am going to be a Douglas County Sheriff's Office deputy. I need to find Alicia, see Mrs. Graham, and contact

Justin. I want to switch all my classes over to criminal justice. I need to sign up for art class; specifically, photography.

Twenty-Five: Preeti

June 14, 2008 5:05 PM
Atlanta, Georgia

More days than not, I think everyone loved high school but me. I listen to salon clients recall bittersweet yet connective experiences; especially fellow women. I feel Douglas County High School robbed me of a traditional high school experience. Douglas County folk are more than mean. They are backstabbing and cruel.

I had not thought that I was a late-bloomer until my freshman year of college. I had attended Berry College for one semester before I had to stop. Becoming a single mom at age eighteen is not the path that I had imagined for myself. I do not want to waste a peak business day at my high school reunion with people asking me, "Hey, Preeti, what did you do with your life?"

I think of my mind as a vast library catalog. I do not like some of the drawers; they hold bad memories. One of the drawers contains an audio file that is on replay this weekend. Mrs. Couch is red-faced and screaming, "I see through all of you like you are panes of cracked glass."

I am cracked glass. What did I do with my life? I did not join the military after September 11th like a few of our classmates. I am not a physician or healing sick kids like Jennifer. I worked in insurance for years but found the schedule too inflexible after I had Nuri. I am enjoying my job during the day and take a class or two here and there at night. I want to own a bohemian-themed salon one day, but I do not have enough of a client base built yet. I live for the precious time with my belly dance troupe: Caravan of the Cherokee Roses.

My sweet husband and I ended up moving further out from the metro Atlanta area two years ago. The city of Temple is the new Douglasville. I am embarrassed that I moved further away from the city rather than closer in, but I needed to follow my clients too. The news media calls it *white flight* which is ironic since I am only half white. Like others, we were chasing less crowded schools and better home prices. With the current economic downturn, it seems like we were wise in our choices.

Even though I feel moderately successful as a good working mom, faithful wife, and homeowner, I feel like I will not achieve the Douglas County High School standard of success until I get my college degree. I do not know why a college degree is so important to me. A person does not have to have one to succeed in life. It is not a steadfast rule, or practical, in every situation.

When I search deep in my heart, I know that a college degree is not the automatic key to happiness that it was trumped up to be by our school counselors, teachers, and coaches. Our principal seemed to be the only one that was completely level-headed and simply asked that we stay out of jail. Well, good; I did. Nuri's biological father did not. He never met her. He dropped off a fat wad envelope of cash when I was about seven months pregnant with Nuri, never to make contact again.

Earlier this week, I had to make a decision that I had not planned on having to make. Melissa called me and said that she had reservations to go to the reunion and wanted to see some people, but not everyone. As always, I took only the briefest of moments to consider an optimal solution.

She is avoiding all of Tommy's friends, especially Alicia, Michelle, and Matt. She proposed that a few of us see each other privately, and separate, from the rest of the class. I was astonished. The high school Melissa would never have considered such a thing. Melissa liked to be seen almost as much as she liked playing fashion police for other people.

Earlier today, on the phone, Melissa said, "Preeti, I love you. You were my maid of honor. But, the truth is that Tommy died a long time ago, and you have no obligations to me. The reunion is not a situation where anyone needs to take sides. But, I feel a tremendous amount of stress coming from the prospect of attending this dog and pony show. I am afraid that Stephanie will think that the reunion is Homecoming: Part 2. I'm sorry to make you choose, but I have reserved a space at the Imperial Fez starting an hour before the other reunion."

Imperial Fez is magical. The interior of the Fez feels like a tent in a nameless Arabian desert on a summer night. The environment makes you want to stay all night and eat as slow as possible. I want to remember the exact taste of the roasted lamb shank and the red harissa sauce on the honey crackers. The cloth tablecloths feel luxurious. I never use a cloth tablecloth at home; just flannel-backed vinyl until the kids become more reliable with self-feeding. Here, you throw towels over our shoulders and eat with your hands.

After we arrive, time moves at the speed of light, and it feels like it is almost midnight and I am Cinderella. Matt and Michael join us along with a few other friends that received telephone call invites from Melissa. We wish Stephanie all the best, but we are thoroughly enjoying our impromptu affair. Knowing that we would be sitting on the floor, like preschoolers, we all wear comfortable clothing for the humid night. There are no prom dresses here.

"Preeti. You haven't aged a day. How has it been ten years? How are you?" Matt asks.

"Fine," I say. I look down and stir my tea several times. Matt notices, so I continue, "Do you want to know, for real? Or, are you merely being polite?"

"My highlight is that I'm not in jail and two years sober. Your life is more intriguing than that. How is the campestral life in the fair city of Temple? What about your children?"

"Nuri Viola Lambert is my oldest. She turned nine this past March. She'll be in fourth grade this fall. Nuri likes painting and is a freaking Junior Girl Scout like Crystal and Anne were. Let me know if you want to buy cookies this January. My next oldest daughter is Magnolia, but we call her Maggie. Leif is my only son. We celebrated his fifth birthday last weekend at Chuck E. Cheese's. Willow will be a year-old Labor Day weekend."

"What a way to celebrate Labor Day. Too bad Showbiz Pizza isn't still around. Showbiz was the best reason to behave while shopping with my mom at Cumberland Mall." Matt says.

Matt is smiling. I look away. He prattles on about Shakespeare Nuri's middle name as if he had a say in it. That son-of-a-bitch is a deceitful stoner. I cannot trust anything that he says.

Most of our group conversation is focused on the present and not elapsed time. We reminisce a little but focus on our highlights from the preceding ten years. Until I sat down, I did not appreciate how much I had missed my fellow CL English survivors. I feel preternaturally relaxed. It is soul-satisfying to be able to connect with my friends in a deep, philosophical conversation because we have such a common educational background.

We were together in class when our teacher announced the Challenger disaster. We sat in homeroom lines in the gym the morning we found out that the Olympics were coming to Atlanta. We cried in class when we heard about the Oklahoma City bombing our freshman year. On the flip side, we saw all the growth that Douglas County went through in those years. We knew the same people; we read the same books, and we survived similar conditions.

"What are you thinking about, Preeti?" Matt says as he scoots a little closer so he can hear.

"I was thinking about the first time we came here together. We came here for Anne. Do you all remember?" I say looking around the table. There were a few nods.

"Anne wanted us to do something special after taking our CL exam," I say. "We were all so stressed out and took it so seriously. The English Language and Composition exam felt like it was a death warrant if we didn't get college credit for one class. None of us were rich, but we splurged to be able to come to the Fez for Anne that night. I think the entertainment may have scared her a little."

The lights in the restaurant slowly dim. I hear fingers cymbals. A belly dancer in a bra top full of shining silver sequins and jewels swishes towards us with a sword that is on fire. She dances rhythmically and balances the sword on her head while her long dark hair sways around her. The cyclical ceiling fans cast false shadows all over the room. We enjoy the spectacle while sipping on our hot mint tea. It feels like the fans drop shadows and ghosts from our past at our table with us.

For a moment, I know what Melissa was talking about earlier today. When she is with friends from high school, the ghost of Tommy takes a prominent seat. Until someone brought a yearbook tonight, I had forgotten that there was an entire section dedicated to couples from high school. I wonder what happened to so many of them. Did they stay together? What was the yearbook staff thinking? I know that it was meant to be cute; we were only seventeen- or eighteen-years old. How would their spouses feel now? I did not meet Chuck until I was twenty-one. Now, I find that I still may have married young.

In the 1990s, it felt like all girls in Douglas County needed to marry by age twenty-two. There was some idiotic notion that to achieve the vision of the American Dream that our teachers had for us that we needed to be married young, contributing to society, and birthing future taxpayers. Right now, here in the shadows, it all feels overwhelming and dark. Matt shifts to sit next to me and places a hand on my thigh.

Trying to ignore Matt's hand, I focus on the dancing. Matt slips one his shoulders behind mine. His mouth moves towards my ear like he's about to whisper a secret to me. Instead, the stupid stoner pauses and breathes heavy for a moment. He remains silent but gives me a series of soft kisses on a tender part of my neck, right behind my hoop earrings. I do not like where this is going. I excuse myself to the ladies room.

Melissa follows me. There is so much that I am thinking about, and it is hard to find words. I wish I were telepathic; just for one night. I say, "Melissa, I'm going to have to leave. I will make bad decisions."

"Do you still care what people think about you?" Melissa asks in a philosophical manner.

"Well, no. I mean, I don't care what people from high school think of my life today. Of course, I care what my family and boss think. But, we've had such a good time tonight that I wish we could be in two places at once. The other reunion is probably over by now." I say wishing I could teleport.

"I'm sure the room will be full of limited edition Tony Hawk Sidekick phones and talk of who is listening to what on Napster. People will be exchanging business cards and gossiping. Dissatisfied homemakers will be looking to score with some of the guys that peaked in high school but are living off their parents' credit cards today." Melissa rattles off.

My phone rings but I do not recognize the number. I reluctantly answer. A crackling voice says, "Preeti, we have something to tell you."

"Who is this?" I reply impolitely sticking a finger in my right ear to drown out the noises around me. Melissa and I walk to the hallway.

"It's Amanda. You need to come to the Galleria. Meet us at the reunion. All of this second reunion stuff is petty. It's like that D.H. Lawrence poem that we had to read about the snake. What was it called?"

"It was called *The Snake*. If I remember, the man embraced his pettiness in comparison to the regal snake. Right? Hold on! Why are we talking about D.H. Lawrence? What's going on over there?" I say in a raised voice to drown out the background music.

"Shit hit the fan. Finish up what you're doing and get over here." Amanda commands. "Preeti, Mrs. Couch showed up tonight. She handed a box to Stephanie. None of us feel right opening without all of us here. I know you guys must not be that far away."

"What the heck? Mrs. Couch arrives with a mystery box? Should we call the police? I'll ask Melissa."

"One hundred and fifty Tiger alumni are here along with some significant others. I don't know how many are with you, but please bring all them here with you. Most of the people who were belligerent, drunk, or unkind have left. We're just sitting around waiting for you all. Tell Melissa that it's safe. I'll tell Stephanie to make an announcement that everyone is to leave her alone."

"No. I don't think Melissa would like that. Maybe we can just sneak in the back or something. She tries so hard not to draw attention to herself, Amanda. Melissa is different now. She's not the walking embodiment of all-things cheerleader now. Mel is, like, a proper adult and stuff." I say letting a little too much slip. Melissa hears it all.

Melissa and I join the rest of the group at our table. They agree that it is time to connect with the others. We are uncertain of what is happening but speculate a million possibilities during the short drive north to the Cobb Galleria. Did Mrs. Couch booby-trap the box? Is there a dead animal in there? Is it a first edition of Dickens? She always promised that she would cover Dickens. We never did.

Our CL English class did not discuss Austen either. Mrs. Couch intellectually robbed us. In hindsight, I wish that I had taken an English class in college too. I miss discussing Shakespeare; he makes my soul prickle.

As we are walking into the large room at the Galleria, there are just a few people left. The DJ is packing up his equipment. People have pulled chairs around the room and left them here and there. Heather and Nicole have already cleaned up their food offerings. Most of the people sitting around in a vague semi-circle are somehow related to Mrs. Couch either as students or family, as in the case of Brian and Alicia. No one knows what is inside the elegant box.

Stephanie nods at us and offers a quick greeting. She is pouring sweat and dressed in a suit, which I never expected. She has mega large breast implants and possibly a new nose. Heather's hair is red and Nicole looks much older. David has lost weight. He keeps rubbing a woman's belly. They must be expecting their first child. Looking at an unfamiliar guest, I can see that he is carrying a concealed gun. It does not seem to bother anyone else, so I am going to remain calm. He may be an off-duty police officer, working security, or passing through.

The suspense grips the rest of the group more than Melissa and me. Heels have long been kicked off. Hair has fallen out of place. Seth is sitting next to Heather and rubbing her shoulders. The room smells like school cafeteria tater tots. Jennifer, Jeremy, and another man are nursing clear drinks in the corner. In some ways, this scene could have been from ten years ago, just before the CL exam.

"I don't have a speech. Mrs. Couch handed this to me and then left. It was weird, y'all," Stephanie confesses with a furrowed brow.

"Well, open it," Jennifer shouts from the corner.

"I think she had a sacrifice to the composition gods and put the ashes in there," Michael says.

"You're right!" I gasp. "It's probably the remnants of some of those old blue composition books that we had to write in. Those things were awful, and the spacing was terrible. Do students still have to write essays in blue books?"

"Quit being melodramatic, Preeti," Amanda gets after me.

I almost did not recognize Amanda. She is wearing a strapless micro-dress that highlights her shocking number of tattoos. They appear permanent. I appreciate that it is thousands of dollars of wearable art, but some of us do not have money to burn like her. She probably does not have children to house, cloth, feed, and support.

"I bet its educational Blockbuster videotapes that she never returned!" Brian snorts.

ABSENT ON SCHOOL PICTURE DAY

"No, no. I got it! It's paperbacks with Book Crossing. She'll tag, label them, and then tell us to travel the world with them so she can see all the places we go," David says sarcastically.

Stephanie unties the extra-wide mesh ribbon to open the box. Her eyes are big for a moment and then look deflated. She starts, "Well, that was some stupid crap to pull on us. *Ugh.*"

Looking quizzically, we all peer into the box. There is a yellowing envelope with the handwritten words "c/o 1998" in blue ink. Underneath the letter, there is a smaller package that is wrapped in printed tissue paper and tied with unbleached butcher's twine. It must be something from the kitchen that she just happened to have on hand. Anne's brother, Robert, walks over.

"Does it look like anything in there could be evidence in connection to Anne's murder?" He is breathless with anticipation. "I have to know. If there is any possible evidence, we need to handle it with care."

"I don't know, Robert," Stephanie says and places a calming hand on his. "You of all people should go through this box now. None of us know what was in here. I asked Brian earlier. He said that he hadn't regularly seen or talked to his mom since high school either."

"We thought the navy and gold mystery box was going to be something related to class. If you think it's connected to Anne's death, take the damn thing," Jennifer says. She and Anne had worked on the newspaper together and were close.

Robert looks at the letter and holds it up to the light. It appears to be a single piece of white paper. The small book-sized package beneath it has some weight to it. We assume from the physical size that it is more substantial in length than Virginia Woolf but less than J.K. Rowling.

An additional letter is attached to the book-sized package. The letter is not yellowed at all. It must be recent. It reads, "Open at the twenty-year reunion."

"What gives with leaving a note to open up more crap in ten years? She's bat shit crazy. Let's burn it all!" Jeremy yells in anger.

Looking at the envelope one last time, Robert hands the entire package back to Stephanie. Stephanie makes a couple of offers to let anyone else open it. Several of us hesitate to say anything but the truth is that we secretly want someone to open it. We do not care who has the honors. Heather steps forward.

"While the rest of you were at lunch that day, I saw her write this," Heather says. "I had come back to the classroom to see if she was okay. Mrs. Couch was in the process of writing this letter. I thought she was teasing. I didn't know Lady Macbeth was going to nuke the fridge! I would have paid more attention or said something. You know I don't mean any offense when I say this, Brian.

But, I would have mentioned it earlier if I didn't think she was just temporarily insane."

"What happened, Heather?" I ask. Robert gets out a well-used spiral bound notebook.

"It seems like it was so long ago but it could have happened five minutes ago too. We left the classroom for lunch. I decided to double-back before I reached the Upper Banks stairwell. I pretended that I had forgotten my lunch money.

"Mrs. Couch was sitting at the student desk at the front of the classroom. It was the one she liked so much. I mean, I never saw her sit in the teacher's desk, did you? She was writing it as fast as she could. If I'm not mistaken, I think she wrote the letter on regular notebook paper. She didn't even clean up the edges."

"The paper does look like three-hole-punched notebook paper," Robert admits.

Heather starts shaking and holding her hands together. She used to do that before cheering at middle school football games. Both Heather and Nicole crisscross their arms when nervous, embarrassed, or both. It is strange to see Heather fall into the same habits now that she is an adult.

Finally, Heather opens the envelope. She reads the letter.

C/O 1998

Here, let me hold a mirror up to your faces. Let me tell you what I see. I see a mutilated, deformed glass class. I have toiled, turned, and broken my back trying to raise you all these past two years. But, you have learned nothing. Your gut reaction was to bite the hand that feeds you. What contempt!

In your futures, I see life and death. I see happiness and despair. I see it all. I see all infinite possibilities at the same time. It's like I have a crystal ball; and, while I cannot tell you the details, I see the big picture. I can see the forest while living among the growing trees.

I see the seeds that you are sowing now and know the harvest that you will reap. I see pain, immaturity, selfishness, and greed. I see backstabbing, lust, laziness, anger, pettiness, and pride.

You are swirling in a storm that will become your own layer of hell. It's a hell of your design, and you will have to figure out a way to undo that self-created prison. You have birthed a fictitious viper made of social constructs, spite, wrath, greed, overindulgence, self-entitlement, and slothfulness. It will wrap around your throats until it chokes you to death. Until then, you're all locked in here, in hell, with me.

If you figure a way out, find me.

Mrs. J. Couch

Heather sits down. She passes the note around to let everyone comment on it. Robert keeps a watchful eye on the paper. David refuses to touch it. Alicia snorts at the letter as she exits to smoke a cigarette. I do not know why Alicia is here. This written reprimand was not intended for her.

"What a rotten self-indulgent bitch!" Amanda vocalizes.

"I'm sorry. Mom loves a well-placed semicolon." Brian says as he shakes his head.

"If we read it backward, will it tell us some celebrity is dead?" Jeremy jokes while choking on his drink.

"We called her Lady Macbeth, but maybe she was one of the witches." Seth muses.

"Pettiness, huh? If I'm guilty, so is she." I say.

"What do we do with this? Do we go ahead and open the package?" Matt asks.

"No. That's what Lady Macbeth wants. She wants us to prove that we're impatient and lazy. Did you all not sit in class with her for two years?" Jennifer says in an accusatory tone.

"I think I'm going to call Will," Jeremy says and steps away from the group.

"David and I are going to go now." Carrie chimes in with a wave. Uneasy glances flicker between David and Matt.

"I'm sorry, brother. It was good to see you for a few minutes." Matt says while keeping his distance. "I'll go to the stage area and call Justin maybe."

"Who will keep the package for the next ten years? Is that practical?" Alicia asks.

"Just you wait. Matt will have a big long discussion about this on his podcast." Melissa says with one swinging knee crossed over her stationary one.

"His what?" I ask. We walk away from the group to talk more privately.

"Matt has a podcast that talks about all sorts of conspiracy theories related to Douglas County. Have you not listened to it?" Melissa says. Her eyes dart back and forth between Alicia and us.

"What does he say?" I press her.

"Goodness gracious, girl. Matt's Douglas County Dirt Diggin' podcast is how I keep with what is going on around here. Stephanie listens to it too. She's all the way out in California. You need to get iTunes and start listening."

"Is it gossip? I get enough of that at the salon." I say and flip my hair.

"No, no, no, Preeti. Matt has all kinds of theories about scandals going back ten-to-twenty years. Its teachers, politicians, law enforcement, and all manner of people in bed together. He thinks Anne was lured out to Cobb County for her murder. He says Tommy's death is connected to Anne's. Matt claims people were paid off with campaign donations. It's dark and profound, girl.

Listen to it. It's too salacious to be true, of course, but still a good listen." Melissa shares.

"So, Matt is a career podcaster now? Is that a career? Is it a thing? Where is he getting his information?" I ask and shrug my shoulders. Devious Matt hooked Melissa too.

"Matt worked on the Joe Couch campaigns with Tommy, Stephanie, Justin, Ryan, David, and Brian. So, I guess he met enough people who are connected. Besides, who does an independent pharmaceutical engineer not know?"

"Is that what we're calling drug dealers these days? He's a druggie. He's dangerous." I plead.

"Matt provides access to affordable medications these days. He makes runs back and forth to Canada for people, including me." Melissa says with scrunched brows.

"Please excuse me," I say and pause. "If Matt's here I'm certain Stephanie is snorting something questionable in the ladies room. David may have gotten high before reaching his car. The one deputy is off-duty and won't arrest him. You're all deluded."

"When you're ready to hear his story, find him online," Melissa says with a gentle wave.

"He's the snake in the garden. He will twist, plot, and deceive any Eve." I say with authority.

"If he's D.H. Lawrence's snake, then maybe you're the narrator, Preeti. Think about it."

"I don't feel honored by his presence. I will finish him off." I think silently but bite my tongue before my lips open.

When I reach the door to the ladies room, I stop. I do not want to be the same high school Preeti to dawdle after Stephanie to the toilet like I am her mother. I do not want to wipe someone else's cocaine into my hand and flush it down the toilet; again. Being a teen mom made me grow up quickly. I need to get home, back to my reality, and back to parenting my children. I am making the long drive back to Temple tonight. Unfortunately, I have to drive the entire length of Interstate-20's Douglas County section to get back home.

Twenty-Six: Amanda

March 30, 2016 12:57 PM
Carrollton, Georgia

North Korea, Nancy Reagan's failed drug policies, and Matthew Young can all kiss my grits. I thought I would burn in hell before stepping a single wedge heel back on the University of West Georgia's campus. The only shame I am wearing on my face today is Urban Decay's Sheer Revolution Lipstick in the shade Shame.

The lecture hall where I am standing looks almost brand new; which is surprising for a university that thinks it's as notoriously old as the University of Georgia. Matt asked me to help David Baggett's wife, Carrie, introduce Anne McWhorter's cold case during a criminal justice symposium. Carrie thought someone who knew Anne should present the case. Her brother, Robert, should be here. But, Robert is working day and night while police-turned-politicians run for sheriff back home. The vacant room is evidence of how few people remember her.

Carrie turns the lights brighter and then adjusts them to feature the single podium at the center of the small stage. There is seating for about two hundred students and faculty. I doubt that many will show up today; extra credit or not. Carrie, a non-tenure criminal justice lecturer, signals to a student to bring some extra chairs on stage. Jennifer, Preeti, and Melissa were kind enough to travel to be with me today.

"Amanda, I have a bottle of water for you. I know that the presentation will be emotional and challenging. I cannot think of anyone more equal to the task. Please let me know if there is anything I can do to make you more comfortable." Carrie says in a gentle tone.

Carrie is a survivor. David does not discuss the details of Carrie's story, but her empathy level is admirable. She loves her fellow humans. It is easy to feel like she is a sister to the rest of us. Some of us went to school together for thirteen years and still dislike each other. I met Carrie for the first time at David's wedding. She was kind and gracious when I showed up wearing Atlanta clothes in the Great Smoky Mountains.

Like a slow tap, students dribble in. Imaginary butterflies flutter in my stomach. The stage lights feel hot. There the front row is reserved for faculty and representatives from the school media. For my generation, it would have the college newspaper. Melissa squeezes my hand for assurance as she sits at a table to my right. Melissa will join Carrie, Preeti, and Jennifer as part of the panel discussion after my presentation.

Anne would say that this would be the perfect yearbook photo. We all look professional and represent the best that Douglas County High School has to offer. We are each unique and are a good crosscut of what adulthood looks like for our Millennial generation.

We did not have college yearbooks by the time I went to university and graduate school. That would have ridiculous at Georgia Baptist. There were so many media outlets that I had not dreamed of, even five years ago. I know someone will Periscope lecture. My pulse is rapid. I can sense my heart falling into a tachycardia rhythm. I try to think of something calming.

Taking a sip of water, I let Carrie give me a lovely introduction. I feel honored that she thinks so highly of me. I am dressed conservatively today. The polyester suit jacket itches around my neck. I feel a hair sticking out of my bun near my neckline. I have tried so hard to be as perfectly polished as Stephanie, but I have never been equal to the task.

I think to myself, "Speak slowly and clearly or they'll know that you're not a real Southerner."

Almost tripping on my way to speak, I try to make a casual joke, "Oh, you can take the girl out of Georgia, but you can't take the Georgia of out the girl. I almost tripped over an imaginary bulldog at my feet. That's a little *Midnight in the Garden of Good and Evil* humor for you. You don't have to remember that later for a test or anything."

Grateful that there are some low laughs from the faculty that are more our age, I look out at the students and try not to become intimidated. I lick my dry lips, hesitate, and start my speech.

"My story isn't completely my story. I'm joined on stage this afternoon by some robust and persistent women. They are like sisters to me. We have been through the good, the bad, and the ugly together. We could talk about so many things, the four of us. But, the five of us are here today to talk to you about what it's like to be friends with a dead person."

The crowd shifts uneasily and some students come in and move closer toward the middle of the room to let additional students sit down. I exhale deep and I hear the feedback on my lapel microphone. The students think I am deranged. At least the students are looking at their phones and not at me.

I start again, "There used to be more of us. You see, when we were eighteen, one of our friends was murdered. Her murder remains unsolved. Her death affected each of us in a different way. After Anne died, I moved back home. I left the small bougie college that I was attending and came back home to be close to my family and watch over my family a little bit. I don't know why I did that. Anne wasn't murdered on a college campus or anything.

"Well, that's not entirely accurate. We don't know why someone killed Anne. The crime still seems so random. I didn't know if the same thing could happen to my little sisters. For at least a decade, I looked for the boogie man around every corner. Not knowing what the boogie man looked like was a problem. It even occurred to me that the boogie man may not even be a man, but a boogie woman."

The students laughed. They can feel my hurt through my shaky voice. I hope their patience lasts. I want them to get to know Anne. "Our friend, Anneewakee, was a waitress at a local steakhouse called Lickskillet Junction. They were part-grill and part-live entertainment. The chain closed down years ago."

"I had my eighth birthday there then they closed," a young man shouts. I can't see his face because his camera side of his cell phone is facing me.

Preeti steps up to my lapel mic for a moment to say, "The last restaurant of the chain closed in 2006. But, we don't believe it was related to Anne's murder."

"Yes, our friend, Anneewakee," I begin again. "We called her Annie when we were younger and then Anne in high school. But, there was so much more to her than what the headlines say.

"You see, it feels like her story was cut short. We were eighteen-years-old. Many of us were reveling in the first stages of self-discovery. Anne was a people-person and loved seeing people at the restaurant. She got to see old friends and teachers almost every day. Our sweet Anne was the type of person who never met a stranger and, so, was able to meet new people too. I cannot imagine all the conversations that she was a part of during that period. It must have been exciting.

"We graduated in 1998. Without sounding like an old lady, things were different back then. People were more trusting and social. There were no status updates to discuss virtually. Anne was one of the few people who even had email when we graduated. I think she was the only person to write her email in people's yearbooks. We had no idea how technology would grow. Everything ahead of us in life was a mystery.

"Her death remains her greatest mystery. The day after Christmas, while the rest of us were on winter break from college, Anne was hard at work. She was at another location of the restaurant where she worked. We assume that it was to pick up more hours. Shockingly, in 1998, there was enough work to go around, even for otherwise untrained teenagers."

Carrie interrupts from the table microphone, "Yes, students. High school students used to work after school."

"Ain't no jobs now!" An angry student sounds from the back. "It's a capitalist conspiracy, man. Feel the Bern!"

"Thank you, Huntsley. You can forward your political agenda after the panel discussion." Carrie condoles.

"Since you mention it," Melissa interjects. "At the time of Anne's death, Bernie Sanders and John Kasich were both representatives in Congress. Hillary Clinton was First Lady. Donald Trump was a Republican without a television show. If you want to be the change, help us solve Anne's murder. Let's get back to Anne."

Blinking a few times and trying to reset, I begin again. "When I think about Anne, I think she should have either gone to work at the library or the newspaper. She loved reading and writing. I don't know why she stopped going to college that first semester. I think maybe she just needed more time away from school to discover who she was.

"The rest of us jumped in feet first simply because that was what our parents and teachers told us to do. Anne wanted to wait until the right time. She wanted her educational pursuits to be on her own terms. I honor her foresight. There is nothing wrong with that. At the end of the twentieth century, conventions were different. There was a horrible stigma around people who didn't go directly to college and become immediately successful in their chosen field.

"The Class of 1998 wanted to be best at everything at our high school. Our self-competition was intense and the teachers, parents, and administration only fostered that competition. But, somewhere around ninth grade, that competition among ourselves became unhealthy and we started to turn on each other.

"We started to shun fellow students who started making different choices for themselves. The students who took the CL English track made derogatory comments about the students who took CL Chemistry during the same class period. It felt like the school was telling us that we couldn't be good at sciences and language, we had to select one. So, Jennifer, Preeti, Melissa, Anne, and I chose the English track."

Jennifer clears her throat and says, "Now, I know what you may be thinking. 'Oh, those snobby girls. What could ever go wrong with them?'"

"White privilege!" A girl with pink bobbed hair says and points at Jennifer.

"There were things along the way that happened during that time that today, now that we have honed our voices as women, we know were wrong or inappropriate. The details are not material. I'm sure that if you're here, sitting in this room, that something must have happened in your life at some point in time where you had to stand up for yourself, or others, and tell the system that it was wrong." I answer on Jennifer's behalf.

The crowd giggles a little but the faculty appear anxious. I continue, "But, we look backward now that we graduated eighteen years ago. If all goes well, you'll be in a similar situation in sixteen or seventeen years. It's been awhile for me. Let me connect you back to 1998.

"One day, in fifth-grade, a teacher told the class that interracial marriage was wrong. We would call that bigotry today. We were on a school club trip once and the boys that were traveling with us wanted to watch a sexist movie from the 1970s. The girls sat mute on the bus and let them do that! We would not dream of that today. In each generation, we try to become more knowledgeable about people so we can better understand each other. We should strive to do right by each other. But, I have to tell you, that Anne was ahead of her time and that is why her death is tragic for me, personally."

An involuntary sniffle comes out of my mouth but I pull it together. A student in the back wipes his eye. He has lost someone too, bless his heart.

I speak through my sniffles to say, "The yet-to-be-identified murderer stabbed Anne in the stomach while she was walking through the Lickskillet Junction restaurant kitchen. She was not kitchen staff. She was wait staff. The thinking, back then, was that there must have been some reason why the killer was allowed inside and into the back of the kitchen."

When I pause to take a sip of water, Preeti says, "We think that it was a person who at least knew Anne; although, she never had any enemies. She was one of the most well-liked people that I ever knew. She was kind, thoughtful, and very understanding. She was the first to sit down and listen to you. I mean: she could authentically listen to you and know your story so well that she could re-tell it through her writing. She had a rare talent."

Choking down the speaker podium's lukewarm bottled water, I continue, "By profession, we are a nurse, hair stylist, speech-language pathologist, sociology instructor, and naturopath. Indeed, I don't think you could get more diverse. Well, in fact, there is one way that we could be more diverse. We could be a nurse, hair stylist, speech-language pathologist, sociology instructor, naturopath, and writer. Who would be the writer? Anne. That was her gift even though it was never her professional career.

"Anne and Jennifer led the newspaper staff together. Anne and Preeti were on the debate team together. Anne and Melissa sang together in the DCHS school choir. Anne and I were on the yearbook staff together before our senior year. Even though they never met, Anne and Carrie both cared about Carrie's husband, David; which connects them in a truly unique way. You see, we're all friends; Anne still connects us all. Her friendship has, in many ways, defied death. The bonds that forged yesterday still exist today, which makes them a touch immortal.

"So, here is how Preeti, Jennifer, Carrie, Melissa, and I are still friends to a girl who has been dead for eighteen years. We connect through Anne's invisible friendship thread. Our life stories are permanently intertwined.

"We're not giving up on finding her killer. We're going to keep her memory alive. When we were growing up, Anne's little brother said that he wanted to be a scientist when he grew up. But, instead, he went to work for the sheriff's office. Anne's death changed his life too. He's woken up every day, for more than half of his life, looking for any inkling of a clue that could lead to finding Anne's killer. Sadly, there hasn't been anything; yet." I conclude.

Carrie stands up at the table to speak, "That's where we need your help, as criminal justice students, and other interested members from this college community. We're asking for your help on this cold case. We want to bring Anne's killer to justice. She died in a time before video could be taken on cell phones and before restaurant security footage was available. Her brother has archived her website in a unique way."

As Carrie sits down, Melissa stands up to continue her portion of the speech. "We have lots of information that we have sorted through for years. But, as the saying goes, fresh eyes are always welcomed. We appreciate any help or expertise that you may bring to the table to help us find justice for our Anne."

Smiling like a used-car salesman, Jennifer interposes, "We hope that if you did not have the pleasure of knowing her in life that you can now, through her writing, despite her untimely death. We hope that you can see the beautiful person that she was and that she had the potential of becoming. My friends and I were not the only ones robbed of a great soul but our entire community and, indeed, the world. Thank you for your time and attention."

Shakily, I step back from the podium. I sit down as Carrie and a student begin to shift the chairs and set-up additional microphones to turn the lecture into a panel discussion. Preeti dots tears from eyes. Jennifer holds my hand. Melissa places some tiny white dots under her tongue.

Carrie is opening the floor to all the students and faculty to see if there is any information that they can dig out of memory banks.

We hope that they are relentless. I see that although David arrived late, he is recording session now. I hope he makes it available to the other friends, family, and classmates that couldn't be here today, including Anne's brother.

A student raises his hand, "Who was the last person to see her alive?"

Preeti answers, "We don't know for certain. She had a knife wound to the abdomen and was found already deceased. She was killed mid-afternoon in between the lunch and dinner rush at the restaurant. The manager claims that the kitchen was empty at the time of her death. We don't know why there wasn't at least one cook in the kitchen. The manager is the last person identified as seeing her alive."

A faculty member interjects with a deep voice, "So, the last person to see her alive, technically, was probably her killer. That does raise a good question. Why was no one else in the kitchen? Was food on the stove? Were there sauces in pots? Anything?"

We all look at each other. Jennifer, Preeti, Melissa and I do not know the answer to that question. Carrie pulls a smaller mic towards her, "Sir, that is an excellent question that we have not considered. We don't know the answer. My husband ate at the Douglasville location of the restaurant chain involved. He stated that the menu contained a variety of beef and pork. I believe there were assorted barbecue sauces. What do you advise?"

"Now, students, I am not telling you what to do. *Ho-ho.* Presenters, I don't want to give you false hope. But, I would seriously question if one of those employees was lying. If there was food cooking, there was a cook in that kitchen. I'm not telling you that as a researcher or professor. I'm telling you that as someone that started off working in the kitchen as a young man. Which," the man gestured to the students with his hands. "As far as you all are concerned, was a mere three months ago."

The students laugh graciously. I lose myself in my thoughts. My contemplations are in another place, another time. We are all thinking about 1998 Cobb County. Our silence spreads like a virus. Phones start to beep with virtual attendees asking their questions.

A young man in plaid stands up, "Who else was there?"

Carrie answers the question for me since she has copies of the case file. There was a cook who was with a waitress removing garbage for approximately fifteen minutes. There was a manager-on-duty but he was not in the restaurant at the time, which defeats the purpose of having a manager. The manager stated that there were not any customers at the time but that could not be perfectly true either. The three witness accounts do not line up.

While I knew Anne, I was not in the county at the time of her passing. There are many details that I am not sure of yet. I try to focus on the answers but my mind is wandering. Today, I am grieving my loss.

This past February was a horrible month for all of us. There is not a bereavement barometer to say who is feeling the worst and why. We are not caught up in a grief race to see who can get to the end the fastest. What would the end of heartache look like for me? Death, perhaps? Yes, February changed me. The silver lining was being able to catch up with David and Carrie. David and I never spoke in school, but I was only too happy to work with the girls on a project for Anne's cold case.

Another student pops up, "Do we have witnesses to interview?"

"Unfortunately, no," I answer. "One of the known witnesses has fallen off the grid. Another one passes away a few weeks ago. Another may have changed her name. She may not know that we are interested in speaking with her again. If she is watching on Periscope, please contact our host, Dr. Carrie Baggett, as soon as possible."

A hearing-impaired student stands up to sign to us. Melissa interprets, "The gentleman would like to know if there was a place that Anne may have kept notes. For example, did she have a favorite book? Did she leave a coded message with a highlighted or under-lined passage?"

Preeti stands up to answer. There is hesitancy in Preeti's voice when she says, "Anne's family shared with us that she had over three hundred books at the time of her death. They went through every book looking for any signs. A few of them had underlined or highlighted passages but we think Anne acquired those books secondhand from bookstores and local flea market. A previous reader may have marked the books."

"What condition did Anne leave her textbooks in?" A faculty asks. "A student's assigned school property reveals a great deal about their habits. What class did you have in common?"

"CL English," I answer. "But it wasn't just that one year. We were in class together for four years of the English program. Some of us went to school together from Kindergarten through twelfth-grade. We lived in a less mobile society back then. Douglas County was considered rural Georgia."

"What did her teachers indicate regarding the condition of her textbooks? They had to be signed out every year. Were they issued in good condition and, then, returned fair or poor? What were her reading habits? Was she an intellect? Was she too busy to read?" Someone else asks.

Melissa says, "I never knew her to mark in her textbooks. I borrowed her book once, during an open-book essay. The only page dog-eared was a Thomas Hardy poem. It was *Ah, Are you Digging on my Grave?* Now we all know the irony in that."

Preeti interrupts, "That is not irony. It's tragedy. The poem was about a dog."

"Think of it this way," a student starts. "If we were to pass Anne's grave, who would we find visiting it?"

"Her immediate family may still visit it," I answer. "But I'm not certain. We could set-up some inconspicuous remote surveillance. It's valid to think someone feeling guilty about her passing may come and go with some frequency. The Cobb County Sheriff's Office didn't have any reason to think a serial killer murdered Anne. There were no other similar deaths in the area at the time, not for a decade before or after."

"Did she have a tox screen?" A girl wearing wayfarer eyeglasses stands with her phone in hand.

"Yes," Carrie steps in and answers. "She was clear of alcohol and illicit substances. Her blood was not a normal consistency, so that may have contributed to her bleeding to death at a faster rate. It is unknown if this was the killer's intention or not. If it was, it shows premeditation. Premeditation would warrant pursuing a first-degree murder charge against a perpetrator."

"Was she the town trollop? Was there violence and slut-shaming in 1998? Did she have a boyfriend? Was someone jealous? Was she, for example, involved with an older man?" A young student in a raincoat asks.

"Thank you, Huntsley's neighbor, for alerting us that you were born in 1999." I comment. Several of the faculty laugh. "Yes, there was slut-shaming in 1998, sad but true. Anne was not the town slut. Several other girls could fight over that title. Anne was a virgin at the time of her death. She had a boyfriend for most of high school, but he was killed in a racing accident our junior year. She didn't have the opportunity to pursue another romantic relationship. She had no known ties with anyone romantically, male or female. There were no notes, love letters, or emails to indicate anyone."

"It had to have been someone that she knew," A faculty member speaks up. "There is an eighty-five percent chance that she knew her killer. That is how the killer was able to get so close to her. She may not have been in a sexual relationship with the individual but the chances are that he or she was known to her. Are you thinking what I'm thinking?"

"Dr. Morgan, are you suggesting that we interview everyone in the high school yearbook?" Carrie asks. She's serious.

"No, I'm suggesting that you start with interviewing the people who were at high school with you all but were not in the yearbook." Dr. Morgan states with conviction.

Carrie asks us a question over the microphone, "Do you recall who the yearbook editor was in 1998?"

Jennifer, Preeti, and Melissa stand up and walk over to me. I am shaking. I look down at my notes, but the words are blurry. I answer Carrie, "Yes, it was me."

"Who was absent on school picture day, Miss Strickland?" Dr. Morgan asks.

Twenty-Seven: Anne

February 2, 1998 10:50 AM
Douglas County High School

For many seniors, like me, the second class of the day is Physics. Unlike most of the science classes that we have had up until this point, Physics is located in the Cloer Building instead of Lower Warner Dorris. There are not too many classrooms outfitted for lab sciences. Science labs are installed and shared, even if the lab is in the vocational training building. I finished all of my math and social studies classes last year so I could clear my senior schedule for what was the equivalent of four years of English in one academic year.

"Anne, how do you know how to do a tick mark every inch? Is it from memory?" Flannel Guy compliments me. Today is a rare day indeed.

"Practice makes perfect. My Grannie McWhorter taught me how to sew when I was little. Oddly enough, all of that came in handy when I started doing yearbook and newspaper layouts. Fate is fickle, though. I don't need these skills now. Things are going digital." I reply with a half-smile.

"Digital? What? Like, Digi Pets?" Justin asks.

"We format our newspaper using software on a computer and electronically upload it the Times-Georgian. I have to scan all of our pictures in one by one and make sure that the TIFF files aren't too big." I say, trying to get through our morning project.

If we finish fast enough, I will have time to look over my English homework before we go to Mrs. Couch's class. She has zero tolerance for sloppy work. I have had a challenging start to 1998, and my homework is not up to her standards. During my last before-school book interview, Mrs. Couch pointed out no fewer than thirteen critical areas that I needed to improve. I wish I had asked her to rank my shortcomings in order of importance to her, the person grading me.

"So, we're supposed to be gifted or whatever, right?" I ask rhetorically while looking at the fire-proof countertop. "Why are we answering questions at the end of each section of a literature book like we're tenth graders? Shouldn't we be writing essays about life or something more substantive?"

"Someday you will need to know the color of the scarf that the lady was wearing in Steinbeck's short story *The Pearl*. Just you wait and see, Anne." Our Physics teacher says. He overheard me and answered sarcastically. He feels the deep pain that is brooding in my soul.

"Well, what color was it then?" I ask. I don't need to know right now, but I certainly did two years ago in tenth-grade.

"Oh, I don't know, but I always choose blue. It's my lucky color. And, all of you Douglas County Tigers that are about to go out into the real world should feel lucky too. The answer is always navy and gold, or, whatever your school colors are. How about that? And, never roll your trash out on Sunday." He laughs.

For a moment I think to myself, "What if I go to college? Will their colors be my lucky colors? What if I go to law school? Or graduate school? Which will I choose? What will be lucky for me?"

After our little experiment, I sit down for fifteen minutes to neatly rewrite my answers on college-ruled paper. I only had wide-ruled at home last night but traded some today with a fellow student that did not care if she had wide-ruled or college-ruled. Mrs. Couch prefers college-ruled.

Jennifer, Jeremy, Flannel Guy, and I walk from the Cloer building through the winding path in front of the historic school and toward the Banks building. We love watching the cars pass by on Campbellton Street. I also like to look up at the greenhouse. I love that greenhouse. It is my favorite spot in the entire school.

Hardwood trees line the front of the school property. Unlike us, the trees are old and mature. It gives the whole campus a college town vibe even though there were no colleges in our little county. I wonder if the exact same trees were here for the first graduates, during the reconstruction era in the New South.

The morning has been foggy and overcast, but we never miss an opportunity for fresh air. Jennifer looks inside the windows of the college and career office as we walk through the front of the school, entering Mashburn Hall. The buildings are all named for teachers that were teaching when my parents were here. I wonder if the teachers that we have now will have buildings named after them one day. I cannot imagine our community loving and appreciating a teacher so much that they would name a building after him or her.

Meekly, I hand in my homework and sit down. I glance over at the desk that had belonged to Crystal last year. I should have said something more inspirational to her when we went to see her at Waffle House earlier this year. Trying to gather my thoughts to be ready for today's discussion, I over focus and hear Tommy whispering to David.

"Yeah, something is going on. Joe Couch worked at Eastern Airlines at Cumberland Mall for a long time but then they closed down and stuff. I mean, they closed when we were in fifth-grade. So, he's been trying to run for a couple of different political offices for a long time now. He's on his third or fourth campaign. He was in the paper again this week. I think she's just jealous. It put her in a bad mood, and she's on a rampage today, dude. You better double-check your work before you turn it in." Tommy advises.

"Hey, why don't you ask Alicia to ask Brian? Aren't they dating now?" David says.

"What's going on is that she's ready for Brian to stop being in trouble. You know Alicia is pregnant, right?" Tommy says a little too loudly.

"Shut up! No. When did that happen?" David says with surprise.

David is one my best friends but also an idiot. I wonder if he knows the origin of babies. His parents never signed permission slips for him to attend Sex Ed at school.

"Oh, dude! C'mon. Like nine months ago or whatever. She's going to have the baby soon. I don't see how her stomach could get any bigger." Tommy says.

We start our book discussion for class. Today it's Joseph Conrad's *Heart of Darkness*. It feels as though it has taken half a lifetime for us to reach Modernism. The sun shines through the windows behind me; except where blocked by old student artwork. I will stay optimistic. The chances of Mrs. Couch being as fanatical about Conrad as she is about Chaucer, Blake, Donne, Shakespeare, Dickens, Austen, and Milton are low.

The filing cabinets give the impression they have the same papers leaking out of them since 1996. All of the chairs seem the same. My fellow students look the same except I think I see a tattoo on Preeti's foot. She probably got it earlier in the year, but I can see it now because we are starting to wear sandals again as winter shoes wear out. Our backpacks are looking worn for this early in the school year. Everyone's packs are slouching by our desks. The clock ticks the same as ever.

"Does anyone have any questions?" Mrs. Couch asks half-heartedly.

"How is this guy British? Conrad is buried at Bonaventure Cemetery in Savannah. Our troop went last year." Seth, the know-it-all, says.

"Seth, you're thinking of Conrad Aiken. Right, Mrs. Couch?" snooty Nicole answers.

"Who is? What?" Mrs. Couch is trying to follow the discussion, but we're tail spinning out of control. It reminds me of a talk that Tommy's football buddy Jason had with us at church a long time ago. We need to try to focus.

"Is Conrad Aiken going to be on the CL exam?" Jeremy asks, making things worse.

"We don't know ahead of time who or what will be on the exam. It is essays, kids. Essays!" Mrs. Couch says.

Mrs. Couch looks flustered and touches her right hand to her head as if to shield her eyes from the minimal light that is coming through the windows. It is mid-day, but the light is not that bright. The gesture does remind of Lady Macbeth in the play that we saw earlier this year. We are not allowed to say Macbeth aloud in the classroom.

"Conrad Aiken is buried in Savannah. He was friends with T.S. Eliot and wrote short stories. He had a very tragic life. But, I don't think there is a connection between Joseph Conrad and Conrad Aiken. The two share a name, so what? If I survive this school year, I'm taking a vacation to Savannah, not a school field trip! A proper holiday exclusively made up of adults. I'm going to sit on a brick patio and tell everyone that I'm retired. I won't retire this century; but, to heck with it." Mrs. Couch says with a lilted moan.

I cannot help myself. Words spew out of my mouth, "Oh! I love 'The Waste Land.' Crystal was the perfect person to have–"

"Don't talk about Crystal, Anne. That was inappropriate. You know my classroom policy on people who aren't here anymore. They're dead to me. Crystal made her atrocious decision, and she'll have to live with it. I forbid you from speaking her name."

"Yes, ma'am," I whisper and pick up a pencil. I squeeze the wood and lead until I think it just might bleed.

"Are there any questions about *Heart of Darkness*?" Mrs. Couch prods. "Did anyone read? I mean, use their eyeballs to actually read it and have their brains interpret the incoming words, and not just peruse the Cliff Notes? I will know if you did."

"Is the River Thames [th-A-m-es] in the story the same as the one in 'The Waste Land' that Anne just mentioned? Is it spelled T-h-a-m-e-s? Because I thought that we read about that one and called it the Thames [tA-mes] river. Mrs. Couch, why are you holding your head?" Michelle says in a direct manner.

"If anyone asks, will you children please not tell anyone that I was your teacher? I've failed. It's the Thames [t-em-z] River or the River Thames [t-em-z]. It doesn't matter. I can't believe the State Department would ever issue any of you a passport. I doubt you could fill out the documents, much less have a photo taken and remember to take it with you to the damn post office." Mrs. Couch starts to shake her head.

"Maybe you should go to Savannah for Spring Break?" Stephanie says, trying to be supportive.

"Or, you could wait until later and take your grandbaby, too," Tommy says with a stupid grin on his face.

I feel sorry for Tommy. He's about to die. We're all going to be on WXIA for the five o'clock news. By then, our teacher will have murdered someone. Maybe I need to take this opportunity to scribble a note to Robert in my journal.

You've been a great brother. Please don't miss me when I'm gone. Lady Macbeth killed me. Tommy and I had it coming.

"You're a horrible person. Who says something like that?" Will screams until he's red in the face.

Will aims, for once, and hits Tommy on the nose. Will was reading a John Grisham book inside his Brit Lit textbook. At least Tommy got hit with Grisham instead of Prentice-Hall. Tommy starts to get up, but the book bounces off Tommy's face and hits Matt. Matt startles and thinks Tommy hit him.

Seeing the surprised look on Will's face, Matt stands up and throws his literature textbook, which we aren't reading out of anymore, at Will. Instead of hitting Will, Will ducks, and the textbook hits the filing cabinet. The filing cabinet has been overload with papers since about 1973. It teeters for a moment before a lot of stuffed-in papers fall out. The drawers slam shut properly for the first time since we started high school.

Mrs. Couch's face flushes red. I decide to lower myself in my desk as far as possible. I know Brit Lit will be particularly invective between now and the lunch bell. In anticipation of being yelled at, I let go and cry a little. I fold my arms on my desk to hide my face. If I were wearing a hoodie, like Matt, then I could pretend to be elsewhere.

I can hear Mrs. Couch exit her desk. Jennifer hits my shoulder for me to look up. Mrs. Couch looks vexed. Her lips purse together. She stands tall and leans over her desk and braces herself on the edges. When she opens her mouth, her teeth are locked like a rabid possum.

"You sniveling little twerps. You idiot children. I am not your babysitter. I am your teacher! How you act and behave, at school and in the real world, reflect on me. Don't embarrass me by intentionally acting stupid. And, if you're genuinely stupid, like Anne is, then I have no patience for it. Not today. Not ever!

"Tommy is just pushing buttons. He'll get his one day. My private affairs are my own. It is no one's business but mine. How would you like it if I went around talking about your personal lives openly? Like everyone knew. *Dammit*!

"I read your writing. I see through all of you like you are panes of cracked glass. I see it when people are screwing around. I know who is doing drugs. I can even smell pot on your paper. Oh, yes. I remember the smell! I know when your parents are away and leave you at home alone. I can discern if you've only had mac n' cheese to eat this weekend because you don't know how to fix yourself a real meal even though almost all of you are eighteen-years-old now! *Dammit.*" Mrs. Couch screeches at us until her voice cracks from strain.

The entire class feels the rage pouring out of her like hot lava. I pick my feet up off the floor a little in case any of the invisible fury spills onto the floor. I am frightened, as though I am experiencing a natural disaster. Shockingly, the calmest people in the room are Jeremy and Jennifer. Having survived an actual disaster, they act like they could have been in their parents' hot tub right now. They did not care; but, they were the only ones.

Amanda looks at Mrs. Couch for a moment but rushes for the door. She does not make it far and vomits in the trash can. She is a quaking nervous wreck. All the teachers see such potential in Amanda; for her becoming a doctor. Up until this minute, she has been pampered and babied her entire academic career. I do not know if the teachers think that they will take a slice of her credit pie when she cures some disease. They seemed to be lined up waiting for her to do something amazing.

Melissa places a hand on Tommy's shoulder, "You went too far. Apologize. Now!"

"Girl! I'm not going to do a thing you say, just because you told me to. Who do you think you are?" Tommy looks at her with condescension.

"Don't talk to her that way!" Preeti yells at Tommy too. "I'll kick your butt, boy!"

"The girls need to sit down and let the adults speak," Tommy starts to smart-mouth.

"Oh, speaking of feminine voices," Mrs. Couch shifts to Tommy's desk.

Looking him directly in the eyes, she gets in his face and starts screaming, "I love reading your writing most of all, Thomas Hood. Or, should I say, Trudy Hood?

"I love reading between the lines about how difficult it is to be married to a man that loves another woman when that woman is dead. I know how that pains your heart. I know how that tears at your soul. I know how you longed for more children, but then there were none. I see how empty your womb is. I know your only offspring is such a disappointment. I see it all. It's crystal clear to me. People living in glass houses shouldn't throw stones, Tommy! Sometimes it hits their beloved mother."

All of this would have been much more dramatic if Tommy could synthesize what Mrs. Couch was saying. She knew that Tommy's mom had been writing for him. A little bit of his mom's soul had leaked out in the loneliness and desire to connect with a reading audience; even if that reading audience was her son's teacher. It is pathetic. Our essays are layers of wretchedness, gross, and disappointment for us all. We are behaving like poorly raised children.

Walking to the back corner, Mrs. Couch grabs the nearest English anthology. She raises it above her head and slams it on the desk right in front of Matt's face. Matt has been unconscious for the entire class, and Mrs. Couch is sick of it. The edge of the book clips Matt's arm. He is awake now.

Matt's invisible social bubble bursts. He had been listening after all. Matt, of all people, is contemplating Mrs. Couch's frenzy. I think he may secretly be smarter than we give him credit.

"Matthew, I know what you nasty, plotting boys are up to with your essays. I'm looking at you, Matt, Tommy, David, and Justin. Brian tried to gaslight me into thinking I was crazy for suggesting that there was a plagiarism ring running here. You little shits!" Mrs. Couch says and throws the British anthology at her replica-sized guillotine.

"Not all the boys are guilty." Matt stutters.

"Oh, no? Jeremy's thesis outline 'Freudian Slips in Beckett's *Waiting for Godot*' is so generic I could have bought it at the damn corner store." Mrs. Couch retorts.

"At least it wasn't a blue light special, eh?" Tommy says nudging Melissa. Melissa sits lifeless, ignoring Tommy.

"I didn't know what to say. I'm sorry." Jeremy says. He dashes out of the classroom.

"What?" Mrs. Couch says and looks at Jennifer. "Are you not going to plead for an exception for you and brother for the millionth time? Act like you don't know the rules because you had to go to elementary school in Carroll County? *Wah, wah, wah.*

"Poor baby. Are you going to sit there, Little Miss Muffet, and behave as though rules don't apply to you today? Like you're some rogue princess sitting high and tight on the outskirts of high school society? No wonder you're friends with Anne. You need empty reassurances. Well, you'll find none in this classroom. The next piece of trash you hand in is going straight into the garbage pail, little miss."

I am not smart. I am stupid. I probably should not go to college. But, everyone is going to college, and that is what is expected of me right now. I will keep pretending. I will fold up my acceptance letter and tuck it away someplace special. But, this is it. I cannot endure anything like this ever again. I am not going to have my parents pay thousands of dollars for foolishness like this to happen next school year. I will pretend that I am going and then simply not go. I am staying home.

Will gasps in fright as Mrs. Couch nears him. She says, "Sad, sulky, Will. Social norms got you down? You think that wrapping pretty paper on lies makes it all better? Well, it doesn't! You may be the only boy in here bold enough to believe that your best is better than buying and copying other students' work.

"Do you ever read what you write out loud? You have disjointed sentences and comma splices from the sixth ring of hell. You are a mess, child. For goodness sake, figure out your narrative viewpoint. If you don't know who you are, how will your audience? You don't need to publish. You need to finish a nice quiet desk job somewhere away from other people. You're all over the place. You're cocky, but honest, Robinson Crusoe. You need just need a trailer on a beach."

Closing my eyes, I try to ignore the venom secreting from Mrs. Couch's mouth. I will live in Douglasville forever. I will be dull but happy. The permits on trailer homes are relatively inexpensive. I hear Carroll County permits are cheaper. There is nothing wrong with living in a trailer park; at least I will not make my parents go in debt. Some other person can take advantage of the HOPE Scholarship money that would have otherwise been mine.

"Michelle. I always forget you're here. You are the most forgettable student in the class. You never say anything worth hearing. You never write anything worth reading. Your opinion is never your own or original, so you lose on both counts. The patience that you alone have sucked out of me this year is equivalent to what my classes of 1971-1972 and 1972-1973 did combined. You're an emotional vampire. Stop it. If you need a pat on the head like a good little girl, then transfer to CL Chemistry. Figures and numbers comfort some people. Knock yourself out." Mrs. Couch orders.

Heather and Nicole huddle together. Mrs. Couch overlooks them although her facial expressions show her disappointment. David and Seth are next to face her wrath.

"David, I'm disappointed in you. You were supposed to be the one smart enough to lift your family out of the cycle of poverty. Shame. Shame on you. You're the laziest son of a bitch I ever saw. You don't know your right hand from your left. Pick one and slap yourself with it." Mrs. Couch says to David with a *tsk, tsk*.

"Seth, you have your mind on what most boys your age have their minds on: girls. That will get you into trouble. Little girls love nothing more than to get little boys into trouble. One day you'll wake up morally corrupt and financially depleted. Don't call me for help when it happens. Your writing is transparent. If you make yourself that open, you risk fragility. Stop it!" Mrs. Couch says.

Seth ignores Mrs. Couch. Next, she sets her sites on Amanda. I mouth a silent prayer that Mrs. Couch does not say anything racist.

"Amanda. You're the great pretender of the group. You're not some goody-two-shoes. You are dark, girlfriend, but you will never be cool. In your attempts to take the road less traveled, you always take the crowded highway. But, silly girl, you never see it! You're the antithesis of original.

"In the seventies, I would have pegged you as a member of the counterculture. But, that's where you're misguided. You struggle with cultural identity, and it is exposed through your writing. You have no authentic voice.

"The newspaper staff asked you to review *Titus Andronicus*? You never read it. I am probably the only person in the county who is smart enough to discern that. *Oops.* Hope I didn't let one of your secrets slip. You are in pain. I see that. I have always seen that. Do you think your ninth-grade teacher bringing home a sliver above minimum wage knew? No. She had no clue. You hid your shit well from her but not from me.

"If you don't get some perspective, you won't last in college. Everyone around here is banking on you being the little Korean girl from Douglas County that makes something of herself. Well, damn if that ain't a tall order for someone so short."

"Melissa, you're an ungrateful little minx. You have what every other girl in your class wants and yet you whine incessantly about it. Michelle would probably cut your throat if it meant that she would have Tommy. I have wondered if I'm going to find your body stuffed in a locker covered in some foul witchy concoction Michelle has cooked up.

"You are in perpetual grief. You imagine the horrors of small-pox outbreaks and other tragedies, but it is not something that has ever touched your life. You are sad all the time and have no reason to be. Your stomach is flat, your tits are high, and your ass is round. Get on your socked knobby-assed knees and thank the Almighty. Goodness. You try the patience of saints. If you turn in one more piece of shit on death and dying, I will hand Michelle a knife, so help me!"

Mrs. Couch swishes around the room back towards the boys. "Saint Michael, you're a holier-than-art-thou hustler. Your father's theology permeates every sad sack of shit you hand to me. Why?

"Why do you put me through that? If I wanted a sermon from your father, I would go to his church Sunday morning. But, you know what? I don't. And, no one asked you either. In pathetic attempt to please your father, you are drowning yourself and every teacher you come into contact with here. I'm climbing on a life raft and leaving you out at sea."

Michael grows bold. He stands up and says, "Thank you for sharing your feelings. But, it's not my father's church. It's the Lord's church. He does with it what He wills. You are still welcome to visit whenever you like. I am offering you grace and forgiveness for today."

"Sit down and shut up!" Mrs. Couch yells at Michael, but the rest of us voluntarily comply.

"I'm offering you unconditional grace and forgiveness, Mrs. Couch."

"Well, I don't accept it, Michael. Up your game or I will throw you out of this program."

The door knob turns. Brittany is at the door. Dribbles of blood cover the front of her shirt. She is holding an ice pack in one hand. Her nose is a puffy purple mess. The entire class holds their breath to see if Mrs. Couch will lay into Brittany. Brittany blinks away tiny tears.

"I have a note," Brittany says. The swelling is moving up her face towards her eyes.

"Everyone has a note. Everyone has an excuse. No one is responsible for any damn thing anymore in this piece-of-shit education system. The whole country is going to hell in a handbasket and the politicians just want us to vote for more school bonds. I am a school bond!" Mrs. Couch laments.

Knowing that either Preeti or myself are next to face her wrath, I clutch my stomach. The Couch and the Lee family are in business together. I doubt that Mrs. Couch will rail on Stephanie like she has the other students. Stephanie crosses her legs and folds her arm. She is putting on her emotional armor. I yearn to be battle-ready at the drop of a hat like Stephanie.

Mrs. Couch heads toward Preeti, "Gypsy girl, you don't have a father figure. You never write about men or male characters. If you're going to survive this life, you have to be willing to work with men. You must work harder than the men because of your gender.

When one woman fails or uses her body to get ahead, then our entire gender suffers. Don't be that girl. Don't be that ignorant ass girl that chases the first di-"

Bzzzzz. The lunch bell sounds. The first period of the third block is over. Brittany backs out of the room with her backpack still on her back. The boys follow Brittany at a swift pace. David, Jennifer, and I are the last to leave the classroom. I have almost escaped.

"Anne, grow up and stop being stupid. The world will eat you alive. Looking cute will not get you out of trouble when you're forty years old." Mrs. Couch says as she flips through her gradebook.

Mrs. Couch does not make eye contact with me. I shuffle out the door. Jennifer puts her arm around me as we leave the hallway. David contemplates going back and telling Mrs. Couch off a few times. After a moment, he joins us heading up the stairs. Jeremy is nowhere to be found.

My dream just died. I need to devise a new life goal between now and when lunch is over. If I fail, I do not think I will be able to walk back into this classroom one more time. I have approximately eighteen-minutes.

Twenty-Eight: Penny

October 2, 2014 3:24 PM
Villa Rica, Georgia

Walking up to the Pine Mountain Gold Museum campus, I see four happy brown-headed rascals running around the outdoor shelter's picnic tables. Tonight is the first night of the gold museum's annual Ghost Train and my parents' high school class has shown up to lend support. Seeing the boys together, I see a spectacular gift. They have siblings. I'll never have any.

My parents' high school friends invited me to attend their annual informal Halloween meet-up. This group has been meeting for over twenty years. While I have met a few of them before, I don't know the women here very well. In a different world, the four rascally boys would be my cousins or step-cousins. Our families are estranged. I'm not certain what to call them.

"Oh! To be sweet-sixteen again! I am positively buzzing with excitement for you, Penny." A freckled woman wearing a gold cross necklace says. "I was sixteen-years-old the summer that the Olympics came to Atlanta. Hush. I am talking like an old hag. What am I thinking? Practically all of us were sixteen that summer. Your Auntie Anne had a July birthday, so she couldn't drive during the Olympics. But, the rest of us were all over Metro Atlanta working and volunteering."

My reasons for visiting with my parents' classmates are nefarious. I want to learn more about them as teenagers. I want to know why my father has forbidden me from dating. I want to know why my mother never talked about her teen years. I know a tiny bit about Auntie Anne. It's odd to hear people talking about her like she is still alive. I know that she loved me and took care of me, but I don't remember her. An unknown assailant murdered Anne when I was an infant.

"Now, Penny, you couldn't possibly remember all of our names." A woman with leathery skin and crow's feet says smiling. "I'm Heather. Your mom and I used to go to church together. You are too young to remember it, but we went to a wedding together once. I looked after you while your mom worked on some flowers at the last minute. Nicole and I work on the paleo food truck. That's why we smell like apples this time of year. As you can tell, Nicole thoroughly enjoyed being sixteen. My situation was different."

"Let's not talk about dead mothers today," Emma says.

I recognize Emma from stalking her Facebook page. She is my father's stepsister although they never lived under the same roof. I am not confident that they have met. Emma went to Alexander High School and is two years younger than Daddy. She walks over to me and gives me a hug. I am not certain what to do. I am not used to women hugging me. I feel awkward.

"Penny, I hope you don't mind. We wanted to invite your aunt too." Heather says with a tentative twitch in her voice.

If my family story were a patchwork quilt, there would be pieces missing. Some of the patches are on top of other patches; those are the lies, omissions, and half-truths. Pieces have been ripped out and hidden. There are colorful, but mismatched, fat quarters that we do not discuss. We do not talk about Emma.

"Hello. I'm Penny Kennedy-Couch. I guess you know I'm Brian's daughter. Well, Brian and Alicia too. Daddy's at work right now. I got a ride after someone invited me. I don't know why I'm here." I say while avoiding eye contact. Emma is intense.

A fifth-grade project required me to research my family history. If I had to give an estimate, I would say that I know less than half of my family history. Daddy does not like to talk about his parents. The Couch family was infamous in Douglas and Cobb counties. My grandmother remarried. She and I have never spoken. In the process of her new marriage, I acquired a step-aunt.

"Our circumstances are unique," Emma says smiling. "But I would love it if you called me Aunt Emma. I am technically your aunt through marriage, but also your aunt by choice. Do you want to meet the family?"

Family? I have a family. I've been in the awkward position of not having any close family for so long that my brain is full of ambiguous words. The words turn into phrases on the tip of my tongue. Those phrases sit there gawkily waiting for my brain to tell them what to do. My words, phrases, and I remain mute.

The one phrase that is lurching on the tip of my tongue is, "Aunt Emma, if you love me so much, why haven't you contacted me before today? Why didn't you call? Why didn't you text? I wish you had taken me shopping for my eighth-grade dance dress. I wanted an aunt, or someone, there when I started my period."

There were years of empty seats on grandparents day at school. I am not certain if my grandparents, on either side of my family, even knew my name. I nod my head at Aunt Emma. She introduces her sons: Julian, Samuel, Giles, and Robert.

Cousin Samuel walks over to me, "Hi. I'm Sammy. I'm four. My brother, Julian, is five. Julian doesn't talk."

Emma looks down at the empty double-wide stroller. She looks tired. She calls the toddlers, Giles and Robert, over for a drink from their sippy cups before we go to the train. She raffles through a diaper bag and seems frustrated. Another classmate joins us. She places a calming hand on Emma's shoulder.

"All of this is a lot for Emma. It's hard to take four kids any-where." A tall woman with a crooked nose says.

"Penny, this is Brittany," Heather says. The two share a quick embrace.

Brittany helps Emma with the toddlers. Emma chases after the oldest, Julian, who has started to become restless. He is not responding to his name. I wonder if the little guy is deaf. He does not look like he has ever had a good spanking either. My parents both spanked me. I did not like it, but I am not a teenage drop-out like my parents either. Both told me that they wished their parents were more involved with them, including discipline.

"Julian has autism. Do you know what that is?" Brittany whispers in my ear.

Not wanting to be her confidante behind Aunt Emma's back, I nod my head *yes*. Sammy is chasing after Julian with a blanket. Julian yelps. Emma wraps Julian in the blanket at lightning speed. She sits down on the grass and starts rocking him. Sammy returns to the picnic area where we are sitting and goes through the diaper bags to find his snack. He feeds himself.

"Did Heather introduce you to Emma? Do you know who she is, in relation to you?"

"She's my aunt. I guess you know my grandmother, Dr. Daniell." I answer.

"Ah, our dear Mrs. Couch, yes. I spent two years with her as a student. It's not the same as being a relation, of course. I did well on the CL exam. I earned four out of five stars, points or whatever. I was able to jump-start my college classes. It was an encouragement to me. But, she was a hard woman. The year that we graduated, she was going through some tough times. It's easy to judge people harshly without knowing their perspective."

"Somehow my birth gave her a hard time," I say. I have heard it from Daddy before.

"No. You mustn't think that. Your birth occurred at the same time as some other things that Lady Macbeth, or your grandmother, was going through. Years from now, Emma will reflect on this day as being challenging. She also met you on the same day. But, you see, she's in the middle of trying to calm her son down. He's experiencing sensory overload. It has nothing to do with you and yet you are here. Some things that are happening outside of your locus of control."

"Locus of control? I haven't heard of that. Are you a psychologist?" I shift uncomfortably.

"Ha! My degree is in psychology, but I run a barre. Are you old enough to go to one?"

"Look at Brittany!" Heather yells. "She's spending all of her nights at the barre."

Heather had been eavesdropping. I whisper to Brittany, "I don't see how that's funny. I think woman-run businesses are great, but isn't bar ownership dangerous? The countryside is crawling with meth heads, alcoholics, and everyone owns a gun."

"No. It's a different kind of barre. It's a fitness studio with a ballet barre. Heather is jealous because she's into cross-fit and eats paleo. You don't have to do all that. Please come and visit me! Your mom was a ballerina. I think she'll approve."

"We're not talking about mothers today, Brittany." Emma reprimands. She's carrying Julian in a tightly wrapped blanket. He looks like a burrito but seems happy.

"You stand here as the epitome of motherhood, and we can't celebrate mothers?" Brittany says.

Brittany takes Julian into her lap and starts to rub circles on his face. He grins wide. I spot a missing tooth. After noticing the missing tooth and dot of blood, I see that Emma's left sleeve dotted with blood. She is shaking. Nicole helps to steady the stroller as Emma finds a plastic baggie for the tooth. If that scene is what having a child lose a tooth is like, I am not certain I want to be a mom. I would faint if someone else's blood splattered on my clothes.

"Look at you, precious," I say, looking at Julian. "With a missing tooth, I bet you could be a pirate for Halloween. You can do all sorts of cool things while you're waiting for the next tooth to come in. You'll never feel it. One day you'll look in the mirror, and it will appear like magic. Maybe you should be a magician for Halloween. You can make your teeth reappear."

"Julian wants to be a train conductor," Emma says in a slow, exhausted tone.

"What do you want to be?" Brittany asks me.

"I'm not going to go trick-or-treating this year. Our church has a trunk-or-treat. I'll wear an orange tee shirt and hand out candy." I say and shrug.

"No, silly, I mean, what do you want to be when you grow-up?" Brittany says with a smile. She's prettier when she smiles.

"My plan is to be a marine biologist. Someone you all went to school with has been mentoring me since Kindergarten. Daddy has put me in all the recommended programs. I snorkeled and helped collect data this past summer." I say with pride.

"Who?" Nicole asks in a harsh tone. "We didn't have any biologists in our class."

"Professor Eason. He's a marine biologist in Charleston. When I was little, I told him that I wanted to be a mermaid. He had some recommendations for me. Now, who else can say that their childhood dreams came true? I'm a strong swimmer too. I placed at the state level but didn't wow at nationals. I half-thought about training for the 2016 Olympics in Rio, but it wasn't meant to be."

"Eason? Who?" Nicole says. "I don't remember anyone at our ten-year reunion being a biologist or professor. My goodness. Brian must have known someone that graduated from night school."

"Will?" Brittany says, with a small amount of recognition. "I haven't thought about Will in over a decade. Since he left Douglas County, I had forgotten about him. He went to college in South Carolina. I don't remember him coming to any of the reunions, formal or informal. Mrs. Couch used to have a First Footin' party on New Year's Day, but he was never there."

"He was that queer little..." Nicole starts to say but falls silent.

"Julian, what is your dream? What do you want to be? A train engineer? You can do that. I want to help you." I offer. "The first step is for you to get comfortable being around trains. Are you ready to ride the train tonight? Will you ride with me? You can show me how to drive the choo-choo?"

Without a second thought, Julian fights his way out of the blanket. He leaves Brittany's lap. Julian takes my hand and starts walking toward the train. We are almost at the grist mill before Emma can catch-up with her stroller full of boys. Nicole and Heather meet us at the small train station.

"Should we wait on Preeti?" Brittany asks the group. "Nuri is almost the same age as you, Penny. She's a sophomore this year. This is her first year at Chapel Hill High School."

"You mean to say that my mom wasn't the only teen mom in the group? Sick."

Nicole starts in on me, "Your mother set an exquisite example, Penny. You should be proud that Preeti chose to keep her baby as a young mother. Times were different."

Heather reins Nicole in, "Nickajack! The term 'sick' is the equivalent of our generation's awesome. Penny agrees with you. Lighten up!"

Brittany, Heather, Nicole, Emma, and I have a good laugh. I am enjoying getting to know these women today. I can see half-inch gray roots popping out of Emma's hair now that she is sitting in the light. Nicole's front teeth are a little crooked, but she does not seem to care. I wonder what they were like twenty years ago. All of them seem intelligent although Dr. Will never thought so. I often wonder how my mother would have aged. Daddy tells me not to think about it too much.

"Julian, my sweet love, is it okay if I ride with your brother, and you ride with your cousin Penny?" Emma says while looking at the Kindergarten-aged boy.

Julian clings to Emma. Emma speaks to me, "You have to hold onto him. He doesn't know that he's in danger. You have to keep him safe. You can't let him fall off the train. I will sit one row behind you."

Brittany interrupts Emma. "We'll all keep an eye on all the boys, Emma. It's still light out. This is the kid-friendly version of the ghost train. I don't imagine that they'll drive the train too fast. It will be over before you know it."

A crisp wind blows through the small train station as we board. Julian and I sit together. I keep my hands on him as promised. We wave goodbye to the dirty bed sheets wafting in the wind at the station and set out for a tour of the grounds.

Mannequins, Halloween decorations, and fake weapons decorate the scenic train loop. I envision a much scarier landscape tonight after the sun sets. I am glad that we came during the day. The Halloween industry is huge in West Georgia. Next year, my senior class will take a field trip to Camp Blood during our fall senior week. For the briefest of moments, I ponder whether or not my College Level English class will be like Brittany, Heather, Nicole, and Dr. Will's experience.

Heather and Nicole each have one of the toddlers. Brittany is sitting in front of Julian. Sammy is enjoying his precious alone time with Emma. I cannot imagine growing up in a house with other children and having to share your parent's attention. I wonder if Emma ever wanted a daughter.

When the train arrives back at the station, a woman is waiting for us. She has been crying and seems distraught. Brittany is the first to hop off the train and talk to her. The others adults hang back and help the children off safely.

Not wanting to impose, I ask Julian to give me a tour of the engine. I glance over my shoulder from time to time to see what the women are debating. I hear a gasp or two. There is a lot of chattering and discussion. Emma's hand is over her mouth.

"How was I to know? We don't have nameplates on the damn things." The distraught woman says through pursed lips.

The women are passing around a two-toned blue yearbook with a tiger cub on it. Based on the mean girl behavior that my mom alerted me to years ago, my guess is the women have discovered bawdy doodles on top of my mother's photo. The tiger seems to be pawing two golden numbers: 98. I hope I am not pouring over my senior yearbook twenty years from now. It is pretty pathetic. They better not be talking about my mom.

"Brittany, you don't know. You don't have kids yet. They go through everything. You have no privacy. I can't put a single dollar bill in my purse because it will be gone. I have to stuff all forms of currency into my bra." The distraught woman says with great frustration.

"You always said you were a gypsy, Preeti. Will you start stealing people's hearts and souls next?" Nicole laughs.

The women never glance over at me. The discussion may not involve me at all. I doubt there have been any high school news flashes since the book came out in 1998. Daddy told me that a few of their friends died after high school. People get old and die. I wonder if they are talking about Anne.

I say to Julian, "There are so many things that I have thirsted for over time. I needed to have an aunt, and now I have one. I wished for brothers and sisters, but none ever came. I prayed for cousins, and now you're here. I'm happy you're here. I wanted for grandparents too, but I don't know how that is going to work out."

After ten-minutes or more, Emma comes over to me to retrieve Julian. She thanks me for watching him. He is turnt. We discuss being careful on the roads after dark. I invite Emma and the boys to trunk-or-treat at my church. She invites me over for Thanksgiving at her house.

"Will Dr. Daniell be at your house for Thanksgiving?" I ask while looking down at my shoes.

"Probably not, Penny. She has the first stages of dementia. She does better with routine and staying in familiar places." Emma answers and then snaps Giles and Robert into the double stroller.

"Did you recently move?" I look up and ask.

"In 2007," Emma says with her hands on Sammy and Julian.

Before long, my dad pulls up in his truck to pick me up. I wave goodbye to Emma, and she walks away. Talking to my dad, her step-brother, for the first time would be too much to manage today. Emma struggles to get out a single sentence at a time with the boys crawling all over her.

Brittany joins me as I walk down the small incline from the museum to my dad's truck in the parking lot. I do not know what Brittany was like in high school, but she is compassionate enough now. I cannot imagine her having been one of the mean girls that my mom warned against.

"Hi, Brian. Thanks for sharing your bae with us." Brittany says to my dad. She walks over to his side of the car.

Thinking that Daddy will want to leave as soon as possible, I start to tell him that I am ready to go. I will make-up an excuse that I have homework to finish or some other such nonsense. Instead, Daddy places the car in park. He smirks at the sight of Brittany.

"Hello, Traveler from an antique land." My father says. I have no idea what he's talking about; he is so embarrassing.

"That's not fair. If I am the Traveler, then you're the narrator." Brittany responds.

"What can I say? I am a colossal wreck, boundless and bare," Dad says with a smile. Gross.

"You are not bare. I can't even." I say and roll my eyes.

Brittany interrupts my disgust, "I have looked on your works, and I do not despair. She's a good kid, Brian."

"Now you're going to make me wish that I could recall Victorian flower language." My dad says. Where is her squad to pull her away?

"Ozymandias was pre-Victorian. Shelley was a Romantic. Your man bun screams romantic too," Brittany says.

"Why don't you educate me, Britt. I think I'm rusty and need some lessons. I can't have my daughter thinking I'm basic."

Oh, my, goodness! My dad is flirting with Brittany. I have never seen him flirt with anyone before. He is shameless. My parents were never married. I have no reason to be jealous on behalf of my mom. Mommy was in a long term relationship with Jason when she died. I am dumbfounded. I have never seen my father take any interest in any girl ever. I never thought that he was gay but classified him, in my mind, as too old to be in a relationship. I do not know what makes Brittany unique. She does give off an air of peace and calm.

I guess "Britt" is pretty for her age, but she is old. I guess she is as old as my dad.

"I offered your beautiful daughter some lessons at my studio. It's a barre studio, not a studio with a bar." Brittany says and giggles. She glances at me and gives a nod of reassurance.

"Is there an upcharge to hear you critique wordplay in romantic poems?" My dad asks.

"My work is physically stimulating, but rarely mentally. I would love to take a lunch break sometime and be able to talk about something stimulating and real." Brittany says and leans in closer.

"Anything that happened in 2009 is off limits for discussion. Can you manage that?"

"Yes, this is not an episode of *Gossip Girl*. I'm not offended. I know why you say that. I respect your boundaries."

"What will we ever talk about, Brittany Allison McIntosh? Is your last name still McIntosh? Will your husband get jealous? I don't need a crazy husband or an ex chasing after me in the street defending your honor. My clients will report me." My dad says. He places his hand on top of Brittany's hand.

"I never married. I became a woman of loose morals. Your mother would be horrified. Besides, I always let them down easy. You should be able to continue your work if you wish. That is unless you're looking for trouble, Brian."

"You always let them down easy until you don't." Daddy says with a sigh.

"Yes, until I don't."

"I've enjoyed following your business page on Facebook."

"Thank you. I have a teenager that I hire out my social media work to these days. It frees up my evenings a little bit."

"Well, that's good to know, just in case you get hungry after lunch some day and still need your intellect fed. What do the kids say now? Call maybe? Text me?"

"Get a room! Dad, you're a textra-terrestrial. Brittany, if you want to see Dad, call him so that his phone rings. I will text the number on your business card for him."

After a few more polite exchanges, we say goodnight to Brittany. The sun set long ago. We're riding in silence. I explain to Daddy what happened with Aunt Emma and the boys. He seems indifferent. I ask him about Heather and why she would want to arrange the meeting. I am always suspicious of people's motives.

"I don't have anything to say about Heather, Penny." Daddy answers me.

"Why not? Was she a mean girl?" I ask while adjusting the air conditioner dials.

"No. It wasn't exactly that. Heather and your mom weren't friends. It's complicated."

"How complicated can it be? What happened? Who threw shade first?"

"If I tell you that, then I have to disclose a lot of other things. Can you please stay my little Penny a bit longer? You are my life's work."

"Daddy, I'm sixteen. What were you and Mommy like at my age?" I demand.

"It was 1996. Things were different."

"That couldn't have been that different, Daddy."

"There is a man that you need to meet. He's a preacher. His name is Michael Vansant."

"What could that possibly have to do with anything? I don't need religious counseling. I go to church, Daddy. I'm a good girl."

"Has Dr. Will ever talked to you about Michael?"

"Uh, no. I don't think so. I meet some of Will's research assistants here and there. He knows some of the other students at camp but not many. Is Michael one of his students?"

"No. Michael went to school with us. He has a letter for you."

"Okay, that's weird. Is Michael a pedophile or something? Did you sell me into sexual slavery?"

"Shut your mouth! I know you're only kidding but don't tease about that stuff. You have no idea the shit I see every day in this forsaken place. People are selling their children into sexual slavery.

It's disgusting. It's vile." Daddy shouts within the confines of his truck cab.

After a moment, Daddy catches his breath. "The letter is from your mother. But, she trusted it to Michael."

"Where's Michael Vansant tonight?"

"He's a recovering alcoholic, Penny. You can't see him alone."

"Where is Michael Vansant right now?"

Twenty-Nine: Heather

◆————————————————————————————◆

September 19, 2009 8:36 PM
Athens, Georgia

My food truck feels oppressively humid today. It does not help that I am jittery. Outside, it is almost twilight on the campus of the University of Georgia. My hand stays on my cell awaiting bad news. I feel as though I am sweating buckets. It started off around seventy degrees this morning, but it got into the mid-eighties today. We are on the cusp of autumn. It is Oktoberfest and the people here are unaware of the humanitarian crisis an hour's drive.

At the invitation of one of mine and Nicole's sorority sisters, I am in Athens today and not my hometown. Douglas County is flooded, along with Fulton and Cobb counties. I have been nervously watching updates on my truck's small television when I can, but I also have to keep working. The hot oil is not going to tend itself.

Many of our classmates have fanned out throughout the West Metro area. I know people in Douglasville, Lithia Springs, Mableton, Powder Springs, Austell, and beyond. The satellite views of the streets are not even recognizable underneath the muddy waters. The Chattahoochee River swallowed Six Flags, an old haunt of mine and Seth's. Roller coasters are underwater.

My cell rings. It startles me. I hope it is not my dad calling with bad news. I have little left to lose emotionally. A wave of nausea hits me as I say "Hello?"

"Heather, it's Jason. Do you remember me? I'm Alicia's fiancé."

"Jason, um, hi. You were the Roman Soldier during our Passion play the year we went through Confirmation Class at church. It's good to hear from you. How are things back home? I've seen the videos on CNN and YouTube. How is everyone?"

"Well, you know that I wouldn't be calling you in Athens if everything was okay," Jason starts crying. "Our cell service hasn't been great here, but I wanted to let you know that Alicia's dead. She's done drown in the flood. It hurts even to have those words come out of my mouth. I hate this. But, I need a favor."

My heart slows to a near halt. I swallow hard. I am sorry that Alicia is dead, but I have had a parent die. Losing a friend and losing family are not quite the same in my book. I try to remain composed and not emotionally involved. Jason must be calling for a reason.

I answer, "I'm so sorry for your loss, Jason. What can I do to help? Do you want me to contact everyone in our class? Her parents? Our dads are lodge brothers. I think Stephanie has an email list or a group or something. I can contact her. Really, please ask anything. I'm happy to help."

"Alicia had more people's numbers than I do. We have the same friends, but she was just better at keeping up with everyone.

It's hard to distinguish in her few things at home who is a friend or client. She kept almost all of her stuff at work."

Jason is sobbing hard. Even though I do not verbalize it, my heart goes out to him. A memory flashes through my mind: Alicia's daughter, Penny. Someone will have to tell Penny about her mother.

"What would you like me to tell everyone?" I say. My voice cracks. "Please tell me as much or as little as you like. I know this is hard on you. When did it happen? Have you made arrangements yet? What's the story?"

"Michael's here at the church with me. His dad couldn't get out of Lithia. FEMA set up some kind of emergency operating station in the church's fellowship hall. Preacher Dan is at a different church now, but I guess you knew that he wasn't in Douglasville anymore. Preacher Dan is inside there with them federal government folks I had to step outside to get a signal.

"Heather, it's not safe to leave Douglas County right now, either coming or going. The perimeter is shut down. You couldn't even get down here if you wanted to. Our situation is dire. We have electricity on and off. But, it's hard to get a cell signal, and I never know when I'll be able to recharge this damn battery." Jason says while snuffling.

If my memory is correct, Jason is an emergency medical technician. Asking him whether or not Alicia is actually dead is pointless. If anything could have been done to save her, he would have been the one to do it. Jason is holding it together but only just. He sounds like he had had a couple of drinks. It is a series of phone calls that no one should ever have to make.

Jason continues, "Heather, it's hard for me to say all this. Please forgive me if I can't quite get it all out in the right order. We found Alicia earlier today. She had been missing. Her whole shop is gone."

"Jason, take your time," I say as I close the front window of my truck.

There were no more clients this evening anyhow. Everyone is glued to their computers watching flood coverage. Behind locked doors, I turn off the propane and sit down on the truck's greasy floor. I brace myself to hear the sad and final tale of Miss Erin Alicia Kennedy of Douglasville, Georgia.

"Alicia went to work like always. It started raining. She said that she was just going to stay and work through the storm. She was at the Beautiful Lee-Dunn Austell location. The recession has been lousy for flower shops. She doesn't make enough money to have anyone help her anymore. At one time, Alicia had two assistants, but she wasn't able to keep even one this year."

"What about Michelle?" I ask.

"Michelle moved along years ago. I think she ended up in South Carolina. The floral business has had a downward turn for years now. I think the Lee family got out at the perfect time. Alicia has had a steady business through the local funeral homes, but one of them shut down not too long ago too. Things are always changing around here.

"The storm worsened. I thought Alicia was safe in the shop. The building has been there since the sixties. I've been working back to back shifts because we're, of course, having an emergency. It's an all-hands-on-deck time. The hours blended into days and then time became all confused because I hadn't slept in about a day and a half. My partner and I were bouncing from one medical emergency to another. It was half-drown kids to the starving elderly to babies being born. It was hard to even get people to a hospital. I thought maybe she just couldn't get ahold of me. Again, the cell service has been spotty. When we had a call in Austell, I thought we might go by and see if the lights were on." Jason pauses.

"The shop was pretty much right on top of Sweetwater Creek. Wasn't it?" I ask. I'm starting to cry because I know that the final result will be the same no matter how the story ends.

"Dammit, Heather!" Jason moans. "The whole shop was gone. There was just a ragin' river where the little store was supposed to be. I couldn't even get anywhere near it. My buddies were trying to tell me that maybe she wasn't even there. And, they were right. There was a chance. We moved on to the next call but then I knew. I knew in my heart that we would be looking for her body in a couple of days. I woke up this afternoon to go to work. I slept about six hours since midnight. Well, shit, I knew. I knew by looking at everyone's faces. They had found her body during the six measly hours I was out."

"Oh, goodness, Jason," I cry. "I'm incredibly sorry. How is Penny? Poor Penny!"

I think about losing my mom and the pain of going through life without a mother. Moms are not replaceable. Remarkable women can come and go from your life, but they are not mommy like your real mom is to you. Oh, Henny Penny. I touch the sapphire earrings in my ear. They feel like they are on fire even though I know that is impossible. I remove them for a brief moment and hold them in my left hand.

"Penny doesn't know yet. We won't tell her until Michael and I finish the arrangements. I don't think the GBI will keep her too long."

"Why is the Georgia Bureau of Investigation involved?" I ask bluntly.

"It's standard procedure, Heather. It falls under the Georgia Death Investigation Act. The Douglas County Coroner looked at the body and contacted the GBI's Medical Examiner's Office."

"I thought Beautiful Lee-Dunn was in Cobb County," I say as I bite my lip.

"It is. I mean, it was. But, Alicia was found in Douglas County."

"Thank goodness! Her case won't end up like Anne's. Jason, that's great news."

"How is it great news, Heather? What the hell?"

"Her murder will be solved. It's in Douglas County. Anne's little brother will lead the investigation and he'll put the pieces together. You, Penny, and her parents won't have to wonder what happened to her. I imagine the not-knowing part would take your breath away. I don't mean to be insensitive."

"Her shop was washed away. The cause of death is drowning, Heather. No foul play is suspected."

"No foul play? Then why did the coroner refer Alicia's body to the GBI?"

"Her death appears accidental. Her death may have arisen as a result of her employment, which is a category that requires a Medical Examiner's Office referral."

"No, Jason. That's not it at all. She was murdered. Alicia wouldn't have stood helplessly by in a building that was being washed away. Are there any witnesses?"

"There is not going to be an investigation. We want to keep Penny's suffering to a minimum. Brian and I want to be able to answer all her tween questions. By the way, Brian knows. He and I want to tell Penny together."

"This cannot be happening." I cry.

"That's what I said," Jason says and cries with me. "What would have happened if Brian walked away? When Penny was a baby? She'd practically have no one. I love Penny, but I don't have any legal claim to her."

"Alicia's death is a homicide. Tommy's death was manslaughter. Anne's death was murder too. It's all connected. Jason, please listen to me. Don't let the GBI write this off as an accidental drowning."

"They have custody of her body already, Heather. There is not much I can do."

"Don't let it go!" I shout into my phone.

"I'm not going to let Penny go. Alicia was working at the shop when Penny lost her first tooth, and I was the one that was with her. She was so upset I wouldn't give her a Band-Aid." Jason explains. He slows his sobbing.

In my mind, I say, "No. I was talking about Alicia's case. Don't let her case go. Don't give up. Don't stop searching. The last remnants of Beautiful Lee-Dunn are now wiped out. Can't you see? Follow the money. Always follow the money trail."

There is a *click-tap* on the other end of the phone. It is Michael. Michael has had his ups and downs over the years. But, to Michael's credit, he is the most available of anyone that I have ever known during a crisis. I do not know how he made it over to Jason at the emergency operations outpost.

"Hey Heather, I hope everything is nice and dry over there," Michael says. "If you're interested in how things are down here, imagine Mrs. Couch on her worst day."

"Are you referencing her impromptu recitation of Jonathan Edwards's *Sinners in the Hands of an Angry God* from memory?" I ask and add a nervous laugh.

"Now, imagine that sermon while she tapped to Yankee Doodle with her pants on fire while high on meth and performing an exorcism. It's pretty dang bad. The river is at a five-hundred-year flood-level. Neighborhoods are floating away. We won't be able to rebuild in our lifetime. The damage is too colossal." Michael says in a shaky voice.

"It is too tragic for words," I say. I'm sitting in the bottom of my truck crying. I cannot see any silver lining to this. Alicia had worked so hard to dig herself out of a hole.

"Contact as many people as you can. Tell them to wait for the roads to be passable. Tell them not to go around the barricades. We'll meet up after the flood recedes. We'll send out a dove or something. Ask them to pray."

"Of course, I will, Michael. Please tell Jason that he's Penny's dad too. I'm not going to say that she's a lucky little girl for having two dads because, hot dang, life isn't fair. Michael, you need to try to build that little girl's faith. Michael?"

"Yeah, I'm here. I know what you're saying. I can't make sense of all this horror. I'll go mad. I can't think clearly. I can't reconcile this in my mind. They pulled Alicia's body out of Sweetwater Creek, Heather. I mean, I can't say too much around Jason. His co-workers are trying to protect him from all of the details. But, Heather, I have to tell someone. It's too much for me to handle. I can't do this. How can I provide comfort in a time like this?"

"You can do this. Leave a copy of the Bible near Jason. He'll figure it out. He's a big boy. That's what my mom's hospice company did for me. They had pamphlets that they didn't directly hand to me but just left near me while I was screaming on the floor. Then they walked away. No one knows how to handle grief. We didn't take a class on it in school." I say while lying flat on the floor.

I wish a storm would come by and take me away too. Better yet, quick transport back home to Douglas County would be convenient too. My preference would be to the far west of Sweetwater Creek and the Chattahoochee River. Never mind that. I bet Dog River is at flood stage as well.

Michael says, "The Lord has answered so many of my prayers over the years, Heather. I'm keeping the faith. But, I'm not my father. I'm not the natural comforter that I'm supposed to be, or, the one that everyone wants me to be. Robert's here, Anne's brother. He must have heard about Alicia from the coroner. Robert's talking to Jason now. I want to throw my hands up in the air and say that I cannot fight anymore."

"Robert will know what to say," I reply. "I was just thinking about Anne the other day. She was scared to death that she was going to burn in hell. Mrs. Couch was so theatrical in her recitations.

She made the sermon feel so real; like our feet were at the edge of that brimstone lake. I think that is what grief is like to me.

"Grief is standing at the brink of the unknown and not wanting to go forward or backward. You're frozen in time and space. I think the profound melancholy combined with the fear of the unknown were my biggest challenges. Of all people, Jeremy was very supportive when my mom died. Even his priest was supportive."

"What did they say?" Michael says. I can hear Robert talking in the background too.

"There was some allegory about a caterpillar turning into a butterfly. The butterfly simply woke up one day and found that he was still himself but, also a butterfly. He wanted to tell his caterpillar friends that he was okay and beautiful now but didn't have a way to communicate with them. I was fifteen and a confused young woman. The butterfly allegory worked for me. I don't know that it will work for Jason. You should tell Penny, though. I think it's a good one." I say.

I look for a stashed box of tissues to wipe my nose. My sinuses are stuffy. It would be nice if a Rhett Butler were in my life and could offer me a handkerchief right now.

Michael starts, "I'll think of something. I'm just weary. I feel bone tired and exhausted. It's hard to even keep my eyes open. The sounds in the background are blurring together. I know Jason and Robert are here but..."

"You can do this, Michael. God chose you for a time such as this. Believe it. Say it. Have faith. Be careful!" I shout, sitting up. "You could be going into shock or something! Alicia's death and the flood are significant trauma, Michael. You need to tell Jason. He'll be able to help. Tell Robert!"

I hear the phone drop. Through the bad connection, I can hear some scurrying sounds, maybe on the floor. I'm holding my phone tightly to my ear to see if I can distinguish any sound. Oh, please, please, let there be something. I hate to think that my advice was so frail that it killed Michael.

Robert picks up the phone. He's breathless as he says, "Heather, I'm sorry to hear about Alicia. Michael's on the floor and, since this old cell can get a signal, we need to let you go. Stay safe. Don't attempt to come back to Douglas County right now, no matter what you think you want to do! Stay away from here. We're at the gates of hell and the gates are opening."

My phone beeps. The screen reads *call ended.*

Not knowing what to do, I call one the few people I know outside of the flood zone: Seth. He answers after a few rings. I ask if he's in a meeting and he says that it doesn't matter. It feels as though we're both working the typical American schedule, which is about one hundred hours a week.

"How many days until Christmas, babe?" He asks. We see each other every year in North Carolina. I count down the days all year.

"Three months and four days," I answer.

"You can survive that long. Do you have a place to stay tonight?"

"Yes, I still have some sorority sisters in town. But, they're all grown-up with husbands and children. I don't want to disturb them."

"You can be cool 'Aunt Heather' for a few days. I can arrange a hotel for you, no problem." Seth says.

"Please don't. I don't want to be alone right now. I received the most astonishing call from Jason and Michael. Alicia is dead. Robert got on the phone and said that it was a living hell there."

"I hate to say that doesn't surprise me. I saw the writing on the wall in eleventh-grade."

"What? I don't understand. She grew into being one of the Goth kids and dropped out, but she had her own business and a career. She was a mom and had a steady domestic partner. When was there a warning that she would die in a flood of Biblical proportions? What about little orphan Penny?"

"Lay off. It's not like speaking ill of the dead. It's just, you know, guy locker room talk about Alicia. Remember that Sex Ed video that talked about sexually active girls being like super-used gym sneakers? That was Alicia. She wasn't sloppy seconds or even thirds. It was more like fourths. No one wanted her, except Brian. We never understood why."

"Is that really what you guys thought? That a girl in her circumstances was like gym sneakers?" I yell.

"Well, of course. Tommy had a lot to say about her. Babe, I didn't mean to-"

"Oh, I'm sure Tommy was the epitome of gentility and manners. What a misogynist! And, you too, Seth! You're a chauvinist, just like Tommy. Here I was mourning for Jason, Penny, and Brian and you can't resist dragging Alicia's name through the mud one last time. How dare you! You're not even human to me anymore."

"*Hey.* I didn't think you and Alicia were besties. You and Nicole were horrible to her in high school too. Where was your anti-bullying attitude then? If I'm a chauvinist then you're a hypocrite, to say the least. How did she die anyway? In a stranger's house? With a needle in her arm? I haven't seen that girl since the beginning of twelfth-grade. I know nothing about who she is today. The last time I saw her, she was wearing a metallic bandeau bra with her Daisy Dukes sashaying around Stephanie's family's floral shop like she was working a street corner. You and I both know that innocent, respectable girls don't do that. She sold her body like she was a two-dollar whore on nickel night."

"I can't believe you. It's like I don't even know you! After all of this time, it's like you don't even know me. May none of us ever stand in judgment for the people that we were in high school. I've grown. I'm a different person. I'm a better person. You obviously can't say the same, and that breaks my heart."

"You have tried to block everyone from your life that knew you before. You tried to block me and Nicole both, at different points in time, and we won't let you. We won't let you give up on the girl that you used to be. Alicia's death has nothing to do with you. It has nothing to do with your mother dying. Don't project your grief onto other people and situations."

"Are you saying that I can't empathize with an eleven-year-old girl who just lost her mom? You're a demon, Seth Bradley Aderhold, and you know nothing about women. If you were so wise about the female sex, you would be married already."

"Don't you see, Heather? I've waited for you for forever and a day. I can't stand to be close to you anymore I'm so sick of waiting. I don't know if you'll ever be ready. If you are ever ready, I don't know that you'll be ready for me. But, I'm hedging my bets. I'm banking on you turning this hissy fit around."

I hang up on Seth. I am not having a hissy fit. He's acting like a typical Douglas County male pig. He thinks that people born with penises are allowed to go out and have sex with no consequences while people born with vaginas are supposed to keep their private parts protected and pure. He thinks we're still functioning in a Puritan society; that ass! I hate him now, and I'll hate him forever.

Not knowing what to think, the first thought that comes to my mind is, "Curse Seth. May he know the pain of having others control your body without your permission. Curse Seth. May he know the struggles that face girls today through the eyes of fatherhood. Curse Seth. May he know the misery that comes from not being able to tell someone you're sorry until it's too late."

Thirty: Brian

◆━━━━━━━━━━━━━━━━━━━━━━━━━━━━━━◆

May 18, 1996 4:54 PM
Mableton, Georgia

The custody arrangement between my parents stipulates that I must see my father every other weekend and for six weeks during the summer. I despise the summer. A single minute spent with my alcoholic, womanizing father is an eternity of torture. The *clickety-clacketing* of electronic typewriter keys bore into my ears. I wish it were possible to run away from my body. If so, I would return in late August when the school year starts.

"Do you want to kiss me, Brian? Too bad, I won't let you." Alicia teases me.

My father is running for office again. This time, he's running for secretary of the county liquor control board. He runs for public office as a profession. It's embarrassing. He trades on my mother's good name in the school system while continuing to be a dirty, manipulative son of a bitch.

"Yeah, that's what your momma said last night too." I retort with a wink at the slut.

I think Dad has illicit sources of income. I feel guilty about every penny he spends to support me, although my mother is the sole provider in the house these days. I have stopped asking for new clothes or video games. I cannot quite put my finger on where certain things come from just yet, but it does not feel right. Most of the money arrives in cash, and leaves as cash too. The envelopes are unmarked. There is an occasional football strategy mark on one or two, but it means nothing to me.

"Brian! Look alive, boy! Answer the phone while I attend to some business in my office." My father says. "Alicia, you need to help me right away."

A fellow Douglas County High School student, Alicia, is interning for my father this summer. Unpaid internships are all the new rage. The adults think that it makes metro Atlanta seem modern; we are not. Dad has brought a lot of students on board for this campaign.

My friend Tommy is here too. Justin is volunteering, but only when he has a ride. He is doing it to stay away from home. Most sixteen-year-olds will do anything to get near Olympics action around Atlanta this summer. Nineteen-ninety-six is the summer to be out moving and shaking, as my father would say. His campaign headquarters is only about ten-miles closer to Atlanta than Douglasville. We are not close to anything, except maybe the international gangs that are moving into the area.

It is a presidential election year. I am shocked that Dad thinks that he needs the same amount of grassroots staff as the Dole-Kemp office down the road. He just wants to be around young people that he believes think he is impressive. He is lame. His ego is bigger than the pyramids at Giza and more bullshit fortified than the Pentagon. Tommy wants to be near him because Tommy is not his biological son. They both love seeing their picture in the newspaper.

The phone rings and I answer. A voice starts, "Watch out for the girls."

"I think you have the wrong number," I answer. There is no way to tell who is on the other end of the line without contacting the telephone company, or dialing star sixty-nine and paying money. Campaign offices get prank calls all the time. Dad does not like giving away money to Southern Bell.

"There are girls coming and going from your office, even at all hours of the night. It's drawing the attention of the police, Joe. You need to watch out for your girls. People notice the girls. Try to keep them dressed and indoors," The voice says.

"Excuse me. This is Brian Couch. Who are you calling for, sir? What is this regarding?" I say, trying to sound authoritative like my mother.

The line goes dead. My heart drops to my stomach. People are watching girls. How strange.

I am sitting at a reception desk and not certain what to do next. I prefer being forced to volunteer during the early morning when Rhubarb Jones is on Y106.7. Weekend country radio is less thrilling than weekday radio. Listening to Rhubarb in the mornings makes the day go by faster. I cannot listen to Rhubarb during the school year. He is the best part of my summer. I sketch a shark cartoon on a sticky pad. I gawp at the phone to see if it will ring again.

After tapping my fingers on the desk for a moment, I decide to head to my father's private office. He has a small space behind rows of empty cubicles. He says that it is because the natural light from the front gives him migraines. He is a drunk and walking migraine.

My shoes scuffle in a slow, uneven pattern toward the back of the general office. I want to be certain that my father can hear me coming. I am always afraid of what I will find when I round the corner. Last year, he laid into me with screaming and his belt. I hurled. I do not want to do that today.

I look ahead and to the side into an empty cubicle. I look into an unplugged donated computer monitor's reflection. I can see Tommy and Alicia. She straddles his lap with each leg on his hips. She lets out a light moan. I almost urinate on myself. Tommy has his face buried into her exposed breasts. Alicia's blouse is open. She is not wearing a bra. Tommy is kissing her.

Holding my breath, I walk backward very slow so that I do not make a sound. I hold my breath as I back away. I wish that I could move faster, but I do not want to risk making a single noise. My urge to urinate on myself increases.

Alicia's grunts become indiscreet. I hear my father in his nearby office giggling like a cocaine addict snorting a line. I will have to tell him about the call later. I cannot bring myself to knock on his door. My feet feel like they are walking on the moon.

There is ecstasy here. Dad is too upper class to have crack, but too behind the eight ball to share his limited supply of cocaine. We keep the good stuff for the high dollar donors, but he samples the little blue tablets with some frequency. I think other people do as well. It is easy to flush if the cops come knocking around.

I feel a hand on my shoulder and almost jump out of my skin. I turn to see Justin. He looks surprised by my shock.

Justin says, "Some ladies that want to see your father. They're here to clean the office. It's almost five o'clock."

"Dad's schedule says that he's here until eight o'clock tonight. Why would they arrive so early?" I say.

"I dunno, man. None of them speak English."

"How many are there? How many people does it take to clean a fifteen hundred square foot office? There's nothing here. There's not even trash to take out like there is at home. I think we have one trash can. I empty the one trash can at the end of the day. What gives?"

"There are five of them. Should we let the girls stand outside? Should they come in and get started? Should we let them sit down? I mean, they're cleaning ladies. Do we offer them a cup of water from the cooler?" Justin says. He shrugs his shoulders. He does not care, or suspect.

I walk to the front of the office again and let five waiting girls inside. There is no way that they are old enough to be custodians. The girls are my age. None of them are smiling. They dress differently than the girls at school. One of the girls emerges. She is older than the others. She keeps her head down. I do not notice the wrinkling around her eye until she looks straight at me.

"You Joe's son?" She says in an accusatory tone. "We here about papers. Now."

Holding the door for the group, they file in like little ducks from the outdoor shopping center's covered sidewalk. The mother duck yells at them in a foreign language. They immediately start walking toward the back cubicle where my Tommy is snogging Alicia.

Wanting to warn my father about his guests, I try to walk faster than Mother Duck, but do not make it in time. I call out to Joe, "Hey, Dad! Heads-up!"

Alicia scurries out of the cubicle holding her Abercrombie and Fitch blouse together. The black choker that she was wearing is half-torn off her neck. She looks confused and is stumbling around in her mom's scuffed office heels. Her dark red lipstick is smudged down to her chin. Her eyes are glassy. The ducks approach the cubicle at high speed. They move fast towards my father's office.

The women are yelling in the foreign language. Much to my surprise, he starts to yell back at them in the same language. I had no idea that my father spoke anything but English. Tommy stands near me. We try to discern what is happening. Papers ruffle. Notebooks open and close. Dad answers the back telephone. It is for his private use.

Alicia, Tommy, Justin, and I hear numbers dialing. Justin looks at Alicia and says, "Do you have the flu?"

"It's a perfect day for a cup of tea, comrade. Comrade Crawford. Comrade Hood. Comrade Couch. Comrade Couch." Alicia says. She starts laughing and then crying. She lets go of her blouse.

"You shameful slut!" My mother yells at Alicia. I had not heard her come in through the front door. We need to tie a small wind chime to it.

"Mom, I don't think Alicia has had a good day. Justin was just asking her if she has the flu."

"She doesn't have the flu, you idiot!" Mom says. "She's smoked some pot. Now her bra has wandered off her body. Isn't that amazing, Alicia? How bras can just fall off our bodies when we're around other people's husbands."

"Maybe I don't need a bra," Alicia says looking upward at the artificial office lights. "We were never allowed to wear them in ballet. We were only allowed our leotards and tights. I can spin for thirty-seconds without falling over. Who wants to pirouette with me?"

Tommy indiscreetly zips up his jeans. My mom hears the noise, looks at Tommy, and cuts her eyes at him. Alicia starts spinning around. Justin holds a fresh paper cone of water from the water cooler. My dad reserves the paper cones for donors, but Justin is afraid of my mom enough to give her one.

"What did he give her, Brian?" My mom asks. The fatty bump between her eyebrows scrunches together. When the facial scrunching happens, I know that she means business.

"She had a cup of tea," Tommy says. He starts laughing, "And I got to cup my hands around her-"

"Iced tea in a glass or hot tea in a cup?" My mother says. Her face looks alarmed.

"There was a Styrofoam cup at the back cubicle," I explain. "There was a tea bag on the side."

"I love a good tea bag on the side," Alicia says in a half-giggle while spinning.

"It looks like it was hot tea, Mom," I say. "You're not supposed to drink hot tea when you have the flu, right? Will she be okay? Should she go to the doctor?"

"Goodness gracious, boys. Young women without bras do not get the flu in May, which goes to show how much you know about the family life. I was already caring for all of my siblings when I was your age. I had six younger children to take care of in addition to myself. I thought you boys were brighter than you let on."

"She didn't hit any x, honest," Tommy says. There is a barely perceptible white powder on his left nostril.

Dad had given Tommy the good stuff. Whatever! I am happy with Matt's homegrown marijuana. Ryan swears that Matt's stash is the highest quality in all of Northwest Georgia. Tommy started smoking before the rest of us and seemed to move up the drug chain without consequence. I think I will stick to my marijuana and be happy.

"Don't be mad at me, Mother. Monsieur Komarovsky just wanted to dance." Alicia says and starts to dance around the office. She has forgotten to hold her blouse together again.

Tommy smiles and starts taunting Alicia with lewd comments. Another volunteer runs to the front door and closes the blinds. Mom intercepts Alicia mid-spin and slaps her hard. Alicia falls to the ground like a butterfly that just had her wings touched and, therefore, broken.

Mom says, "I am not your damn mother, child! Now put your clothes on and let Brian or Tommy drive you home. I will clean up here."

Knowing that Tommy is high, I tell him to stay behind with Mom. Justin stays to take care of Tommy. As I walk across the parking lot, the pavement emits a hot, wet heat. It must have been ninety degrees today. My father keeps telling me that if I am not careful that I will grow up to have to labor under the hot sun, like a real man. He does not think I am cut out to be a real man. If real men hurt their wives, force girls to clean early, and hand out hard drugs like candy on Halloween then, no. By my father's standards, I do not want to be a real man.

I move my car from the outer reaches of the parking lot, where assorted store staffs have to park. I park my Dodge Neon by the campaign headquarters front doors. Justin flips the *open* sign to *closed*. Tommy leans on a support pillar. If you did not explicitly know where my father's campaign office was, you would never find it. He never invests in signage when bumming it in the slummy office parks.

My mom buttons Alicia's blouse up for her. Like a mother, she brushes her hair back into a neat ponytail. Tommy is holding Alicia's small purse. We look at each other while helping Alicia into the passenger seat. Alicia is unconscious.

"Brian," Mom whispers. "Let this be a lesson to you. Your reputation is like glass. Once the glass is cracked, it cannot be repaired. This piece of filth is cracked glass. Stay away from her at all cost. Like a siren, she will snag you and drag you down into the depths of hell."

"That's rather fatalistic. Now that Tommy isn't with us, can I ask, did Alicia get into some contaminated drugs? I thought Daddy had given most everything up. I know that he keeps some things for the donors," I say and then gulp hard. "But I thought he was clean, Mom."

"Your father is a rapscallion. I'm sorry that you carry that ignorant racist lecher's name. It's disgraceful. I will speak with him about what has happened here today." She says.

"What did happen here today? I know you two are more separated now than ever; but, why are you still married? Why do you let him manage his affairs like this? It's all a fraud."

"Brian, you have to understand that I have no control over your father's behavior, actions, health, addictions, or proclivities. He's a jackass. He's always been a lying, cheating scoundrel. Now what I think happened was that your father put some liquor in Alicia's tea thinking he was going to get to enjoy the heavy petting. The warmth of the tea and alcohol either made Alicia too woozy for your father to be interested or he was distracted with other business. Please drive her around until it wears off. Go back to Douglas County, walk around a store. Just don't send her home to her parents like this."

"It never occurred to you that Tommy could have been the one," I say.

Hearing his name, Tommy walks over to the car. He says, "Mr. Couch told me that I should be on blouse control in case her knockers went wild again! Free the hooters! *Hoot, hoot!*"

My mom slaps Tommy. Tommy does not sober from the slap. He continues to jive around the sidewalk for a minute. Justin redirects him into climbing over Alicia into the back of the car.

"At least they live in the same neighborhood, Mom," I say.

Moving to the driver side of the car, my mom leans in and says, "We can't afford to lose Tommy. He brings a lot of coverage to our campaign. It's good for your father and his career. The campaign is a group effort, remember? All of us are all in. I will have to allow Tommy into American Literature next year."

I slump my shoulders. I know what is coming next. I ask, "What about the rest of us? What about the other volunteers here?"

"It can't be obvious that I am covering for your father with favors at school. You, Matt, Alicia, and Ryan need to be out of the AP-track English program. Justin will remain in. I see potential in him."

"But, Mom, we've all worked so hard," I say. I see my future flushing down a proverbial toilet.

"I know, son. But, it can't be helped. We can't have any connection between myself and a girl that thinks her tatas were born free for public consumption. I know my husband's hands roam all over that territory too. I now know that the land was not newly explored thanks to Tommy." My mother says while glaring at me. "I know what happens after Homecoming games. I'm not stupid, Brian. I heard the rumors."

"There was never anything between me and Alicia, Mom," I say. I am being honest. She cannot even see it.

Tommy starts to scream in the back of the car. He's playing air guitar to a random eighties rock band that only he hears. He hits the back of the driver seat with his full body weight. I'm thrust forward into the steering wheel. I lean back and look at Mom.

Mom says, "Why did you take Alicia to Homecoming if you didn't like her? Did something happen?"

"It was all Dad's idea," I admit. "I wasn't even going to go. I would rather stay home and play video games. I'm not full of the tiger spirit like you too. I know that both of you are always all over my case and trying to get me to do things at school. It's just not my thing, Mom.

"Dad said to ask Alicia out because her parents were donors. I was following his orders. I don't even like girls just yet. I don't mind going places, but I'm still a virgin. I don't want to have to date a girl because that's what boys my age do. I see enough drama between you and Dad."

"Hmm," My mother contemplates. "Alicia's parents aren't donors. They're wealthy and politically connected, but they're not donors yet. Maybe your father thought that he wanted them to become donors. That's why he wanted you with Alicia."

"I didn't think too much about it. We had a decent enough time. Alicia wants to take Russian literature. She has a great-grandmother that emigrated from Russia a long time ago." I say, knowing that my mother ignored the important part of what I just told her. Both Mom and Dad see me as a pawn in their political campaigns.

"Well, that would explain why she was referencing *Doctor Zhivago*. Having her choose a class in Russian language and literature would be the perfect cover for her not continuing onto CL literature and composition. Is her family Russian Orthodox? Do they go to mass in Atlanta?"

"No. The Kennedys go to a non-denominational church off Kings Highway." I say. Tommy places earphones on his head and turns up my Walkman. He's still playing air guitar.

"Perfect. I bet Alicia's family is Shtundists. If her parents ask, tell them that you had a spiritual discussion. An awakening! Tell them that you were discussing the bleakness of *Doctor Zhivago* and that is when Alicia got bored and fell asleep. That should work. They'll be too embarrassed by their daughter falling asleep during a philosophical discussion with you that they won't think too much about it."

"Why do I have to say anything? Can I not just drop her off without a concocted story?" I say. I feel anger rising in my biceps as I grip the steering wheel hard.

"No, they'll want a story. Make it a good one. Look sincere when you tell it." She advises.

"I think you're the one that likes to cook up stories around here, Mom. If you're wondering how our story, mine and yours, will end, please know that I will never forgive you if you make me stay with my father for any amount of time this summer."

"You'll be fine."

"I'll go to the press."

"You would never."

"Watch me."

"What do you want?"

"I want to go to summer camp somewhere. I need to be away from both of you." I demand.

"Find a camp that will take you at this late date and we'll talk about it."

I make eye contact with my mother for the last time as her only child. My need for her parenting skills ended today. She is more concerned with cleaning up after my father than with taking care of herself, or me.

Hickeys dot Alicia's neck and chest. Tommy is flailing like a fish out of water. I had hoped to be more of a boy scout, but I am not. It is now my business to take care of Alicia's dancing and Tommy's snorting.

I will wear a cool face mask and lie to their parents. I will compromise and negotiate to get what I want and need. I am not proud of this course of events, but I aim to survive. I will get out of these later teen years alive, even if it is only with a skeleton of my damn morals intact.

Thirty-One: Joe

◆―――――――――――――――――――――――◆

June 14, 1990 3:12 PM
Douglasville, Georgia

"See, I said it would all work out one day," I tell my wife, Judy.

We are sitting in my cousin Hal's law office near downtown Douglasville. Judy's eyes are locked on the bookcases circling the room's interior. She is such a little mousy bookworm; it gets on my nerves. She has always been much more in love with her book characters than me. Fictional men are twerps dreamt up by bored housewives.

"Congratulations," Judy says. "I know that you've always wanted to have this money. It's a sudden windfall to start your political career. It must make you happy, you evil bastard."

"Damn straight!" I yell at her. "My mother worked hard at that shop. Her hands were torn to shreds as long as I could remember. But, she loved working with flowers. She loved that little shop more than me. That is why she kept working until she finally had a stroke.

"Now, what other woman could work seven days a week into their late seventies? She put food on my table. She sent me to college. I was the first in the damn family. She yelled at me when I did wrong. She didn't coddle me. She didn't hold my hand and tell me that things would be alright. Things would be alright if I made things alright. She wanted me to be respectable and powerful. If she couldn't give me what I wanted in life, she can damn well do it in death."

"What are you going to do with the shop now that Mother is gone?" Judy asks. "Are you going to show up with your know-it-all attitude and start bossing people around? Do you see Doug and Belle Lee listening to a word you say? No. You're a bull in a china shop, Joe."

I think for several moments before answering. "Beautiful Lee-Dunn will continue operation. We're silent partners with Doug Lee and his people. Mother liked Doug. Besides, he's good at what he does. I can't arrange any damn flowers myself, of course. That's why mother sent me to college. There is nothing wrong with the flower business right now. People are still dying, getting married, falling in love, and whatever else it is that they want to say with flowers."

"You never say anything with flowers." She jabs at me. "You save it for your cheap call girls."

"Yeah, well, Mother was a florist wasn't she. The markup on the flowers is unreal, Judes. You should appreciate that I saw fit to spend our money in more practical ways." I say to the dumb bitch.

"Our money? You mean my paycheck! You spend it all on yourself; on your bottles." She says. She is lashing out again. "We'll be lucky if we can pay off some of the credit card bills."

"Now, what are we going to do? What do you want me to say? That we're going to have in-vitro fertilization at your age? How are you going to do that at age forty-two and without functioning ova-ries? I know that you've always wanted more children, but it's hard enough with one rugrat as it is. Second-grade is that awkward age where they're potty-trained but not out of the house yet."

"*Oh!* Listen to you, Mr. Know-it-all. You're trying to blame my disappointments on my body. I'm not disappointed in my body! I'm disappointed in the person who I chose as my life partner! And our son is in his last week of fourth grade. You're his father! You should know what grade he's in."

"Dad's don't know that kind of stuff. Dad's don't get involved until later." I answer. I'm right.

"No! You're more useless than a bent-dicked-dog. I bet you think you're going to quit your job and stay at home all day drinking and screwing while I'm out there earning my family a paycheck. No, sir, I bet if you asked Hal he could give you a biography on each of his sons. Go ahead! Ask him!"

"Ask me what?" Hal says. He's also my best friend, fellow high school football alum, and a salve for Judy's soul. He'll help me get her off my butt.

"Hal, how are the boys? How old are they now?" Judy asks.

"Shoot. Those four rascals make me feel like an old man. Chris is graduating from Alexander High School next week. He's going to Oxford at Emory, which my checkbook is none too happy about, Judy. I hope Chris doesn't screw around like I did.

"Rick just got his learner's permit, so he wants to start working. I told him the girls wanted the guys with college degrees, but he doesn't listen to me. I told him to go work at Six Flags, but Rick intends to stay in Douglas County near his brothers. He thinks he knows everything. I think everyone should hire teenagers; they seem to know everything.

"Ryan is crazy because he's twelve and feeling' those old hormones, right Joe? Remember that? I thought he would be looking at the girls already, but he just stays locked in his room, keeps to himself, and writes all day. He's just a puddle of emotion. I don't know what he writes about in that room of his. He's his mother's favorite. Otherwise, I wouldn't let him get away with it. Josh just earned his Tiger Scout badge. He's all boy, Judy. You know about that."

"I bet you gave him his first pocket knife. How old is he?" I say. "Has he gone camping yet?"

Hal smiles, and he says, "Yeah, he's seven now, so it's about that time. I'm waiting until the last day of school. I don't want an expensive knife to get lost in some snot-nosed first-grade classroom on the last day, you know? How is Brian?"

"Fine," Judy and I respond at the same time. An awkward silence follows.

The heat is hot and dry today. There is a vague smell of pool chemicals in the office. Hal must have walked down to the hardware store to pick something up. Lots of people are moving into palatial neighborhoods now with things they call amenities.

Downtown Douglasville has become boring. It's only old people here tending their small gardens and their even smaller minds. I want to be where the next generation is. New neighborhoods are building in communal areas with basketball courts, tennis courts, pools, golf, and club houses. There are endless ways to entertain yourself. My favorite is to watch the teenage girls wearing their first bikinis. It reminds me of when I was young.

"Joe, I'm sorry about your Mother. We all loved Mother Dunn. Shall we get to the business at hand?" Hal says. Judy nods. She's up to something.

"Going through probate has been challenging since you have different last names, Joe. Now, don't get me wrong, I know the exact reason why..."

"I'm technically a bastard. But, I'm about to be a rich bastard, so let's get on with it." I snarl.

"Well, Mother Dunn didn't need a man. She had everything worked out for herself." Hal says.

"She only had herself to rely on," Judy says. She's about to cry, the sentimental wench.

"Well, she was taking care of herself and her boy. She wasn't an airhead. She didn't have her nose stuck in books, buying expensive costumes that are the same price as a month of groceries!" I yell.

"Either that costume was lined in gold or you have a small food budget, Joe. Which one is it? I've never known you not to have the means of taking care of your family." Hal says. He is a sarcastic prick.

"Mother Dunn gave Brian and me money for groceries and necessities that you never knew about, you hateful bastard! She kept on providing. You're just jealous that Mother cut you out of that equation. During the summer, when I didn't have a paycheck she always made sure that I had a new book to enjoy for summer reading and that Brian had money for camp.

"Did you not know? Did it never occur to you where the funding was coming from, Joe? No! You don't even know what our family budget is. You don't know how much food costs. Bread is up to seventy cents a loaf. Eggs are over a dollar dozen now, except that I still buy mine from the farmers market. A gallon milk is over a dollar too, you jackass! I know how to feed my family and your mother did too." Judy screams. She has a tissue in her hand.

Hal comforts Judy with a hug and few pats on the back. He's a slick one. I think for a moment, "The last time I bought milk it was thirty cents a gallon. Who in the world would pay a dollar a gallon? That's obscene. You're a spendthrift."

Judy lunges at me and knocks me out of my chair. The chair topples over. She is on top of me. She screams in pain for a moment. Hal picks her up. She cries, "It's my ribs! I think I broke a rib."

"Yeah, well brittle-boned menopausal women do that, Judes," I say.

I know I should lay off on the meanness but cannot. Every mean word that I spit out at her gives me a little bit of a high. I miss my coke.

Looking on the floor, I see that the contents of her purse have spilled out everywhere. There are decades of embarrassing crap spilled on the plush white carpet. There are birth control pills, a worn wallet, coin purses, hairbrushes, gum, and even a roll of gift wrapping tape. Judy is a mess. The most lurid item is a navy blue book. I almost mistook it for a yearbook, but it is the size of a novel. It is Danielle Steele's *Daddy*. Oh, I will be able to dig into her over this one for the rest of the year.

"Some English teacher you are! You're just a tawdry girl from trashy-ass Newnan reading sleazy novels. Let me guess, does some character have sex with Daddy? Is Mommy not getting any?" I taunt.

Judy's nose is bleeding. Hal is holding her. His lower lip is almost above his upper lip. His daddy used to look like that right before giving me a beating. His father was the closest thing that I had to a father in my life. I do not like seeing him like this. It awakens something primal in me. Judy stumbles in her jelly slippers to her purse. Hal helps her pick up her things.

A pretty lady comes to the door. "Mr. Bearden, I heard a noise."

The shapely young thing is wearing a pencil skirt and white blouse. The white blouse is almost sheer under the fluorescent light. Her bra is white as well. Poor little miss forgot that the blouse was sheer. Respectable women would have worn a nude colored bra underneath. I do not think she is a respectable woman. She has not joined a sorority yet. She is not refined to a razor's edge yet. I like them unrefined.

The lipstick across her lips is freshly applied. It is inconsistent with three o'clock in the afternoon. Her lips have been busy doing something. Good old, Hal. I wonder how Hal has been doing these past few years. I bet his wife does not know. Not everyone can be as honest as Judy and I are with each other. This girl looks about my age. I wonder if she is interested in me. Women are always interested in men with money. I have money now.

White Bra sees Hal and Judy gathering small items from the floor. She helps. I position myself slightly behind Hal's desk so I can see further down the White Bra's blouse. To be young and handle breasts fresh out of the gelatin mold! I bet her boyfriend is happy. I would be happy if I were her steady.

Now I have lots of money to give White Bra things like a new pair of silk hose, red lipstick, or bras. Girls love stuff like that; women like Judy do not. Women of a certain age see those products as necessities, and then they are no longer gifts. They want to pick them out themselves. Then, to save money for other things like trashy novels, they go and buy discount store versions of those things. Five and dime store makeup never looked as good on a woman as cosmetic counter lipstick.

"Did they run out of flesh-colored bras at Rich's, sweetheart?" I say with a smile. I do not try too hard to hide the bulge in my pants.

"Joe!" Hal yells at me. "That's Chris' high school girlfriend, Cassandra. You can't say things like that anymore. It's sexual-ha-rassment. Now, you're family and a client, but I can't have you talking' to her like that. Besides, she's a damn junior in high school, Joe. You're a sick puppy, just like Daddy always said."

Cassandra helps Judy to the waiting area outside of Hal's private office. She is probably taking her to the ladies room. Good. She can put a tampon in while she is at it. Judy can play up her self-inflicted injuries and get a hearty dose of naïve sympathy.

Women love a good gab fest in the toilet. That is where they chitter-chatter all their little secrets. Judy is probably ruining my chances of getting with that girl right now. Instead of seeing me as a man with means, she will see me as weepy Judy's husband.

"Joe, you can't do that. You're not someone rich and famous, my friend." Hal says. "You can't get away with murder or whatever else it is you're plotting. Don't call me from the jail house phone at two o'clock in the morning because someone's daddy caught you up his daughter's skirt!"

"That was one time, and it was college." I defend myself.

"Well, you were in college for a damn long time, Joe. Judy was working and supporting your sorry butt for almost seven years. You tried every major ever offered. A married twenty-nine-year-old man on campus, while pursuing their education, is alright these days. But, you weren't just pursuing an education. What area of study is written on your precious lambskin anyhow?"

"English," I say. I look down at the floor. The plush carpet bends into the funny shapes of the items from Judy's purse. She does leave a permanent impression.

"You're joking? You have an English degree!" Hal says. His mouth is open.

"Oh, c'mon, Hal. You know that Judy didn't have a brain to get a degree in something' like architecture. She was working slave hours at school those first few years. She hardly had any time to come home and help me. It had to be in her degree field, of course. Her teacher stuff limits me and my dreams."

"You are lower than low, my friend," Hal says. He's shaking his head now. "You're shameless. I don't know if I should even continue this paperwork to give you the little amount of money that your mother left you."

"Little? I thought she left me everything!" I say as my lips purse right around my front two teeth. I start breathing heavy and sweating. I think I could still take Hal in a fight even if he is three inches taller than me. We're both still pretty short for modern times.

"All told, it's almost sixty-thousand-dollars. It's nothing to sneeze at, Joe. You need to understand that it's not enough money for you to retire right now; at age forty-seven. You're going to need to keep your job. You're going to need to save for retirement. Trust me and put aside some money for Brian to go to college. It's getting more and more expensive every year."

"I always thought Judy would just quit her high school job and go work at a college where Brian could get free tuition. That money is mine, not his. I don't want him to end up being an entitled brat like your kids." I say. I hate Hal for all that he has, and everything given to him.

If I had a hot wife, like Hal, maybe I would have four boys as well. I would be living the abundant lawyer life and boating on Lake Lanier. I would drink as many beers as I want and wave to my hot wife waiting for me on the shoreline. That is every Georgia boy's dream. You work hard, go to college, meet a hot piece of ass there, get a job, marry the hot piece, have smart kids, and go hang out on the lake for the next thirty years. Judy robbed me of all of that. She was hot, and then it faded away after she had Brian. If I could do it over again, I would do things differently.

"What are you thinking about?" Hal asks. "I hope you say your future."

"Nah, I was thinking about Lake Lanier," I say.

"Oh, Linda and I love to take the boys to Lanier," Hal says. I hate him even more.

"Georgia poet Sidney Lanier is Lake Lanier's namesake," Judy says on her return. She loves to interrupt conversations and bring them all back to her and her expertise.

"You only know that because you have to teach it!" I retort. Hal and Judy look away.

"Judy, Mother Dunn left you some money too," Hal says. My jaw drops in disbelief. "She wanted you to have your own money in a bank account with your name on it. She stipulates that you must open an account at a local bank with me as the only co-signer. That is, of course, strictly if something happens to you, and you are incapable of going to the bank and attending to your business. It's more like a power of attorney. Mother Dunn and I had it worked out ahead of time."

Judy's eyes sparkle. She is thinking of a hundred possibilities of what to do with the money. I bet she will want some new shoes. How much money could Mother have possibly left her? Everything was supposed to come to me. It is not fair.

"Now, Joe," Hal says. "I'm not to disclose the amount to you. Judy, you're not to tell him. Judy, your bank statements will be sent to me. I will drop them off for you at school. It's no trouble, and it is on the way home. At least, it's on the way for now."

"What? Are you moving' out of your family house off Rose Avenue?" I ask.

"There's a new subdivision called Chapel Hills. It's off Chapel Hill Road. There's going to be golf and a club. You should come out and take a look. We're getting a five bedroom house. Each boy will get to have his own room, even when he's off at college. Now, isn't that something?" Hal says. He is prideful. I want to rip his larynx out.

"We're happy for you, Hal," Judy says. She's staying off into the corner. "We'll miss you all being close to downtown."

"There's nothing off Chapel Hill Road, Hal," I say. "You'll have to drive thirty minutes to get to the grocery store. There's just that one gas station. If you go too far down Chapel Hill Road, you practically fall into the Chattahoochee River at the edge of the county."

"Joe, you're exaggerating. Now, I need to finish up some business with Judy. Can I trust you to be a good boy and go sit in reception with Cassandra?"

"I'm her husband. Any of her business is my business." I protest.

"Sure, except when your mother says otherwise. Mother Dunn knows best." Hal says while shuffling me out the door.

The old white door clicks shut. Hal thinks he's a fancy lawyer, but he is just a big fish in a small pond. I have some money now, and I need to make it count. There will be a reliable income from the floral shop too. I think I can quit my job.

Working at the airport has been tedious. The commute gets worse every year. I waste my entire day sitting in my car trying to get somewhere. I am determined to go places, and this money is going to get me there. They say money cannot buy happiness but watch me. I will never stop trying. I think I will start my pursuit of happiness with Cassandra.

Thirty-Two: Julian

◆————————————————————————◆

December 23, 2020 4:44 PM
Winston, Georgia

"Granny," I say in my softest voice. "Please sit down. You are always by the window, but it's frigid today. Mama is afraid that you'll catch a cold. She says it will make your rheumatism worse."

"I'm all right, boy." Granny hisses at me. "Go play a game, or read a book. It's Christmas break."

My frail grandmother is wrapped tight in a heavyweight tartan. The pattern represents the Anderson clan. My grandfather bought it for her when they visited Scotland. I didn't get to go. I was only a toddler. Mama says that Granny came back changed, for the better, after the trip.

"Do you want me to read to you?" I ask and touch her shoulder softly. "I know you like Robert Burns, but I'm not ready yet."

My grandfather made a big deal about purchasing a tartan belonging to the clan with Granny's maiden name. He always wanted her to feel independent. She had worries about him because he is younger than her. Marriages like that did not happen in her time. Now, it is less unusual.

"No. No Robert Burns today. I'm teaching American literature this year. Which textbook are we using now?" Granny says.

Granny has a strange sense of *now*. Her version of now is not the same from minute-to-minute. Some days she wakes up and thinks that she is still teaching. She goes to the driveway to look for her car to drive to school. Sometimes she wakes disoriented and wants to attempt an almost twenty-mile walk to Douglas County High School. There are no sidewalks in rural Douglas County. It is not safe for her, even if she was healthy enough to make the journey.

"Yes, ma'am," I say. I usually comply with Granny's prerogative to be called 'ma'am.' "Would you like a cup of tea? English breakfast? Milk or no milk?"

Inside the old farmhouse, it could be 1980, 2000, or 2020. The rolling farmland goes on forever. There is not a car in sight. If I stay still for a moment, I can hear the horses neigh and the wind beat against the shutters. Granny's breathing is shallow. It hurts her to stand too long. I drag a rocker to the window for her. It's heavy, and my eleven-year-old body cannot manage the bulk.

Granny yells at me about dragging furniture across the floor. "You should like you're moving Confederates through hell and half of Georgia. Pick it up off the floor. Honestly. Who are they hiring in the county's plant department these days?"

My grandfather has not changed much of the interior of his house since his parents lived here in the 1950s. Granny found it quaint for the first few years until she got annoyed. She wanted new appliances, broadband, and a stove that didn't operate on hand-chopped wood. I smile at the thought of the stove. Grandpa said that the stove was not negotiable. The family stove stayed. I wonder if I should put another log on even though my parents told me not to touch it.

"Do you have enough money?" Granny asks. I nod my head *yes*. "I mean, do you have enough money for the things you need but not always the things you want?"

"Yes," I say. "You took care of us, Granny. You took care of me. You did a good job."

"Joe! That wicked woolgathering bastard was always bad with money. He would drink it in and piss it out." She says and pulls her tartan tighter.

"Granny, it's Julian. How about we get to our lessons?"

"What grade? Bring me my literature books. Why aren't you in school?" She asks, again.

"It's Julian, Granny. You homeschool me. We're working on sixth-grade literature, the old fashioned way. I'm on the copper-level book." I say and hand her the book.

"What? Homeschool? No. I would never allow one of mine to be homeschooled. You need to be at school with your friends. It's cold outside. Is it Christmas? Should we go to The Farmer's Table before they close for the afternoon? I need some blackberry preserves, grass-fed beef, duck eggs, honey, and a Fraser fir."

"You're the only teacher that I've ever had. At least, you're the only teacher than I can remember. We've been together since Kindergarten." I say.

What year is it right now in Granny's mind? I do not know. I start to cry. I miss my Granny so much. It is unfathomable that there is not a cure for dementia yet. The medicine worked for a long while but stopped suddenly this fall. I overheard my parents talking about Granny having a virus when she was younger. The doctors think the virus made the dementia worse, or so they whispered. Mama and Papa blame Joe.

"Jules? Is that you? My Julian? My sweet Ju Ju with the pudgy cheeks. Oh, sweetheart. Come. Sit with your Granny by the stove. We'll read. Don't tell your brothers that you're my favorite, okay? What book is this? I remember sixth-grade literature and composition. Where were we? Winter break? Are we on poetry or oral tradition? No, it's nonfiction. Isn't it?"

Granny hobbles to the stove. Her tartan shawl drops but I pick it up. I scamper to get her another rocking chair right before she starts to sit down. Granny was going to sit on the floor. If she does, I will never be able to get her back up again. I guide her into her rocking chair. I sit on the thick rug next to her. I sit Indian style and close my eyes.

"Here is 'A Backwoods Boy' by Russell Freedman," Granny says with her most tender voice. "It's a story about young Abraham

Lincoln. That's what I loved about teaching out of these books. There were plenty of good stories in here for boys. I know all about raising boys.

"Common Core ruined the art of teaching literature, Jules. They had cheap ghostwriters write the material, so they didn't have to pay legitimate authors what they earned. We're going to have illiterate guppies on our hands and then what will we do? Society will go to hell in a handbasket."

"Don't read to me right now, Granny. Please, tell me a story. Tell me a true story. Tell me a story about you." I beg her. I know this lucid period is short.

"Do you know who else was a farmer boy, Julian? Your grandfather is a farmer boy. He grew up on this farm. He's continually invested in it over the years. He turned a blind eye to the '90s commercial boom in Douglasville. Most of the old roads that I used to travel are now six-lane roads. Your grandfather and I loved those roads. We didn't know it at the time. We took some things for granted back then."

"Was it before I was born?" I say with a smile. I love stories from before I was the born the best.

"Yes, sweet love. Believe it or not, a lot of things happened before you were born. Can you believe that I just said that? I said *a lot*. Well, that's ridiculous *a lot* is something that you build a house on, isn't it? It's the evilest adverb. I took off millions of points from students over the years for those two wily words. Sometimes the students were only poor spellers. I took off more points if they made *a* and *lot* into one word. I've wasted my whole life editing crappy to mediocre work. Now, who will remember me when I'm gone?"

"I will. I will remember you, Granny." I say. I wrap my arms around her wool skirt covered legs. She is shivering.

"Julian, please remember me. I wish I could teach you long enough to read and edit what you have to write. I can always tell what a child will grow up to be by their writing. I want you to remember your parts of speech and not get lazy. Never use pronouns, love."

"I'll pretend that I'm writing with a cursed quill, like in *Order of the Phoenix*," I say.

"Phoenix? What is that? That's out west." She says. I am losing her.

"We read the whole Harry Potter series last year, Granny. We made wands, and you sewed a cloak for me for Halloween. You love costume days at school, Granny. Remember?" I say.

There is a pause in Granny. She is thinking. I can hear the tick-tock of the grandfather clock. The clock sounds slow too. Granny's brain is wandering again. I want to put a ball and chain on her mind and keep her here with me.

After a minute, Granny says, "Costume day at school; yes. I remember costume day. I had a beautiful green gown. I made it for Halloween 1989 when we could still call it Halloween instead of book character day. I worked on it all summer and then two months of evenings. I loved that gown more than any wedding dress. I wore it until I retired. I had kept it in my closet in the classroom. I donated it to the theater department at Douglas County the day I cleaned out my classroom. Donating my costumes was hard to do, but it was the right thing to do. Lots of average high school girls are a size medium/large. My wardrobe will fit many young actresses over the years. It was practical."

"You did like to do things that were practical, even when they didn't feel good. I've learned so much from you Granny. I have been organizing my allowance in cash into envelopes like you taught me. I don't like the feeling when one envelope is empty, especially the 'online credits' one." I say. I like that my Granny has taught me the old-fashioned way of doing things.

"Envelopes," Granny says. She becomes agitated. "Envelopes and envelopes of money sat on his desks. He thought that he was so important. He thought that money was going to save his soul. He couldn't appreciate humble beginnings and the fine art of saving a little over time. He didn't want to shop at the thrift stores and wait for sales at the grocery store. None of that was fast enough for him. He wanted power and influence. He thought those envelopes of cash were going to get him there."

"Granny, I think I know who you're talking about." I comfort. "But, I think you might be in shock still. Please, don't get too upset.

It will be awhile before everyone is back. Mama, Papa, and Grandpa are out repairing a fence right now. We have Brunswick Stew in the slow cooker for when they get back. Doesn't it smell good? You and I canned those tomatoes together this past summer. I think it will taste like summer. At least, I think it will after I pick out all of the beans."

"Don't be so picky, Julian." She admonishes me. Her eyes are stern. "You don't always get to choose the way things go in life. Many a time I've had beans dumped into my life's stew. The beans stuck to me and muddled things up. It's all about how you handle the beans and the envelopes. What day is today?"

"It's the Wednesday before Christmas, Granny. Christmas is this Friday. You used to tell your younger students that today was Christmas Adam since tomorrow is Christmas Eve." I say. I sit up onto my knees and hold her hand.

Granny squeezes my hand back. "When I started teaching, all of the students celebrated Christmas. The one or two Jewish students I had in the seventies knew about Christmas. Often their families celebrated it too. I gave them a Happy Hanukah card. They were thrilled that I remembered them. There were no other teachers in the school that were as progressive as me back then. I started student teaching the 1969-1970 school year. I was twenty-two-years-old when I earned my own classroom."

"What were things like that first school year?" I ask. I know that she is teetering on the edge of being angry. Her respirations have increased, and her mind is wandering a little again. A good question, well-timed, is a pot of gold; or, so Granny would say.

"The students were distracted, even back then. They worked after school, all over town. Some of them, the girls especially, were reliable babysitters for me when my son was born. Many of them smoked pot. No one advertised it at the time, of course; but, what they smoked was organic, locally sourced, and non-GMO. Ha! Students didn't have synthetic drugs to get into back then. It was before slacker drug addicts invented Meth. I'm not certain if we even had pseudoephedrine." She says. There is a smile on her face.

"Tell me more about the seventies. Were the kids smarter?"

"No, but yes. My colleagues were more intelligent in the seventies. I had better-prepared students entering my classroom. By the time I retired, I had had to let so much go. I was not receiving the quality of students that I was used to in the previous decades. The 2009-2010 school year had to be it for me. The gifted CL students that I had that year were of a much lower quality than I had my first years of teaching mainstream freshmen English. Did you know that I had to start off at the bottom and work my way up? To find a better position at the high school level, I even had to teach a few years of eighth grade English."

"How am I coming along, Granny?" I ask.

I look over at the boiling stew. I hope everyone will return soon. Her agitation can come on suddenly. I don't want her to hurt herself.

"Your writing is marvelous. You just happen to be writing on a second-grade level. Just think of where you have come from, Julian! Those stupid preschool teachers didn't know what hell they were doing. Your mother cried her eyes out when they threw you out of that little church preschool. Public preschool helped a little. I took you under my wing. I've nurtured both your creative side and academics. I couldn't be more proud. You'll always be ahead in literature. I apologize I haven't been able to advance you too much in science. There will be time for that later."

"I like science and math," I say. "Were there magnet schools back then?"

"Oh, no, Jules. Douglas County didn't have anything fancy like that. We didn't need it. The principals routed certain students to certain teachers. The process wasn't official or formalized. We wanted each student to get the best. Students lacking in composition skills went to my office neighbor, Mr. Bailey.

"Bailey wrote science fiction under a pen name. The boys especially responded to his firm grammatical rules. He had a way of explaining things. Students going to liberal arts colleges to focus on literature came to me.

"I was always a good editor, but I was never a writer. There were times, early in my teaching career, when I would sit and write poetry during lunch break. I might pop out a limerick or a short poem. But, it was nothing worth publication. Where are my papers now? Where is my desk?"

"We're in the old farmhouse, Granny. You keep your office things upstairs, in the blue bedroom. You haven't touched those boxes in at least ten years." I say.

"I must go there to my desk. Right now, Julian" She says and starts to stagger to the stairs.

Granny had a small stroke sometime in the past year. Her right foot drags behind the rest of her body. Watching her decline is sad. Even when I am eighty-years-old, Granny will always be the strong-willed spit fire of the family.

We labor for almost a half hour to get up the stairs to the spare room. Granny and Grandpa don't sleep up here anymore. They do not need the guest bedrooms, but use them for some storage. Granny can't clean up here anymore, so the doors are kept shut to keep dust out. She puts her weight on the lever handle and pops open the door.

Granny gasps at the sight of the room. There is a twin-sized white wrought iron bed covered in a frilly duvet with a flat matching pillow. It may have belonged to my great-grandparents. There is a single window covered in drapes that match the duvet. Granny shakes them open. Even through the overcast sky outside, I can see the dust fly everywhere. I sneeze. Granny ignores me. She used to say *Gesundheit*. I like when she says it because no one says that nowadays.

Yellowing papers cover the writing desk across from the foot of the bed. Granny is a stacker. Some people organize in folders, like my dad. Granny likes a good stack of papers to flip through. She goes to work quickly flipping through everything. Despite rheumatism, she seems very at home among her papers. I go to the door to turn on a light for her, but there is no switch. The room does not have electrical wiring.

"Remember? Remember the route?" She says.

Granny is becoming more and more disconcerted by the minute. "There was a very specific route that I had to take after school. I did it for almost ten years. It was the same path. I would leave school, go to the floral shop, pick up an envelope, and take it to the campaign headquarters.

"We all had a route so the police wouldn't suspect anything. I wonder what office he'll run for next year. He always comes up with something clever. On the outside, you would think that everything was legitimate. He was even in the newspapers...until he wasn't. I never want to see him in prison. Why would I? What obligation did I have to him? He wasn't loyal to me, so why should I ask more out of myself than I out of him?"

"I don't know, Granny. Did you unearth the item you were looking for?" I ask. I cannot leave her up here to go get help. She will not be able to manage the stairs.

"I must correctly route the envelopes. The money comes and goes out. Don't you see? I'll teach you. You take the money skimmed from the shops. My job was Beautiful Lee-Dunn, unless I was sick or school was out. Then, things would look fishy if I went. I parked a couple of blocks away too. It really was a rather small amount on a weekly basis, less than two hundred dollars except during holidays.

"The money goes to the treasurer at the campaign headquarters. It doesn't matter who is running for what. You classify the money as walk-in donations. You put that money into payroll. But, here's the thing. The students are all volunteers. The checks are made out to dummies.

"Yes, you lose money to social security and taxes that way, but the money is clean and not traceable. Joe cashed the payroll checks. I mean literally: cashed. It took Joe a long time to figure out how he wanted everything to work. For the longest time, he would just give me the money. I would spend it on groceries, a new dress, shoes, car maintenance, and other minor household things. But, at the advent of people going cash-free, things got tricky.

"Did you know that we used to have to pay for almost everything in cash? I pumped my own gas and took my purse inside the store to pay, in cash, for my purchase. Isn't all that unbelievable now?

By the time we were on Joe's fifth campaign or so, people started getting suspicious. We had to change counties. We tried to stay out of the Atlanta news media outlets. That was when Joe began to get into things that I didn't approve of at all. I didn't know the names of the crimes. I'm not a criminal justice expert like Coach. He reads crime novels when he's not reading Westerns.

"It all started with the envelopes. I shifted envelopes for years. Joe paid people off. He was bribing and doing the needful. We did the needful back in those days."

"Granny, does this have to do with Anne?" I ask hoping the answers is *no*.

"Yes," she says. She steadies herself on a chair at the desk. She clumsily pulls it out and sits. She starts to stare off into space again.

Granny looks at one of the envelopes. "Anne was here...for a time. Then, like so many others, there were envelopes. There were years of envelopes until Ricky killed himself."

"Who is Ricky?"

"Never mind that boy. Ricky made mistakes. He had to go. The cotton mill fire was perfect."

"What about Anne? I want to know more?"

"Anne was a mistake. She was an innocent lamb thrown onto the sacrificial altar of millennial witchcraft and hearsay."

"Don't be dramatic, Granny," I chide. "There was not witchcraft. You're thinking of the Scottish play that cannot be named. Please don't be dramatic. Tell me about the envelopes again. Tell me about Anne's envelopes."

"There was one to lure, one to bait, one to bribe, one to hide, and one to chide. That's how you cover your ass when someone has died." She says. "Or, you'll be fried."

I hear footsteps coming up the stairs. It is Grandpa. He looks at me first and then to Granny. She is crying at her desk. She is confused and shuffling her papers around again. Grandpa is angry with me for bringing her up here.

"Where are their essays? It's Christmas break. I need to finish grading the essays. There are several classes of senior English students. I have at least a hundred essays to grade. Where is my pen? I need my red felt-tip pen!" Granny says.

"Judy, come downstairs with me. Your show is going to be on." Grandpa says.

"I have to grade papers. What show?" Granny says with a muffled yelp.

"Whatever show you want, Granny," Grandpa says patiently.

"Why don't we watch the 2015 version of Macbeth?" Mama provokes.

Granny shoves stacks of papers off her desk. She releases a guttural blood-curdling scream. Mama knows that Granny cannot stand to hear *Macbeth*. It was mean of Mama to provoke Granny. As Granny is distracted, Papa and Grandpa take Granny under her arms to the stairwell.

"Sorry, Jules. It's not safe for her up here. She could break a hip. You know better." Mama apologizes to me. I believe her.

A cold wind beats against the western side of the farmhouse. Boards squeak beneath my feet. I start picking up papers and envelopes. Granny kept the hundreds of senior essays written for her over the years. Periodically, Grandpa brings her a stack of papers to edit again. She has been re-editing the same papers for at least ten years.

Sparks fly in my brain. Connections are forming. I think in thought bubbles. I am constantly trying to connect my thought bubbles. I have not read *Macbeth*, but I know that I have seen it written somewhere before.

"Macbeth," I say to Mama. "Macbeth. Macbeth. Macbeth. Macbeth."

Mama runs from me to the stairwell, "Daddy! It's Jules. He's having a spell again. Help!"

All my parents hear is me repeating Macbeth and not knowing what it means. I clutch an envelope close to my chest. My fear is that I will lose the envelope while going down the stairs. I think it is the key to solving a murder.

Macbeth. Lady Macbeth. Macbeth. Blood. Macbeth. Help me, Granny. I am about to be lost in the woods again.

Thirty-Three: Anne

February 2, 1998 12:07 PM
Douglas County High School

"I'm alright." I say from the floor of the hallway of the Lower Banks building. "I need a minute."

My classmates stare at me for a moment and then ignore me. I know I fainted. I am passing it off as a blood sugar dip from skipping lunch. I am lying on my back when David and Justin help me up. Vague memories of morning's Physics class dance through my psyche, but things are blurry. Justin does not care for me or my writing.

Oh, no. Now, I remember what happened before lunch. Can I pretend that I do not remember anything from this morning? My skull did not make contact with the floor. I landed on someone's backpack that was near the row of lockers. I think pretending to be dazed and confused would be easier than going back into the classroom.

Principal Daniell looks at me. He is not certain what to say, so he just moves on. In his mind, I am just a girl and girls faint. In a pretend office inside his brain, a little old man probably took a file folder of information on what he witnessed. The little old man filed my spell under 'The mysteries of female anatomy.' Now he will promptly forget about it like it never happened. He does not know my medical history. I don't feel the need to tell him to use a walk-ie-talkie to call the front office to call my parents.

"So, you kids are smart, right? You can look in the classroom and see that your teacher's not here. But, you're here to learn and so we're going to go back inside and keep learning." Principal Daniell says as he twists his master key into the classroom's door lock.

Mrs. Couch guards her classroom like a sacred, ancient church. She treats its contents like a holy grail of all things senior English and British literature. The classroom is a tomb of past projects from students who graduated, or had otherwise left the school, from the last twenty years or so. I can see a cardboard Dickens village that looks lonely without Mrs. Couch in the classroom. Principal Daniell glumly walks in and looked around.

Everything had changed since before lunch. On reflection, the classroom has not changed. I have changed. The generic Shakespearian costumes hanging in the back of the classroom on a cabinet that has not been opened this decade seem extra dusty. A puzzle of The Cathedral of Westminster sits nearby on a table with fake grass that has started to attract grime.

We all sit down in near perfect silence. We know that each of us has a hand in our bad behavior. Mrs. Couch did not tell the administrative office that she was leaving. Heather decided to tell the principal, discreetly, what transpired. She isn't a tattle-tale. Mrs. Couch's mental collapse and verbal thrashing is a real-life emergency.

Sitting down in my resin and metal desk, I look at the chalkboard in the front of the classroom. No one in our class has ever seen Mrs. Couch use it. I do not think anyone in the school even knows the condition of the chalkboard in her room. The chalkboard hangs covered in student artwork. The chalkboard has been pinned onto and taped over for years with student art. There are charcoal drawings, pencil drawings, watercolors, and even a mosaic piece of Jesus as faux stain glass. It is all from students that had desperately wanted to impress her. The former students left little pieces of their souls in the art and, in that way, it is like they are perpetually locked in the tomb with us. Mrs. Couch has made us her preserved, silenced mummies captured at the peak of our youth and potential.

I am analyzing the art for the first time. I see that all of these past students wanted to give their best to Mrs. Couch. It wasn't about getting a good grade for them as much as they wanted to express their appreciation for her work by giving their best work.

For the past two academic years, I had sat in this classroom and, yet, never noticed the work of my fellow students. If I converse honestly with myself, and do not try to cover my heart in secrets, then I can see that my class and I have not been giving our best. Our best work does not hold a candle to the work of the students of the past. Mrs. Couch does have high expectations of us, but she also has seen what can happen when students push themselves. We had not been pushing ourselves enough.

Interested in seeing what a newbie could do driving the train wreck that was now our CL English class, none of us utter a syllable as the principal tries to figure out where to sit down. Amanda has pointed to the student chair, but Principal Daniell is at least a foot too tall to sit there. He pulls a rolling chair from behind the county-issued teacher's desk. The chair squeaks as he rolls it out.

Principal Daniell jokes, "I didn't know that they still made these. It's retro."

"No, sir, it's vintage," Stephanie says with a bite in her voice. "That's probably original. Mrs. Couch wouldn't allow anything fake or copied in her class."

Looking to his side, he sees the square television attached to the corner of the room with wires hanging down and across the overstuffed room. He asks if we are watching anything. Will replies that we are not. Principal Daniell does not know that the television is broken, yet Mrs. Couch refuses to let anyone into her classroom to fix it. She is more than happy to wheel in the old television and VCR cart.

Michelle speaks up and says, "Mrs. Couch doesn't like us to watch too many movies because it will not help us become good writers."

Principal Daniell nods his head and looks at the desk. He takes an envelope and slips it into Mrs. Couch's massive gradebook. The entire monstrosity swells with overstuffed papers, yet it still looks a little organized. He rubs the dark green spiral-bound record of our past two years. For either sentimental or masochistic reasons, she has kept a record of all of our work from the previous year. We were never allowed to write about the same topic twice.

Principal Daniell nudges the edge of a clay chess set that has been hand-carved into little figures from the Civil War. It is most likely a project from Mrs. Couch's American Literature class that covered Crane's *Red Badge of Courage* one year.

Principal Daniell asks, "What happened? Did she not get over the war?"

We all involuntarily giggle. Amanda looks wounded and quickly says, "Sir, that's a project that my brother, Isaac, made for *An Occurrence at Owl Creek Bridge* years ago. He worked very hard on it. I helped him warm the clay by hand."

"Oh, is that Crane?" he asks trying to remember some English class from long ago.

"No, that's Ambrose Bierce," I say.

I hope Isaac feels honored that Mrs. Couch kept his middle school-level work. Amanda seems to be proud enough of it. Mrs. Couch's expectations of students appear to have increased over the years.

"Use this time to study, write an essay, or read a book. Look, I coached golf until the beginning of this school year. After dealing with everyone's parents this year, I feel like I have one foot in the grave. I am counting the hours until Spring Break." Principal Daniell says.

Without warning, I notice Jennifer and Jeremy standing in the classroom doorway. She looks confused. Jeremy tries to hide behind Jennifer, but it does not work because he is several inches taller than her. I look at their backpacks sitting next to their desks. I am glad that I did not have to carry that heavy load for them. I would have fallen over with twelve hardback textbooks.

Jennifer says, "You didn't send me with any paperwork. ISS rejected me. I offered to tattoo a barcode on my butt."

"Well, crap. I don't have time to make it formal. Just take a seat and read something like everyone else. I can keep an eye on you here." Principal Daniell says motioning Jennifer to sit.

The principal looks as exasperated with us as Mrs. Couch. There must be something wrong with us. We are defective students. For the first time in Douglas County High School history, we will be known as the class that was not ready for the May CL Exam or college in general. The local colleges and universities will block our admission based on our sour reputations.

Will and Michelle look at each other. With the greatest silence, they pull out the books they have been reading. Will retrieves his John Grisham and opens a random page. I am not confident that Will ever reads John Grisham. Will only wants everyone to know that he intends to become a showy prosecutor in a quaint Southern town that is more genteel than Douglasville.

Michelle is reading *Anna Karenina*. Russian authors are not part of our high school level literature classes. There is a special class to learn Russian, and one on Russian literature, but it is not available if you are gifted-tracked. Michelle knows that she needs to prepare for World Literature, as required by the State of Georgia, at the college level. She is ahead of the rest of us.

Jennifer and Jeremy bump elbows and use hand signals to discuss something. I feel left out when they communicate in twin-speak. I know it is self-centered of me to want my best friend to talk to me too. I feel like my mind is bubbling over. I have no way of working out all the thought bubbles popping up. I wish Crystal were here. At the very least, she is exceptional at handling the unexpected. She always knows what to say.

Brittany is in the back corner of the room looking at the door. She appears so though she is ready to run away. Unfortunately, there is a whole-classroom length wall shelf holding a thousand books. The county couldn't afford real shelving. The shelving is unsecured cinder blocks and wood planks. The plans have started to bend. I think most of us would bend under the weight of twenty-five-years with Mrs. Couch. Trophies line the top of the bookshelves. I have no idea which sports they represent because they are so high up. Mrs. Couch may have sponsored an athletic team before Brian was born.

Clearing her throat, Brittany says, "I never say anything. I'm scared. I'm scared that I'll always be wrong. I'm scared that my answer will never be enough. So, rather than being wrong, I just don't say anything."

Looking both confused and contemplative, Principal Daniell continues to sit in the rolling chair next to the desk. He doesn't know what to say. None of us do. Of all people to speak up next, it is Matt. He has not said anything since ninth grade. I do not know why he comes to school.

Getting up from his desk, Matt says, "It's all a scam. Art is subjective. Reading and writing are art. It's not for one person to say whether we'll live or die by our pens, or keyboards."

There was finally something tangible in the ethereal heavens choking the classroom that the principal could grab onto to rebuke. Principal Daniell latches onto Matt's idea and formulates a generic response, "Education is never a scam. We want you all to-"

"Stop," Nicole says crying. "Don't placate us. I want to hear what Druggie Matt Young has to say. Because you know what, Druggie Matt, I think you're a loser and a dopehead. I can't believe you haven't dropped out already. So, I want to know exactly how you are making an A- in this class while I struggle to get a C. I do everything right. Everything."

"Nicole, it's not personal to you." Matt answers. He puts his hands out to calm her. "It genuinely is all a scam. You weren't invited to participate in the scheme. I regret that. It would have been more inclusive to persuade everyone into joining us. But, you're a tattle-tail that can't be trusted."

Everyone in the class remains silent. A few moments ago, we were under the impression that Matt was exposing a profound philosophical truth. We train our eyes on the back of the room; on Matt. The principal rolls back and forth from the main desk to the student/teacher desk at the front of the classroom.

Principal Daniell's left eyebrow rises involuntarily, "How much of a contrivance is this? Do I need to take notes?"

"You all are stupid for not figuring it out. That's why I'm sick and tired of this place. Everything is so false and contrived." Tommy says. None of us knew Tommy was listening.

"As if!" Melissa says. "Mrs. Couch just went off on you for turning in your mother's writing."

"Oh, my mom didn't write that," Tommy admits. He shrugs his shoulders a little.

"What do you mean 'your mom's writing'? What did Mrs. Couch accuse you of, Tommy? You know that this could have an impact on your graduation status, right? It could affect your ability to finish out the basketball season. Or, heck, you may not even be able to play baseball." Principal Daniell says.

Like a hardened police officer, Principal Daniell is investigating us by letting us do all the talking. He knows that we will crack.

He does not have to separate us to find it all out. Our mentality to-date has been that we need to sling mud at each other to survive. The boys need to shut their traps.

"Mrs. Couch thought my mom wrote all my stuff; but, undoubtedly, she didn't. She does all my science and social studies projects, but I didn't need her to help with English. Matt and Brian had me covered." Tommy says. He is letting everything spill. He should have played dumb, as usual, but he loves holding the attention of the entire class.

"Look, it wasn't my idea," Matt says defensively holding his hands up from the desk and away from his body. "Brian has access to all of the old essays from like thirty-years of students. Mrs. Couch couldn't possibly remember all of that. She tries to hold everything in the front of her mind like she's some Brit Lit divine seraphim. She can't.

"No one could hold that much information at one time. How is she going to know? You take a copy out of the filing cabinet, see if it matches up, and *boom*. You simply recopy the work in your own handwriting. Or, better yet, you could always type it at a computer. I mean, of course, if you have one at home. You don't want to do that in the school library with the librarians looming over you like Ringwraiths." Matt says with a gentle nod.

Principal Daniell sits with a hefty stillness and an air of suspicion about him. Nicole stands up to hurt Matt, but Heather grabs

Nicole's right elbow. Both Nicole and Heather are average size girls, but Nicole is still muscular from years of cheerleading.

Nicole drags Heather with her toward Matt while Heather is still half sitting in her desk. Nicole grabs a book off Preeti's desk and throws it at Matt. She misses her target, but Matt gets the idea. Nicole adds a variety of curse words to make sure that Matt understands. None of us have ever seen Nicole pissed off before. She and Michael are the senior class's resident saints.

I breathe in deep for a moment and try to calm myself. My hands are clammy and shaking. Heather is walking Nicole out of the classroom when Nicole's last insult to Matt is unleashed, "You are a toad, ugly and venomous. You think you wear a precious crown on your ugly head!"

Stunned by the outburst, Principal Daniell thinks for a moment and says, "Shakespeare?"

Seth is utterly annoyed by Principal Daniell's lack of literary knowledge by Mrs. Couch's standards. Seth says, "If Nicole wasn't so angry, she probably meant to quote Shakespeare to Matt. We had to read *As You Like It* over the summer. I didn't think it was that good. I far preferred *Much Ado About Nothing* when we went on the field trip earlier this year."

"Know-it-all," screams Justin. "You just found out that at least Matt and Tommy were cheating with the help of Brian, and you decide to give us a theater review, Seth. You're as dumb as Anne. If it weren't for her, Mrs. Couch wouldn't have gone off on the rest of us. Stupid, Pollyanna Anne."

Justin puts his noggin on his desk like a Kindergartner. He pulls his flannel shirt over his head. That is why we call him flannel guy. He was part ostrich too. I can see his white tee shirt advertising Lewallen's Body Shop. I didn't know he worked there. I think people who are living in the real world and working are taking the cheating news much worse. I know I am.

"Does Mrs. Couch know? Is that why she yelled at you and left?" Principal Daniell asks.

"No," Tommy says. "That's why I let her keep yelling at me. I didn't care. Her accusations would be difficult to prove. Cute girls, usually sophomores, type my papers. It would be difficult to say who typed them, right? I mean, it could have just as easily been her or me. That's why Mrs. Couch never recognized the papers that Brian gave to Matt to give to me. I simply re-typed handwritten essays."

"I think we accidentally gave ourselves the biggest insult of all," Jeremy says wistfully.

Principal Daniell settles in his chair and leans to the left, onto Mrs. Couch's preferred desk. He narrows his brows and pinches his lips so as to not say anything. The rest of the class sits thinking about Jeremy's observation for a moment. After Jeremy, I am the second to come to the horrible realization.

"Oh, no!" I say. I start crying, and words come out with a mumble. "That is the worst thing that anyone could say about us as writers. Our writing is indistinguishable and forgettable. We didn't leave a single ounce of ourselves on the paper. Hemingway had said some admirable things about writing that we talked about last year. But, the one unifying concept that we talked about last year was that we should show our passion and emotion in our writing. The students who came before us didn't do that. Now, we're continuing to disappoint Mrs. Couch by following the same pattern. We're generic. We're insipid. We're bland."

I take a deep breath and several people comment on and off. Mrs. Couch specifically called Michelle out for being forgettable, but the same applies to the rest of us. High school intimidates us so much that rather than using it as a practice grounds for college, we froze under the slightest pressure. Principal Daniell coaxes me to continue explaining.

I say, "If we had been on target, authentically writing for ourselves this past year and a half then Mrs. Couch would know our writing. Just like she would be able to look at a passage in a book and recognize the writing as Kipling, Milton, or Shaw. We should all have different voices. Our voices should be influenced by our education, our family background, our reading preferences, and even ethnic background if that is something that we want to let peek through the lines."

After sitting for a moment and staring blankly out the half-covered windows outside, Stephanie is looking straight at me. She says that the bell has rung and that I had to follow her to newspaper staff for our next class. I could not speak or move. I feel trapped in a continuous loop of thoughts. I can't escape. I can't even breathe correctly. Everything is off, like a *Twilight Zone* episode.

Principal Daniell comes over to me, "You did faint, Anne. Can I call your mom? Can I ask someone to take you home? You may need to lie down. I wouldn't feel good about letting you drive home."

"Robert," I say in a barely audible voice.

Jennifer approaches me with our backpacks. "Anne, Jeremy went to get Robert. I'm going to take you home. I've already talked to Mr. Worthan. He doesn't mind and hopes you feel better. We're not going to miss anything in class. He's teaching the freshmen and sophomores about copy. He was going to let us work on scanning pictures, but you have better equipment at home. Okay? C'mon."

Thinking that nothing could get stranger that today, I shuffle outside. The air feels too cold. My disorientation grows while walking through the parking lot. Jennifer parks in the main Selman Avenue parking lot close to the old gym. My car is in the senior parking lot off Campbellton Street. I am tripping over the uneven pavement. The sun leaves spots in my eyes. My feet are numb but feel wet. Jeremy and Jennifer take me on either side while Robert carries our backpacks. The wind whips down the steep Selman Avenue hill and up through the parking lot near the gym. I can smell the fertilizer on the nearby golf course.

Half of the old lower parking lot has been demolished to make space for a new gym. I hope it's lovely. It is a new gym that we will never see the inside of or be able to use. That is fine. After working at the Red Cross blood drive inside our current gym, I smell blood whenever I go in there. It is a brain reflex I cannot shake.

Jeremy buckles my seatbelt for me in the back of Jennifer's navy blue sedan. We are all checked out of school today, yet I feel like I accidentally left part of my soul in the classroom. I am treading water in an ocean where sharks are nipping at my ankles. The sharks I envision are mostly college, parents, and teachers; but, just for good measure, I think there was probably a Stephanie shark in there too. I need to hurry and scan our photos for the next issue.

Bump, bump.

Jennifer is driving. She tells the three of us to hold onto her car's grab handles. Jeremy whistles *Dixie* for a brief moment. Suddenly, Jennifer is navigating her small car on the gymnasium sidewalk! Oh my goodness. Oh, no. Oh, yes! *Woo-hoo!*

I am sitting in the back with the window rolled down. The air is whipping through my hair like I am in the eye of a hurricane. Jennifer is working her way through the construction zone going at least fifteen miles-per-hour. She moves onto the Banks Building's sidewalks.

The car flies right by the exterior of Lower Banks and Mrs. Couch's classroom! Jennifer shoves her left hand out the driver side window and flips a bird with her middle finger. She laughs like a maniac as Jeremy pokes his left hand through the sunroof to match his twin's gesture.

Holding tight to the safety of my seat belt, I start laughing with abandon. I stick my face out the window to feel the sun on my face. I gulp in big choking mouthfuls of fresh winter air. Jeremy asks me what I wanted to do. He says that Jennifer will take us anywhere. She has a full tank of gas. We could go to Alabama if we wanted to.

Where do I want to go? I want an ice-cold vanilla milkshake from the new Chick-fil-a on Fairburn Road. I want to swing wildly from the old rope hanging over the deepest part of Sun Valley Beach's massive pool. I want to race golf carts at Chapel Hill Golf and Country Club with shade overhead and sun warming my bare arms. I want to laugh with my friends in the parking lot of the dollar movies. I want to dance to bluegrass music on the banks of Sweetwater Creek. I want to hold my breath as I drop safely from the top of Six Flag's Great Gasp.

I want this beautiful, singular in-between moment to last forever. I want it all right now. Because, I know that when I wake up from this shock that I will be a bona fide adult, and there is no returning to this rapturously balanced moment after that.

Note from the Author

Thank you, beloved reader, for joining me on this adventure through a very real time and place with my fictional characters. *Absent on School Picture Day* is the first novel of a trilogy. You have assurances that you have invested your precious reading time well as the final two books are already written and awaiting editing.

My beloved characters were each carefully crafted over more than a year through a methodical process. The majority of the first names were chosen from the U.S. census popular baby names lists. The last names were borrowed from old graves in Douglas County, Georgia. Thank you to the Douglas County Cemetery Commission for maintaining records on the county's historic burial grounds. The names are intended to be authentic to novel's setting while also being generic to the story's time period.

To make my characters as real as possible, I wrote biographies for each individual; no matter how minor the character. This process is not my original thought and one widely discussed on National Novel Writing Month (NaNoWriMo) boards. Each of my characters has a birth date, death date, cause of death, family lineage, and history, even if it is not entirely revealed in the novels.

As a tribute to the real people that I have known and appreciated over time, I wanted to integrate special aspects of them into my characters. I have tried to give certain people better endings than what they were dealt in real life. It is my way of saying, "I saw you. I see you still. I empathize with your story. You were special to me then. You are special to me now."

Absent on School Picture Day is a labor of love and work of fiction. Please understand that my characters are my own. They are not based on any individual person; living or dead.

My senior English teacher's name is Mrs. Brenda Carroll Yates. The fictional character of Mrs. Judy Couch is not based on Mrs. Yates, either personally or professionally. To the best of my knowledge, Mrs. Couch has a very different fictional storyline than Mrs. Yates. As a former student, I would like to thank Mrs. Yates for her dedication to her work and the generations of students that she taught at Douglas County High School.

My novel does takes place in the real world. As a result, there are many pop culture and literary references made by the characters. A list of literary references follows.

For personal photos, exclusive content, sneak peeks, and more, please connect with me on:

YouTube (A. Hollis)

Facebook (www.facebook.com/1998Series/)

Twitter (@1998Series)

Literary References

Adler, Warren. *The War of the Roses*. New York: Warner Books, 1981.

Andersen, H. C., Lisbeth Zwerger, and Anthea Bell. *The Little Mermaid*. New York: Minedition/Penguin Young Readers Group, 2004.

Andrews, V. C. *Flowers in the Attic*. New York: Pocket Books, 1979.

Austen, Jane. *Pride and Predjudice*. Pennyslvania: Franklin Library, 1980.

Beckett, Samuel. *Waiting for Godot: Tragicomedy in 2 Acts*. New York: Grove Press, 1954.

Berendt, John. *Midnight in the Garden of Good and Evil: A Savannah Story*. New York: Random House, 1994.

Bierce, Ambrose, and Donna J. Neary. *An Occurrence at Owl Creek Bridge*. Mankato, MN: Creative Education, 1980.

Brontë, Emily. *Wuthering Heights*. London: Oxford University Pr., 1930.

Burns, Robert, A. Noble, and P.S. Hogg, eds. Noble, A; Hogg, PS, eds. *The Canongate Burns: The Complete Poems and Songs of Robert Burns*. Edinburgh: Canongate Books, 2003.

Chaucer, Geoffrey, and Walter W. Skeat. *The Canterbury Tales*. New York: Modern Library, 1929.

Coleridge, Samuel Taylor. "Kubla Khan." *Christabel ; Kubla Khan, a Vision; The Pains of Sleep.* London: John Murray, 1816.

Conrad, Joseph, and A. N. Wilson. *Heart of Darkness.* London: Hesperus Press, 2002.

Crane, Stephen, Rosemary Border, and Tom Briggs. *The Red Badge of Courage.* Hong Kong: Oxford University Press, 1989.

Dahl, Roald, and Joseph Schindelman. *Charlie and the Chocolate Factory.* New York: A.A. Knopf, 1964.

Defoe, Daniel, and N. C. Wyeth. *Robinson Crusoe.* New York: Scribner, 1983.

Dickens, Charles. *The Mystery of Edwin Drood.* Leipzig: Tauchnitz, 1870.

Edwards, Jonathan. *Sinners in the Hands of an Angry God.* Phillipsburg, NJ: P & R Pub., 1992.

Efimova, Aleksandra, Peter Ilich Tchaikovsky, and Elizaveta Efimova. *The Nutcracker Ballet.*

Ende, Michael, and Roswitha Quadflieg. *The Neverending Story.* Garden City, NY: Doubleday, 1983.

Flaubert, Gustave. *Madam Bovary.* Westport, CT: Easton Press, 1975.

Freedman, Russell. "A Backwoods Boy." *Prentice Hall Literature: Copper.* Englewood Cliffs, NJ & Needham, MA: Prentice Hall, 1991.

Goggin, Dan. *Nunsense: A Musical Comedy.* New York: S. French, 1986.

Grandin, Temple. *The Way I See It: A Personal Look at Autism & Asperger's.* Arlington, TX: Future Horizons, 2008.

Hansberry, Lorraine. *A Raisin in the Sun.* New York: Vintage, 1994.

Hardy, Thomas and Katherine Kearney Maynard. "Ah, Are you Digging on my Grave?" *Thomas Hardy's Tragic Poetry: The Lyrics and The Dynasts.* Iowa City: University of Iowa Press, 1991, pp8-12.

Hemingway, Ernest. "Hills like White Elephants." *Men Without Women.* New York: C. Scribner's Sons, 1927.

Joyce, James. *Ulysses.* New York: Random House, 1961.

Kirkman, Robert. *The Walking Dead Compendium.* Berkeley, CA: Image Comics, 2009.

Lanier, Sidney, Mary Day Lanier, and William Hayes Ward. "The Song of the Chattahoochee." *Poems of Sidney Lanier.* New York: Scribner, 1891.

Lawrence, D. H., and William York Tindall. "The Snake." *The Later D.H. Lawrence. The Best Novels, Stories, Essays, 1925-1930.* New York: Knopf, 1969.

Levitt, Steven D., and Stephen J. Dubner. *Freakonomics: a rogue economist explores the hidden side of everything.* New York: William Morrow, 2005.

London, Jack. "To Build a Fire." *Best Short Stories of Jack London.* Garden City, NY: Sun Dial Press, 1945.

Lowell, Amy, and John Livingston Lowes. "Patterns." *Selected Poems of Amy Lowell.* Boston: Houghton Mifflin, 1928.

Malory, Thomas, H. Oskar Sommer, and Andrew Lang. *Le Morte D'arthur.* London: D. Nutt, 1889.

Marshall, Catherine. *Christy.* New York: McGraw-Hill, 1967.

McCourt, Frank. *Angela's Ashes: A Memoir.* New York: Scribner, 1996.

Meyer, Stephenie. *Twilight.* Roma: Fazi, 2008.

Miller, Arthur. *The Crucible: A Play in Four Acts.* New York: Viking Press, 1953.

Mitchell, Margaret. *Gone with the Wind.* New York: Macmillan Company, 1936.

Morrison, Toni. *Paradise.* New York: A.A. Knopf, 1998.

Murkoff, Heidi Eisenberg, Arlene Eisenberg, and Sandee Eisenberg. Hathaway. *What to Expect When You're Expecting.* New York: Workman Pub., 2002.

Nabokov, Vladimir. *Lolita.* Kunst Hochschule Berlin: Hans Reitzel, 1957.

Pasternak, Boris Leonidovich. *Doctor Zhivago.* Franklin Center, PA: Franklin Library, 1978.

Rawls, Wilson. *Where the Red Fern Grows: The Story of Two Dogs and a Boy.* Garden City, NY: Doubleday, 1961.

Rowling, J. K. *Harry Potter and the Order of the Phoenix*. (Harry Potter Series, Year 5.). New York: Scholastic, 2003.

Sewell, Anna, and Alice Thorne. *Black Beauty*. New York: Grosset & Dunlap, 1962.

Shakespeare, William, and Alexander M. Witherspoon. *The Tragedy of Titus Andronicus*. New Haven: Yale University Press, 1926.

Shakespeare, William, and Claire McEachern. *Much Ado About Nothing*. London: Arden Shakespeare, 2006.

Shakespeare, William, and Kenneth Muir. *Othello*. Harmondsworth, Middlesex, England: Penguin, 1968.

Shakespeare, William, and Lawrence Mason. *The Tragedy of Julius Caesar*. New Haven: Yale University Press, 1919.

Shakespeare, William, and Thomas Goddard Bergin. *The Taming of the Shrew*. New Haven: Yale University Press, 1954.

Shakespeare, William. *As You like It*. New Haven: Yale University Press, 1954.

Shakespeare, William. *Hamlet*. Cambridge: University Press, 1948.

Shaw, Bernard. *Pygmalion*. New York: Dodd, Mead, 1939.

Shelley, Percy Bysshe. *Ozymandias*. New York: J.L. Weil, 1992.

Steel, Danielle. *Daddy*. New York, NY: Delacorte Press, 1989.

Steinbeck, John. *The Pearl*. New York: Viking Press, 1947.

Thackeray, William Makepeace. *Vanity Fair, a Novel without a Hero*. New York: Heritage Press, 1940.

Tolstoy, Leo, and George Gibian. *Anna Karenina*. New York: W.W. Norton &, 1970.

Wilde, Oscar. *The Picture of Dorian Gray*. London: Ward, Lock, 1891.

Wilder, Laura Ingalls, and Garth Williams. *Little House on the Prairie*. New York: Harper & Bros., 1953.

Williams, Tennessee. *The Glass Menagerie*. New York: New Directions, 1999.

Wright, Richard. *Native Son*. New York: Harper & Bros., 1940.